Tired of Being Amazing

RACHEL'S STORY

Tired of Being Amazing

RACHEL'S STORY

JUDITH MINKOVE

Tired of Being Amazing:
Rachel's Story
© Judy Minkove
2023
judyminkove.com

Distributed by Epigraph Books

Photo credits:
The front cover image was taken at Sam's wedding (2010) by Zush Photography.
The author photo is by Keith Weller Photography.

Published 2023

ISBN: 978-1-960090-11-9
Library of Congress Control Number: 2023903622

CONTENTS

FOREWORD ix

CHAPTER 1   *Signs*   1

CHAPTER 2   *Recalibrating*   21

CHAPTER 3   *Hope v. Fear*   35

CHAPTER 4   *Turbulence and the Power of Music*   53

CHAPTER 5   Chesed–*A Supportive Nest*   75

CHAPTER 6   *New Normal*   103

CHAPTER 7   *A Delicate Balance*   125

CHAPTER 8   *New Normal, Again*   145

CHAPTER 9   *Challenging the Odds*   153

CHAPTER 10   *'Man Plans, God Laughs'*   173

CHAPTER 11   *Glimmers and Downers*   183

CHAPTER 12   *Renewed Purpose*   197

CHAPTER 13   *Getting Back on Track*   229

CHAPTER 14   *Grappling with Loss and Travel Plans*   267

CHAPTER 15   *Final Gifts*   285

EPILOGUE   *Ripples*   297

AFTERWORD 307

ACKNOWLEDGMENTS 311

AUTHOR BIOGRAPHY 317

EPIGRAPH

The Sky

If you look at the sky,
Sometimes it's dark.
It has a misty light.
Look again.
See a blue sky,
Light,
And the sun shining bright.

Rachel Minkove
6th grade English assignment for Ms. Irene Gordon
Beth Tfiloh Community Day School

Foreword

By Zipora Schorr,
Director of Education
Beth Tfiloh Dahan Community School
Baltimore, Maryland

My dear Rachel, my beautiful Rachie,

I miss you; we all do.

Those seemingly simple words mask a sea of emotion, a depth of feeling, a statement of profound loss and pain.

And yet, we all know that you never wanted the pain, the symptoms, the diagnosis to define you. And it most definitely did not.

What defined you was your essence: your smile, your faith, your encouragement of others, your fortitude, your strength. And, without doubt, you would want to be remembered for all of those things, since that is how you helped all of us get through what was a wrenching and tragic time for you and for us.

You never looked at it as a "battle" or a "fight"—words of struggle so often used to describe the trajectory of a journey that began with the word Cancer.

You took each day, each challenge, each new symptom or news as something that had to be dealt with, and you did that with the extraordinary support of your family, your friends, and ultimately, your faith.

Your life began way before the ominous diagnosis that would propel you through your last months, and I remember your years growing up—really good years.

You never passed me in the halls of school without flashing me that megawatt smile, shy at first, and gaining confidence with time; always surrounded by friends; always doing the right thing (your brothers thought that was boring!); and always with that spark of intelligence and understanding in your eyes.

Remember when I visited you when you were spending your gap year in Israel? I still have this picture of you bounding down the steps in the Old City of Jerusalem, and you grabbed me in an embrace, whose warmth I still feel. I was so touched that you wanted to meet me for coffee (what kid wants to meet their Principal, when they are not in trouble?!) and we had a chance to talk about the seminary you were attending, your life goals, and your recommendations for future graduates for the program that was right for them. You never wanted to talk only about yourself; it was not about you, but about how your experience could inform and help others with their decisions.

You did the same thing when you came back to Beth Tfiloh to work in our library. You needed to be in Baltimore for your treatments, and found a way to continue to spend your time meaningfully—of course, helping others, because that is just what you always did.

No wonder you chose social work as a calling—and how much

you would have helped others by sharing your deep wellspring of compassion and sensitivity and understanding. You did that anyway—by your ongoing example, and by just living your life day by day, minute by minute, crisis by crisis.

Even the last time I saw you was not marked by upheaval or emotional turmoil. It was a Shabbat afternoon, and there was a sign on the door that announced that this was not a time for visitors.

That certainly did not deter me, since I wanted to see my Rachie one last time. I walked in and saw you lying there in your last moments on this earth.

You were at peace, and as I said the words of the Shema, I am sure I detected a smile at the corner of your lips. At least, I like to tell myself it was there.

Because it is ultimately that smile—of hope, of compassion, of kindness, of joy—that defined you, and continues to inform our memory of you. That smile, that heart, that soul that lives on for all of us.

The call came that night, and your funeral was on Tisha B'Av, the saddest day of the Jewish year, now doubly sad, and doubly mournful.

I have told you all, each one of my students, that there was nothing I would not do for any of my "children." Only one thing I do not ever want to do: eulogize you. And that is what I had to do as I spoke the final words of farewell to you.

I feel your presence every day, and that is why I mention you each year at our opening meeting, and at our graduation ceremony—because I want others to feel your presence and know that the world was better just because you were here.

I am supposed to say, "May your soul be bound up in the bonds of eternal life"—and it will.

But I miss you; we all do.

CHAPTER 1

Signs

We'd just finished dinner when Rachel called. We were excited for the nightly call from our daughter in Los Angeles, where she'd relocated two years before, during the summer—of 2006—from Baltimore to pursue a degree and a career in Jewish education. Now, after a Day School Leadership Training fellowship in LA and a stint teaching elementary schoolers, she was teaching middle schoolers at an LA Jewish Day School. I put the phone on speaker, and my husband Judah and I crowded around. Initially, we'd been worried about her adjustment; Rachel had a couple of cousins in LA, but otherwise didn't know anyone. But her bottomless vitality and megawatt smile had quickly resulted in a wide circle of friends, and we were thrilled that she was already thriving socially. Of course, we were hardly surprised; back in Baltimore and in College Park, where she'd gone to college, she was also always surrounded by friends, convening people she loved and hosting friends with their friends for Shabbat meals.

But that night, the conversation was different. Judah and I leaned in closer. Rachel said she'd been struggling with constant itching—not the kind that comes from changing laundry detergents. No, it was far more intense, enough to awaken her in the middle of the night. Calamine lotion had proved useless. Judah, an internist, listened intently as she described feet polka-dotted with welts.

Rachel, our middle child, had porcelain skin that tended to be dry, so perhaps it was that, or maybe caused by bedbugs, lurking in the used mattress she'd bought from a friend. But there were no bugs, and the itching became a regular subject of our nightly calls. She'd been to a dermatologist, she reported, and the doctor blamed delicate skin or stress. When the creams he gave her proved useless, she saw another dermatologist, who said the same thing. Rachel resigned to dealing with exceptionally sensitive skin, finding that weaving toilet paper between her toes provided some relief. But the itching persisted.

It was a few months later that Rachel let us know that she was struggling to find her work fulfilling. She hoped, she told us, to line up a job teaching or working at a Jewish organization in New York, where she could make a difference. But she would fly back to Baltimore to spend some time with us first, which relieved us because, admittedly, we'd grown concerned. On our nightly calls, Rachel had begun telling us about odd new symptoms that were revealing themselves: a slight cough, for example, and a tendency to get easily fatigued. We were glad she was coming home.

And for good reason: the moment Judah saw how thin and weary Rachel had become, he knew something was terribly wrong. Three decades into his medical career, he was already coming up with possibly diagnoses, but had one of his partners examine Rachel. A chest x-ray was needed—STAT.

With aching clarity, I recall that Friday, in October 2008, when my work phone rang. "Daddy doesn't like my chest x-ray," Rachel told me. "He sees fluid and lots of lymph nodes. He thinks I have lymphoma." I sat at my desk, tears barreling down my cheeks and two *oh no's* escaping my mouth, the words otherwise stuck in my throat. "We love you," I reassured my daughter, "and we will support you."

And so begins this story about our daughter's ride on one of life's most terrifying roller coasters: A time during which—held by her faith, her family, and, meaningfully, by hospital staff and caregivers—she surprised everyone around her by doubling down on finding her purpose.

A week after Rachel's CT scan, a biopsy confirmed the diagnosis: stage 4 Hodgkin's lymphoma. The unbearable itching, we learned, had been the result of histamine release, caused by the disease. A common symptom of lymphoma, doctors don't typically make the connection in otherwise healthy young adults like Rachel, who was almost never sick.

In the wake of this news we were shaken to the core. How was it possible that our vibrant daughter was grappling with a life-threatening illness, just days after her 25th birthday? We'd celebrated with dinner out and a big cake, after which she'd gone out with friends. But our hearts ached. This was something that happened to other people, not to us. My father was a rabbi, so I knew from experience that families got through the initial shock of receiving awful news. Eventually, we would lean on humor, find our coping mechanisms. But right then, I had no idea how we would do it.

Rachel, too, was crushed. In the first days after the diagnosis, she had several meltdowns at home, but, from go, was determined not to let the diagnosis define her. She wanted to begin treatment as soon as possible, she said, "so I can get on with my life."

All we knew to do then was to make it clear to Rachel that we were a team.

Jon and Sam, Rachel's two brothers, showed up immediately. Jon came from New York bearing five custom-made T-shirts featuring a family photo of us huddled around our kitchen table under the word "Cha-*raych*." The guttural "Cha" prefix is short for *charedi*, which means pious, or strictly adherent to tradition, Jon having coined the teasing nickname when Rachel returned from a gap year of study in Israel more religiously observant than when she'd left. My own nicknames for her had been "Silly Goose," or "Miss Goose," tributes to her silliness and sense of fun. Now, though, I generally opted for "Beautiful Rachie."

Rachel had long turned rabid sports fan, thanks to her father's and brothers' collective obsession, and Jon and Sam ramped up their wacky trivia questions and sports banter. Watching Ravens and Orioles games together were a welcome distraction from her impending treatment.

And there was hope, we thought. We clung to it as an appointment with a Johns Hopkins Hospital oncologist neared. Between Judah and me, we had ample connections at the hospital; by then, I'd been employed as a writer there for seven years, frequently inspired by testimonies from patients who'd had positive outcomes, interviewing them and the physicians who managed their care for newsletters, and Judah often referred patients to the hospital's esteemed cancer center. Rachel would be in good hands.

Our community showed up immediately, too. Family, friends

and colleagues brought favorite foods and offered practical help and boundless moral support. We heard from or about people who had been diagnosed years before with Hodgkin's and were now doing well. "At least," people would say, "she has the 'good' kind of cancer."

Indeed, of all the cancers a person can suffer, a diagnosis of Hodgkin's lymphoma comes with encouraging outcomes. Most commonly occurring in early adulthood, the blood cancer has a survival rate of about 80 percent, according to The American Cancer Society. And, thanks to advances in treatment, survival rates have improved over the past few decades. The five-year relative survival rate for all patients diagnosed with the disease is now about 86 percent; the 10-year relative survival rate, about 80 percent.

Rachel began chronicling her cancer journey by way of regular email updates to her family and friends on Oct. 15, 2008, the day after her biopsy. In addition to being adjacent to her birthday, the biopsy fell on the joyous holiday of Sukkot—the Jewish equivalent of Thanksgiving:

> Wed, Oct 15, 2008 at 8:36 PM
> Dear Friends,
>
> Chag Sameach! [Happy Holiday!] As many of you know, I've been under the weather for a while now. Between my perpetual itching and chronic cough, I haven't felt like myself in a while. When I just went home to Baltimore on Friday for the chag, I got a chest X-ray. It showed enlarged lymph nodes. Over the next few days, I got more tests. I had a surgical biopsy yesterday, which revealed I in fact had Hodgkin's lymphoma.
> I will be in Baltimore for the next month or so.

Hopefully, after my first round of chemo, I will be healthy
enough to go back and forth to New York. If any of you are
on the East Coast and would like to visit so I'm not bored,
feel free to call me, and see if I'm home. I will be staying at
my house, not the hospital. I apologize for the impersonal
nature of this email, I've just been through a lot in the last
week. You can call my cell, but I may not always answer,
but I will receive your messages. Thanks for being good
friends. Please forward this to anyone I missed.

Rachel

The following Friday, we met with a young oncologist who was cordial but reserved. He introduced us to the oncology fellow, a woman who was young, pretty and smart, like Rachel, and apparently at the beginning of a promising career, prompting a *why me* moment, picturing Rachel naturally connecting with students as a mentor, impressing colleagues and parents with her sweet demeanor and professionalism. But God appeared to have other plans for our daughter.

This impeccably dressed oncology fellow would manage Rachel's care: Outpatient chemotherapy every two weeks for six months—standard treatment for Hodgkin's—and regular tests and follow-up appointments. Symptoms usually respond quickly to the meds, they assured us. This gave us hope, but there was no denying the fear and uncertainty we felt for our girl, whose suffering had arrived right at the prime of her life.

We steeled ourselves as we embarked on our sobering new reality.

On any given day, as many as 180 patients pour into Johns Hopkins' outpatient infusion center for cancer treatments or blood products.

Another 100 come in for follow-up visits Sometimes there are no seats. Long waits are a given. Just waiting for a phlebotomist to draw blood to ensure white blood cell counts are high enough for receiving chemo can take more than an hour.

For us, this was one of the scariest times of our lives, but for the staff, it was pretty much business as usual.

So we found our own rituals and routines. On treatment days, I'd take Rachel to outpatient oncology. En route, I'd load her favorite mix CD. As we rounded the Pepsi sign on I-83, Rachel and I would exchange tired smiles in anticipation of Leona Lewis' refrain: "It'll all get better in time." A half-hour later, we'd arrive for Rachel's biweekly fix. In response to encountering occasional rudeness as we tried to navigate the red tape of the hospital system, Rachel also found a treatment day uniform: A red T-shirt emblazoned with the words: "Smile—it confuses people."

At the infusion center, patients are escorted back to one of six "pods," where they spend the next several hours hooked to an infusion pump. Nurses and techs scurry about in the open space, taking vital signs, changing IV bags whenever the pumps beep and keeping an open eye for sudden nausea.

Walking into the crowded waiting area and then the pods, you enter the world of the unwell—sitting hairless alongside their loved ones, seeming oddly suspended between despair and hope. *How can this many people have cancer?* I wondered, no less buoyed knowing that Rachel was getting treatment at a hospital that attracted people from all over the U.S. and around the world for their care.

Rachel's heart-patterned bag held an armamentarium of distractions—computer, snacks and DVDs to help her endure the hours-long infusion. But even distracted, she was terrified of needles, and her veins often proved too thin to access, requiring several attempts.

So, before leaving the house, she'd pop a sedative, grab a bite and hope the warm packs on her arm would coax her stubborn veins.

Thankfully, her phlebotomist, Linda, was as natural at positioning a needle as she was at smiling. With each successful IV insertion, she'd laugh with Rachel and hug her, intermittently chatting about their shared Baltimore Ravens fandom.

And Katy, Rachel's primary nurse, was warm, soft-spoken, patient and even-tempered, but also honest about what Rachel could expect in terms of side effects. And indeed, nausea and fatigue followed, but after several treatments, Rachel's itching had nearly vanished, and her blood counts and energy level soared. But upon seeing concerning results to a pulmonary function test, Rachel's oncology fellow took her off the chemo drug with potentially harsh side effects to her lungs.

In the week between treatments, Rachel rallied—hopes restored, blue eyes brighter. She made plans with friends and even kept some of them. By December, Rachel was running more than half a mile.

Then, a small blow—about halfway through her treatment course, Katy suffered a freak accident, and the nurse who subbed for her was somber and negative. This impacted Rachel, making the treatments harder to bear. Still, Rachel's doctors barely felt any lymph nodes. Though nausea, fatigue and a slight cough remained steady companions, Rachel toughed things out, hopeful for the best.

The outpouring of love from family and friends, meanwhile, continued at full volume. Our refrigerator filled up with Rachel's favorite dishes—soups, lasagna and brownies. Flowers and plants brightened our dining room and den.

But Rachel missed her friends and social life terribly. Talking on the phone was exhausting, so she often let her phone ring, turning instead to emails and social media—then in its infancy. She'd plop her computer onto her lap and begin her two-fingered pecking. I still don't know why she never learned how to properly type on a keyboard. No matter: she typed at a furious clip.

Mon, Oct 27, 2008
Hey Friends and Family,

Thanks so much for your amazing support during this not so easy time. I wanted to let you all know that I went to my oncologist on Friday. I will be starting my chemo on Thursday at Hopkins. It will be every other week for 6 months. Hopefully, I will be finished all my treatments by mid-April. I will be up for visits in between chemo treatments. Please call in advance and make sure that you don't have a cold if you want to stop by.

It was determined that my disease is Hodgkin's stage 4. Although stage 4 is alarming, the treatment is the same, and as responsive. They treat stages 1-4 exactly the same way. I have the best doctors and will be getting great treatment. Again, I appreciate all the phone calls and emails. My cell is always on, although on silent if I'm asleep.

Hope to have good news for you all soon. Enjoy the rest of your chag!

Rachel

Mon, Oct 27, 2008 at 12:14 PM
Hey Everyone,

I have been getting so many emails and phone calls from people wondering about my first round of chemo, so I figured it's time to write an update. I want to first thank everyone for being so amazing. I apologize if I have not returned emails or phone calls, but just know that they mean the world to me. I have really seen what an extraordinary group of friends and family I have through this time.

On Thursday, I had my first round of chemo, not such a fun day. Not being such a needle person, they had issues with my IV that didn't thrill me. (Apparently, I have tiny veins.) But, I have begun my war against the Hodgkin's in my body, so it will all be worth it. 1 down, 11 to go! Once they successfully worked my IV, the chemo drugs were in me for a few hours. Following chemo, I was exhausted and dizzy for a few days, but each day I am getting stronger. In fact, yesterday I was able to walk a mile for the first time since chemo. My next chemo is not for another week and a half so I have ample time to feel like myself again. Thanks again for your continuing concern and support, and I will continue to update with any news or changes. As of now, my body is in the midst of fighting, and will continue to do so.

Rachel

Despite all these healthy approaches to our new reality, the cancer shadow loomed large and had begun to wear on all of us. There was unspoken angst we each grappled with and carried with us. Some days it felt like lugging an overstuffed valise without wheels. I was taking off days from work but still feeling pressure to stay connected. And, my fatigue and worry sometimes resulted in careless errors in my work. But we bore on, determined to support Rachel through her ordeal.

Cancer had haunted my family when I was growing up, too. My mother—as a result of having a sister die of colon cancer—lived in perpetual fear of any kind of cancer. She could hardly even say the word *cancer*, only ever whispering it.

My mother had endured a great deal of suffering herself, one of six children growing up in an argument-riddled tenement on New York's Lower East Side in virtual poverty. Her parents had brought their large family from Poland, and my mother was the first American-born child. Diagnosed with scoliosis at an early age, she wore a brace and required multiple back surgeries over the years. Despite all of this, she excelled in school, and it took me many years into adulthood to realize that she'd also been depressed.

Thankfully my father, a pulpit rabbi, was a jovial, kind man who hailed from Chicago and met my mother for a blind date, when he was in New York for a rabbinical convention. My mother was charmed by his abundant optimism, and they were married in New York on a snowy day in late December 1947.

As they raised the five of us, Dad always had a joke or Talmudic saying ready when we needed it most. One of his favorites was *Gam zeh yaavor*. "This, too, shall pass."

But even my father shared my mother's worst fears about cancer. Wherever my father served congregations—whether in Tennessee, California, Rhode Island, Indiana or upstate New York—his hospital or home visits always included people who were "dying of cancer." He'd say special prayers for them, but more often than not, weeks later, he was writing eulogies on index cards held together with paper clips.

In the 1960s, we were living in Rhode Island and had driven to New York to visit my aunt, who, by then, was nearing the end of her life. I was eight and couldn't stop staring at the stick-figure legs emerging below her distended belly. She reminded me of an ostrich, and I was afraid to go near her for fear that I would "catch" the cancer myself. I could barely communicate with her anyway, as she mostly spoke Yiddish. It strikes me now how cruel this kind of fear is: the fear of getting close to someone who is suffering. After these visits, my mother's eyes glistened and her mouth quivered.

As I grew into my teenage years, I began to realize that every family seemed to be touched by cancer—some more than others. Still, the subject haunted me. I tried to use my rational brain to shrug it off, but the messages of my childhood were there to stay.

When I was a junior in high school, I saw cancer up close again. A girl in my gym class suddenly started wearing head scarves. Before long, she was the only one of us allowed to use the one shower with a curtain. That was because she had *Cancer*.

Small wonder my mother would always utter the word in a whisper: *CAN*-cer. I often thought to myself: *Could there be a worse fate*?

Of course, its prominence strengthened bonds. By the time I got to college, I found myself listening sympathetically as I learned about friends whose parents, siblings and other relatives were "battling" cancer. I now realize that using "fight" metaphors like these makes it seem as though a person has a choice in these matters—that one might not be "fighting" hard enough. Yet, that was the way cancer treatment and one's response to it always seemed to be presented.

At the time, I accepted the "fight" metaphor—indeed, embraced it—but I came to realize how flawed it was. Even the most compliant patients can't deter cancer cells from proliferating. Now, I try to avoid fight metaphors for cancer, even though they seem to empower some people.

The topic found its way into my early courtship with Judah. Seniors in college, we spent a great deal of time on the phone between dates. After a particularly vulnerable call I received one night in the fall of 1976, I knew I would marry him. He told me about the greatest source of pain in his life: when, as a senior in high school, he got news that his mother would need a mastectomy at age 43. The call was the longest we'd had so far, and Judah did most of the talking. His voice cracking, he shared how scary the biopsy and surgery were; the dreadful treatments that made his mother retch; and her difficult path to recovery. I was drawn to his empathy and depth of feeling that night, and I had a feeling he'd gotten it from somewhere.

I was right. His family, I learned, was incredibly close. At its core was the woman who would become my mother-in-law. Bea "Bootsie" Minkove, the woman Judah had told me so much about, was a force. The quintessential matriarch, she presided over holidays and family gatherings, almost always located at Bootsie and Mickey's modest semi-detached Baltimore home. Never fussy, these events featured abundant hugs, tasty food and family stories. And no matter how many times we heard those tales recounted in Bootsie's quasi-Southern, nasal drawl—so different from my mostly Midwestern accent—we'd laugh uproariously. Soon it felt natural to call her Mom.

From the moment I joined the family in 1976, she enveloped me with affection. At 22, I knew little about keeping house, running a kitchen, balancing work and dealing with my husband's grueling medical training. I learned to cope by studying her ways.

Things had been a little different in my household growing up. Although my mother was deeply devoted to her five children, her back pain made things more difficult for her. As a rabbi's wife, she was also consumed with cooking, baking, and supporting my father's congregants. On top of that, she often worked double shifts as an L.P.N. She simply didn't have much time to spend with us, except at the Shabbat table, though she didn't sit down for long. She needed to sleep before her evening shift. I reflect now on the emotional and physical toll the pressures of life took on my mother, and feel a deep admiration for how much she was able to accomplish under all that duress.

My experience of my mother made it so that I paid close attention to other women of her generation, and the first thing I noticed about my mother-in-law was how organized she was. Every week, in flawless teacher's script, she'd make her shopping list and take care of her parents' needs and any other commitments.

Her husband, "Mickey," a man of very few words, worked alongside her. He baked challah for the Sabbath; she made babka; she washed the dinner dishes; he dried. Wednesday evenings, dishes scrubbed and dried, they'd hit the grocery store. When they returned, he'd wash the fruit and let it air-dry. All she had to say was "Mick," and he'd be there, attending to a stuck drawer or the fridge's temperamental thermostat. I marveled at the efficiency of that household, punctuated by loving glances or private laughs—never a harsh word, at least in my presence.

Most nights around 7 p.m., Bootsie would call to see how we were doing. She could detect stress a mile away. When I'd confess to feeling overwhelmed, she'd listen and offer advice, frequently ending with the Hebrew expression my father often cited: *Gam zeh yaavor*—"This, too, shall pass." Truth be told, there were times when I resented hearing that aphorism. After all, she couldn't possibly appreciate the strain of balancing Judah's on-call schedule, my job, and, before long, child care. Besides, sometimes I felt smothered by her calls. It seemed as though she wanted to know exactly how I was doing and to offer guidance, even as I convinced myself that I had everything under control.

But every time I saw her again and felt her warm embrace, I'd set aside my irritation. When our first son, Jon, was born, she'd relish watching him one day a week while I worked. When I'd come to pick him up, she'd be reading to him or playing with him on the floor, her eyes twinkling with joy. At those moments, I felt blessed to have such a doting mother-in-law, or *Savta*, as my kids came to call her.

Our lives fell into something of a happy routine. But alas, it was short-lived. Cancer had struck again, and neither Bootsie's son the doctor, nor her brother the doctor, nor her physician nephews could halt its progression. As Mom soldiered through the brutal treatments, we watched her steady decline, feeling utterly helpless. Her death at 54 rocked our world. Hundreds packed the funeral home to hear eulogies befitting a queen.

Oddly, in March of 2009, as Rachel neared what we hoped would be her final treatment for Hodgkin's lymphoma and was feeling much better, we marked the 25th anniversary of Mom's death. I felt her presence more than ever. Maybe it was because I was then the same age she was as she left this world. I'd think about this when I caught my father-in-law's eye across our dinner table every Friday night. As he lifted the monogrammed sterling flatware I used weekly to honor her memory, I wondered if he'd made the connection, too.

I felt Mom hovering over Rachel as she battled cancer. We have a lone photo of Savta holding her first granddaughter—a beautiful creature with arresting eyes and delicate skin. They'd had only five short months to bond, yet I'm certain something mystical transpired between them. Rachel displayed the same fortitude and optimism we saw in Mom throughout her battle.

Cure rates for breast cancer, I reminded myself, had risen dramatically since Mom's death, and we had reason to be hopeful that Rachel's cancer treatment for lymphoma, too, had good odds for success.

By the time the joyous Jewish holiday of Purim of 2009 arrived, Rachel had only two more chemo sessions left of her six-month treatment. Hopeful, we gathered in the kitchen, as we did every year to bake hamentaschen. As we gathered the ingredients, Rachel took off her rings. Rachel had purchased one of them in Jerusalem after she witnessed a bombing, when she was studying there in 2004. The Hebrew inscription etched into the silver band reads *Gam zeh yaavor.*

I realize that many families have a cancer story, but when you're part of a medical family, as my husband is, it's hard not to think about worse-case scenarios. So often, I'd hear Judah discuss an unnamed patient with his uncle or cousins and hear the words, "suspicious for a mass," or "metastatic cancer."

Judah is not a loquacious man, though he has a wicked sense of humor and can quickly make a pun of pretty much any word or name. But the pain I saw on his face the day of Rachel's chest x-ray was palpable.

Those two shared a special bond, beginning with their identical coloring: white, freckled skin that never tanned—scorched by even seconds in the sun—and crystal-blue eyes that blazed intelligence. But Rachel was smilier, and when she succeeded in making Judah laugh, I saw the totality of their resemblance. They'd talk sports and joke about Lady Gaga's outrageous ensembles so much that Judah took a liking to Rachel's pop music, too.

These exchanges melted me, even when I felt an occasional pang of jealousy for their animated banter and private jokes about celebrities, sitcoms and sports. But in the unnerving rhythm our lives had taken on, I was grateful to witness any humorous aside.

Nov. 11, 2008
Hey Everyone,

I just wanted to start off by thanking everyone for their generous donations to Team Rachey and for Avi for spearheading such an amazing cause. In less than a week, over $6,000 was raised for lymphoma research. That is quite a feat, and I am really touched by this whole project.

I had my second round of chemo on Thursday. Luckily, they found my veins on the first time this round, which was only minimal discomfort. (The drugs also helped immensely.) The side effects were very similar to the first time, and will continue to be so for the rest of treatment. I am basically weak and dizzy for the first four days following treatment, and progressively improve each following day. Today, I was able to go out a little, only having fatigue as a side effect. By the weekend, I should be feeling like myself again.

Yesterday, I received some great news from my oncologist. I had a CAT scan earlier in the day which revealed that my lymph nodes had shrunk significantly. My biggest node had shrunk from 2.5 CM to 1.1 CM, more than half the size. My body is responding well to the chemo, and it's only been one cycle. If I have improved this fast already, I'm excited to see my results after a few more cycles. Despite all my uncomfortable side effects, my body is fighting this cancer and winning. Knowing that the chemo is working is a strong impetus to upkeep a positive attitude.

Thanks again for everyone's continued support. You are all helping me get through this difficult time. I'll continue to keep you posted.

Rachel

Hey guys,

I just wanted to share some poetry with you all. These are some of my reflections from the past month. Have a good Shabbos. I'll write an update shortly.

Rachel

THE ROLLERCOASTER

Up and down
Up and down
Up and down
The rollercoaster glides through time, each day spanning
    an eternity.
The passenger shrieks as the coaster reaches its highest
    elevation,
knowing what follows . . . The Dreaded DROP
At the lowest point, the passenger emits a whitish hue
    and is ready to
get off this frightening journey.
The only thing holding her back is the exhilaration of
    staying high forever.
Is that a possibility? She ponders.
The passenger has quickly learned that anything is
    possible in this
rollercoaster of life.

LEAVES

Colorful, radiant leaves create images of paintings
    coming to life.
Rich reds, yellows, orange, and greens, illuminate the
    streets with
their breathtaking beauty.
Yet, as you begin to take in these unbelievable images, the
    leaves
start to exfoliate.
The trees wan, and eventually become bare.
Perhaps, instead of a depressing occurrence, it is neces-
    sary for the
health of the tree.
The radiance may fade during the cold, bleak winter.
However, come spring, there is renewal and appreciation
    for the leaves
and the new healthy tree.
Although monochromatic, along with the effervescent
    sunlight, hope and
new beginnings are linked to these trees.
The natural shedding of the trees expunged the harmful,
    albeit
beautiful, leaves.
And only time could renew a full and vibrant tree to
    restart a new
cycle of life.

IN AN INSTANT

In an instant, your world can drastically change.
All preconceived notions and expectations can be shat-
    tered within seconds.
One day, you can be living your trite, routine life.
You can be partying with friends and adjusting to the
    nuances of big city life.
Then, in an instant, that all changes.
You receive news that puts life in a new perspective.
You start to appreciate the value of family and friends
    and shiver at
the thought of being without them.
You see beauty in what you used to consider mundane.
And the opportunity to return to a normal life not only
    seems
appealing, but a goal to strive for.
Sometimes, it takes only one instant to gain that
    perspective.
And, hopefully with time, even the most boring days will
    seem perfect
        after overcoming the hurdle that simply took an
    instant of time.

CHAPTER 2

Recalibrating

O n March 26, 2009, budding azaleas greeted us as we loaded the car with cheesecakes for the oncology staff to celebrate what would be Rachel's last chemo. We were upbeat, but once in the pod, an emergency cardiac arrest there frightened us. The oncology fellow seemed more subdued, too. She expressed concern about Rachel's elevated LDH serum level, suggesting a possible blood flow problem. Finally cracking a smile, she told Rachel, "Glad this is your last one."

Two weeks later, on the eve of Passover, we learned that the oncology fellow's original somberness was warranted. "There's some bad news," said the doctor, calling with the PET scan results. "You have significant progression of the disease." A torrent of unwelcome words followed: *No time to waste, stronger chemo. Bone marrow transplant.*

I was in the kitchen shredding bitter herbs for the Passover *seder* when I heard Rachel sobbing in the den. She showed me the damning words on her PET scan. Engulfed in grief, we limped through the holiday. Once again, loved ones rallied. My close friend Liz burst through our front door and into our kitchen, hugging me and seizing the grater and bowl from my hands. "*Go*," she said. "You need to be with your daughter."

We wasted no time scheduling the next available appointment with Dr. Richard "Rich" Ambinder, an expert in lymphoma and leukemia. But first, we had to get through the holiday.

Passover, aka *Pesach*, marks a defining moment for Jews; a transition from bondage to freedom. Preparing to escape Egypt, after 200 years of enslavement, the Israelites couldn't wait for their bread to rise, so we eat unleavened bread, or matzo, throughout the holiday.

The *seder* is rife with symbolism: *matzo*, bitter herbs (to represent the bitterness of having endured two centuries of slavery), salt water (tears), *charoset* (the apple and wine mixture that resembles mortar for the pyramid bricks), just to name a few.

Everyone reads and sings through the *haggadah*, recounting the story of the events that united our people. Midway through the recitation, we eat a festive meal.

Passover is also very labor-intensive. All *chametz*—unleavened products—must be removed or locked up and the entire house cleaned.

On April 2, 2009, as we prepared for the second *seder* in the wake of such terrible news, we continued to lean on community. Our dear friends Mitch and Janice, who joined us annually for the *seder*, asked if we still wanted them to come. Rachel said she'd be OK with that, though I hesitated. When they did end up coming, we felt buoyed by their presence.

Jon, in an effort to infuse the evening with humor, announced a bitter herbs contest. Picking up the horseradish root from the table, he challenged Sam to see which of them could consume/tolerate the most.

Normally, when her brothers launched into outrageous antics, Rachel would roll her eyes and then laugh a little out loud. But on this *seder* night, she was uncharacteristically subdued. But as they traded dares, Jon telling Sam, "I'll see you one piece of *maror* and raise you one," she began to brighten.

By then, the boys were as red as ripe tomatoes, tears streaming down their cheeks. And our collective laughter erupted into gasps, then wonder. I couldn't imagine a more unabashed act of filial love. And, I've no doubt Rachel was moved to the core.

But as Passover drew to a close, the upcoming appointment at Hopkins loomed large.

For all his world renown, Rich Ambinder, director of Johns Hopkins Hospital's Division of Hematologic Malignancies—a deliberate man with wavy, silver-touched hair—was unusually accessible. He greeted us warmly, as the attractive oncology fellow looked on. Then their faces turned grim.

"You have chemo-resistant disease, and a 40 percent chance of a cure with salvage therapy—high-dose chemo—and a bone marrow transplant," Dr. A. told Rachel. He also recommended radiation to her chest following the transplant. More dreadful statistics followed. By then, Rachel, her father and I were unable to stop our tears.

Rachel suddenly broke the silence. "What about my fertility?"

"Forget about your fertility!" the fellow shot back. "We need to save your life!"

My heart instantly sank: I'd always envisioned a future with beautiful children for our only daughter, who had a gift with kids and often shared her dreams of being a wife and fun-loving mom.

As Judah and I poured out our concerns, Dr. A. listened and then paused—he's given to long ones. He locked eyes with Rachel. *"Despite this bad news,"* he said. "You're young and strong, and I have good reason to think that you will do well. For sure, you're better off going in younger."

Still, he cautioned, Rachel's cancer had proven aggressive. "So, we'll all have to keep a close eye on your symptoms." Soon we'd come to depend on Dr. Ambinder and his perceptive and soft-spoken nurse, Jane. After a bone marrow aspirate in preparation for seeking a match, Rachel would need to begin a high-dose, three-agent chemo regimen.

First, however, Rachel insisted on seeing a fertility specialist. Two days before her bone marrow biopsy, she had an ovary successfully extracted and immediately stored in a freezer vault. She named the ovary "Olga" and warned me to take care of myself, because in a few years, I'd become a grandmother to her triplets. I laughed out loud and assured her that would be my greatest pleasure.

Greeting us warmly, Dr. Garcia—an accomplished OB-GYN with much experience and self-assurance—told us he'd seen many cancer patients recover and go on to have healthy babies following in vitro fertilization. He pulled out a sheet of paper and drew two circles. The outer one, he called the cortex; the inner one, the ovary.

"After taking the ovary out," he said, "we make sections"—he drew three rectangular boxes—"and freeze them. Four to five years later, we reinsert them using a small incision into the ovary. It's like an autograft."

There is limited ovulation, he went on, "but the hope is that you can fertilize the eggs. *OR*, if that doesn't work, we can put pieces of the ovary in the forearm. The tissue would take three months to have fresh ovulation; four months to produce an egg." Rachel and I laughed out loud, imagining a pregnant forearm. We didn't quite grasp how this all worked.

"You were born with all the eggs in your ovary," he explained. "Genetically, the eggs are in a dormant stage—completely immature." But with chemo, all the eggs are completely gone, he noted. This was her only chance to preserve her fertility. Rachel winced at the news that the surgery could cause shoulder and abdominal pain, but she was determined to go through with it.

On April 15, Rachel's right ovary was removed successfully. Afterwards, Dr. Garcia flashed a victory smile and reported that it had gone perfectly.

But the next day, Rachel was doubled over in pain. Her doctors were hardly pleased, knowing that the very next day she would need a bone marrow biopsy from her back. That meant she'd have to lay flat on her belly—the source of her most recent surgical anguish.

On the day of the bone marrow extraction, Rachel was anxious and still weak from the ovary extraction. We gave her lorazepam for her anxiety and a painkiller. Still, as the needle entered her back, Rachel's face crinkled. "Ow, ow, *OW!*" she cried. I felt tears welling up but forced myself to tighten my grip on Rachel's hand for reassurance.

The bone marrow nurse moved swiftly, and, before we knew it, the procedure was over. But she wasn't done for the day. Next up was the insertion of the Hickman catheter to her neck, so that drugs could course through her veins through a port. She actually welcomed the procedure. After all, it meant that they wouldn't have to coax and poke stubborn veins any longer.

After six months in the hospital's outpatient infusion area, we knew the routine. Once in pod C, amid the cacophony from pumps, TVs and conversation, a sea of calm prevailed in Jane, who'd been an outpatient caregiver since 1998, and would review and explain the labs to us.

As his primary nurse, Jane stayed in close touch with Dr. Ambinder's lymphoma and leukemia patients. That meant understanding the intricacies of standard and experimental treatments and knowing which drug interactions or side effects can prove life-threatening. Any time Jane caught a puzzled expression on our faces, she'd ask if we understood. Then she'd paint a clearer picture of how, for example, low potassium can spell trouble for heart muscles.

"I love what I do because of the patients I treat," Jane once shared as we grew closer to her. "An incredible number have touched my heart." But the other thing that brought Jane to this work was the fact that her husband was diagnosed with leukemia at 33, and then died from a brain tumor at 54. "I understand what patients are going through," she told us. "Cancer is a scary place to be. I want them to know that we're not a big, cold institution."

A strong bond was also evolving between Dr. Ambinder and Rachel. When a scan came back with worrisome cancer or when side effects escalated into infections, doctor and patient would negotiate the need for admission to the hospital. Sometimes Rachel convinced Dr. A. to let her stay home. "I expect that you'll get through this hurdle," he'd say, "but," he'd say with a grin, "you're *complicated*."

Meanwhile, our strapping sons charmed the phlebotomists, bantering about who would be best suited for the role as bone marrow donor. Sam ended up a perfect match; Jon a half-match. We were elated by the news. She joked that she and Sam would be DNA twins, and jubilantly sent out an update to her friends.

> Hey all,
>
> Thank you everyone for your overwhelming support and warm wishes during this difficult period. I apologize for not getting back to everyone's emails individually, but they really do mean a lot to me. In the last few weeks, I have found out some better news than my pre-Pesach disaster. My brother Sam is a perfect bone marrow match, which was the doctors' ideal situation for success. Additionally, through doctor examination, it appears that my lymph nodes have shrunk, and this new potent round of chemo is working. I will have concrete evidence of this progress at the end of the month with a CT scan.
>
> I also have my dates for the hospital and transplant. My hospital stay will be a long 4-5 weeks. Visitors are allowed, and I would love to see people, just stay away if you have any type of cold or infection. I will be admitted to Hopkins on June 17, and the transplant should take place on June 23. Following which, I will recuperate in the hospital. This process is happening a lot sooner than I anticipated. They are only giving me one more round of the chemo regimen I'm on now, which was another piece of good news. I'll be getting chemo tomorrow-Friday all day long. That should hopefully be my last outpatient chemo.
>
> Thanks again for the amazing outpouring of support!
>
> Rachel

As for me, I always prided myself on coping well, but at this point, I was beginning to feel unraveled. My job as a newsletter writer/editor for Johns Hopkins Medicine required setting up time for interviews. I was expected to write compelling stories for diverse audiences and, sometimes, more complex stories for physician newsletters.

Shortly after I disclosed Rachel's health woes, my boss seemed sympathetic, but not long after, he appeared to resent my absences and lackluster writing. Then, one day, without warning, he foisted a writing project on me: to serve as editor/primary writer for a biweekly employee newsletter. It seemed particularly cruel, as the newsletter's release dates coincided with Rachel's biweekly cancer treatments.

My creativity was also at an all-time low, and it didn't help that I was perimenopausal. I now knew exactly what people meant when they described having a visceral response to stress. Since early childhood, overeating has been a source of solace to me, and I've struggled with my weight ever since. As Rachel got sicker, I turned increasingly to food, trying to stay balanced, with the help of Weight Watchers. I felt a little better knowing that hormonal changes, along with aging, often cause weight gain.

But my body was reacting to stress as never before. Simultaneously, two things began to occur: My fingers developed unsightly warts, and my periods became especially intense. The excessive bleeding made my blood count drop, which caused overwhelming fatigue. Marjorie, my closest friend at work, called my troubles "biblical—Job-esque." She remained an anchor as I sank into a perpetually exhausted, demoralized state.

Keeping up with all this physical and emotional stress became a herculean task. Judah insisted that I see my gynecologist. I feared my doctor would recommend surgery, which is precisely what he did.

The following week, my poor husband had to take me to Hopkins early for my endometrial ablation, an outpatient procedure that stems heavy bleeding by removing the lining of the uterus.

I don't recall much from that day, except for when I opened my eyes in the recovery room to discover Judah and Rachel standing over me. Rachie flashed her electric smile. Eyes sparkling from the overhead lights, she exclaimed, "Hi, Mommy! Now it's *my* turn to visit you!"

Instantly, I was overcome with gratitude and wonder. But I knew that recovering from my surgery would be a cakewalk next to what my daughter was about to endure.

The appointed day for the intensive pre-bone marrow transplant treatment arrived as I was recovering at home from surgery. I was heartbroken not to have been able to support Rachel in person, but I was determined to be there for the latter part of her chemo. The outpatient, weeklong ICE treatment, an acronym for ifosfamide, carboplatin and etoposidephosphate, is the standard approach for refractory Hodgkin's patients. It precedes the bone marrow transplant, in hopes of beginning a calculated attack on cancer cells.

According to the National Center for Biotechnology Information, part of the National Institutes of Health, chemotherapy given in combinations of drugs usually works better than single drugs because different drugs kill cancer in different ways. We were warned, however, that side effects would likely intensify.

Knowing that the treatments would make Rachel's hair fall out, I scheduled an appointment with Fagie Rosen, a lovely, soft-spoken woman who sells stylish wigs in her home. Her clientele is mostly religiously observant married women who cover their hair, but she also serves customers who are losing their hair because of chemotherapy.

It took Fagie only a few minutes to find a human hair fall nearly the same color as Rachel's hair. It looked so real that over time, even I began to think of it as her own hair. The wig was expensive but worth every penny: I saw almost immediately how much it boosted Rachel's confidence. The best part was that Rachel wouldn't have to use a flat-iron, as she often did with her naturally curly hair. Her new wig was stick-straight. She loved it.

Still, before going to bed, as Rachel carefully placed the fall on the Styrofoam wig stand, I couldn't help but notice how quickly her own hair was vanishing. Sometimes, when I caught her looking at herself in the mirror wistfully, I had to turn away, and not only because I didn't want her to see my reaction. I found myself saddened to realize that her naturally beautiful sandy-blonde hair that she so prized would soon fall out. As a baby, Rachel's tight blonde curls had framed her face, but over the years it had grown thicker and longer, and she took pride in all the time she spent—especially before Shabbat—making her hair look straight and shiny.

⁓

Rachel's first ICE treatment took place on April 22, 2009. By then, I'd begun to keep a journal to chronicle her treatment, along with how Rachel was responding to it.

Also, though, the journal was a way to document my own emotional journey alongside Rachel's; what our family was going through at that time.

Friday, two days after the treatment, Rachel developed blurry vision, nausea and fatigue. That Shabbat morning turned out to be sunny and mild. After breakfast, Rachel insisted on going for walk. We did, but forgot to bring along a water bottle. The sun, no longer mild, was getting hotter by the minute. Rachel had to sit down to catch her breath, looking faint, as her lips turned blue. As we struggled to make it home through the backyard of our neighbor's house, she began to collapse. Suddenly, I looked up and saw our neighbor Mindy, who'd been heading to synagogue but dashed back to her house when she saw us, returning immediately with a water bottle. Then she helped me support Rach en route home, safe and sound.

In that moment, I imagined how Hagar must have felt in the Book of Genesis when she realized her son Ishmael was dying from thirst, and God sent an angel with water. Mindy was our angel. I was incredibly grateful and relieved.

The ICE treatments continued to make Rachel sicker, and I silently wondered how much more her poor, thinning body could take. She looked so frail, as if even the slightest breeze could whisk her away. At times, dreams of Rachel struggling to survive, gasping for air, frightened me, though more often than not, thankfully, I'd fall into an exhausted sleep, sans dreams.

We'd had a crash course in pre-transplant prep and what to expect—the good, the bad and the ugly—mostly the last two. Knowing that both Sam and Rachel were about to experience some discomfort saddened me, but I was so proud of them both.

Rachel would first need a spate of tests: A CT scan of her sinuses, EKG, blood tests, heart scan. Thankfully, the person who explained this to us was Lacy, who was not only Rachel's social worker, but someone who was also becoming a trusted friend. She was patient and thorough about letting us know what to expect, and supportive in the face of insurance snags. "We want to make sure it's safe for Rachel to undergo the transplant," she explained. "Then, six days of chemo, then transplant, then four days of chemo to kill any remaining cancer cells."

She then explained that Rachel's hospitalization post-transplant would last three to four weeks. Sam, however, would be able to leave the hospital a few hours after the transplant. The plan was that my sister-in-law Niti, who'd driven to Baltimore from New York that morning with my father-in-law, would drive Sam back to his apartment in New York, where he was enrolled in a master's degree in health program.

"After the transplant," Lacy told Rachel, "you can see people, as long as they're healthy." She went on to explain that the bone marrow team would watch her and give her transfusions if her blood counts plummeted. Following her release from the hospital, Rachel would need to head to the IPOP (inpatient/outpatient unit) every day for one to two months to monitor her condition.

Days 14-21, she explained, are called "engraftment," where you start to see some recovery after the transplant.

We still had about two months before Rachel needed to be admitted, and there were days we could almost forget that she was sick. She seemed eager to move forward, running errands and taking short walks. On one of those walks, she stopped at Rite-Aid to buy a birthday card for Judah. The front of the card showed a 10-year-old girl dancing with her dad. The words below the photo read: "Little girls love their daddies …" Inside: "…even after they're all grown up!" And then this, from Rachel:

> *"Happy Birthday! You can't get rid of me yet! I'll*
> *always be your little girl. I hope you have a very happy*
> *birthday. This is going to be a good year for all of us!*
> ,
> Rach"*

Judah opened the card as soon as he came into the kitchen … and wept.

Not long afterwards, Zippy Schorr, the head of the Jewish school our kids had attended, called to invite Rachel to help out in the library. "I just I want her to feel useful while she's recovering," she said. "I daven for her every day."

Admission day loomed large, and when it ultimately arrived, the sun was shining through a brilliantly blue sky. Rachel, visibly anxious, came downstairs wearing the "Cancer Sucks" shirt she'd received from a friend. En route to the hospital, she slipped in the CD mix tape she'd created for the occasion, which included Akon's "Dangerous"; Gloria Gaynor's "I Will Survive"; Kanye West's "Stronger"; Madonna's "4 Minutes"; Pink's "So What"; "Hero," by Mariah Carey; and Rihanna's "Live Your Life."

Once we arrived on Weinberg 5 and entered Room 1, we were relieved to see a spacious, clean area, especially after having spent so much time in crowded communal hospital areas. We'd been advised to bring things from home that provided familiarity and comfort, and we unpacked Rachel's quilt. A large calendar on the white board made it easy to check off the days until the transplant. The nurses, attentive and compassionate, asked regularly if there was anything we needed.

The first chemo treatment would be delivered at approximately 4 p.m. (actual time: 5:15). Blood draws would take place all through the night. Rachel's oncology fellow stopped by, as did the head of the Bone Marrow Transplant Unit.

I managed to sit and work on a story for a newsletter. A knock at the door brought someone in our community who was delivering a homemade meal of macaroni and cheese—true comfort food, and one of Rachel's favorites.

The next day, I bumped into Lacy. Her face, resolute, beamed reassurance. She reminded me that Rachel's pluck would position her well for the bone marrow transplant. I knew she was right, but I dreaded the suffering Rachel was about to endure.

The reality that chemo alone wasn't enough to keep Rachel's bone marrow from producing defective blood cells hit hard. We knew that her immune system—what was left of it—would have to be "rebooted," reengineered with Sam's healthy bone marrow, the spongy source of all blood.

I tried my best to stay positive, but it was hard, and my words were often choked with emotion. Meantime, Judah walked around crestfallen, his head low and brows furrowed, barely speaking. His father's health had also begun declining, compounding our stress and uncertainty even further.

CHAPTER 3

Hope v. Fear

Seeing our daughter look weaker with each passing day made it hard to accept that Rachel's blood counts would continue to plummet until Sam's bone marrow took root and started making new platelets. It was a scary time: The risk of infection or fever was great, so we all had to be vigilant about hand hygiene and exposure to germs.

Rachel's suffering intensified. The treatment ushered in a host of side effects: mucositis raw mouth sores low into her throat, so excruciating that she required a morphine pump; gastrointestinal upset; rashes and overwhelming fatigue.

Shepherding patients through a bone marrow transplant demands constant—but *honest*—cheerleading. From day one, there were loving messages on the white board and excitement at crossing off completed days. Applause greeted Rachel when she completed laps around the unit. Surprise massages arranged by the unit's nurse manager lifted Rachel's spirits on particularly awful days leading up to the transplant.

On another white board opposite Rachel's bed, in multicolored markers:

> Hey Ms. Minkove— your 5A nurse Teresa is here to bring a few smiles ☺ your way
> Hoping I can help you have a better day!!
> -------------GOD BLESS-------------

For his part, Sam was elated that he could provide lifesaving bone marrow for his sister. When he'd beat out his brother as the closer match, he'd truly acted as if he'd won the lottery, seemingly unfazed by the likelihood he'd feel pain and soreness from the extraction. And, though he didn't verbalize it, I could tell that his love for Rachel transcended the blood donation. Sam, ever the younger brother, used to follow her around—she always played the teacher; he, the obedient student, completing "homework" she assigned.

As Sam grew older, his big brother would yank him away for baseball games and sports trivia, but Sam continued to spend time with Rachel when Jon wasn't paying attention. Now, though, both boys were eager to do anything to save their sister's life.

Their love for Rachel touched me beyond words. Jon and Sam once took pride in teasing her about her ignorance about sports or some of the people she called friends. With each passing year, though, the three of them had common friends and had grown closer. Now, my sons were emailing or texting their sister regularly. They g-chatted funny stories and other nonsense to distract her—and themselves—from the cruel realities of this time. Throughout the day, her phone buzzed with the same message from them: , "How you doin', Charach?"

We all were hyper-focused on helping Rachel get through her ordeal. But we knew we had to turn our trust over to the hospital staff and hope for the best.

Rachel's team of caregivers were attentive and kind. "OK, my sweetheart," nurse Carla would announce as she breezed in, "we're going to get you out of bed today, so we can get you out of here faster." And when the physical therapist didn't show up, she gave Rachel her own PT session. In between them, Carla regaled us with humorous stories about her family.

On one horrific side-effect night, a nurse named Greg sat down with us and said gently, "When you manipulate the immune system like this, you have to expect the possibility for anything to happen." Out of consideration for sleep's restorative powers, Greg would draw Rachel's blood early, so she wouldn't need to be awakened at night.

During this time, the bond between Rachel and Lacy continued to deepen. She and Rachel discussed things like coping with long hospitalization and managing fatigue, and Lacy was a compassionate listener, but she was so intuitive around Rachel, it seemed as though she could read her mind. It was clear to me that Rachel had had some difficult conversations with her, in which Lacy gave Rachel permission to express her fears, and I felt so grateful for Lacy's empathy and support. Lacy, it turned out, was also something of a role model, as Rachel described in an essay:

> While my friends were out partying, dating, getting married, and having babies, my new goal was survival. I had little time to think about future career goals and plan, when I was feeling so ill from chemo treatments.

These were trying times for me. Fortunately, there was someone to whom I could vent my frustrations and who could assist me in the weakest hours.

Walking the halls of the bone marrow unit was a compassionate, understanding and approachable social worker. She arranged support groups among the patients and families, in addition to speaking individually with each patient about their feelings. After meeting with her a few times, my future plans became clear.

I was determined to beat my cancer so I could reclaim my life, become an oncology social worker and help others in my position. I could use my own experiences to relate and sympathize with my clients. My career path was only realized through my own adversity. My social worker motivated me to apply to school, offering to review my qualifications and essays. She was there every step of the way.

Throughout Rachel's prolonged illness, our family wrestled with fading hopes and legitimate fears. For solace, I turned to books about hope and offered them to Rachel. "Ugh," she'd say, eyes rolling. "Hope books depress me. I just want to live my life."

Families climb onto the roller coaster with patients. We certainly did. I'd start the day feeling optimistic, but despite my abiding faith in God, by evening, fear, anger and dread would consume me. I knew my husband was also struggling. He knew too much about what could go wrong. It pained me that he seemed utterly incapable of clinging to hope. But Judah didn't want to discuss his feelings. It occurred to me that he was exhausted from insomnia and stress. I also sensed that his faith in God was teetering. On occasion, he would admit to having those feelings. But most nights, once his head hit the pillow, he had no interest in rehashing our situation.

For my part, I continued to try desperately to stay hopeful, if nothing else, for Rachel's sake.

The trouble with hope, though, is that it's so fleeting. Rabbi Maurice Lamm said it best in his book, *The Power of Hope*: "We know in our bones that hope is everything. In the back of our minds, we suspect that it's nothing at all." Without thinking, we use the word "hope" daily in conversation or emails: "Hope to see you next week." But who knows if we'll even make it through the day?

Those grueling weeks in the hospital were also particularly difficult for Rachel because she thrived on socializing. Even as a little girl, she was almost never without friends, her teachers often telling us that she was extraordinarily friendly towards her classmates—not cliquey. Unfortunately, Rachel was too weak to entertain friends at the hospital, nor did we want to risk having them spread germs, but she relied on virtual contact with friends to get her through. Her phone pinged all day long with loving comments from her brothers, friends and relatives.

Unfortunately, the effects of the pre-transplant high-dose chemo— diarrhea, vomiting, mouth sores, overwhelming fatigue and bouts of fear—made it difficult for her to even talk on the phone. Being sequestered on the bone marrow unit with barely any contact with the outside world seemed to be crushing Rachel's spirit. Even though it was her best hope for recovery, it was the kind of isolation that seemed the cruelest kind of prison for Rachel.

What always replays in my mind are the unit's doors slamming as people entered. I suppose the idea was to create a barrier between the main ward and the unit that held some of the most immunocompromised people in the hospital. But every time someone entered the BMT unit, I'd hear that door slam—even from Rachel's room down the hall.

I had always loved the show "Get Smart," whose opening sequence featured bumbling private eye Maxwell Smart walking through door after door, each slamming behind him. For so long, that had been my primary association with slamming doors, but now, the sound had morphed into a worrisome omen, portending bad news—a doctor coming in to share a bad test result. The sound of each slammed door made me shudder in fear that another figurative door would close on our girl.

More sights and sounds from that summer still reverberate in my head: the antibacterial gel dispensers every few feet that would often run low; the infusion pumps patients pushed ahead of them as they walked laps around the unit; the mops always in motion, scrubbing the floors clean of vomit and shoe detritus.

Then there were the twisted tubes filled with Rachel's blood—like licorice ropes dancing around the pump's wheels, as Rachel mustered her strength to round the halls. The pump's rhythmic beating, like a grandfather clock. The kind voice asking *"May I help you?"* whenever Rachel pressed the nurse call button. But that didn't mean someone would show up right away. It could take as long as a half-hour before someone would enter Rachel's room. Sometimes, when I felt indignant enough, I'd head over to the nurses' station myself to find out why the beeping was ignored. Apologies would follow, but so would the news that a patient had experienced an emergency, requiring more nursing assistance. And that would distress me just as much.

Days on the bone marrow transplant unit passed slowly. And yet, we continued to mark the big calendar facing Rachel's bed with X's. But the idea of marking time … oh, how I wished it didn't seem like a prison sentence.

On the night before the transplant, Rachel took an Ambien and slept from 10:30 till 4 a.m., a fairly long stretch, by hospital standards. I jotted down as much as I could in my journal to document her symptoms and the cascade of kindnesses that followed us into the hospital. Friends poured into the unit bearing gifts, including books, magazines and art projects. The aroma of a lovingly assembled home-cooked meal wafted into the hallway.

At last the big day—June 16, 2009—arrived. And, of course, bursts of sunlight poked through the clouds. I had to believe it was a good sign. Sam, delivered by Niti, looked great and had passed his bloodwork tests. He didn't seem the slightest bit nervous about the procedure. Sam and Rach bonded, joked and enjoyed each other's company. I wished Jon were there, too, but I knew he'd be coming for Shabbos.

Later in the day, Rach had trouble with hot flashes and then diarrhea—a common side effect with Cytoxan. She seemed unchar-acteristically claustrophobic with so many people around, but overall, acted relatively calm about what lay ahead.

Inside me, hope and terror wrestled with one another. As a way of coping, I recorded every detail I could of that day in my journal:

> 6/16/2009
>
> Super-Sam matter-of-factly put on the blue Superman shirt I picked up for him at Target, davened and went right to the car. But first Niti gave him a big hug and said, "It feels like the first day of school." Indeed. A new beginning for all of us. May all go seamlessly for Sam and Rach. Hope you're listening, God.
>
> The receptionist on the third floor is Betty Flowers, a name that comforts me—with a pleasant voice to match.
>
> 9:40 a.m. Waiting for them to take Sam back. The P.A. came by and said it would be another 20 minutes.

Judah just joked, "Tomorrow Rach is going to wake up and say, "Trivia question" every hour.

Sam, meanwhile has been testing Jon and Rach on sports trivia. Jon actually tried to call, but we can't use cell phones here.

10:10 a.m. Still waiting for them to take Sam back. Judah said that one of us should see Rach. Good thing. As I was entering her room, she was calling me because she had just thrown up for the second time. She'd also had diarrhea during the night. She's on Compazine now and holding a warm pack to her stomach. Now she's watching "Lost," and is fighting sleep. Beautiful, peaceful, sweet face.

11:10 a.m.
They finally took Sam back. 11:45 was the actual start time for the harvest, once the spinal block took.

2:20 p.m. Marrow delivered to Rachel's room. She was too tired and nauseous most of the day to notice, but we took pictures. A physician's assistant extracted enough bone marrow from Sam's hips to fill a 2-liter bottle of Coke. Shuttling between floors to check on the siblings was both anxiety-ridden and exhilarating. It took four hours for the drip to finish. Looked like tomato-sauce droplets from an upside-down, old-fashioned water bottle. Incredible.

As it happened, Sam didn't actually come out of recovery until after 6 p.m. Weak and barely able to walk, he did manage to plop into a wheelchair to see Rach. I captured that on my camera, too. He got a second wind at home, where he ate most of a delicious take-out dinner and had two friends over to watch a game.

Rachel also recouped enough strength to walk around the ward twice. Unfortunately, right before Sam left, she threw up worse than she had in the morning. We'd been warned that the symptoms would intensify immediately before and after the transplant.

But the "rebooting" was behind us, at least. I thanked God, uttering the *Shehechayu* blessing for a pivotal occurrence, for God's having allowed us to reach this particular moment in our lives.

All that said, our girl was perpetually exhausted. The blood draws three times every night didn't help, and Rachel's shrinking body was ravaged by side effects. Still, she mustered the energy to drag herself out of bed daily to walk around the unit. "We encourage 25 laps around the unit per day," one of her nurses told us, warning that venturing off the unit would increase the risk of infection.

When your child is morphing into an adult, it's hard to strike a balance between mothering and fostering independence. In this case, of course, we had no choice but to stay vigilant—to protect Rachel from overextending herself.

To be sure, there were moments when she cried about how unfair it was. The "it" always hovered: Illness striking a vibrant young woman simply shouldn't ever happen. I had little consolation to offer her, except to acknowledge that she had every right to feel this way. And, when I finally turned in for the night, I wondered how much more her poor body could take—not to mention how much more reserves I had left in me to provide hope.

The ups and downs unnerved us. Rachel suffered nosebleeds so bad she needed platelets. Her fatigue was relentless, even as she continued her walks around the unit. She was ravenous and ready to try solid food, but even eating very slowly, she threw it all up.

I ran into her attending doc in the pantry, and to my astonishment, he told me that Rachel was doing well. "I'm not trying to mitigate her suffering from these symptoms," he said, "but once those counts start rising, she's going to do well. We see it here all the time."

Nevertheless, my heart ached for her—as my journal reminds me:

7/5/2009

Rach is in a major funk. She has no energy, and she's list-less and short-tempered. Even Sheera's presence doesn't seem to be helping. Judah is saying that if it's mostly psychological, she needs to get past it, or they won't send her home, which would make matters worse for her. Yet she is starting to realize—no doubt—that once she gets home, she has a long road ahead of her. Small wonder she's depressed.

Yet her white count has reached 350 and her ANC, 105. She needs platelets again. Her taste buds appear to have changed, too. She ate ¼ of a bagel—if that—and some chocolate milk, but she said, "Nothing tastes right."

Sheera and Talia spent a good portion of the day with Rach. They saw a big difference between the way she looked Friday night v. today. She's much more exhausted today. And yet she walked around the unit six times with Sheera and five more later, with Judah. With two black eyes and ghostly pallor, Rach looked utterly spent. She didn't smile much today. Everything was an effort, and she had diarrhea.

Despite her struggles, Rachel opted out of taking morphine that particular night and for several others, so that she could be more awake. And she asked for pasta with sauce, so Judah and I went home for a while, and I grabbed a box of pasta and pulled together a home-cooked meal. Rachel devoured most of the container of the pasta. But, clearly, something had shifted for her emotionally. She shivered a lot and didn't have the energy to get dressed. Rachel also turned her friend Leora away that night. I told Leora I would take her again in the morning.

I had to admit: Rachel's pallor frightened me. I hardly recognized our girl.

On our way out the next day, Judah said to me: "They put her on the brink of death. This had better work." I had to believe it would.

This also wasn't the only time during that prolonged hospitalization when I didn't recognize our beautiful girl, be it physically or emotionally. My mind would transport me to Rachel's healthier days. It was so rare for her to be sick that I couldn't even remember her bad case of chicken pox. I must have been upset by it, but so much has happened since. But now, as I ruminate about her medical history, certain moments are surfacing that give me pause.

When Rachel was around 10, she discovered something strange about her hands. Even on a mild day outside, her fingers would feel cold and within seconds turn white. She'd rub them together. They would turn red, then white again. She thought it was quite a feat to see her hands turn colors, like my old mood ring I told her about.

She'd run over to us, holding her hands up like a bandit, laughing while exclaiming: "I have a disease! I have a disease!" As if it were the coolest thing in the world. Instinctively, I'd invoke the old Jewish aphorism *al tiftach peh l'Satan.* "Rachie, don't open your mouth to Satan!"

Judah assured her that she had a common condition, known as Raynaud's disease. There's not much you can do about it, except wear gloves, even on fairly warm days. Judah and I are also susceptible to the disorder. I carry gloves in every coat.

I had another flashback in the early days of Rachel's hospital stay that dogged me in its unnerving prescience. One morning, I opened the window shade, and as sunlight pierced her cerulean eyes, it hit me.

As a teenager, Rachel made a friend at camp, Devo, who lived in Miami. The year after they met, when Rachel was in ninth grade, she got a call from Devo about her mother, who had just been diagnosed with leukemia and was coming to Baltimore for a bone marrow transplant at Johns Hopkins Hospital. Of course, we volunteered to help.

Devo's mom Lori and I instantly hit it off. Despite her pallor, she wore a curly blonde wig and fashionable clothes. Her eyes sparkled when she spoke, and she had a wicked sense of humor. After the transplant, she wasn't allowed to leave Baltimore for three months. During that time, her son was scheduled to have a bar mitzvah in Florida, which they ended up scaling down and hosting at a synagogue in Baltimore. Lori was radiant—albeit pale—during that recovery period, and things began to look up.

But some months later, we learned that the transplant had failed. The week before Passover that year, while I was on my way to see Rachel play in an after-school softball game, I got the news that Lori had passed away. I knew I had to tell Rachel, but my heart was broken, and my eyes kept welling up.

It was still early spring, so cold winds accompanied the bright sunshine. As I inched closer to the field, I saw that Rachel was up next. She wore a blue baseball bomber jacket, and as she walked to the plate, her ponytail bobbed through the space at the back of her hat. Then she positioned herself and focused her gaze on the pitcher.

Suddenly, a whack as Rachel hit a triple. Jubilant, she rounded the bases. A smile wide as a watermelon slice lit up her face. I cheered and jumped up and down, overcome with joy. Then our eyes locked, and I experienced a vivid flashback to my first date with Judah. *That smile! It was the very same one that had won me over.* I couldn't help but notice how much our daughter's features and mannerisms mirrored his. I felt a profound love for them both.

As I went to hug Rachel after her softball triumph, I felt beyond proud. But how was I going to tell her about Lori?

Like a film clip, that scene on the baseball field often resurfaces.

The irony of that feat rankles. Yet picturing that smile comforts me all the same. Sure enough, Rachel was shaken by the news about Lori, which I finally shared with her once we got home. I hoped she could cling to the memory of achieving that triple. Would victories like these be enough to soften the blow cancer treatment brought— not just the side effects, but the roller-coaster hopes that accompanied the protocols? It was a question I was incapable of answering.

Four days later, I saw a transformation in Rachel. She was ravenous for every meal and mustered the energy to walk 25 laps around the unit. She also seemed engaged in every conversation. One night, our good friends Barbara and Craig came by, and Rachel talked to them about her time in L.A. for more than a half-hour. It was the most animated I'd seen her in weeks. But the highlight of the day was when she decided to write Oprah about her cancer experience, urging her to do a show on young adults with cancer. I remained frightened about Rachel's uncertain physical state, but I felt a bit of relief.

Meanwhile, the bond Rachel shared with her brothers was growing. They were coming back and forth from New York to see her.

Jon, who was pushing 30, was working at a law firm and dating sporadically (though we never knew who or for how long). Sam was in his medical training, studying day and night for boards. Still, all three kids stayed in close touch.

Once again, sports, the great equalizer, became an anchor. They texted often, discussed trades, upsets, and baseball trivia, which proved a welcome distraction. "Trivia question!" Jon would suddenly announce. "Which pitcher had the most shutouts during the 2008 season?" Several more questions would follow. I felt elated whenever Rachel answered correctly. They would banter and joke, taking turns answering questions, such as, *What was the most awkward moment with guests during a Shabbat lunch at our house?*

Rachel's hospital stay lasted 32 days, about average for a bone marrow transplant. To the bitter end, she would need six final days of high-dose chemo. When we heard that the transplant had finally taken root, we were heartened. There was no stopping this girl, and everyone she touched believed that, though doctors and nurses have undoubtedly learned not to be overconfident.

As her last day in the hospital neared, we began thinking about Rachel's new life—trying hard to calm our demons. The transplant had been successful, though terrifyingly low blood counts became the rule, requiring daily platelets and blood transfusions.

Only a few times did she seem demoralized and defeated: during a stretch of unrelenting fatigue, diarrhea and mouth sores. She would rail, "It's not fair! It's not fair! When am I ever going to feel better?" Yet, more X's appeared on the whiteboard calendar with each passing day, each representing a set of incremental milestones. And, as the days wore on, we talked about what would happen once Rachel could finally come home.

What she most looked forward to in the immediate future was a daily shower in her own house and the luxury of getting up when she pleased, though her body didn't always cooperate.

About five weeks later, Rachel sent out an update that left me no choice but to believe in the potential for remission.

July 24, 2009
Hey,

Sorry for my lack of communication in the past few weeks. I have been home from the hospital 2 weeks now, and I'm loving being out of there. I can finally sleep in peace. Following my in-patient stay, I was going into the hospital every day. The nurses would check my blood counts, and I received platelets almost daily. I have now graduated to three times a week at the hospital, and am finally starting to produce my own platelets. My white cells continue to increase daily, and I am working toward becoming a normal, healthy person again.

Physically, I am feeling a lot better, and rebuilding my strength with daily walks. I am finally reemerging into the world, taking short outings in not crowded places. The fatigue is still overwhelming, but I am now able to get through the day without falling on my face.

I received great news from my day 30 post-transplant blood tests. After a mere 30 days, I am 100% Sam. The transplant worked! There are no traces of my own DNA in my bloodstream; it is all Sam's. The doctors were hoping for at least 50% Sam by day 30 and 100% by day 60, so I'm ahead of the game. Now, Sam's healthy cells need to destroy my cancer cells. I will be getting another scan at day 60, which is in the middle of August, to determine if the cancer has shrunk. I will keep you all posted on that front. But, it is certainly refreshing to know that the transplant took. I also have developed some rashes, which the doctors have identified as probable graft versus host disease, which in acute cases is great for killing my tumors. So, all in all, things are looking up!

Rachel

———◦———

Rachel's next PET scan, imminent, hung like a shadow over us. As a mother, I had never felt so bereft or helpless. A life-threatening illness in a young person just seemed entirely wrong and shockingly unfair. I wanted so badly to assure Rachel that she'd be fine, knowing that I desperately needed to believe it myself. Though some days brought debilitating doubt, I had to hope Rachel's body had finally responded to treatment.

At long last, as the summer of 2009 drew to a close, we were elated to learn that Rachel had a complete response to treatment. Dr. Ambinder suggested radiation just to shrink lingering nodes and to prevent recurrence, but four weeks later, assuming all went well, Rachel could get on with her life.

> *Aug. 26, 2009*
> *Hey everyone,*
>
> *I am officially in remission! My PET scan showed no evidence of any cancer remaining. This is the news I've been waiting to hear for a while, and I am elated. I could not have won this fight without the help of G-d, my family, and friends. Thank you all for your support during this nightmarish year. My parents have been there with me through thick and thin. And it's always nice to have my strong younger brother fight for me. Thanks for the bone marrow, Sam. My brothers don't let anyone mess with their sister.*
>
> *In order to prevent a recurrence, my doctors have recommended radiation. I really don't want to deal with Hodgkin's again, so why not? I will be starting radiation after Labor Day 5 days a week for 3 and a half weeks.*

After that is completed, I can really celebrate. I am hoping
to move back to NY after the chaggim and start living
my life again. As much as Baltimore has been good to me,
it's time to move on. If anyone has any leads on jobs, that
would be much appreciated.

Thanks again for everything. Keep me in your thoughts
to prevent recurrence. I am looking forward to starting
the next chapter of my life.

Rachel

Up until that September, I had never stepped foot in Radiation Oncology—nor did I want to. Rachel had already been through so much. But in light of Rachel's complete response to treatment, radiation had the potential to seal the deal.

When we arrived there for Rachel's first day of treatment, we noticed an oddly shaped piece of steel dangling near a wall in a waiting area. We wondered what it was, until we saw a patient strike it like a gong. Then we realized that we were witnessing a momentous rite of passage: the end-of-treatment bell.

The bell rings every day; it can even be heard in the adjoining Weinberg garage. But it's hard to say what's louder, the bell or the ovation from oncology patients that ensues.

Up to 140 patients a day come through the unit for treatment. Used as an adjunct to chemotherapy or as a definitive treatment to control malignant cells, radiation therapy requires patients to lie motionless in awkward positions, while red lasers pinpoint the site to be treated.

Marian, the unit's nurse manager, acknowledged that the therapy would be pretty grueling. Patients return daily for four to eight weeks of treatment, which can bring on side effects, such as burning, itchy skin, nausea and fatigue.

Marian was responsible for the end-of-treatment bell's presence at Hopkins. She'd read about an end-of-treatment bell at the hospital where she'd formerly worked in Houston—about how it boosted spirits and became an instant hit with patients and staff. At her suggestion, the bell was installed 10 years before Rachel's treatment. The unit also held a poetry contest—the winning poem would be framed and posted next to the bell.

I was curious about how that tradition started, so I decided to write about it for the Johns Hopkins Medicine employee newsletter. "We all thought Marian was crazy," recalled radiation oncology clinical associate Roz Watson, who, like several others, feared that no one would go near the bell. "What if patients have a relapse and need to come back for more treatments?"

But Roz told me that the bell had been an incredible addition to the unit. She has frequently heard her patients say things like, "When it's my turn, I'm gonna hit that thing so hard!" Another nurse, Maggie, in remission from cancer herself, told me, "I know what it's like to go through this. It's such a wonderful thing to watch patients hit that bell. People fly in relatives, take pictures and bring in cake."

And my family was no different. On the last day of my daughter's treatment, I felt like my heart would burst. We invited 20 friends and family members. One of our guests, who herself had battled Hodgkin's told me, "You'll remember this day like you'll remember her wedding."

It was the culmination of a dark year-long journey when Rachel rang that bell, and she hit it with every ounce of strength she could muster. I can still conjure the sound and Rachel's words: "I feel like it's ringing in a new year—a fresh start—a time for health and happiness."

CHAPTER 4

Turbulence and the Power of Music

By the time Rachel was home after her bone marrow transplant—October of 2009—I'd been employed at Johns Hopkins Medicine for six years, where I continued to write stories about employees at all levels who made a difference in their departments, as well as grateful patients who'd experienced exceptional care.

I found myself reminiscing, back to 2002, my first year as a Johns Hopkins Hospital employee, when I worked as outreach coordinator in the Comprehensive Transplant Center (CTC). My job entailed writing newsletters, interviewing the director and writing his column, updating brochures and managing events, and working closely with patient volunteers.

The CTC covered kidney, liver, and heart transplants. I was told that I didn't need to update the bone marrow transplant brochure, however, because demand for these treatments was rising, so the Department of Oncology's communications team was taking that over.

It was an uplifting job in many ways. The wonder of transplantation endures. And grateful patients generally seemed eager to share their stories. I even had the chance to scrub in on a kidney transplant between two sisters. I'll never forget the moment the surgeon entered the operating room cradling a silver bowl with the healthy kidney he'd just extracted—precious cargo.

Then, as rock music blared, I watched him and the other doctors gently implant the healthy kidney into the young patient's abdomen. Their blood-soaked gloves were about to choreograph a miracle.

Suddenly, I saw urine stream out as an unfurled ribbon, the dull pink ureter morphing into a glowing, pulsating bright red. Cheers erupted, but I was still frozen in place, awestruck by the transformation I'd just witnessed.

Breakthroughs like these—or the research that would lead to them—unfolded every day in this behemoth institution.

Distinguished by its iconic dome, the original Johns Hopkins Hospital/School of Medicine has continued to expand, with research buildings, a children's center and cardiovascular tower. Today, the institution consumes much of East Baltimore. Other than the state of Maryland, it's the largest employer in the city.

On more than a few occasions, while en route to a meeting, I've stopped to observe the sweeping old brick buildings juxtaposed to brand new ones. Some 40,000 employees, from floor sweepers to M.D./Ph.D.s, pour into the hospital every day: a city unto itself.

Hundreds of patients and their families from near and from all over the world traverse those doors every day.

And, though The Johns Hopkins Hospital can be a complex place to navigate—literally and figuratively—its history of caring for people from all walks of life for the past 135 years offers patients and employees alike a legacy of hope; or, to quote its former tagline, "the promise of medicine." More recently, the tagline was updated to "Forward. For all of us."

From my first day on the job, I was in awe. But it wasn't until Rachel got sick that I truly empathized with patients' and families' hopes that they or their loved ones' health would be improved.

And suddenly, here I was, six years after witnessing that successful kidney transplant between those grateful sisters, overcome with gratitude myself. I had, after all, just seen Rachel restored to good health, following her cancer and bone marrow transplant ordeal. But could the hospital really *promise* that she would stay well? I had to believe so.

Judah, on the other hand, incapable of trusting that claim, seemed to be waiting for the other shoe to drop. I worried about his negativity, even if he kept it to himself. To be fair, he'd seen enough recurrences to feel skeptical.

But, as Rachel finally began reclaiming her life, she looked so radiant and healthy that we owed it to her to believe that she would defy the odds. We knew that the rug could easily get pulled from under us again, that all it would take would be a few lurking, undetected cancer cells. But, with every ounce of my strength, I pushed those thoughts aside.

Thankfully, we suddenly had a great distraction. In December 2009, Sam proposed to Nikki, a lovely girl he'd met at the University of Maryland and who, like Sam, planned to pursue a medical career, six months after their graduation.

Having been at Maryland three years ahead of them both, Rachel had already gotten to know Nikki, and they'd often eaten Shabbat meals together at Hillel and in friends' dorm suites.

We were also already fond of Nikki and her quiet, cerebral ways. Over Shabbats she'd spent at our house, she actually enjoyed curling up with textbooks.

We were very excited about their August 1, 2010 wedding, just hoping and praying that Rachel would be well enough to walk down the aisle.

But summer seemed so far away, especially when Baltimore got socked with two back-to-back Biblical snowstorms: On February 2010, the skies dumped 25 inches of snow on a large swath of the East Coast. The following week, 19.5 inches fell.

The storms shut down almost every service in the city. Roads were impassable. Our street, a cul-de-sac, wouldn't be plowed for another week. We were frantic—not because of the idea of being shut in together (fortunately, I had plenty of food), but because Rachel needed to get to Hopkins for bloodwork. It took some brainstorming, but Judah remembered that one of our neighbors/good friends, the Spieglers, have a son-in-law, Michael, who had a four-wheel-drive vehicle and lived a couple of blocks up the hill behind our house. He offered to lend it to us.

I will never forget our trudging through the imposing snow mounds. Judah, cradling Rachel in his arms, reminded me of Harrison Ford rescuing a young lady. We charged through it, huffing, puffing and laughing. When we reached the apartment complex behind our house, we spotted Michael standing next to his cleared-off SUV, like a mirage, flashing a big smile. He handed Judah the keys and we thanked him profusely.

The trip to Hopkins was an adventure like no other ... more like a mission. It was also eerie, as we were among only a handful of cars on the road. Thankfully, 83N was desolate but clear, and the streets near the complex were passable. We were frazzled, but Judah drove carefully, and we made it to the hospital, relieved we'd arrived safely and that Rachel wouldn't need to miss her follow-up appointments and blood draws.

We returned home safely, too, as Rachel's drugs started kicking in, which meant keeping Zofran—the miracle anti-nausea pill— handy. In the following days, Rachel's good friend Mira, who lived a few doors down, came by in a snowsuit. The two girls built snowmen, drank hot chocolate and laughed uproariously together, as the sun began to melt the snow and restore Baltimore to some normalcy. Ah, normalcy ... I wondered what that would be like.

To our relief, the chemo appeared to be working. Rachel's energy level improved dramatically. At the end of February 2010, much of her strength and optimism restored, Rachel moved to New York. She was excited to have landed a new job as a personal assistant to a prominent rabbi. We were so proud and dared ourselves to be hopeful that her health would remain stable.

But on Saturday night, March 2, 2010, just two days before she was to start her new position, she felt horrible. She had a fever of 104 and a painful cough. It was the eve of Purim—that joyous festival marked with feasting and toasting and costumes.

Why, WHY was there always a medical crisis for Rachel on a Jewish holiday? My questions for God were beginning to pile up.

Her brothers scrambled to get Rachel on a train from New York to Baltimore. When she arrived, we were shocked to see her—chilled but burning up with fever, devoid of color and bent over and coughing. The next morning, we took Rachel straight to Hopkins. She'd lost eight pounds.

A few days later, she had a CT scan, which my diary tells me "was worse." Her doctors said she might need an open lung biopsy. Rachel's fever persisted, leveling at about 101.

The pulmonary team, led by a kind doctor with a reassuring smile, explained that when they looked at the scan, they saw nodules and an insidious infection.

After they left, Rach took out her phone and played the songs "Telephone," by Lady Gaga and "Bedrock," by Young Money. She told me the Young Money song had been in her head on the train back to Baltimore. I laughed and rolled my eyes as the song played: "Call Mr. Flintstone—I can make your bed rock." Our taste in music couldn't have been more different, and I marveled at Rachel's ability to turn to songs, even with those with lyrics I found silly, for escape.

Moments like these, however, were becoming rare, as Rachel's health deteriorated.

Fortunately, I loved Rachel's nurse, Toni, who had taken care of her once before. Another expert RN, Mikaela, who'd been both an army nurse and a pediatric oncology nurse, succeeded in getting an IV started. It took two sticks, even after unsuccessful attempts by others the night before, but she finally accessed a vein. Rachel kept wincing. "Ow, ow, *ow*," she moaned, as she squeezed my hand.

Sonye, the pulmonologist, told us that this latest setback could be a combination of muscle weakness and whatever was causing the cough. The infectious disease doctor favored bronchoscopy.

Dr. Ambinder was blunt. "Two scans show the biggest change," he told us. "Something is blocking her lungs—it could be a fungal infection or more cancer. Either can be very aggressive."

The full story would be revealed after the bronchoscopy the next day, followed by a possible lung biopsy two days later. It was hard to accept this setback. But there wasn't consensus on the diagnosis. Nearly everyone on the care team suspected that it was fungus. And Dr. A told us he'd seen Hodgkin's recur in lymph nodes, not in lungs. We had to hope for the best.

Ultimately, however, the bronchoscopy revealed cancer in Rachel's lymph nodes and pneumocystis pneumonia, caused by a yeast-like fungus in people with weak immune systems. The cancer had spread to her lungs, an uncommon finding in Hodgkin's patients.

While working on this memoir, I stumbled on a yellow legal pad page recording that interaction with Dr. Ambinder during this visit to the hospital documented above. In my haste to rush to Hopkins that night, I'd left my journal at home. The yellow paper is crumpled, and ink runs here and there from a water spill, and probably a few tears. My handwriting looks frantic.

By that point, Judah and I were in a state of shock. A numbness had washed over me. I feared things were worsening fast. And I had good reason to think so. Judah's pained expressions validated my hunch.

If that weren't enough, Rachel started having hallucinations.

She reported seeing animals bursting from a painting facing her bed. It turned out that etinostat, one of the experimental drugs she was taking to help prevent the proliferation of cancer cells, was likely the culprit.

But Dr. A provided hope about the experimental drug. "It's different from any drug you previously have gotten," he told Rachel. "The early results have been pretty encouraging." Then, he added, "You could go into remission. It's a bit of a long shot. But you can't have active infection. We have to work out how pneumocystis factors into that. If there looked like there could be a long delay, we could go with a donor lymphocyte infusion [which would mean a blood transfusion from Sam]. It's faster to get the drug. That's the update I have for you now. You're going to need a line for a blood draw—Hickman or Port. We're into serious trouble, and even chemo is likely not to work."

At this point, my face was drenched with tears, mirroring Rachel's. "There are two possible outcomes," he continued. "It doesn't do anything at all, or it works great. The other question is whether to do some old-fashioned chemo to shrink things down. We need to see where you are with oxygen. For sure, the washing, bronchoscopy causes a little bleeding and compromise. It's healing up."

Hot tears kept racing down my cheeks. Judah's face was frozen in concentration. I knew he had to process all this as a physician, but more terrifyingly, as a father.

Then, Dr. A. went on to say this: "Another thing we should consider is thalidomide—quite a remarkable drug. I've treated 15 Hodgkin's patients with it in desperate situations. One responded dramatically. The drug has a cousin—lenalidomide [Revlamid]—a much newer drug. I've never had any experience with it. Your CT scan shows infiltrate—more nodular than it's been."

Judah's face drained of color, as, I'm sure, did mine. It was a lot to absorb. I wondered how much Rachel could take. The unknown loomed ahead, and so did Rachel's refractory disease. I couldn't imagine having to treat such sick patients on a daily basis, especially young adults who never had a history of serious illness. And I couldn't help but wonder what Judah was thinking. *How does he deal with giving bad news like this to patients?* To his credit, Judah never discussed them with me.

One thing was certain: Judah trusted Dr. A. completely. The difficulty Judah had with Rachel's care had more to do with the slow pace of hospital care—hours-long waits for blood draws, for example.

Given his medical experience, he knew how to serve as a quarterback and had a fine reputation. He also had little patience for inefficiency. Sometimes he expressed those concerns to staff members. It didn't always make a difference. Yet we both knew that, overall, Rachel was receiving superb care.

On one level, for me, ignorance about all that could go wrong was bliss. I was determined to greet Rachel with a smile and provide a positive outlook, but I, too, harbored fears. It was exhausting to remain upbeat, but I had to emulate Rachel's hopeful persona. Yet even she looked more despairing. What could I possibly do to cheer her up? I knew it would be her friends who would make the difference. Still, I sensed that some of them were withdrawing, fearful that things were looking bleak. Could I blame them?

Honestly, there were times I wanted to bolt from this nightmare. But guilt and determination to stay strong for Rachel tamed my escapist fantasies.

After eight hours in the hospital, I'd come home and try to do mundane tasks, then collapse. I had troubling dreams, but most of the time, I managed to sleep through the night.

Not Judah, though. Sleep eluded him. The pressure between us, not to mention the strain on the family, was bubbling up. That much was obvious, though he barely spoke about what was going through his mind. We'd begun to fight over stupid things, like what to bring Rachel to cheer her up. I just wished he would verbalize what he was feeling. Perhaps he was too scared to share his deepest fears. He knew way better than I did how quickly a diagnosis could plummet, even with "good" cancers.

Finally, Rachel was released from the hospital. The ensuing few months were trying, as fear and uncertainty hovered over everything. Rachel's concerns were mounting, too, as she tried to find her way back into the rhythms of her everyday life again. The night before another appointment with Dr. A, she'd expressed her fears about the future. "No one will want to date me once they learn I'm battling cancer," she said hopelessly.

On arriving to Dr. A's office, she began asking him pointed questions: "How long can you live with Hodgkin's? What if none of the treatments work? How long can you live without treatments?" ("A long time," he answered.) He even went on to say that with the newest treatment about to come out, she could be among the first to go into complete remission.

Yet the latest PET scan revealed that, while the tumors in her lungs were gone, new tumors under her arms had emerged. It felt to me like a macabre game of "Whack-a-mole."

It was time for Rachel to start taking Revlimid, the thalidomide derivative Dr. A had recommended at the last appointment. I winced every time we discussed it. Thalidomide, a drug developed in the 1950s to reduce morning sickness, was found to cause death and birth defects in children and taken off the market, because of massive pressure from the press and public. The fact of this contributed to our escalating stress. But at least there was a treatment left to try. Rachel had to fill out a long consent form in a crowded, noisy chemo area. Almost every line warned about the potential for birth defects while taking this drug, and that the safest behavior was abstinence. I knew we didn't have to worry. It wasn't as if guys were banging on our door to go out with her. That realization made me feel a little sad, yet relieved, for the time being.

The following week, Rachel seemed to have acquired a second

wind. She made plans with friends. And, at her insistence, we—Judah, Rachel and I—packed up and headed to Rocky Gap Lodge, in Cumberland, Maryland, for a gloriously relaxing Shabbat. The weather was perfect, and Rachel managed to walk a fair distance.

Most of the time, we sat outside reading and talking, doing our best to avoid the topic of Rachel's health. On Sunday, we went paddle-boating, taking in magnificent views of the mountains. En route home, we hit the outlet stores. Rachel found a great bathing suit. By the time we arrived home, we were tired but refreshed, thanks to Rachel's determination to break from our stressful routine.

Days turned into weeks, as the Revlimid caused side effects, including nausea. But we were pleasantly surprised by Rachel's energy level. She and Judah went for longer walks; she went out with friends for snowballs and lunches. Dr. Ambinder seemed pleased and said her counts were looking much better.

On July 16, Jon and Sam came home for "Tour de Court" (TDC) weekend, a game Jon invented one lazy summer afternoon back in 1995, when he was looking for something to do with friends that didn't require a car. It started out as a single two-on-two basketball game but eventually would morph into 24 three-player teams and both a men's and women's tournament draw. The tournament requires players—regardless of age—to ride to each game site on a bicycle, and each site is either a neighborhood or backyard basketball court. The event, in all of its lighthearted camaraderie and play, became a genuinely fun way for the community to get together, and grew into an annual summer tradition for much of our community.

Jon had no idea all those years ago that he would unwittingly create a basketball tradition that would grow into something that united our neighborhood, something profoundly uplifting. By 2008, the low-tech biking/basketball tournament they had created from a long summer of boredom would turn into a major fundraiser for the Leukemia & Lymphoma Society to support people like Rachel.

Now, Jon opened the box of T-shirts he ordered for TDC players, with a new tagline for the 2010 tournament: "We tour for Rach." Seeing everyone at the opening ceremonies in front of our house as Jon, Sam and our rabbi paid tribute to Rachel, moved me beyond words.

TDC was just one many ways Rachel's brothers showed up for her during this time. It moved me to watch them both go to such great lengths to support Rachel and to ease her stress. As their mother, I clearly remembered times when the connection between my sons and their sister was more ambivalent—like when Rachel was born, and Jon, adjusting to the arrival of his sister, repeatedly asked me, *Mommy, is Rachel good or bad?* Or the extent to which both boys teased her when they were young, which Rachel mostly took in stride until she'd reach her limit and yell, *I'm telling!*

But despite childhood teasing and squabbles, I'd watched their bonds deepen over the years, particularly when Rachel embraced the world of the sports her brothers had always loved so much. The three of them had bonded in play, so TDC was an especially fitting show of support for their sister.

In the weeks following a rousingly successful TDC, despite one disappointment after another, Rachel found ways to harness her hope. Rachel had always succeeded in life by relying on her ability to make a plan and then stick to it. And, though her protracted illness continually derailed her plans, she persevered. Even though the job with the rabbi was no longer possible, she refused to let her illness or recurrences define her. She remained in close contact with friends and got out as much as she could.

One of the primary ways Rachel stayed in touch with hope during that difficult time was through music. Music—especially fight songs—emboldened her. She'd dance around the house, singing, "I'm gonna start a fight ... *na-na-na-na-na-nana!*"

It heartened me to see Rachel connecting to music in such important ways.

From an early age, I, too, was captivated and empowered by music. I come from a musical family, and I'd sing along and harmonize with my siblings to Peter, Paul and Mary, Joni Mitchell and Simon & Garfunkel. I had a special bond with these musicians. Their music focused on relationships and social justice. They had profound insights, I believed, into my emerging life.

Our phonograph's turntable rarely rested. When our sixties music wasn't playing, my father would play cantorial recordings by Moshe Koussevitzky, Richard Tucker, and his favorite, Yossele Rosenblatt. My dad would sing along with the cantors daily—even as he shaved— in a clear, resonant way that made me feel that he truly believed every word. So pure was the sound, it seemed he had a direct line to God.

My family's musical roots may have been largely cantorial, but our paths had crossed significantly with another musical lineage entirely. In 1947, my newlywed parents moved to Memphis and shared a two- family home with the Presleys—yes, *those* Presleys—for six years. Four of the five Fruchter children were born in Memphis, myself included.

We lived upstairs in an old duplex my parents rented from the kosher butcher; Elvis, his parents and grandmother rented the apartment downstairs. During those years, my parents were struggling to make ends meet as our family grew. We were poor, but the Presleys were worse off—so much so, that my parents quietly paid their water bills.

Serving as the rabbi of a small synagogue, my father would later become founder and principal of the Memphis Hebrew Academy. They knew Elvis when he was a teenager, between the ages of 15 and 18. My parents' experiences with the Presleys are chronicled in several Elvis biographies.

"He was the finest boy you'd ever want to know," my mother would often say, wistfully.

During the day, my mother would come downstairs and chat with Gladys over coffee. Mrs. Presley confessed her worries about her son. "She wanted him to give up his singing career to become a doctor," my mother said. "But I told her she shouldn't worry. One day he would make her proud, no matter what career he chose."

Mom would remind Mrs. Presley that Elvis was a good boy. He worked at a gas station after school and every Friday would cash his paycheck and turn the money over to his mother. And, whenever my mother would come home from the grocery store, Elvis would run out to help her with the packages and bring them upstairs for her.

"He was so respectful," my mother often said. He used to call my father "Sir Rabbi." In our house, Elvis was known as the "Shabbos goy," the kind gentile who would turn on lights for us on Friday nights or Saturdays, when Orthodox Jews are forbidden to light a fire, which in time evolved into not turning on lights. Despite numerous offers for compensation, Elvis refused to take any money for those services. He also accompanied his family to church every Sunday, dressed in his finest threads.

Handsome young Elvis would frequently pull out his guitar and serenade girls on the porch swing. My mother told us he was always a clotheshorse and had been setting aside money for a pair of cufflinks he saw at a jewelry store. My mother surprised Elvis and bought them for him as a high school graduation gift.

My parents also allowed Elvis frequent use of our record player and invited his family for meals at our home—and in our sukkah (outdoor shelter) on the Jewish Feast of Tabernacles each fall. I found myself both inspired and star-struck by this connection.

The warm friendship between our two families continued through early 1955, when we moved to California. I was a newborn, making me the fourth Fruchter child. My father's meager salary could no longer support all of us. The synagogue was struggling, too, so he accepted a position in Oakland. A couple of years later, my parents saw a headline in the local paper: "Elvis Surrounded by Thousands of Girls." My father looked at my mother and asked, "Do you think it's the same Elvis?"

Indeed, it was. My father called George Klein, Elvis' agent, who had celebrated his bar mitzvah in my father's synagogue. Backstage on concert night, Elvis greeted my father with open arms and made a big fuss over him. My mother, unfortunately, couldn't attend, as she was unable to find a babysitter that night.

That unforgettable reunion would be the last time Elvis and a member of my family would see each other. But the press remained fascinated with Elvis' humble beginnings and sought biographical nuggets. Years later, we learned that Elvis made generous contributions to Memphis Jewish charities because he recalled a Jewish family that had helped his family when he was younger.

My mother was convinced that Elvis turned to drugs because his mother died so young and the two had been extremely close. Mrs. Presley once told her that Elvis had an identical twin who had died at birth, likely factoring into Elvis' devotion to his mother.

When my mom heard the news on that sad August day in 1977

when Elvis died, she was inconsolable. She spoke not as a disillusioned fan but as an old friend: "He was one of the biggest *mensches* I've ever known."

I have no recollection of that time, as we left Memphis when I was but three weeks old. But the Elvis connection has become part of our family's folklore. My kids thought it was one of the coolest things about our legacy. I like to quote a newscaster who interviewed my mother: "Be nice to your neighbors, 'cause you just never know!"

To this day, we talk about this auspicious Presley family connection, because music has always been so central to my family. It was certainly an anchor in my household growing up. We'd sit around the Shabbat table and sing *zemirot*, hymns and acrostics celebrating the joy that the weekly day of rest brings. My sisters and I would harmonize as we washed the dishes, my mother sometimes humming along. My brother, Harold, had taught himself how to play guitar, and we'd often gather together to sing Jewish and popular songs.

We also played records every day and sang along. It proved to be a great escape from our isolated lives as rabbi's children. During my freshman year of college, every day after class, I'd play Carole King's *Tapestry* album and other "classic rock." But I also loved Jewish music.

In college, Harold performed as lead singer in a Jewish rock band, called Ruach Revival. They produced several albums, which my parents played often, especially as we prepared for the Sabbath. Now 70, Harold—aka Chaim—still has a beautiful voice and continues to perform as lead singer for Kol Chayim Orchestra, at weddings and conduct High Holiday services. We sometimes joke that he was touched by Elvis—literally. In July of 1952, when my parents pulled up to the house with their newborn third child, Elvis asked my mother if he could have "the honor of carrying him upstairs."

My husband and sons, though appreciative of music, prefer

spending most of their down time on sports. Thankfully, Rachel inherited my family's love of music. She had a lovely, sweet, melodious voice. Even as a toddler, she loved singing and dancing to records and tapes. Her favorites were "Joelly Billin" (Billy Joel) and Wionel Witchie (Lionel Richie).

Music would always hold a prominent place in Rachel's life. She so enjoyed singing popular songs with her friends from camp and school and watching any TV show that featured music. We did have concerns, however, when we were on vacation and couldn't peel Rachel away from MTV (which we didn't pay for at home). I feared she'd embrace that culture of provocative music and scantily clad icons. So we compromised and let her watch only in short installments.

I needn't have worried. Rachel graduated from Beth Tfiloh High School in 2001. She did well academically and, like many of her friends, planned to spend a year devoted to Judaic studies at a seminary in Jerusalem before starting college.

Though we have many family members living in Israel, Rachel was mostly cloistered in her dorm and would travel the country and visit family when she had down time.

On Sept. 11, 2001, we—along with the rest of our nation—were devastated to learn about and see live coverage of the bombings of the Twin Towers in New York. Rachel, frantic with worry, called to ask if we were OK and if we wanted to come to Israel. Though Jon was at Yeshiva University—just miles from Manhattan—he was asleep when the national tragedy occurred. Sam was still living at home.

Three months later, Rachel was sitting in a café on Jerusalem's Jaffa Street, enjoying hot chocolate with friends, when a pair of suicide bombers simultaneously detonated explosive devices just a few hundred feet away.

"I've never been so scared in my life," Rachel told a *Baltimore Jewish Times* reporter. "One of my friends was being lazy and taking her time leaving the restaurant. If she hadn't, we would've been at least hurt. There were still nails flying toward us."

Thankfully, when things were a bit more stable, my sister-in-law Dena and her husband Walter, who live in Israel, picked Rachel up and brought her to their home, until it was deemed safe enough to return to Jerusalem.

One day, en route to Hopkins for treatment, we were discussing a spate of bombings that had just occurred in Israel. Rachel recalled that terrifying episode in her life. Then she turned to me and said, "Mom, can you believe I'd ever experience anything worse than *that*?" She'd rendered me speechless. Choking back tears, I patted her leg and replied, "No, beautiful Rachie."

In 2002, after her year of intense Judaic study in Jerusalem, Rachel started college at the University of Maryland, College Park. She majored in history and amassed friends, as honey does bees. She made some friends at Hillel with whom she launched an a capella group called Rak Shalom ("Only Peace") that would rehearse weekly and perform at various events. Over long Shabbat gatherings, they would harmonize, snap their fingers and mimic instruments.

One night, we traveled to College Park to hear the group perform. Rachel was excited to have been asked to sing her first solo in a song called "Hafachta." The lyrics originated from Psalm 30. King David, fresh from a victorious battle with an enemy, praises God for saving his life. *Hafachta mispidie li'michol li*, "You (God) have turned my suffering into joy."

Wonder and pride filled my senses as I heard Rachel's sweet voice project those words. Seconds later, as the collective finger-snapping continued, that big, warm smile emerged, and she continued swaying to the beat. Our girl had found her groove socially and academically.

Periodically, Rachel would bring home friends she'd met at College Park for Shabbat who grew up in Atlanta, Chicago and New York. The singing, harmonizing and giggling did my heart good and made me feel both younger and older—simultaneously.

Not long before moving back to Baltimore from L.A., Rachel had even tried out for a role in musical production. For her audition, she sang "I Dreamed a Dream," the song from *Les Miserables* sung by Fantine, the destitute single mother who is forced to give up her child: "But there are dreams that cannot be, and there are storms we cannot weather." Rachel got the part, but by the time she heard, she'd already made the decision to move back East and find a career that suited her better than teaching elementary school.

One day, as we listened to that song on en route to Hopkins, Rachel turned to me and said, "Mom, that's kind of my life right now." I felt staggered and speechless to hear it.

Rachel pointed out that her life was beginning to mirror Fantine's—rife with disappointment. The lyrics gave me chills: "But the tigers come at night ... with their voices soft as thunder; as they tear your hope apart ..." Ever since then, I haven't been able to listen to the song without breaking down.

As her spirits flagged with each small or large setback, friends continued to be the best medicine for her, often virtually. Even when she was not with friends in person, Rachel's optimism and sense of humor still shone through, as in this g-chat with her close friend

Sheera (who sent it to me years later, knowing that I might enjoy reading it):

3:53 PM	**Sheera**: hello
3:54 PM	**Rachel**: hiiii
3:57 PM	**Rachel**: hiii. hows work?
3:59 PM	**Sheera**: going alright today.
4:06 PM	**Rachel**: i hear that i ve been stuck at hopkins all day.
4:07 PM	**Sheera**: that sucks. how come? what are you getting?
	Rachel: i couldnt breathe and i need platelets and potassium
4:08 PM	**Sheera**: are you feeling better now?
	Rachel: a little im on oxygen which helps
4:09 PM	**Sheera**: good
	Rachel: so theres a really cute guy across the room from me getting chemo ive never seen him before
4:11 PM	**Sheera**: hahaha. so you should go say hi
4:13 PM	**Rachel**: hes w/his dad its kinda awkward and im w/ my mom
	Sheera: hmmm ok, perhaps another time then
4:14 PM	**Rachel**: yea hopefully we can run into each other in a nicer place
4:18 PM	**Sheera**: definitely try

Through it all—the treatments, weekly to Hopkins, unexpected high fevers, need for transfusions, lung infections, coughing and nausea—Rachel surprised us with her resilience. That's not to say our nerves weren't frazzled. We were plenty scared of the next potential crisis. But if she could stay positive most of that time, we had to at least try to do the same. The main thing was that she was receiving regular care at Hopkins and had overcome her most recent lung infection.

Still, Rachel's cough worsened, and she constantly struggled with overwhelming fatigue. By this time, prednisone had become her best friend. It would almost immediately silence her cough. But it also kept her up at night.

More than ever, music continued to be a grounding force. Rachel's friends—most of them living outside of Baltimore by now—made her CD mixes, including one her favorites, Lady Gaga, in all of her outrageousness. Rachel loved not only her music, but also her self-made backstory and feistiness. And Rachel's love of pop music was infectious; even I had to admit that Gaga was extraordinarily talented and fun to watch.

The great thing about music is that it never dies—and, over and over again, it invites us into its soaring melodies and hopeful refrains.

Music, while a solace, couldn't change Rachel's troubling new reality: Her coughing fits intensified and woke her up at night. She had to be readmitted for a lung infection and needed yet another bronchoscopy. But our girl wasn't willing to sit still. She combed the Internet, seeking potential treatments. Although she'd been through several treatments that worked initially, the tumors in her lungs would resurface, forcing Dr. Ambinder to seek yet another approach.

CHAPTER 5

Chesed–
A Supportive Nest

There are certain words in the Hebrew language that almost defy translation. *Chesed* is one of them. Perhaps that's because it's so emotionally powerful. In its simplest sense, *chesed* is the attribute of grace, kindness or love, aka *loving*kindness, between people. It also refers to the piety of people toward God, mirroring God's attributes of love, mercy and grace toward humanity.

From the outset of Rachel's prolonged illness, we were overwhelmed by the outpouring of love, support and efforts to ease our stress. Our neighbors, synagogue and close-knit community provided tremendous practical and moral support, from meals to rides to the hospital, especially when my medical leave ran out. And, I was so touched when my wonderful colleagues even offered to donate their sick time to me. Fortunately, that wasn't necessary. We were managing financially, though we feared that the latest experimental drug cost a fair amount of money.

It was hard for me to be on the receiving end of all this *chesed*. Given my father's rabbinic pulpit, I'd grown up fairly isolated; we'd moved around a lot, and there weren't many people who wanted to be "friends" with the rabbi and his family. So I wasn't very accustomed to being the regular recipient of lovingkindness.

Of course, as Judah and I settled into our Baltimore community and acquired more friends over the years, I took great pleasure in cooking for others during a difficult time or surprising someone I cared about with a favorite book or a scarf. It was a natural extension of our neighborhood's and community's response to life events: We celebrated births, bar and bat mitzvahs and special birthdays together in a big way. And, when someone needed surgery or suffered the loss of a parent or the worst-case scenario—a child—we found ways to provide support one another.

Until Rachel got sick, we'd been fortunate not to have needed help from others. Yet we could never have imagined the myriad, unusual ways people would ease our burden. We'd experienced it to some degree when my mother-in-law died, but the outpouring for Rachel was 10 times more generous and unexpected. I continued to feel uncomfortable about accepting help and other kindnesses, though most of the time I accepted it, regardless.

One evening, a couple of weeks after Rachel learned of her first recurrence, we received a call from our dear friend and neighbor Liz. She wanted to know if she and a mutual friend, Sherri, could stop by to talk to us. They were volunteers for an organization I'd heard of but hoped I'd never need to tap into: The Jewish Caring Network (JCN).

Founded in 2006 by a group of people who came together to

support a close friend dealing with a medical crisis, JCN provides practical help and emotional support to help families through trying times. I knew of it but couldn't have imagined the lengths the organization's volunteers went to—making sure to pinpoint the *specific* needs of each family.

The two women sat on our couch, notebooks in hand, asking *exactly* how they could help. At the time, though I was on medical leave, it was running out quickly, and much of my time was spent helping Rachel deal with her symptoms and treatment. We were also looking out for my aging and increasingly frail father-in-law, who lived alone in a nearby apartment and came to our house for Shabbat dinners. He would have eaten alone otherwise; his second wife had passed away in 2008.

Liz and Sherri asked pointed questions. Though I cringed at the reality that I needed practical help, I let them know our favorite foods—and most importantly, Rachel's. We also told them about Rachel's love for chocolate, pasta, massages, music and movies, as well as the chance to go out with friends for coffee or lunch.

And so, despite my discomfort with being on the receiving end of *chesed*, I swallowed my pride and acknowledged that I couldn't continue doing as much as I was accustomed to. I needed the help. There was no denying that Rachel's symptoms were affecting our everyday lives.

The roller-coaster of symptoms leading to crises and minor triumphs was speeding up. We did our best to stay focused. I willed myself to stay positive, though in private, I never stopped wondering why this delightful girl deserved such a horrible fate. Despite this worsening reality, she continued to surprise us with her resilience, magnetic smile and efforts to look her best. Our friends adored her, too, and continually sought to brighten her days. She sometimes felt well enough to drive herself to Hopkins, but most of the time, she had rides.

I knew how much she missed her independence and hoped that one day, when her health seemed more stable, we could buy her a used car.

One warm sunny Sunday in March, when I arrived at the strip mall on Reisterstown Road to pick Rachel up from her hair appointment, she came out singing, "I'm a blondie, I'm a blondie!" Her hair had grown back enough to have it shaped into a pixie, but I didn't know she was getting highlights. At this point, Rachel was feeling fairly stable, having adjusted to Revlimid's side effects. She looked adorable and so happy. From there we went home. Then she went out with Mira for a drive, and when she got home, we ate delicious ziti with spinach that a friend had brought over, and took a walk down the block, where we caught up with neighbors. It had been a delightful and active afternoon, and Rachel was exuberant.

But when we got home and sat down in the den, Rach discovered that Lyn, the research nurse, had called. Apparently, Rachel's liver enzymes were elevated, drawing into question her eligibility for the latest study on an experimental drug. Rach tried to call her back and left a message. Then she left a message for Dr. A.

We were a bit shaken by this development. But the protocol said that even with elevated enzymes, the doctor could make exceptions for admission to the study for otherwise eligible patients. We waited. And worried. Good thing the NCAA tournament was on—Rach kept busy looking at her brackets. I watched her deftly distract herself, somehow staying busy and positive in all of this, and felt awed.

And, there were moments when—often unbeknownst to us until later—Rachel took matters into her own hands. One morning in late March, while I was at work, she went out by herself and walked to the Atrium shopping center—about half a mile from our house—to get a manicure. She ran into several of our neighbors. Then, Rachel made her way to our friend Pam's house—a good ¾ of a mile. Later, Rachel called and asked me to pick her up there. The delight on Pam's face immediately soothed my spirits.

The days seemed to fly by faster. Rachel invited friends over, and she continued to muster enough energy to continue taking walks. I had to take that as a good sign.

But I knew we were all thinking about the date: March 26, almost exactly a year prior, that Rachel had what we'd hoped—expected—would be her last treatment. Her follow-up appointment that day with Dr. A. revealed little. She was pretty much status quo. Her weight topped 101. It was better than being under 100, but in her healthier days, she'd weighed at least 15 pounds more than that. The new normal seemed to include accepting side effects and infections, which was also the case for other patients with refractory Hodgkin's. We just prayed that Rachel's symptoms wouldn't become serious enough to require a hospital admission.

Meanwhile, she continued to tutor when she felt up to it. There were times I could tell she was wistful about how her health was derailing her life and her chances for a more "normal" future. I felt dejected, too. I wanted to see my daughter living a life not dictated by parents, medical professionals, and treatment.

Rachel had begun the protocol Dr. A. had prescribed weeks earlier. And Passover was fast approaching. Dr. A. reported that Rachel's liver function was back to normal. But her skin was getting drier. He ordered a thyroid test. "I expect good things from you with this study," he told Rachel. But the treatment made her weak, tired and achy, and she developed a low-grade fever. She took a brief trip to New York shortly thereafter, accompanied by Jon, who had come in for a visit. Rachel had a great time but was utterly exhausted.

Two weeks later, Rach received an email from Dr. A. "I'm concerned. I want to schedule a CT scan." The report came back with a vague assessment.

"It's not so bad, but you're *complicated*," said Dr. A. "The report is saying that things are better, but it's not clear how much of it is pneumocystis and how much is tumor. But there's new inflammation. My concern is that the tumor was starting to grow back, but it's not clear. Though not likely, it could be allergies—transferred from her donor."

Rachel continued to spend her days reading, g-chatting with friends and making plans to get back to New York and L.A. Of course, we grappled with our fears about letting her travel, but she was so determined not to be defined by her illness. I'll never forget the day she read something aloud on Facebook that incensed her:

> Stupid cancer ... Some of us want a new house ... a new car ... a new mobile home ... To lose weight ... But someone battling cancer wants just one thing, to get better and win the battle. 97% of my friends won't repost this, but 3% will. Let's see who does. Please repost this in honor of someone who lost their battle, or for someone fighting it now.

Her face turned beet-red. "That's SO not true!" she yelled. "I don't define myself by my cancer. I go about my life like other people, make plans to go places and spend time with friends and family, study with the rabbi and attend events when I feel up to it."

The outburst made me so proud. I couldn't have agreed more.

And suddenly our summer calendar was filling up. In addition to preparations for Sam and Nikki's upcoming wedding, we learned that a special *chizuk* (literally, strength; support) event at Rachel's high school was underway. Friends of ours had organized the program to show communal support for Rachel. It was something we'd never experienced and were so touched by the idea and the efforts behind it.

We'd also received the exciting news that Rachel was selected to throw out the ceremonial first pitch at Cancer Survivors Day the following Sunday, June 13th, at Oriole Park. Our wonderful friend Mark, who'd performed Rachel's biopsy, had recommended her to the planning committee. She was ecstatic to have been selected. But, as we kept a sharp eye out for symptoms and complications, Rachel's self-esteem was beginning to fray.

One late April night, over a pasta dinner a friend had brought over, we were talking about people who were particularly skilled in one area or another. I'm not sure how the topic arose, but Rachel suddenly voiced a troubling observation: "I took ballet, piano, volleyball and was never good at any of them."

It pained me to hear our normally confident girl sound so insecure. That may be true, I acknowledged, but I assured her that she excelled at one thing, more than most people: she's always been good at *life*—coping, making friends and enjoying it to the fullest.

Still, I knew she was anxious about the next day's treatment. I tried to direct her to a more positive state of mind: "We're gonna kick cancer's butt tomorrow, right?" She gave me a wan smile and nodded before dragging herself upstairs for the night.

Spring was budding all around. As usual, the azaleas popped up first, and I took it as a hopeful sign that positive change was possible. But destructive thunderstorms were leaving broken tree branches blocking the path to our cars. Lately, everything seemed fraught.

But *chesed*—those acts of boundless kindness from friends and neighbors—consistently lifted our spirits and Rachel's: One friend, Joanna, stopping by to see her and update her on their classmates' lives. Another, Shoshi, to catch up, joke about their brothers, and watch *Grey's Anatomy*.

After much debate about Rachel's threshold for the aforementioned study, we learned that Rachel's platelets revealed that she was up for it. But she needed red blood cells to raise her hematocrit. By this time, gallons upon gallons of blood had coursed through her veins. I think about the nameless good people who donated blood to extend lives.

Because of their selflessness, I became involved in marketing Johns Hopkins Hospital's blood drive campaign. There was a time when I couldn't donate blood because of my low hematocrit, but now I make a point of donating at least twice a year and/or volunteer to help people register at the blood drives.

By late spring of 2010, we'd begun to experience the angst of watching Judah's aging father struggle with health issues. My parents had passed away years before; both were 79 when they died. My father-in-law was our only living parent left, and every Friday night, after he ate with us, Judah would walk him home.

Mickey Minkove was a man of few words who relished his independence. But he was in his 80s, and we worried about how thin and frail he was getting and whether he could be trusted to continue living on his own. Both The Jewish Caring Network and our circle of friends were well aware of our situation. Once again, we found their support to be indispensable, especially one beautiful Friday afternoon in May, which happened to be Judah's birthday.

Judah came home that day at 1 p.m., a little while before he had to take Rachel to Hopkins for an appointment. I left at around 2:30, hit the grocery store and returned home to prepare for Shabbos. After I put a roast in the oven, I decided to check for messages. The second message came from Judah's father: "Hi, this is Dad. How's Rachel? Just wanted to let you know that I've been on the floor for 24 hours. Can Judah or Samuel come over and help me get up?"

I was dumbfounded. First, I called Judah, who had—seconds before—heard the same news from his brother, Josh. But Judah had *also* just heard Dr. A. tell Rachel that he wanted her to get a chest X-ray (which wound up showing pneumonia). He wanted to admit Rachel for IV antibiotics. Rachel wouldn't hear of it. No beds were available anyway. She was put on a drug called Avelox.

Amid the chaos of the call from his father and the latest about Rachel, Judah called his brother Josh in New York. On the phone, my husband's voice cracked: "I can't deal with this now! I just can't!" Josh reassured Judah that he would handle the situation, and called our cousin, Shaindy, asking her to go to Dad's apartment immediately. I called Liz, who kept an eye on the roast and promised to pick Jon up from the Bolt Bus at 5:30, so that I could go see my father-in-law.

Sure enough, Judah's Dad was on the floor, his leg splayed as we waited for the paramedics. I asked him why he hadn't called us sooner, and he said he hadn't wanted to bother us. Apparently, he had been on the floor since 5 p.m. the night before, and never thought to press his emergency bracelet.

It turned out he'd broken his hip. It was only after this that I heard from Judah what was going on with Rachel at Hopkins, and when I did, I felt not only an acute sadness, but utterly overwhelmed.

Somehow we emerged from that crisis intact. Our lives continued in a rhythm defined by how Rachel was feeling on any given day. We'd come to expect good days and God-awful, scary days. Rachel began to look thinner and paler to me by the day, but in her unrelenting insistence on spending time with friends, she continued to refuse the role of sick cancer patient. I recall her telling me about an organization called "I'm Too Young for This!" a cancer support group focused on the needs of young adults with cancer.

Sometime later, we learned about "Stand Up for Cancer," an organization that began in Hollywood. One night we watched stars on TV perform at a fundraiser for the organization. Closer to home, in Columbia, Maryland, we learned about The Ulman Foundation, which also supported young adults with cancer. I wondered why it seemed so many more young people were getting cancer.

In part, it may have been that awareness about cancer in general had increased and continues to increase. Despite this, it felt natural to me that young adults would see themselves as invincible, the prospect of something like cancer unthinkable. It is also not uncommon for physicians and caregivers to under-recognize symptoms that might ultimately reveal a cancer diagnosis.

The numbers tell the under-recognized tale: As of this writing, according to the American Cancer Society, about 80,000 young adults aged 20 to 39 are diagnosed with cancer each year in the United States. About 4% of all cancers are diagnosed in people in this age range. And, approximately 9,000 young adults die from cancer each year. Cancer is the 4th leading cause of death in this age group, behind only accidents, suicide and homicide. It's the leading cause of death from disease among females in this age group, and is second only to heart disease among males.

Young women are more likely to be diagnosed with cancer than young men, but young men and women are equally likely to die of cancer. What's especially troubling is that survival rates for cancer in young adults haven't changed much in recent decades—unlike the improvements seen in many cancers in children and older adults. Survival rates can vary a great deal, based on the type of cancer, stage of cancer and other factors.

In Rachel's case, having been diagnosed with stage IV Hodgkin's lymphoma greatly reduced her odds of survival. And yet, we clung to hope as she continued to show extraordinary resilience and determination to comply with her treatment and follow-up care.

As the trips to Hopkins became more regular, the wait times became less bearable. Bloodwork results took at least an hour and a half. And Rachel had begun throwing up her breakfasts and lunches more often, partially due to side effects from her medicines and chemo.

Life outside of Rachel's illness continued in its own complications, too, That May, Judah had cataract surgery, which went well, but that same day Judah's father was agitated and confused. No doubt it was because the following morning, he was scheduled for hip replacement surgery, as a result of his recent fall.

I continued to work mostly full time and arranged for friends to check in with Rach by phone. Visitors continued to stop by—our rabbi, relatives. But Rachel's shortness of breath concerned us all. The *Pneumocystis* pneumonia (PCP), a serious fungal infection that weakens the immune system, was still messing with her lungs, causing nearly constant shortness of breath.

Compliments of my wonderful co-workers and supervisors, Rachel and I managed to escape one day to a spa one Friday in late May for massages. It was a lovely way to usher in Shabbat. But the following morning, Rachel was extremely tired and short of breath. Family and friends had become the most reliable key to lifting our spirits, so we visited with as many loved ones as we could.

Rachel was encouraged by the steady influx of exciting summer plans. On top of the upcoming Orioles game Cancer Survivors Day pitching event, she received surprise tickets to a Lady Gaga concert, courtesy of Jewish Caring Network; and, of course, Sam's wedding was nearing.

But Rachel's health issues had intensified. She was coughing more, and her blood counts had plummeted, leading to a hospital admission and the need for two units of blood. Concerned, Dr. A. wanted to schedule a bronchoscopy to see if she had PCP again or another kind of pneumonia. He came by the next day at around 1 p.m., saying he was "puzzled." The CT looks the same, he continued, so he didn't think it was a "galloping" tumor, but noted that he could be wrong. Rather, he thought it could be breakthrough (resistant) PCP or some other infection. Regardless, Rachel needed a sputum test and bronchoscopy.

As always, visitors poured in. Rabbi Silber dropped off a chocolate cake his lovely wife, Aviva, had baked; Barb assembled meals, and her daughter—Rachel's good friend Mira—picked up a Carvel cake and drove Sam and me back to the hospital. The cultures came back as *Pseudomonas*, a bacterial infection. Dr. A. told us that Rachel would need to stay in the hospital for at least a few more days and would need IV antibiotics for two weeks, which could be administered at home through her port.

I asked Dr. A. if he'd seen Hodgkin's patients go into remission after this many setbacks. He responded: "Absolutely. That's the great thing about Hodgkin's. It's one of the few cancers that can respond and where people go into long-term remission." I felt relieved but also a bit doubtful, especially when I discussed the topic with Judah. He always seemed to focus on worst-case scenarios. Yet how could we not be hopeful when our daughter used every ounce of positive energy she had to cling to hopes of a complete remission? It wasn't easy, especially for Judah, who knew way too much about what could still go wrong.

Finally, on May 22, Rachel was released from Hopkins. But she needed a portable oxygen unit at home to help her breathe. Seeing her tethered to the unit pained me, as did her stooped posture, as she walked gingerly through the house.

Rachel and I had been invited to Nikki's shower at a restaurant in New Jersey, but of course, Rachel was too sick to attend. My dear friend and neighbor Malka—who had family in that New Jersey suburb—drove me up and back that day, another of the many acts of *chesed* that helped get us through. Wonderful as the shower was, I got choked up as I thanked the hosts and guests; it pained me that Rachel couldn't be there. I couldn't help but think that she might never be blessed to be in a relationship that would warrant a bridal shower.

Still, it was finally hitting me that Sam and Nikki's wedding was imminent, and that there was also much to be excited about.

And when I returned from the shower later that night, Judah reported that Rachel looked better and had enjoyed more visits from friends.

The next night, after we'd watched *The Bachelorette*, we headed upstairs. I helped Rachel get into bed. Suddenly, a cascade of angry words tumbled out: "I'm fed up with being sick and dependent on oxygen!" She felt like she had a leash, she said, and like she was under house arrest. She just wanted to get dressed and go out with friends.

I told her that she had every right to be angry and upset. It really wasn't fair. The next day, brows furrowed, Rachel typed furiously to update her friends.

---------- Forwarded message ----------
From: Rachel Minkove <rminkove@gmail.com>
Date: Sun, May 23, 2010 at 1:42 PM
Subject: update

Dear Friends,
I know it's been a while since I've sent an update. I've been through a lot of obstacles, but I'm finally getting back on track. I was released yesterday from the hospital after a five day stint, including Shavuot. After having difficulty breathing for the past month, and my oxygen levels going down to 80%, I was admitted. The doctors were concerned that the Hodgkin's had progressed in my lungs, making it difficult for me to breathe. They performed another bronchoscopy on me, revealing I had a bacterial infection called pseudomonas, another type of pneumonia. Thankfully, that was the sole cause of my breathing troubles. I am now back home, albeit still on oxygen and high dose antibiotics. I should be weaning off the oxygen, hopefully in the next week.

There is a big disconnect with how I have been feeling and my progress. Fortunately, the silver lining with all my recent discomfort is that the cancer IS getting better. My recent petscan showed dramatic improvement and significant shrinking of the tumors. My chemo is working, and I hope to remain on the study and get into remission again. I'm still receiving the oral chemo pills every other Friday. I have another treatment this week. The drug seems to be working well with Hodgkin's patients, and hopefully this will be the answer. Once I'm finished with this pneumonia nonsense, I'm headed in the right direction.

Thank you all for your continued concern and prayers

and amazing chesed for me and my family. I'm continu-
ously amazed at what wonderful friends and family I
have. On a totally separate note, I have been
asked to throw out the 1st pitch at the Orioles game on
June 13 for Cancer Survivor's Day. It's always nice to have
something to build up to and work toward for feeling
better. Now, I just need to practice throwing. Additionally,
if anyone is in the Baltimore area on June 6, there will be
a shiur and program in my honor sponsored by Midreshet
Harova. I have included a flier with details.

Thanks again for everything. I'll try to be better with
these updates. I just haven't had the energy to write in
a while, but hopefully there will be only good news from
here on out.

Rachel

Looking back on the totality of the kindnesses bestowed on us, I realize how varied they were—and often unexpected. The "shiur and program," referenced in Rachel's email, is a prime example. Rachel's friend Jamie had approached Rav Milston, the principal of Midreshet HaRova, the seminary in the heart of Jerusalem that the two girls had attended, with an idea: How about if he came to a community *chizuk* event in Baltimore to show solidarity with Rachel and rally support for her through *divrei Torah,* or words of Torah, spoken and studied together? Rachel could even address the group herself.

The idea, Jamie told us, delighted Rav Milston, who said he was heartbroken to learn about Rachel's illness and happened to be coming to America in June. Plans advanced quickly from there. Our old friend Bernie handled logistics, arranging to hold the event at Beth Tfiloh, Rachel's high school, spending hours making sure the setup and program would proceed without a hitch. The speakers would include Zipora Schorr, head of Beth Tfiloh Community Day School; Rabbi Milston; Rabbi Silber; and Rachel, if she was up to it.

I recall the raised eyebrows when people heard about the idea. Some thought it was strange; morbid, even, knowing how much Rachel's health was declining. But I reasoned that it was not unlike the frequent impromptu *Tehillim*—reciting Psalms together at gatherings in synagogues when someone took ill or if there were a community crisis. United in prayer, people would speak about the power of prayer and solidarity to help someone through illness.

Truth be told, Judah and I were skeptical. We thought it was a little weird that Rachel would be speaking at an event centered on her healing. *Would she really be up to speaking?* More than that, we fretted about the event turning depressing—not uplifting.

We needn't have worried. A crowd of some 250 friends, family and acquaintances filled an auditorium on that early June day in 2010. Rav Milston spoke about the power of studying Torah in the merit of those who are sick. He also shared lovely remarks about our family's Hebrew names and their significance—as well as their power—to provide hope for a *refuah*, a complete recovery.

Rachel and her parents, he pointed out, had strong names. *Rachayl Tova*, literally meaning "good ewe," is a testament to her character, her capacity for goodness and positivity. The Biblical Rachel, Jacob's beautiful, beloved wife, is considered the matriarch of the Jewish people. My Hebrew name, Yehudit Esther, he noted, honored two heroic women who helped to save the Jewish people during times of annihilation: Judith, who killed an invading Assyrian commander by getting him drunk and beheading him in his sleep (something I doubted *this* Judith could have done!); and Esther, the Persian Jewish queen who saved her people from the wicked decree of the evil prime minister Haman.

Rav Milston went on to talk about Judah's full name, Judah

Avraham, and his namesakes. Derived from the Hebrew word for "praise" the Biblical Judah was the fourth of the 12 sons of Jacob and Leah and the ancestor of the tribe of Judah—the seat of the Israelite monarchy. The lion became the tribe's symbol, derived from Jacob's blessing to Judah, conveying leadership and strength. My husband's middle name, "Avraham," Rav Milston noted, honors the first Jewish patriarch, who embraced monotheism and practiced humility and hospitality.

Then, Rabbi Silber spoke. The words poured out of his heart. He began by focusing on "the *chizuk* we all get from Rachel—from her radiance and the way she handles illness." Then he went on to say lovely things about our family. Afterwards, our dear friend and neighbor Sammy, who is blessed with a beautiful voice, led us in the recitation of *Tehillim*, or psalms. It struck me that the courage and gratitude to God in such lyrical terms by the psalms' author, King David, remains a timeless and powerful reminder of believing in what's possible: the essence of hope.

But, of course, the star of the program was Rachel. My journal reminds me that when she got up to speak, she was incredibly poised. Her luminous eyes twinkled as she described the communities that support us and continue to nurture us. Here's what she said:

> Being a cancer patient and a patient in general means you do a lot of waiting. I guess that's why you're called a patient. There are times I wait for hours before I am called in for my scheduled appointment. During these waits, I often observe and scope out the waiting room. Most of the patients are elderly and have people next to them caring for them. But there are always a few patients who are anxiously waiting with no one to support them. I feel for these individuals. It's difficult enough dealing with cancer, but to do it alone, I honestly cannot fathom.

I am aware that I am extremely fortunate in that realm. My parents dote on me and take care of my every need. They are waiting with me and are present for the positive and the negative results. We have been through all the ups and downs together as a family. I often wonder how they deal with everything on their plate and still remain positive.

And then I remember the broader picture. My parents have an amazing network of friends and community who support them. Each area of the cancer equation, I've discovered, needs their own support system; from the patient, to the caretakers, family, and community. We all feel each other's pain collectively. But it was not until I got sick that I realized the profound power of community and how it continues to surpass all my expectations.

Rabbi Silber and I recently studied the story of Shimshon [Samson]. I couldn't help thinking about what a tragic figure he was. You often associate him with his strength, but he was completely alone. Shimshon separated himself from the Jewish community, so the Pilishtim thought he was acting alone. Because he alone was protecting the Jews, he had no support. His loneliness ultimately led to his demise. He fell for Delilah because he desperately craved to be loved and have someone love him. Strength can only get you so far when you don't have the support and love from others. This story saddens me and inspires me at the same time. Shimshon may have had Divine strength, but imagine how much more he could have accomplished with the support of his community. To me, having faith in G-d is tantamount to healing, yet at the same time I depend on family, friends and community to help me to overcome daily physical and emotional challenges.

Today's event unites several communities that have

sustained me throughout different periods in my life. We are currently sitting in the school where I developed and first identified as being part of the Jewish community. Beth Tfiloh provided me the foundation and values necessary to perform in the world at large, and I am forever grateful for that. Many people I know feel little or no connection to their schools, but I always feel like I'm coming home when I walk into this building. Mrs. Schorr and the faculty have done an extraordinary job in making their students feel proud to be graduates.

Additionally, this event came to fruition in large part through my seminary, Midreshet HaRova, where I spent a transformative year after completing high school. They are truly a beacon for Torah values and knowledge. When Rav Milston contacted me about creating a day of learning in my honor, I was really touched. As an alumna, I still feel connected to the HaRova community, and clearly they do to me as well. When one of their former students gets ill, they rush to provide chizuk. Midreshet HaRova embodies chesed—extreme kindness —and I am so honored that Rav Milston has come to give this shiur.

Finally, my family and I are so fortunate to be part of the astounding Baltimore Jewish community, including friends, family and the Jewish Caring Network. We are inundated with food deliveries, pick-me-ups, phone calls and emails. Each one of those gestures means the world to our family. Suburban Orthodox is an extension of that community and has been wonderfully supportive, orga- nizing various tehillim services. Additionally, as I noted earlier, I have had the pleasure of being a chavruta with Rabbi Silber. The rabbi, the shul, and the entire commu- nity have made it possible for my parents to spend the necessary time with me. All of these communities assist us *in ways we could not even imagine. One act of kindness surpasses the next, and I am so grateful.*

I would also like to personally thank Bernie Kozlovsky for all of his dedication in organizing this wonderful event, down to the last detail. Also, Sam, I wouldn't be here without you. Thank you for your marrow, and I am so thrilled for you and Nikki and can't wait to dance at your upcoming wedding. And, Jon, you have been there for me every step of this process. You both are such great brothers. Most importantly, I could not do any of this without the love and support of my parents. I can never thank you guys enough for everything you have done for me.

As I sit and wait for the doctors, I have peace of mind that all my communities are working 24/7 on my behalf, while keeping me in their thoughts and prayers. I often wonder how those people alone in the chairs handle everything. Seeing them always reminds me of how fortunate I am to have so much support of family, friends, and community as a whole both local and from afar. You are all part and parcel of my recovery. G-d willing, all of these amazing facets of my life and community coming together will bring a speedy and permanent recovery.

I was utterly blown away by Rachel's self-possession and heartfelt words, and beyond proud. As she spoke, I noticed many people reaching for tissues.

The response to Rachel's words was overwhelming. She received a standing ovation. Zippy Schorr ended the program with a beautiful message about hope and resilience, not a dry eye in the room. As for us, we felt tremendous pride and gratitude. But most of all, like everyone else in that auditorium, we were awestruck by our daughter's eloquence.

In the days that followed, Rachel continued to astonish us with her focus on building strength, but she was clearly exhausted. Her eyes were droopy, and she moved more slowly than usual. It occurred to me that she'd worked hard on writing her speech, and the cumulative effect of chemo was beginning to wear her down. But the big pitch at Camden Yards and Sam and Nikki's wedding were both around the corner, and would buoy her spirits.

We tried to find ways to make Rachel more comfortable at home. Her back ached, and we realized that she spent a great deal of time on the couch. So we decided to purchase a leather chair and ottoman for the den. Elan, a handy friend and neighbor, helped to schlep it from the store and assembled it within a half-hour. Oh, how I treasured our generous neighbors! Within days I saw improvement in Rachel's posture.

Fatigue, however, continued to plague her, and she started feeling anxious about her pitching debut in Oriole Park, just a few days away. Seeing Judah practice with Rachel in the backyard—her eyes focused on the ball and Judah's swing—gave me hope. I so loved this passion-for-baseball bond they shared.

Dr. A, meantime, became something of a second father figure to Rachel. Amid the day-to-day stress, one of the hardest parts was not knowing how Rachel would feel on a daily basis, and our rhythm became that when one regimen would prove problematic, e.g., cause her liver enzymes to spike, Dr. A. would try another route. I lost count of the number of times he called her "complicated." Sometimes she'd feel frustrated by his long pauses. She tested him constantly, asking when she might be stable enough to travel again, for example. He was someone she trusted enough to push against, and his being deliberate and cautious provided more peace of mind for me and Judah.

Sunday, June 13, 2010, the day of Rachel's pitching debut, was blisteringly hot and humid, just as we'd feared. But that didn't scare our daughter, decked out in her Oriole jersey and leggings, the excitement from the day's events all over her face. All we could do was hope for the best and make sure she stayed hydrated. During the 25-minute ride to the stadium, Jon and Sam teased Rachel about what might potentially happen when she pitched, like how she might accidentally hit the batter.

When we arrived at Oriole Park at Camden Yards, we were directed to a lovely air-conditioned suite. Laid out before us was a whole spread of kosher ballpark food (Camden Yards is among the few stadiums in the country that offers it). We were too excited to eat much.

Rachel was already short of breath, even just having walked to the park from our car. We weren't even sure she'd be up to walking out on the field. But then we saw her trademark fortitude take over, beaming her megawatt smile as we walked onto the perimeter of the field. We were heartened by the turnout, quickly spotting many friends and family members rising in the stands to cheer us on. Another cancer survivor had joined her in the lineup for the "first pitches."

When it was Rachel's turn to pitch to 6'8" pitcher Chris Tillman ("Cute," Rachel declared), she wound up and threw an overhand pitch that Jon recalls couldn't have been more than seven miles per hour. "It was more of a shotput technique she'd developed for Beth Tfiloh softball," he jokes. But for a 95-lb. young woman with stage 4 cancer, she'd mustered all her strength to keep that ball in the air.

The sun had forced her eyes into slits (*Why didn't I make her wear sunglasses, I asked myself?*). My concern was erased the moment

I heard the thundering applause. Rachel flashed one of the biggest smiles I'd ever seen from her. She looked utterly jubilant. This was a dream-come-true for her. The Orioles ended up giving up five runs in the first inning, losing to the Mets, 11 to 4, but no matter: Rachel was triumphant, empowered in a way we hadn't seen in years.

With July suddenly upon us, our days became consumed with plans for Sam's *aufruf*, a traditional celebration that falls on the Sabbath a week before marriage, wherein the groom is called up to the Torah for a special blessing and to read the weekly portion from the prophets. Upon completion, everyone throws candy at the groom and sings "*Siman Tov u-Mazel Tov*," a joyous, celebratory song.

In addition to wedding preparation, we'd planned to host family and friends for Sam's *aufruf*.

The prospect of feeding hordes of family members was somewhat stressful, but mostly, it was, at last, a *good* problem. This kind of preparation made me excited, even as I felt the pressure of the task. As the event approached, Rachel helped me fill the bags of candy we'd throw at Sam when he was called up to the Torah: joyful work.

But my biggest stressor, which I willed myself not to verbalize, was how Rachel would be feeling. Even with a wheelchair, in the sweltering heat that was expected for that weekend, could she handle the walk to the synagogue? The thought that she might suddenly need to be rushed to the hospital remained a legitimate fear. Her weight was dropping again, and even witnessing her short coughing fits made us wince.

As the threat of another medical crisis nagged at us, Dr. Ambinder suggested it was time to reassess, and Rachel needed to gear up for yet another dreaded PET scan. When she told me what it was like to have one, I was stunned. I had no idea just how taxing it was. I told her she should try to describe it to people—in detail—to give them more insight on what she was going through. So she did, and it turned out to be cathartic for her. It also broke my heart to read it.

From: Rachel Minkove <rminkove@gmail.com>
Date: Thu, Jul 8, 2010 at 2:25 PM
Subject: PET scans and I just don't get along
To: <rminkove@gmail.com>

Dear Friends and Family,
I've always been averse to PET scans. Not only are they grueling and uncomfortable; they usually give me bad results. The test lasts for two and a half hours, with 45 minutes of sitting still, while being forbidden to read, talk, listen to music, or "think." Then, you have to have your arms tied over your head in a claustrophobia-inducing machine for an additional 45 minutes, topped off by drinking a putrid, milky, barium concoction. I'm getting nauseated just thinking about it. My scans usually interfere with Shabbos, Yom Tov, and now American holidays. This July 4th was not my favorite. My oncologist informed me that my cancer had progressed. The lymph nodes had grown in most areas, and some new ones had formed.

After meeting with my doctor yesterday, however, there was some good news. The nodes that were previously in my lungs had disappeared as result of this last chemo. So, these last 4 months were not a complete waste of my time. I now have no organs involved, which is an improvement. I just wish that the new ones hadn't developed and progression hadn't occurred. That is where I am at right now. I was very disappointed, but

I've come to expect that with these tests and this process in general.

In terms of what comes next, I had a lengthy meeting with my doctor, where he presented a new plan. I will be starting a new oral chemo pill in the next week, which I can administer daily to myself at home. It supposedly has minimal side effects, so I should be feeling pretty well while taking it. Additionally, in a few months Sam will help me out again. I will receive something called a Donor Lymphocyte Infusion, where my bone marrow donor, Sam, gives me a unit of blood. It is performed like a simple blood/platelet infusion, which will hopefully cause some graft versus host disease for me to build antibodies against the tumors.

This next process has no "end" date. If the pills don't work, we will try something else. It looks like I will be in Baltimore for a while. For those of you here, I would love to be more social. Also hopefully, I'll have some more flexibility and strength to travel a bit. Although my cancer journey does not look like it is ending just now, I have accepted it. I will keep doing what I need to do and am confident about the care I am getting. I wish I had better news to share. But I am hanging in there.

Thanks, everyone, for checking in on me and showing that you all care.

It really means a lot.

Rachel

As much as it pained me to read this, Rachel remained a compliant patient, and Judah and I did our best to stay supportive. Setbacks had become the norm, however. Our spoken and unspoken concerns about Rachel's health remained fraught. Everything revolved around what kind of day or week she was having.

Being religiously observant means not only celebrating Shabbat, holidays and other joyous times but remembering tragic ones as well. Tisha B'Av, the saddest day on the Jewish calendar fell that year just a few days before Sam and Nikki's wedding. Tisha B'Av is a fast day that commemorates the destruction of the Temple in Jerusalem: twice: the first Temple was destroyed by the Babylonians, in 586 B.C.E., and the second Temple by the Romans, in 70 C.E.

On Tisha B'Av eve, Rachel awoke early and was perky again all day. She heard me pounding chicken breasts for the aufruf Shabbos meal, and told me that friends were taking her out that day for lunch.

Feeling buoyed by Rachel's apparently high spirits, I went for a swim and then headed out to buy shoes for the wedding. But that evening, after we finished eating our pre-fast meal, she showed me a passage with the quote:

"And God sent his wrath on the daughter of Judah." It was creepy, but the sages say it refers to all of Israel. Just a weird coincidence, but it gave us heavy pause.

———— ❦ ————

At last, the *aufruf* weekend arrived. Once again, our friends outdid themselves with their generosity. We hosted 26 family members and friends at our house on Friday night. My dear friend Faith—a gifted Renaissance woman with a wicked sense of humor—created center-pieces for the tables set up in our living room and dining room. It's hard to capture the profound joy we felt to have reached this moment. Nikki and her family were also with us.

Rachel ate well and reveled in the company of all those close relatives and friends. But we were still concerned about the weather. The forecast had called for extraordinarily high temperatures and humidity. We don't drive on Shabbat, and the synagogue is a mile from our home.

Sure enough, walking outside that day felt like entering an oven. But we managed to make it to the synagogue intact. Rachel had insisted on walking some of the way, before she consented to sitting in the wheelchair.

The Kiddush spread was elaborate and plentiful, prepared by Fishel, the same caterer who had catered Sam's bar mitzvah more than a decade earlier. He didn't disappoint. In addition to crudites, chicken drummettes, turkey salad, sesame noodles and broccoli salad, there were assorted cakes, cookies, candy, nuts, and fruit. And, at the last minute, he'd ordered ices for everyone. He knew the forecast was horrific—high nineties and possibly triple digits. Before the feast, Rabbi Silber gave a shout-out to Rachel. "Not a day goes by," he said, "that Rachel is not in our prayers."

All weekend long, people gathered around our living room and den to catch up while perusing old photo albums. Bursts of laughter emerged as we reminisced about what a terrible baby Sam was. And now he was about to be married and begin a long journey to a career in medicine.

Seeing the joy on Rachel's face and hearing her talk about other things besides her illness did my heart good. I also caught the awe on many faces as they watched Rachel act as the proud big sister, not the ailing cancer patient.

Our extended family and friends showered us with affection. Our Benhurst Road neighbors—whose children grew up on the block with our kids and felt like a second family—hosted a lovely and sumptuous Saturday evening meal a few doors down from us, in our adjoining back yards. But Rachel left early to rest. That journey to the synagogue had begun to catch up with her.

The next day, everyone was bone-tired from the heat and excitement. We were expected at a wedding for Michelle and Harry, Sam and Nikki's close friends. Rachel was also invited. She looked pretty but pale, and her coughing had intensified. Still, she was animated at the wedding, delighted for the chance to leave the den and to catch up with friends.

But our subconscious minds reveal what it means to be human. Sometimes they bring a burst of hopeful energy; other times, dread. The day after Michelle and Harry's wedding, Rachel told me she'd dreamt that she and I had flown to New Zealand for a new treatment that lasted six months—and it cured her. The place was beautiful—on a beach. If that's all it would take, to simply imagine such a thing, I'd go immediately. My hopes were flagging from all the ups and downs. I suspected she was struggling, too, but I knew we both wanted a miracle so badly.

As the day wore on, I came across a *dvar Torah*, a brief sermon, in which a rabbi quoted a cartoon he'd just seen. A bird says to a human: "I don't sing because I'm happy; I'm happy because I sing." It reminded me to find joy every day, to *sing*, in spite of unsettling realities. But could I sustain the effort? There were days I felt utterly defeated, and other times when I could conjure Rachel's compliance and pluck— and *willed* those treatments to finally put her in remission.

CHAPTER 6

New Normal

After Shabbat, my inbox started filling up. At least three people wrote to apologize for not being able to attend the *aufruf* because it would have required walking in such extreme heat. I chuckled to myself, instantly recalling Rachel's insistence on walking as much of the way as she could.

We kept reliving highlights from the *aufruf*. The joy we saw on so many friends' and families' faces was uplifting. And were touched by the warm public welcome Rachel received from Rabbi Silber.

As we slid into late July of 2010, things continued to heat up, literally and figuratively. The weather remained well past 90 degrees, with stifling humidity. There was no question that we felt genuine joy as Sam and Nikki's wedding neared. But Rachel's symptoms remained unpredictable and uncertain. Some days she seemed shockingly pale and emaciated. Other days, she was bursting with energy. Of course, we realized that the higher doses of prednisone to treat her cough likely triggered her higher energy level. At the same time it made her sleepless at night.

And yet, though we didn't admit it to each other, there were days when fear consumed us. Judah was mostly silent, but I saw new worry lines on his face. By then, his sleeplessness rivaled Rachel's. Thankfully, I was so exhausted by day's end that on hitting the pillow, I fell asleep instantly.

Meanwhile, the abundant outpouring of *chesed* continued. There were chocolate cakes, checks to cover parking at Hopkins, gift certificates to a nearby coffee shop and flowers for Shabbat. These kindnesses were so moving, and always so necessary.

The days leading up to the wedding felt like they were both speeding toward us and dragging endlessly at the same time. They felt especially long when Rachel suffered coughing fits and overwhelming fatigue. I wondered how she'd endure an entire day of preparation away from her bed, the, "hurry up and wait" time that typifies weddings until they officially begin.

Yet I saw purpose emerge once she recouped some strength from a fitful night of sleep. Grit: There it was again. It was obvious that she wanted to look glamorous and healthy for her brother's wedding—not to evoke pity. After all, it was her younger brother's big day—the guy who'd extended her life through his selfless bone marrow donation. She started taking more walks and tried to eat more, despite the likely nausea that would follow.

But first, our immediate family would spend the Shabbat before the wedding together at the Pearl River Hilton, in New York—the site of the wedding. It would be the last time Sam would be with us as a single young man. And Nikki was cocooned with her family in West Orange. We noticed that week that Rachel's coughing was punctuating nearly every conversation. She was sick of taking steroids, but not taking them meant more coughing, and we wanted so much for her to enjoy the wedding.

We enjoyed a gloriously relaxing Shabbos at the Hilton, where the wedding was to take place. The weather was magnificent, and we watched someone else's outdoor wedding unfold as we felt our own excitement build. On Shabbos afternoon, we played Bananagrams, and Judah won almost every round. A sense of calm and joy washed over me.

Finally, something wonderful was about to take place. We were all so happy.

When we awoke on Sunday morning, my youngest child's wedding day, we were greeted with sunshine and a cloudless sky. Rachel, never much of a morning person, dragged herself out of bed to grab a bite before the makeup application. Her two years in LA fed her passion for glamour and sparkle, and within minutes, the makeup artist was having a blast glamming her up. The gifted stylist also perceived that Rachel didn't want pitying looks. Our girl wanted to look damn good—*and healthy*—for her brother's nuptials.

Some 20 minutes later, the transformation was complete. Rachel looked fashion-model gorgeous. Her eyes glittered, a contrast to the washed-out hues we'd grown used to seeing on her frighteningly pale face. And, the custom-made royal blue silk gown she wore intensified her eyes' beautiful brightness. Rachel's radiant smile, outlined in pink lip liner and gloss, turned electric every time she greeted someone that day.

Make no mistake: Despite her suffering, our daughter's joy was palpable. It wasn't only out of happiness for the couple but because she'd had an entire day to feel like a normal person. She'd taken an extra prednisone pill to control her cough and boost her energy level, as well as a low-dose steroid pill, which helped her feel well enough through the long exciting day.

Rhoda and Bruce, Sam's new in-laws, were gracious and loving. Rhoda, a highly organized early childhood teacher, had handled almost all the details, knowing my time was constrained and unpredictable. She'd also had some practice: It was the third wedding for their family. We'd heard plenty of horror stories over the years about *machatunim*, or in-laws, but from the outset, ours couldn't have been kinder and more supportive.

I had to pinch myself: Miraculously, the wedding day had finally arrived, and we were all together and healthy enough to participate fully. And the weather was magnificent. So much had happened during the last nine months, but God gave us a break to celebrate a special couple. It was a time brimming with love—and hope.

With her styled pixie haircut, in her makeup and her custom-made gown, Rachel looked regal. She flashed a big smile as she took careful but confident steps down the aisle in silver four-inch heels to "Better in Time," by Leona Lewis. I was glad we walked behind her; otherwise, my makeup would have disintegrated in seconds from the sight. All evening, she dazzled people and danced the night away. Her stamina was incredible. The steroids kept her up late, but we were all wired anyway. As my journal reminds me:

"What to say about Sam and Nikki's wedding? So much love, beauty and unabashed joy. The couple looked radiant and beautiful. We all did. At last, a simcha."

The next day, we saw the newlyweds briefly, then headed to

Riverdale, N.Y., to visit Judah's father, who was living in an assisted living facility. He looked really good. We could tell he'd had a wonderful time at the wedding. Though he rarely showed emotion, I saw his eyes well up as we discussed some of the highlights. He'd surprised us by walking down the aisle despite his recent health problems, with the help of Dena and Josh, his daughter and son.

After the visit, we ate dinner at Rachel's favorite kosher restaurant in New York: Noi Due. To my delight, she devoured a rich pasta dish. En route home to Baltimore, we played Leona Lewis' song again, but Rachel had fun rewriting the refrain: Instead of "It'll All Get Better in Time," Rachel belted out, "It All Comes Back to Jon!" She was referring, of course, to our collective and teasing obsession with envisioning Jon settling down with someone next. We all laughed heartily, except for Jon, who let out a chuckle but then rolled his eyes. Rachel coughed as she cackled, which made me squirm, but overall, the weekend had been triumphant: Sam's wedding had elevated us all.

Alas, the high we'd experienced was short-lived. A mere two weeks after Sam's wedding, we were distressed to learn that some of Rachel's previous symptoms had reemerged. She mentioned that her legs sweated at night, and she was more tired than usual. Sam scheduled a trip to Baltimore for a donor lymphocyte infusion for Rachel.

During our next appointment with Dr. Ambinder, he mentioned that he'd been talking to other doctors about Rachel, and had concluded that if she didn't get a response from Revlimid, he would consider another bone marrow transplant. I wonder if he heard my muffled gasp.

With the wedding behind us and with these disconcerting

developments in Rachel's health, the day-to-day stress and uncertainty came into sharper focus. Rachel continued to experience good days and horrific ones. Meanwhile, my supervisor told me that she wanted me to come to the office as much as possible because I was more focused there. I knew my professional writing was becoming lackluster, in large part because it seemed so unimportant, relative to what we were going through. I acknowledged that the quality of my writing would likely improve if I didn't work from home or while I was at the hospital, as Rachel was getting treatment. But my heart ached to leave Rachel alone.

Granted, since the infusion providing hope for some prolonged "normalcy," it felt good to have some semblance of a routine. But my angst persisted. As I wrote in my journal, "Can I trust Rach to be responsible? Would she overextend herself on outings with friends? Would she eat as well when I'm not home? More importantly, can we count on the latest medication—and God—to pull her through these long days? One can hope."

On August 11, 2010, my father-in-law turned 88. I can still hear Rachel's sweet voice on the phone: "Hi, Saba! Just wanted to wish you a happy birthday!" That call no doubt lifted his spirits, even as his health deteriorated.

That same evening, Rachel looked pale and coughed more than she had in previous days. But she managed to muster the energy to go out with her friend Adena. Later, we walked around the neighborhood. She mentioned several times that she was tired.

Severe thunderstorms and, no doubt, worry, had cheated Rachel out of a good night's sleep. Neither Judah nor I had slept well either.

Rachel was exhausted for the rest of that day, but she looked forward to a weekend trip to New York she'd planned. Naturally, Judah and I fretted about her stamina. Yet we knew she needed to get away from us and enjoy some quality time with people her own age. We did have some peace of mind knowing that she'd be staying with two friends, Talia and Leora, both of whom happen to be nurses.

So we let her go. Judah and I had a quiet and restful Shabbat, while, we later learned, Rachel had found little opportunity to rest. Not that she'd wanted to. Talia had invited four friends over for dinner on Friday night, followed by dessert at Jon's apartment, a few blocks away. The next morning, Rachel went to *shul* and ate lunch at Talia's, along with six friends. Then, she told me, she walked about 20 blocks to meet up with her friend Jamie and her two children. After that, she headed back to Jon's place.

Later, on recounting the highs and lows of her trip, Rachel admitted to having experienced night sweats. The lack of sleep had resulted, in part, from the hallway light and noise that filtered into the bedroom where she stayed. All that said, she'd had a wonderful time. I suppose it was worth the risk, but my mixed emotions resurfaced after I bade Rachel a good night.

By this time, we'd come to understand that Rachel's being called "complicated," meant that her response to treatment was inconsistent. Sometimes her body would respond for a bit, and we'd see an energy burst. But within a couple of weeks the tumors would metastasize her bloodstream like a tornado, knocking her down physically and emotionally. And, as we'd come to expect, a crisis would often arise on Shabbat or a Jewish holiday. Rachel continually joked that her body was antisemitic.

Reading provided a welcome escape for all of us. I relished being part of a book club that met every six weeks. We read all kinds of books, mostly contemporary fiction and nonfiction. Judah, a voracious reader, was beginning to get the hang of reading on a Kindle during long hospital waits.

Rachel, meanwhile, enjoyed popular fiction, some of which made me wince—especially her latest obsession: *Fifty Shades of Gray.* The violence and misogyny consuming hundreds of pages troubled me. But she eagerly awaited the arrival of each sequel and polished them off in days.

Alone in her room every night, she also rediscovered the children's books on her shelf. Having taught elementary school, she treasured these books' simplicity, illustrations and nuances.

Her all-time favorite was Eric Carle's *The Very Hungry Caterpillar.* On nights when she was feeling especially tired and defeated and couldn't muster the strength to even hold the book, I'd curl up with her and read it aloud.

We both loved Carle's musical lyricism:

"In the light of the moon, a little egg lay on a leaf. One Sunday morning the sun popped out and out of the egg came a tiny and very hungry caterpillar. He started to look for some food. . . . "

As I turned the pages, Rachel and I would lock eyes and smile at the illustrations. We tested each other on exactly what the caterpillar ate on each day. Then, when we finished reading the pages about his Saturday feast, we laughed out loud, especially when we messed up the order of the foods he binged. By then, "he was no longer a tiny caterpillar. He was a big, *FAT* caterpillar." In that moment, we'd crack up together, even as my heart was breaking.

Soon the book became a talisman—required reading every night. Though we didn't verbalize it, I'm certain we both knew that the cocoon metaphor mirrored Rachel's existence over the past few years. And, with every reading, on the last page, upon reaching the final words, when the caterpillar morphs into a *"beautiful* butterfly," Rachel and I would once again lock eyes and exchange smiles. It was hard to choke back my tears.

We longed for a cure that would bring her freedom from this relentless cycle of setbacks. Carle's book epitomized hope, and reading it had become a sacred ritual, along with some of her other favorite books. Rachel had no intention of giving up, I realized. My awe for her intensified daily.

Since the wedding, she'd managed to continue going out with friends. One day, our wonderful neighbors surprised her and took her to a water park. She had a blast.

As I noted in my journal on Aug. 25, 2010, Rachel started looking better and seemed more energized. She took a walk to the mailbox to send off her Netflix (*Dexter*) and ended up walking about a mile. Later, she went out to dinner with her friend Mira. She ate only half of her wrap because, she said, it was soggy. *Better that as a reason, than loss of appetite*, I mused.

I didn't end up spending much time with her that night because we needed to pay a *shiva* call to a friend whose father had just died. Then I had some cooking to do and phone calls to return. Finally, at 10:30, I made my way upstairs and shared a humorous article with her, followed by reading Eric Carle's timeless book aloud.

Upon entering Rachel's room, I noticed that she'd put away a lot of her clothes that were typically strewn on the floor and over her desk chair. That she'd found the energy to do so was encouraging. Even Judah, who had by now become increasingly pessimistic, told me she looked good that day. "Cute" was his word. When he came home, Rachel was wearing a Ravens hat with a tiny ponytail sticking out of the back. I was delighted to see that her hair was finally growing back.

Meanwhile, another young adult in our community was grappling with advanced cancer. Nineteen-year-old Gilad Schwartz, who'd been diagnosed with liver cancer, had been feeling progressively worse over the summer. His mother, Michelle, an articulate woman whose angst about her son's advanced disease was palpable in her writings, had kindly reached out to me when she heard about Rachel's diagnosis. I hated that we shared this horrible bond as parents of children with life-threatening illness. Gilad's sister was in Rachel's class in elementary school. Though the Schwartzes weren't close friends during those early years, cancer had bonded us. Michelle, her husband, Eddie, and their three other children, were going through hell.

Early the next morning, a phone call from Liz brought news I'd been dreading. Gilad had passed away. The funeral was set for 3 p.m. that day. The news of his death wasn't unexpected, but it was heartbreaking and shocking nonetheless.

I considered attending the funeral. Yet I knew I couldn't muster the strength—and not just emotionally. Urinary retention, something that had plagued me in recent weeks, had struck again. I was in agony. Judah saved the day by prescribing an antibiotic and antispasmodic. And, in yet another show of kindness, a colleague at work ran out to the drug store near my office to pick up the prescription. I could barely walk.

I wondered to myself, *Was it the news I'd heard that locked me up inside? The cumulative effect of all the ups and downs?*

Even before the phone call, it had been a particularly stressful day because two colleagues were out, and I needed to cover for them. On top of that, I had to leave early for my Dental Clinic appointment. The crown for my rotted tooth had come in. Life for all of us marched on, with all its demands, often at inopportune times, as Rachel's symptoms raised concern. Her cough, pallor and fatigue persisted, though there were days when she'd push herself to get dressed and head out.

I returned home early to find Rachel on the couch scrolling the internet, her computer balanced on her belly. She looked dejected and utterly spent. When she told me she went to Gilad's funeral, I was dumbstruck. We hadn't discussed whether or not she should go. I assumed she wasn't up to it and stayed home. But Rachel had called the Estersons for a ride. I couldn't imagine that she would feel compelled to go. She didn't know him well. More worrisome to me was that it would likely depress her terribly.

My hunch proved correct. "It was the saddest thing I've ever been to," Rachel said. The funeral chapel was packed, and beautiful tributes by the principal of Gilad's school, Gilad's two brothers and his mother followed.

Later that night, Rachel and I enjoyed a homemade mushroom pizza. As we ate, she looked at me intently. Then she said: "I'm going to beat my cancer for Gilad." I was in awe of Rachel then, but couldn't deny the tug of doubt I felt, knowing that as much as she desperately wanted to beat her cancer, it wasn't something she could actually control.

As our angst over this loss and Rachel's ups and downs persisted, so did my urinary retention. I knew that stress and grief were visceral. How many times did I see a pimple emerge right before a presentation or deadline I needed to make? Thankfully, I had the pills Judah prescribed to relieve my symptoms.

Paying a *shiva* call to the Schwartzes was something I dreaded but knew we had to do. Rachel insisted on coming along. Michelle told her that she had to "beat EFF-ing cancer." Pulling me aside, Michelle told me that watching Gilad slip away was worse than anything she could have imagined. My eyes filled up. I grabbed a tissue and told her how profoundly sorry we were and that everything was in God's hands, only half-believing it. Could I trust God to save Rachel's life, after He'd allowed Gilad to slip away? Once again, my questions for our Creator were piling up. Topping the list: *Why are so many young people's lives cut short?*

Afterwards, we spent the day with Sam and Nikki. Jon came over with a new girlfriend, who seemed lovely. Rachel, meanwhile, announced that she'd developed painful mouth sores, a sign that the donor lymphocyte infusion could be taking root. "Welcome, graft-versus-host," I wrote in my journal. "Let this be IT!"

The next day, Rachel's dear friends Naomi and Mike arrived from LA. Rachel was so happy to see them, and from the back seat of their rental car, she gave them a little tour of Baltimore. Dr. Ambinder had advised Rachel to take Valtrex for a few days because her lips were puffy. She looked good and was smart enough to stay out of the heat.

Mike and Naomi's visit was absolutely medicinal. They hit Dunkin Donuts, a movie and the State Fair. I was pleased to see that Rachel's appetite had resurfaced, but she did admit to feeling tired. And, she showed me an angry poem she'd written a few hours after making that *shiva* call to the Schwartzes. It was wrenching to read, but I was glad her anger came through. Writing these sentiments down *does* help, I thought. And we were both writing through it: Me, in my journals, and Rachel, in her emails, which were becoming a vital record of her experience.

During Mike and Naomi's visit, Rachel took them to the Newseum in Washington, a museum devoted to journalism and one of my favorites (it closed its doors, sadly, in 2019, due to lack of funding). She loved it, though she was exhausted from having walked so much.

We also received a dose of humor during Mike and Naomi's stay. They'd taken Rachel to her weekly appointment for a pregnancy test, which was required just because Revlimid can cause birth defects.

Her regular bloodwork was also performed. But her urine and blood test proved positive for pregnancy.

At first she thought the positive blood test was hilarious and outrageous. "It must be immaculate conception," she said. There was simply no way this was possible. But as the day wore on, we worried that something was causing an estrogen release that wasn't normal.

On the heels of Mike and Naomi's visit, Rachel made plans to spend Labor Day weekend in New York. She was eager to catch up with her friends and brothers. *Here we go again*, I thought. I fretted about all the germs she'd catch on the Bolt Bus, but I was now in the habit of recognizing that there were times when mental health trumped risks like these. Our plan was to drive up to N.Y. on Sunday to pick her up.

Judah and I spent a quiet Shabbat at home, something we desperately needed. Our friends on the block invited us to dinner with two other couples, which felt refreshingly normal. It was also a good distraction, as I tried not to think about how difficult it had been recently for Rachel to catch her breath as she walked. I knew there was no getting around the need to walk for blocks on end in N.Y. Rachel could barely muster the energy to pack for that trip, so I helped her, trying my best not to make her feel dependent on me.

After Shabbat ended, we spoke to Rachel from our car, en route to Highland Park, NJ, where Sam and Nikki were now living. Rachel said it had been a glorious day out and she'd walked to shul for Kiddush and, after lunch, to Central Park. Coming back, she got tired and short of breath. "I coughed a lot," she admitted, "but Talia took good care of me."

Of course, Rachel overdid it and got little sleep.

We arrived at Sam and Nikki's that Sunday at around 1 p.m., talked for a little while, and then looked at wedding proofs before turning in for the night. Scanning the apartment, I swelled with pride. Everything had a place, and the couple seemed so natural together. But Nikki kept stealing away to study her medical textbooks.

This was just the beginning of their long road ahead to become doctors. I couldn't imagine how hard it would have been had I also wanted to pursue a medical career, in addition to Judah, who was a freshman in medical school when we got married. Yet I had no doubt that Sam and Nikki would pull it off.

Once we settled back into our fraught routine at home, our plucky daughter continued to seek escape from her increasingly dire illness. Rachel connected with old friends, mostly by phone, but was spending more time with her fellow College Park friend Julie, who'd recently married and lived a few blocks from us. Both girls shared a love for *The Bachelor*, and watched it together weekly at Julie's.

Word got out that Lady Gaga was performing in Baltimore, and our Jewish Caring Network liaisons took note. One day, our doorbell rang. Standing on our porch were two young girls—volunteers from Jewish Caring Network—bearing big smiles and a huge basket full of goodies. Inside were two tickets to the concert. Rachel gasped with excitement. She immediately chose her friend Joanna—an equally star-struck Gaga fan—to accompany her. I was in awe of this organization, filled with gratitude for thinking of uplifting distractions for Rachel that we were too exhausted to consider.

While they were at the concert, my journal reminds me, I imagined she and Joanna were having a blast. She'd looked beautiful walking out the door: a long black shirt and black leggings with silver accents. Midway through the evening, Rachel called us and excitedly held up the phone so we could hear Gaga perform a song.

The next day was the eve of Rosh Hashanah, the Jewish New Year. It was a busy time, but I took a few moments to record in my journal my wishes for a better, healthier year for Rachel and for all of us. I was about to light candles to usher in the holiday when I realized I hadn't heard from her in a while. Sure enough, I discovered that Rachel could barely move out of bed after her shower. She'd spiked a fever of 102.5. Our Rosh Hashanah dinner guests arrived within the half-hour. Thankfully, Rach got through the meal—on the couch.

But she was beginning to feel miserable. We didn't quite know what to do, so we sat tight and gave her Tylenol. Over the holiday, the fevers went up and down. Finally, Rachel decided to call Dr. A. He was in London, and she woke him up (it was about 3 a.m. there). He told her to see him on Monday, when he gets back, that she probably had a "Hodgkin's fever."

Setback, hope, setback. *How much could our girl take?* I wondered aloud to Judah. The roller coaster appeared to be speeding up. Her cough had worsened, too.

Judah shared his theory with Dr. A.: that Rachel seemed to develop fevers on the seventh day after being off the drug. So, Judah suggested, perhaps it should be increased, or, she should take the drug continuously. Dr. A. mentioned that her night sweats keep not only Rachel awake at night, but him, too. I was touched by this confession. He also suggested that Sam might need to return for another donor lymphocyte infusion. The topic of another bone marrow transplant also came up. Rachel was direct, as usual. "Can I survive another one?" He said yes, and that her organs—*even her lungs*—were in good shape. He also noted that he has two patients in remission following their second transplant.

Later, when I returned home, Judah told me Dr. A reached out to him after I left to go back to work. He'd asked how Judah was holding up, that he didn't know how Judah did it. Judah told him, "We take our cues from Rachel. She's the strong one."

We—and anyone who heard about what Rachel was going through— were in awe of Rachel's resilience. But as time went on, she tired of hearing people tell her how inspired they were by her. Choking back tears, she reiterated her frustration, her words becoming a refrain: "I'm *tired* of being amazing! I just want to be a normal 27-year-old."

A week after her 27th birthday, I had a procedure to stem my incessant uterine bleeding and urinary retention. On that same day, Rachel had a CT scan. It just didn't seem right or fair that caretakers like me should have their own health crises. I worried that it would limit my ability to help Rachel out, and about how it would affect my already challenging work situation. Writing stories had become a major source of stress. But the most wonderful thing happened after I awoke from anesthesia: The first person I saw running toward me in recovery was Rachel. She'd "snuck" back there, she announced proudly.

And, despite Rachel's worsening cough, she learned that her CT showed no change. I felt hopeful, especially because Sam and Nikki had arrived for Shabbat, and the weather was gorgeous. Naturally, Rachel had insisted on walking to shul. She needed to stop a few times to catch her breath, but recouped enough strength to attend a friend's wedding in Potomac, to which our entire family was invited. It felt so

NEW NORMAL : 119

uplifting to celebrate a joyous occasion with friends and family. As a bonus, my brother Harold and his band played at the wedding.

A couple of days later, Rachel sent out an update on the two-year anniversary of her diagnosis. These missives not only informed her friends and family about her health, but provided insight to them—and to us—about how she was dealing with her fragile state.

---------- Forwarded message ---------
From: Rachel Minkove <rminkove@gmail.com>
Date: Sun, Oct 10, 2010 at 10:27 PM
Subject: 2 years...

Dear Friends and Family,

Today marks my two-year anniversary of being diagnosed. I was hoping that at this point in time, I would be well into remission, living my normal life again. But, life doesn't always work with your expected plans. Luckily, I am feeling pretty well and stable. I have started working again part-time at Beth Tfiloh and just celebrated my 27th birthday with friends in New York [previously] and Baltimore. I'm trying to create a new reality for myself that is not centered around my illness.

Of course, the holidays don't tend to agree with me. As Rosh Hashanah started, I began having fevers, which went up to 103 at one point during the holiday. Fortunately, the fevers subsided on their own. On Yom Kippur, I was weak and wheeled to shul for a bit, but was not feeling so well. My liver functions were elevated, and I received a transjugular liver biopsy on erev Succot. The procedure was more painful than I believed it would be, but thank G-d there were no tumors.

In fact, when my doctor presented me at a bone marrow conference, it was decided that my liver issues were probably Graft Versus Host Disease (GVH), which *was the reaction we wanted from my Donor Lymphocyte Infusion. Hopefully, the GVH will fight the tumors and help shrink them. For now it's wait and see for a little while. I am on steroids and anti-rejection drugs, but we are hoping the GVH helps cure me. There are a few options of what chemo I will go on next after we see how the GVH works, I'll keep you posted.*

Since Succot, I have been feeling much better. I was able to go up to the West Side for Simchat Torah and partake in the festivities there. I walked and went to shul. So, I don't have much to update right now but wanted to let you all know I am stable and working toward recovery. My liver functions look pretty normal now, with the treatment I've been getting. I would not have been able to get through these past two years without all of your love and support. Thank you all for everything!

Rachel

Normalcy at all costs became Rachel's mantra. She continued to tutor. It amazed me that all this time she'd found the strength to do so. One day, she told me that the girl she was tutoring must have been scared by her constant coughing. But she added that it felt great to work again, and that she felt validated by a grateful letter from a parent about how her student had benefitted from their sessions together and how her grades had improved.

Daytimes, Rachel made plans with friends, and at night she read novels and relaxed in front of the TV alone or with friends. She and Judah would bond every night in front of *Jeopardy!* And much to my delight, Rachel was capable of scarfing down three slices of pizza.

Even amidst the continued roller coaster of lab values and symptoms, Rachel refused to sit still. She continued searching the Internet for news about treatments for refractory Hodgkin's and made more travel plans to catch up with close friends who lived out of town. At the same time, she was thinking about how she could rework her resume so that it didn't show a gap in her trajectory. A legal career, like that of her older brother Jon, intrigued her. Or, she mused, "Maybe I should become a social worker to support young adults with cancer, like me." The more she talked about this, the clearer it became to me that this was what she really wanted to do. I so hoped she could. I knew she would shine in that role.

It occurred to me that perhaps Pamela Paulk, then vice president for human resources at Johns Hopkins Medicine, could be of help. Having written about her many times over the years, I'd come to value her not just as a leader, but as a friend. She'd sent me a lovely email saying how sorry she was to learn of Rachel's illness. So I shot her an email.

I hadn't even necessarily expected a response, but in yet another extraordinary act of *chesed*—this time, from outside our community—Pamela met with Rachel and me. She gave Rachel advice I never would have expected. "You don't have to note on your cover letter or resume that you were ill over the past two years," Pamela assured her. "Just write that you needed to take some time off because of a close family member's illness." The meeting ended with two warm hugs and renewed confidence for Rachel. I was beyond grateful.

Rachel wasted no time investigating graduate programs in law or social work. By sharing her plans, it seemed that Rachel was reassuring all of us about her important mission: to survive and get on with her life.

A few weeks later, frustrated by the status quo about her treatment, Rachel took matters into her own hands. Dr. A. had mentioned that a new immunotherapy drug had come out, but that Hopkins hadn't been among those receiving it just yet. But, he noted, it had made its way to

NYU Medical Center as a clinical trial. Rachel immediately perked up and began typing an email to the oncologist leading the trial.

From: Rachel Minkove
Sent: Oct. 25, 2010
Subject: Interest in the study for Bentuximab Vedotin
(SGN-35)

My name is Rachel Minkove. I am a patient of Dr. Richard Ambinder at Johns Hopkins Hospital in Baltimore. I have heard that you are involved in a study for the new drug, Brentuximab Vedotin (SGN-35). It's possible that Dr. Ambinder has already spoken to you about my case, but I wanted to introduce myself to you and fill you in on my situation and hopes that you will consider including me in your trial.

I was diagnosed with Hodgkin's Lymphoma in October 2008. I received 6 months of ABVD treatment, which did not bring me into remission. Afterwards, I had two treatments of ICE and an allogeneic transplant from my brother. I received mantle radiation and went into a short remission in October 2009. I had a recurrence in my lungs in March 2010. After trying Entinostat for around 4 months, there was some progression. I then tried Revlimid for 2 and a half cycles and received a Donor Lymphocyte infusion from my brother this past August. Currently, I am stable but far from remission and am encouraged by your study.

I wanted to know if there was any way for me to join your study, despite the fact that I received an allogeneic transplant. I know the new drug is also being considered an orphan drug, so if there are any exceptions to be made, I would love to be one. If not, is there any way to receive the drug at Hopkins, or at your institution off-study? I am willing to travel anywhere to take part

in this. I really wish to be part of this trial, and want a full remission. I am 27 years old and ready to live my life again. Dr. Ambinder may contact you, but feel free to contact either of us. You can reach me at . . .
Thanks!

Rachel Minkove

The upshot of this effort was a trip to New York with Judah and Rachel to discuss her becoming part of the study. I stayed behind, hoping and praying that finally a treatment would save Rachel's life. But it was not to be. The trial had closed. The kind oncologist assured them, however, that the drug would soon become commercially available.

My worry came in waves, like grief. *How soon would the drug become available?* And what if *that* didn't cure her?

The stress was taking a toll. My work began to suffer again. I could barely eke out a sentence. And my skin, my rosacea, flared up. Red spots speckled my face. I looked as if I'd suffered burns, which I realized, was true—figuratively. Yet I knew we had no choice but to cling to hope.

How could we not? Despite all the angst and devastating developments, our girl continued to fight her disease. But there was no denying how dire things had become.

CHAPTER 7

A Delicate Balance

By late October of 2010, people knew we were in serious trouble. We remained in awe of Rachel's resilience, but the setbacks were chipping away at our hope. We received more intensely pitying looks. Our rabbi was organizing regular gatherings to recite *tehillim* in her honor.

Rachel continued to tutor, go out with friends and entertain a steady stream of visitors over Shabbat and holidays. One crisp autumn Sunday, her friend Joanna took her to a Ravens game. Their dazzling smiles in the photo Joanna's husband, Ryan, captured that day convinced me that Rachel needed to get out even more. That picture quickly became the wallpaper on Rachel's phone.

Interactions like these seemed to sustain her. Yet there was no denying that our daughter was becoming more fragile, beginning to look skeletal to me in a way that shocked me so much that I had to turn away. I wondered what she thought when she looked in the mirror.

I sensed that when people saw Rachel, they presumed she was either anorexic or afflicted with cancer. It was so distressing that I'd sometimes need to dash into a bathroom and weep. Then I'd feel shame for acknowledging that if I didn't have a daughter with stage 4 cancer and seen a girl looking that bad, I probably would have thought the same things.

The tests of our threshold continued. For his part, Dr. Ambinder continued combing the literature on refractory Hodgkin's and weighing the value of treatments to cure her. Things weren't looking good, but Rachel took note of how much he cared, sometimes in light of things he clearly *didn't* say, things that could have dashed her hopes entirely.

As the roller coaster of attempted normalcy and worrisome lab values and symptoms continued, I clung to the intermittent glimmers, especially on days when Rachel looked healthier. Through it all, Rachel continued to stay in touch with friends regularly. By sharing her plans, it seemed that she was reassuring all of us about her important mission to go on with her life.

October of 2010 was nearing its end. Most of the leaves had fallen, carpeting our steps and lawn with golden hues when the sun shone and morphing into slick paths when it rained. Rachel decided she needed to get away to New York again before winter weather could disrupt her plans. When she told me this, I'm pretty sure I gasped. Then I reminded myself that Rachel was an adult and deserved some measure of independence at this obscenely unnatural juncture. Still, I had to rein in my fears.

I marveled at Rachel's focus. She'd lie on the couch at home or in a chair-bed while getting an infusion at Hopkins. Computer perched on her belly, she would commence two-fingered clicking—responding to emails, preparing for tutoring or writing updates. Her typing was intense. It sounded like a woman in heels running to catch a bus. The metaphor sent shivers down my spine, as I pictured Rachel's desperate rush to reach her "destination": restored to good health.

It occurred to me that prednisone could have been fueling this productivity. But I saw something else emerge in Rachel: a renewed sense of urgency, determination to achieve some semblance of normalcy. And, of course, there was hope, that slippery emotion that had once again sprouted, despite the cancer cells' resurgence.

Though I feared the effect all these activities and her insistence on going to New York would have on her stamina, we caved—and allowed her to make the trip. There was no question that it would buoy Rachel's spirits. Her nurse friends—Talia and Leora—looked out for her when she was there, as did Jon. But when she returned home, she looked especially washed out. Her coughing and itching seemed worse to me. Sure enough, Liz told me that Rachel coughed and scratched all the way home.

And suddenly, Election Day was upon us. Rachel tutored twice, once in the morning and later that afternoon and then worked in the library. "I made $60 today!" she boasted. Afterwards, she went to vote with Judah. At the polling place, she became short of breath and exhausted and sat in an empty chair intended for other volunteers, and when one of the volunteers got upset about this, it distressed Rachel. Once the woman learned that Rachel wasn't well, though, she relented.

En route home, Rachel's cell phone rang. It was Dr. Ambinder. Rachel had left him a message about helping her get a spot in the brentuximab, aka SGN-35, study in New York. He told her she didn't qualify. After a series of long pauses, he told her that he thought she should start another round of bendamustine ASAP. He was concerned about her itching and coughing.

Rachel was crushed. She remembered the awful side effects from the drug: nausea, coughing vomiting, GI problems, fatigue. He went on to say that he expected her to do well with it. But then he added, "We're running out of options."

Hopes fading, I wondered once again how much more of this alarming news we could take. I felt as though I was sinking, and that with every attempt to get out, I sank deeper.

In the rare, quiet moments I had to myself, I closed my eyes and whispered, "*Please*, God, *please*," and then I conjured my father's spirit. I knew that doing so had the power to lift me up, even if the feeling would falter in the face of so many threats to Rachel's health. Nevertheless, I indulged myself for these momentary escapes to harness some strength.

In the summer of 1965, my family moved from Warwick, Rhode Island to South Bend, Indiana. My father was pleased to have landed a rabbinic position at an established, albeit struggling, Orthodox congregation. In Warwick, we were among just a few Orthodox families at the Conservative synagogue. Finally, in South Bend, we were bound to feel more in our element.

As Dad optimistically said, quoting the sages: "*Mishane makom, mishane mazal*" ("When you change your place, you change your luck.")

We were especially pleased about the upcoming move because Chicago, where my father was born and raised, was only 90 minutes from South Bend. Finally, we were within reasonable driving distance of extended family. But first, we needed to acclimate to our new lives in Indiana.

An architectural gem, the domed, turn-of-the-century shul—a mile from our house—was showing signs of disrepair. And, its membership was dwindling because increasingly, Jewish families were moving into more spacious homes that were being built in the northwest part of the city. The new reality was affecting daily Shabbat attendance negatively. Dad's salary wasn't sustainable either. But he felt more at ease serving in a position where most of the congregants were religiously observant. My mother would need to find work as a nurse's aide to supplement his salary.

Dad led services twice a day. Come Shabbos, he'd leave the house early, sometimes with my brothers, for the long walk to shul. About an hour later, my mother, my two sisters and I would head there. By then, it was almost time for the Torah reading.

Looking regal in the oversized tallis draped over his shoulders, Dad opened the ark and cradled the velvet-covered Torah. We sang in unison as he led a procession of men. Gingerly, they placed the scroll on the large, angled table, centered on the *bimah*.

For the first "*aliyah*" (being called up to the Torah) blessing, old-timer Max Cohen slowly ascended the *bimah*'s two steps. My father used the filigreed silver pointer to show him the Hebrew words where he was to place his *tallis*. Then, Mr. Cohen would bring the tallis to his lips and kiss it before saying the blessing. The sacred scrolls are too holy to touch with bare hands, so the tallis provides a buffer. In a scratchy voice, Mr. Cohen uttered the ancient words, *Barchu es Hashem ha'mevorach.* "Blessed is the Lord who is the eternal source of blessing." We in the congregation responded in unison: *Baruch Hashem hamevorach le-olam va-ed.* "Blessed is God, forever and ever."

And then, my father leaned into the Torah with the pointer while responding to the blessing with a musical, elongated "Amen" to commence the time-honored chanting. Enunciating every word in his booming, melodious voice, Dad made the Biblical narrative come alive.

I followed along in the *Chumash*—the Torah in printed form— periodically looking at the English translation. Instantly, I found myself transported to Egypt, where Joseph's brothers threw him into the pit with his defaced, torn multicolored coat.

After the Torah was returned to the ark, the congregation sang an uplifting song about how the Torah is a tree of life. Then came a collective hush before Dad began his sermon.

As always, he opened with a smile and two words that immediately put people at ease: "Dear friends." (Years later, I came to realize that he treated everyone as a dear friend.) Then he shared a joke before diving into the essence of the weekly Torah reading (*parsha*). His voice echoed through the congregation as he drew parallels to contemporary life and its challenges, citing lessons the *parsha* offered.

One particular Shabbat, sibling rivalry and honoring a legacy were the *parsha*'s predominant themes. There was no denying, Dad said, that by being boastful about his ability to interpret dreams and having witnessed how his father favored him, Joseph aroused jealousy. Following this, he suffered at the hands of his brothers. But, ultimately, his resourcefulness and faith would save the Jewish people— and the Egyptians—from a deadly famine. Over the next two Torah portions, Joseph rises in ancient Egypt's ranks, so powerful, as to be unrecognizable by the brothers who discarded him until he ultimately reveals himself to his father and brothers—one of the most poignant moments in Biblical history.

"It was all part of God's plan," Dad observed aloud to the congregation. "Yosef was destined to greatness, but first, he had to experience many trials." I wish I could remember how he tied it all up. It went something like this: "May we be imbued with the spirit of Joseph to overcome our obstacles and remain steadfast in our faith …"

Dad seemed completely at home up on the *bimah*. At 6-foot-2, with large, expressive hands and round cerulean eyes, he cut a commanding presence. To me, it seemed like he had a direct line to God, but with a sense of humor— *Tevya-esque*. On high holidays, Dad would stand for hours in his white *kittel* (a ceremonial robe worn over a suit) and oversized *yarmulke*, leading the congregation in prayer and speaking eloquently to convey important lessons.

Yet there wasn't a condescending bone in his body. He greeted everyone with a broad smile and a hearty "Good Shabbos!" or, on holidays, "Good Yom-tov!" and could often be heard saying, "That reminds me of a joke." Whether in shul or at home, he was the most nonjudgmental person I've ever known.

Dad often quoted from *Ethics of the Fathers*, a Hebrew collection of aphorisms. Among his favorites was the one stressing the importance of giving people the benefit of the doubt, and "Who is rich? He who is happy with his lot."

We Fruchter children—then between the ages of 8 and 17—relished seeing our father as an admired leader. My mother, too, who was naturally skeptical, seemed happier in South Bend, where I was lucky enough to see that beautiful smile of hers I loved so much. But she was perpetually exhausted from working as a nurse's aide, cooking for us and helping Dad with the shul bulletin. Her back, congenitally curved from scoliosis, became more hunched with each passing year. Yet she continued to work long hours; sometimes double shifts. It wasn't until years later that I appreciated her resilience.

Our dark green-shingled house on Edgewater Drive—owned by the shul and directly across the street from a river—was the most spacious home we'd ever lived in and featured a lovely, gated front porch.

At that time there were no Jewish day schools in South Bend. Providing their children with a Jewish education was important to my parents, and at last, we lived near a thriving Jewish community that happened to be Dad's homestead—Chicago. My older sister was already boarding there with cousins and attending the Orthodox day school; and my older brothers, at the yeshiva in Skokie, where my father received his rabbinic ordination.

We looked forward to visits with our extended family, after having kept in touch over the years via my Aunt Blanche's newsy letters and periodic phone calls.

Initially, however, my younger sister Hannah and I attended public schools and Hebrew School in South Bend. We were new and unpopular, though things would improve for us socially in time.

The sixties were raging with anti-war demonstrations, psychedelic drug abuse and the music that would later be known as "classic rock," not to mention the folk music I'd come to love. My parents were remarkably tolerant of our obsession with those secular songs, but they wanted us to socialize with teenagers who were religiously observant.

Debbie, the oldest of us, would come home to South Bend intermittently for weekends, as did my brothers, from the Skokie yeshiva. Harold's roommate had taught him how to play guitar. We looked forward to Saturday evening Monopoly and Scrabble marathons and *kumsitzes* (singalong gatherings), to which we invited some friends. (I would later end up spending my sophomore year of high school in Chicago.)

Because Orthodox Jews don't drive on Shabbat, our walk to shul sometimes felt endless to me. It generally took about 45 minutes.

But seeing my father on the *bimah* and hearing him chant the Torah and share his insights always lifted my spirits. For his part, my father seemed delighted to be serving a more religiously observant congregation than his previous posts.

Following services, we'd partake of the modest *Kiddush* in the social hall before heading home for lunch. Some four to six hours later, depending on when the sun set, my father would need to walk back again for the afternoon and evening services, no matter the weather. I was too young to appreciate how difficult that must have been. His being obese didn't help. Yet he never complained, nor did he have any interest in losing weight.

My siblings and I also struggled with body image, and sometimes wanted to diet or lose weight. When we arrived in South Bend, I was 11, overweight, socially awkward and friendless. In the era of Twiggy and other stick-figure models, it felt like there was a lot of pressure to be impossibly thin.

But when we would diet, Dad would remind us of the verse in *Deuteronomy*, "*V'achalta v'savata*," part of the sacred "*Shema*" prayer we recite daily. It means, "You should eat and be satisfied." He always seemed to have a quote from the Torah or sages at his fingertips for every situation. He never wanted us to deprive ourselves.

Dad's even temper also made him approachable; his laugh was infectious. People instantly took to his good nature. I knew my mother thought he was often *too* kind and didn't stick up enough for himself. She'd often chide him about that.

As for his family, he loved us all unconditionally. Still, as one of five children, I knew I had to compete for his attention, especially when I was feeling dejected.

One wintry Shabbat, when I was in 8th grade, I seized an opportunity to have his ear to myself. I asked if I could accompany him back to *shul* for the afternoon *mincha* prayers. He was delighted to oblige. We'd enjoyed our usual festive Shabbat *lunch*, then went upstairs to rest and read. I kept checking at the clock. Finally, when 4 p.m. arrived, I dashed down the steps to grab a snack and bundle up for the walk back to *shul* with Dad.

I can still conjure his chapped, enormous hand encircling mine as we navigated broken sidewalks. We talked about school; I whined about my math struggles and lack of friends. He responded with a parable from the Talmud. Then he turned to me, smiled and said, "Don't worry so much, *Jude-ala*. Things will get better in time. *Gam zeh ya-avor*; This, too, shall pass." Instantly, though I'd heard those words many times before, I felt reassured.

After a brief silence, he started singing a favorite Yiddish song, by Yossele Rosenblatt, whom he revered. Called "*Aheim*," Yiddish for "home," the song tells the story of a lost bird who finds his way home to Israel, the Jewish homeland. As my father picked up the song's tempo, at first, I rolled my eyes. But within seconds, a peaceful feeling swept over me. I smiled up at Dad and found myself humming along.

Dad's faith in God was so pure, so genuine. I often wondered how he managed to go about life with a perpetually upbeat disposition. How I cherished moments like these, when I had him all to myself!

Once we settled into a routine in South Bend, we'd make frequent trips to Chicago, as long as my father didn't have to officiate at a wedding or a funeral. It felt good to finally see our relatives on a regular basis, especially my father's beloved sister, my Aunt Blanche, and her husband, Rabbi Aaron Rine.

From the moment we were buzzed into the Rines' upstairs half of a two-family home Uncle Aaron's accented greeting echoed through the chamber: "Come in! Come in! I haven't seen you since I saw you last!" We paraded up the stairs, eager to enjoy catching up with our beloved *mishpacha*. The sound of that Hebrew word for family always felt like balm to me.

Uncle Aaron, a slight man with thick, black wavy hair, mustache and big doe eyes reminiscent of Groucho Marx, was a study in contrast to my 6'2, fair-skinned, heavyset father. Uncle Aaron clearly adored his wife, my wise Aunt Blanche, who was almost a head taller than her husband.

"Make yourself homely!" Uncle Aaron would command, as we entered the dining room. Shuffling her slippered feet behind him, my pale but regal aunt would embrace my father, her youngest brother. "So good to see you, Elya," The Yiddishized nickname sounded way more endearing than Dad's given name, Alfred, or "Al," as my mother called him. Sometimes my beloved uncles were also there.

Over dinner, Dad and Uncle Aaron would catch up and exchange corny rabbi jokes. The comic volleys always began with my uncle, who'd emigrated to the U.S. with his family from Lithuania to escape persecution. It wasn't until years later that I came to realize how Jewish humor can serve as a powerful antidote to antisemitism—and stress.

My grandmother, whom we called Bubbie, sat in a wheelchair, speaking mostly in Yiddish. Her descent into dementia had begun. She and her blacksmith husband, my Zaydie, who'd died before I was born, had made it to Chicago in the early 1900s from Sighet, Transylvania/Hungary/Romania—the same village where Elie Wiesel was born and attended yeshiva. Only now does it astonish me that Bubbie, having been widowed at a young age, raised a family of five boys and one daughter.

When Bubbie and her family initially arrived in Chicago, horses were being replaced by cars as the chief mode of transportation, so my Zaydie pivoted from his career as a blacksmith and became a grocer. "Fruchter" is the Yiddish term for fruit peddler. Essentially, it seemed, he was returning to his family's trade in the old country generations earlier.

Thankfully, my father, the youngest of five brothers, was born in Chicago. Blanche arrived two years later. There was also a half-sister, Rose. Dad and Aunt Blanche took elocution lessons. Both were articulate and had a natural gift for English and its complicated grammar. Dad was a stickler for upholding English and Hebrew grammar and made sure to alert us whenever he heard it misused.

From her wheelchair, Bubbie spoke mostly in Yiddish. Eyes vacant, she'd smile at times but seemed oblivious to much of what we were saying. Many years later, I would learn all about her infamous condition, Alzheimer's. Little could I fathom then that my father and two of his brothers would suffer the same fate.

As our time in South Bend wore on, my older siblings bonded with kids from similar backgrounds in Chicago, but my younger sister Hannah and I remained in South Bend and found it difficult to make friends, knowing that we couldn't socialize much on weekends, given our religious commitments. Financially, we were also struggling—even with tuition subsidies for my older siblings.

I often wondered how Dad always managed to go about life with such an upbeat disposition. There was never enough money to pay the bills, it seemed, without help from an uncle who was extremely close to my father. On top of that, my mother's back was getting more hunched by the day. She was taking courses to become a licensed practical nurse, cooking meals for all of us, doing housework and helping my father with the shul bulletin and other projects. And she loved to surprise people with her delicious baking gifts.

Meanwhile, we worried about Dad's girth (well, everyone except my mother, whose hobby was pushing food). He simply loved to eat. It never seemed like he was binge-eating out of stress; he just had no intention of cutting back. No matter our voiced concerns: he'd laugh it off, noting, especially on Shabbat and holidays, that it was a *mitzvah* to eat.

With each hurdle we encountered, be it in school or at home, he assured me and my siblings that *Gam zu latova*. "Everything works out for the best." No matter that I had few friends and struggled with my weight. But when my teenage brain allowed it, those aphorisms soothed my spirits.

Then, one bitter-cold day in February of 1967, our house caught fire. We learned the culprit may have been a short circuit in a pole lamp in our living room. I'll never forget that day when my father picked us up after school and broke the news. He drove us to the house, though it was uninhabitable. The first thing that caught my eye was our overturned couch and other furniture in the snow. The porch was a sea of ashes.

But what shocked me most was seeing the charred birdcage, lined with cinders. Our four colorful finches—Zippy, Tippy, Hippy and Lippy—along with our white parakeet we'd named "Beautiful"— hadn't stood a chance. Those little birds were so musical that when my father's cantorial records would play, they'd sing and chirp along, on key. "Beautiful" was especially gifted that way.

I thought my heart would explode. Hot tears streamed down my cheeks. But then, Dad reminded us how lucky we were—that, thank God, none of us was home when flames ripped through the living room. My parents had gone to the drug store to get a few things before my mother's hospitalization that day for a hysterectomy. Because of the pervasive fire and smoke damage, we needed to live in a hotel suite for what seemed like an interminable five weeks, while the house was repaired and cleaned.

By then, my adolescent brain had begun to grapple with questions for God. Six months earlier, Howard M., the 18-year-old son of a beloved congregant, was driving to a summer job when his car was struck by a train. In those days, there were very few signals warning of oncoming trains, and the young man—my brother David's friend and classmate—was killed instantly.

David had answered the phone early that morning, as he recalls vividly. Mrs. M. asked to speak to my father, who'd already left the house for morning prayers. Then, her voice cracking, she told David, "We lost Howard today." Initially, the news didn't sink in for my brother, but once it did, he told her he was deeply sorry and that he'd make sure my father got the message. Howard and his family were such wonderful people. We, along with the entire community, were heartbroken.

The unanswerable question rankled: *Why? Why did God punish these good people?* Our house fire ultimately reminded me that yes, thank God, we escaped harm. I kept thinking: *We could have died, too.* But why are others struck down in the prime of their lives without explanation? And the Holocaust? *How to make sense of wholesale genocide, torture and suffering?* Dad would often admit that he had no answers to questions like these, but he always had hope for a better world. In the meantime, he would insist that we count—and celebrate our blessings.

Today, more than half a century later, I still have no answer to those questions. Yet I can't help but wonder: *What would Dad have said about Rachel's illness during the prime of her life?* Her suffering seemed relentless, "Job-esque," as my dear friend and colleague Marjorie continued to say whenever I told her about another setback. I've no doubt Dad would have offered some wisdom from the sages but ultimately would have confessed that he had no explanation.

During my sophomore year of high school, I lived and attended school in Chicago, and my siblings and I would sometimes take a train back to South Bend for Shabbat and catch up with my younger sister, Hannah. I'd enter our house ravenous, following the scent of my mother's freshly baked cinnamon babkas. Not infrequently, I'd scarf down an entire one in one sitting.

Although we were finally getting into a groove, and making friends, the South Bend shul was still deteriorating both physically and financially and our household and tuition expenses were mounting. So, in 1970, my father accepted a position in Watertown, New York, at a Conservative (despite the label, "conservative" in this context means far more liberal than Orthodox) synagogue. By then, my oldest sister, Debbie, was at Stern College; David was at Indiana University; and Harold had started Yeshiva University. Hannah and I moved to Watertown with my parents.

To our knowledge, we were the only Orthodox family in town. We attended the local public schools and had kosher meat and chicken sent from a kosher butcher in Syracuse via Greyhound Bus. My new friends turned out to be kind, religious Christians who "prayed for my soul." It seemed that the Jewish kids had little interest in befriending me. Whenever I tried to be friendly to one of them, they would snub me, saying things like, "Sorry, I need to run; I forgot something in my locker." They were either cliquey or averse to the idea of befriending a religiously observant girl—or both.

The small house the shul owned was on the same property catty-corner to the shul. That meant no more long walks with Dad. But by then, I was too consumed with homework, college prep and National Conference of Synagogue Youth (NCSY) "Shabbatons" (weekend gatherings) throughout New York State to feel wistful about it.

In 1972, during my freshman year at Stern College in New York, my parents and younger sister relocated to Troy, NY. My father had accepted a position at an old but beautiful-in-its-day Orthodox synagogue, a couple of blocks from Russell Sage College. I'd come home periodically from Stern, where I'd majored in English.

During my senior year, I was editor of the biweekly college newsletter and made extra money working in the Stern kitchen, serving Shabbat meals. It was there that I met my *bashert*, or the person destined to be my spouse. I thought it both strange and wonderful that Judah's name was the male Hebrew version of mine. It's been confusing people ever since.

My father officiated at our wedding on December 26, 1976, in that historic Troy shul, just as he'd done for my older sister the previous November. A major snowstorm that began the night before socked the East Coast, so a number of our guests couldn't attend. Flights were canceled, and stress was mounting. At the last minute, Judah's family arranged plan B: travel from Baltimore via a chartered bus for everyone including the groom. In good weather, it would take 7.5 hours, but it ended up taking even longer. Ultimately, they arrived at 2:45 a.m. The wedding was to take place at 2 p.m.

Of course, my father remained optimistic that the wedding would go on. The entire congregation was invited. And miraculously, it did go on, sans the janitor, who never showed up, so my brothers had to clean the bathrooms. Snow is far less daunting for residents in upstate New York, so, thankfully, seats filled up. We were also grateful to discover that New York City guests had braved the elements.

The age-old traditions—poignant words from my father under our *chuppah*, spirited Israeli dancing, well wishes and tasty food—magically erased some of the stress from the snowstorm. By then, I'd also grown fond of Judah's warm, close-knit family.

After spending the night at an understated hotel, Judah and I headed to Williamsburg, Virginia, for a few days before his winter break from his first year of medical school ended. I was eager to begin my new life in Baltimore, working as a proofreader, and tried to make our Pikesville top-floor, two-bedroom apartment on Clark's Lane *haimish*, or homey. Once the semester resumed, Judah cracked the books and excelled. Before long, he was on call every third night during his internal medicine residency.

Of course, the stress, constant studying and sleep deprivation sometimes dogged him. On his nights on call, I missed him terribly, though I'd begun to get together with friends in his absence. Knowing how focused, astute and charismatic he was, I knew he'd make a fine doctor. What he seemed to like most was interacting with and assessing patients, and then identifying the most effective treatment. Meantime, I'd begun my job as a proofreader and editor, and also freelanced for book publishers.

Four years later, on April Fool's Day 1980, which also happened to be the first day of Passover, we joyously welcomed our first-born son, Jonathan. And, though Judah wasn't home much during Jon's first few years, by the time Jon turned 10, they'd grown close, chattering incessantly about sports.

Rachel arrived three and a half years later, Oct. 3, 1983, via C-section, as she was breach—feet first. I was struck by the profound connection that quickly emerged between her and Judah. She'd not only inherited his round face, delicate skin and translucent eyes; she seemed to smile the most whenever he held her. At that time, Judah was chief resident in medicine at Union Memorial Hospital and had become adept at overseeing trainees' schedules, taking histories and caring for patients.

Sam was born on June 5, 1986. A few months earlier, we'd purchased a house that was under construction, but wouldn't be ready for two months. When we learned that the home construction was delayed for two additional months, we rented a house in the neighborhood from a family who was overseas. When they returned, we moved into my father-in-law's basement. Sam, who had chronic ear infections, cried incessantly. We were sleep-deprived, stressed and essentially homeless.

By the time we finally moved into our home, it felt so good to be settled in our own place, despite the lack of front steps and a few of the windowsills. And little did we know, we were about to become part of a neighborhood of extraordinary friends who made us feel like extended family.

By this point, late fall of 2010, we'd experienced much of the usual family stress childrearing brings. It didn't seem possible that we had adult children building their futures academically, professionally and personally. But Rachel's diagnosis had changed everything, upending not only her adult life but ours, too.

Judah had by now become numbed by our new reality. He still barely spoke, and when he did, he seemed so fragile, quickly expressing his frustration. I was frustrated and stressed, too, but I mustered smiles whenever I could, for Rachel's sake. As had been the case throughout our ordeal, Judah remained incapable of staying remotely optimistic. He knew how bad things could get—even with the so-called "good" cancer. They already had. But there was nothing good about cancer.

Nevertheless, I clung to hope relentlessly and as much as I could. Whenever I felt on the verge of collapse from the stress and fear of more setbacks for Rachel, I'd close my eyes and summon Dad's chapped, protective hand encircling mine, as we navigated those broken sidewalks near the old South Bend *shul*. The Yiddish songs, corny jokes and predictable aphorisms could easily have evoked my cynicism. But in Dad's loving voice, they soothed my spirits. They'd become anchors.

If only they could cure my ailing daughter, I thought.

Then, one day, as I watched Rachel type an upbeat email to friends and family, I had a revelation: Rachel's resilience and irrepressible optimism were part of *her* DNA, thanks to her grandfather. Luckily for her, she'd inherited an extra boost from my mother-in-law's fortitude.

Yet the thought of Judah's mother's suffering and shortened life due to breast cancer reminded me of that part of our legacy, too.

CHAPTER 8

New Normal, Again

The fall of 2010 continued to bring bursts of color. We took short walks, kicking the crunchy leaves that lined our path and inhaling the crisp air. Most of that time, Rachel mustered the energy to endure her worrisome symptoms. Fall had always been my favorite season, until that dreadful day, almost exactly a year before, when Rachel heard those damning words about her diagnosis: "You have refractory stage 4 Hodgkin's lymphoma and need salvage therapy—high-dose chemo and a bone marrow transplant."

Meanwhile, the subprime mortgage crisis throughout the U.S. that began in 2007 had reached a cataclysmic point. By 2009, banks were lending money to more high-risk borrowers, and housing prices soared. Jon and his law firm represented many of the high-risk borrowers who were in default of these mortgages.

I felt proud that Jon was doing impactful work, in addition to staying in close touch with us and with Rachel. But greater demands on his time made it more difficult for him to visit her as often as he might have liked. And Sam was studying incessantly for a master's degree in health sciences and had applied to medical schools. Around that time, he was elated to learn he had an interview at the University of Maryland School of Medicine, as were we.

That said, by this point, Judah and I were teetering. It was becoming increasingly difficult to stay positive about Rachel's condition, even for me. Judah's exhaustion from sleepless nights was also taking a toll. Most Friday nights, he could barely make it past 9 p.m. Rachel teased him constantly about it. As she took more prednisone to calm her cough, the drug also kept her wide awake. And she wanted us to keep her company.

One Friday night in late October, a couple of hours after Shabbat dinner, Judah said he needed to get into bed. Rachel followed him upstairs, and after I cleaned up a bit, so did I. I walked into our bedroom and saw father and daughter propped up, reading books. Judah's eyelids became heavier by the second. Suddenly, Rachel started teasing him about how little energy he had. I plopped onto the bed, and we all started laughing together.

It didn't take long for Judah to say, "OK—*enough*! I need to go to sleep." Rachel would have none of it. "Big baby Judah!" she said in a fit of laughter. "Big baby Judah!" I laughed right along with her, even though my heart broke for my stressed-out and sleep-deprived husband. After all, in addition to ensuring that Rachel was taking care of herself, he managed dozens of patients every week, many of them elderly. And he couldn't talk to me about any of them, given HIPAA and the protected, confidential status of information between doctors and patients.

After about 10 minutes, Judah did fall asleep. It struck me that— sick as she was—our daughter had more energy than Judah and I did, combined. But I noticed something else that night: Rachel's voice was becoming hoarser. The cough emerged intermittently, competing with her delicious laugh.

When Rachel and I finally acknowledged that Judah was asleep for the night, I followed her into her room as she got ready for bed. As was our tradition, we curled up with *The Very Hungry Caterpillar*. I just hoped Rachel didn't perceive my fear that her condition was at a stalemate or possibly worsening. I just couldn't shake my anxiety about this new vocal hoarseness.

As we read Eric Carle's final words "… and he was a "Be-*YOU*-tiful butterfly," we once again exchanged smiles. I kissed her, told her I loved her and gently closed her door. Then I crept into bed and cried myself to sleep.

Thankfully, some good news on another front arrived. I returned home from a book club meeting to learn that Sam was accepted into the University of Maryland School of Medicine—just as his father had been 35 years before. I'd always known Sam had the same kind of resilience and drive. Jon had earned a law degree from the University of Maryland School of Law, a couple of blocks away from the University of Maryland Hospital. I was so proud of both of them and grateful to be living in a city that offered abundant academic opportunities and nationally acclaimed hospitals.

As for Rachel, inspired by her experience and her social worker, Lacy, she had decided to focus her future on helping young adults with cancer—"an underserved, forgotten population," she argued, as she well knew. So she began looking into the program at the University of Maryland School of Social Work in downtown Baltimore.

I was incredulous but so proud of our plucky girl and her renewed sense of focus. But part of me felt like Rachel, with her stage 4 cancer diagnosis, was setting herself up for disappointment. At any time, her condition—already weakened by setbacks—could turn dire.

By this time, November of 2010, Rachel had some semblance of a rhythm to her life. She seemed perkier, and her itching had subsided. But her cough had worsened, in part because she'd begun weaning herself down from steroids. She managed to tutor and to keep her weekly visit to Julie's house to watch "Gossip Girl." It all seemed quasi-normal to me.

On top of that, Rachel was encouraged to learn that Dean, someone she knew who had relapsed Hodgkin's, reported that the huge tumor growing in his neck improved dramatically after one treatment with bendamustine.

Though Rachel's fatigue and shortness of breath continued to dog her, she insisted on driving herself to Hopkins for bloodwork. Her platelets were finally increasing, and her itching seemed less intense. One night, while cooking dinner, I heard uproarious laughter in the den. Rachel and Judah were watching *Amadeus*. It was so infectious that I put down my spoon and dashed into the den to laugh right along with them.

My hopes and worries continued to waver, depending on the day. Rachel seemed to test our limits, insisting that she spend time with friends in Silver Spring. Despite our concerns, we caved, and she always had a great time. On top of that, she was weaning herself off of prednisone to relieve its dreadful side effects, mainly insomnia.

Here we were, well into November of 2010, two years since her diagnosis, and Rachel was still grappling with symptoms.

By this time, she'd become fixated on improving the odds for young adults with cancer. So I arranged a meeting with Terry

Langbaum, administrator of the cancer center, who'd overcome Hodgkin's lymphoma herself many years before. I'd set up the meeting to discuss young adults' needs and support and how to open the lines of communication about topics like fertility and hair loss.

The meeting, which also included Hopkins media relations reps, gave us hope. They were all upset to learn about our experience prior to the fertility consult, immediately before Rachel's chemo began (that horrible moment when the oncology fellow said to her, "Forget about your fertility! We need to save your life!"). Terry said she'd speak to the team about how to communicate with more sensitivity. We bounced some ideas around. Then, they asked Rach if she'd be willing to speak about her experience at a national cancer network meeting in North Carolina. She told them she was more than willing. It turned out that the organization had decided that very same day to set new guidelines for young adults. (Since then, the Leukemia & Lymphoma Society continues to offer many resources for this demographic, including videos and online chats.)

Two days later, we headed to New York together to visit my father-in-law at his assisted living facility, while Rachel spent time with friends on the Upper West Side.

While we were in the city, I accompanied Judah's brother Josh and his wife, Niti, to a pre-Thanksgiving shopping trip at Fairway. The moment we entered the busy market, the sun's rays cast a spell over me. My eyes popped at the bounty: deep purple eggplant, Indian corn, squashes in myriad sizes and golden harvest hues.

Hordes of shoppers weaved through the market on that crisp fall day. Everyone seemed to be in high spirits. The temperature was falling, but it wasn't quite bitter-cold yet. All that lush produce and a general sense of camaraderie rekindled my hopes. I'd gone from a shockingly black and white life to a Technicolor one, albeit way too briefly.

That night, we ate dinner at a kosher Moroccan restaurant with Jon and his latest girlfriend, who seemed lovely. I was on my best behavior and tried not to "interview her too much," as Jon surely feared I would.

On the long ride home, Rach seemed agitated. She talked about how she belonged in New York (her frustrations with the city notwithstanding). Judah assured her that we would certainly revisit that idea when she got to a more stable place—in a good few months. Winters in New York, we reminded her, are so brutal anyway. But I felt my heart lurch.

Rachel had gone to several parties in the city the night before and mentioned that she'd met a cute guy named Ben. Along with another one of Rachel's friends, they'd shared a taxi back to the apartment where she was staying. Ben asked to be her Facebook friend. It pained me to hear her say that she'd decided to block him and other people from certain information because she didn't want him to know she had cancer—at least at this point.

On the heels of my energizing Thanksgiving shopping trip, we talked excitedly about our forthcoming Thanksgiving dinner at our dear friends', the Wolfs—an annual tradition, and guaranteed to spark lively conversation. As we discussed who was on the likely guest list, Rachel suddenly declared, "I'm bringing home three guys!" Though I knew it wasn't true, I laughed out loud and said, "That's fine with me!" But I felt a tug of disappointment for Rachel, knowing her social life was so fraught because of her health.

Rachel spent much of Thanksgiving Day watching the Thanksgiving Day Parade. A friend came to visit her but stayed way too long—several

hours. Rachel, clearly exhausted, was too polite to ask her to leave, and I suppose I didn't have the heart to do it either. I just wished someone would write an etiquette book about how to support friends with cancer respectfully.

With everyone home, the house was overrun with stuff—coats, Jon's gargantuan shoes, garment bag, legal pad covered in his chicken scrawl. But it was happy clutter and chatter. Hearing sports talk among the Minkoves restored a sense of normalcy.

Our den was awash in purple and black. From the kitchen I heard the clapping and cheering: The Ravens had beaten the Tampa Bay Buccaneers 8 to 3. To this day, though I have little interest in sports, I've come to appreciate its power to distract, uplift and unite people—and indeed, entire cities.

We headed to the Wolfs shortly thereafter for Thanksgiving dinner. As the door opened, sweet Shoshi Wolf ushered us in. "Shosh!" exclaimed Rachel, who shared a special bond with the Wolfs' third child. Both were the only girls in their respective families. They seemed more like sisters, which mirrored how I felt about Faith.

Faith, of course, had cooked enough to feed a battalion. The table was magazine-cover gorgeous, replete with china, silver and crystal. Whimsical touches softened the formality: mini-turkey placecard holders, fall leaves sprinkled here and there, cornhusk dolls. The most memorable part, though, was feeling enveloped in love after so many years of sharing this tradition with what has become our second family.

On that night, after all we'd been through, it felt so good to be out of our house, which seemed to have morphed into a medical unit. The den was overrun with alcohol swabs, tissues, thermometer, yellow plastic bins for Rachel to throw up into, bottles of water—some half-full; others that had slipped under the couch.

CHAPTER 9

Challenging the Odds

The day after Thanksgiving, Jon insisted on giving us a break and taking Rachel to the outpatient chemo unit at 8:30. It was so crowded that morning that Rachel had to stand until a seat became available. She and Jon didn't make it home until about 1:30. Rachel was wiped out, but tolerated the chemo fairly well. But, having weaned herself down to 5 mg of prednisone, her coughing was worse.

Right before Shabbat began, Rachel was feeling utterly exhausted. She'd insisted on showering and getting dressed, eager to wear her new pink and gray argyle dress from Old Navy, and she put on a little makeup as we awaited our dinner company, which would be followed by a little celebratory party for Sam on his being accepted to medical school.

Rachel looked beautiful that evening. She announced that she might as well look good, so that she might feel good, too. The strategy seemed to work. She clearly enjoyed the evening and ate well, sans her usual nausea.

But, just as we'd come to expect, things turned worrisome. At around 10:30 the next morning, she insisted we go for a walk. She practically sprinted to keep herself warm from the biting wind. At first, it felt brisk but tolerable. En route home after walking about three-quarters of a mile, Rachel struggled to walk back up our street's incline. Soon she was gasping for air. Thankfully, we made it home. That weekend we also attended an engagement party for our close friends' son, Aeli, and his fiancé, Sonia. Rachel looked radiant, but seemed out of sorts. Afterwards, Rachel joined the guys to celebrate.

And the next day she scared the hell out of us. I suspected she'd overdone it with all the socializing. I was on the phone when Sam burst into the kitchen to tell me that Rach was on the bathroom floor and couldn't get up. She'd tried to take a shower but suddenly felt very dizzy. Judah blamed it on the lower dose of prednisone she was on.

I sprinted upstairs to help her up. She hadn't quite fainted, but her pallor alarmed me. I helped her back into bed, and came back later to make sure she was OK and to help her get dressed and escort her downstairs. Nausea dogged her. It seemed like an eternity, but once she got settled on the couch, at least some of her color returned.

The long weekend was ending with everyone but me watching the Ravens game. There was so much to do in the kitchen, and I wasn't that interested in the sport, though I continued to be grateful for the welcome distraction football and other sports provided. The sheer physicality of it stood in contrast to Rachel's declining reserves.

Most of all, I was moved by the sight of Rachel sprawled on the couch wearing her oversized Ravens jersey, the boys sitting close to her, Judah leaning in—the four of them riveted by the game. I found my phone and snapped a photo. To this day, that moment evokes joy.

From the kitchen, I heard the clapping and woohoo-ing: The Ravens had beaten the Tampa Bay Buchaneers 17 to 10. As soon as the game ended, Sam and Nikki headed home to New Jersey. It gave me tremendous pleasure to assemble care packages for them to take home. Neither of them looked like they'd eaten much lately.

And so, we were back to three adults in our household. It had been an uplifting, albeit chaotic, time together—a reprieve from our usual angst-filled rhythm. But we needed to brace ourselves: Another chemo regimen was about to begin. Rachel sent out an email update saying that she had a "good feeling" about this treatment. Then she began looking at airfares to LA. I cringed a little, but, by this time, realized that socializing was as critical for her survival as her meds were.

The week was racing by. It was the first night of Chanukah—commemorating a time of miracles. Our hopes were rekindled: Rachel's weight had climbed to 106. After her shower (I stayed outside the door this time), she told me that it was the first time in a long while that her hair was long enough to pull around to her nose so she could inhale that clean, fresh post-shower scent. Once again, I was struck by the simple pleasures we take for granted. Rachel, meanwhile, had asked to throw a Chanukah party for her friends at the house.

We went about our lives, trying our best to create some normalcy. During the day, while I was at work, Rach continued to go out with family and friends. At night, we'd bond in the den, watching TV together; at that point, she adored *Glee*. I shuttled between the kitchen and the show, checking on the three baked zitis I'd made for Rachel's Chanukah party, scheduled for that Saturday night.

About 25 people were coming. Judah and I would need to

skedaddle, of course. We wanted so much to empower Rachel—to give her a sense of living independently, without worrying about our eavesdropping. Going out by ourselves would do us good, too, I realized. The Chanukah party turned out to be a blast, as she and her friends reported.

Snowy days and ice warnings followed. I was grateful that we could enjoy some down time together during the winter holidays. The glistening snow brightened our views and spirits. And suddenly, 2011 was upon us: a new year, renewed hopes for a cure ... or so I prayed.

The push-pull hope engine cobbled forward. Things continued to look up: Rachel's platelets were on the rise—a good thing, as Rachel had made plans to head to LA in early February for the Grammys, thanks to tickets Joanna's husband had received as a gift from a client. Rachel was ecstatic when Joanna called to invite her to join them. By then, of course, Judah and I were concerned that Rachel was on the verge of collapse. The see-saw seemed to be teetering more every day, and the angst seeped into our daily lives. But then Rachel would rally and make me believe she was on the path to better health. Rachel's *Pseudomonas* pneumonia continued, yet the symptoms had abated, and she was on Cipro. All I could do was hope for the best.

When she arrived in LA, the weather was sunny and holding steady at 76 degrees. Her dear friends Mike and Naomi hosted her. By the time we spoke to her later that night, she'd already met up with her close friend and former teaching colleague Jessica and two girls from the school where they taught. Soon, Rachel would need to hang up, as she was preparing to go out to dinner.

But I fretted over the realization that she still hadn't conquered the *Pseudomonas* infection. On top of that, I'd heard about two more young people in our community who had just been diagnosed with cancer. I couldn't make any sense of it. *When would this end? What are You trying to tell us, God? Why, WHY?*

I'd recently read that out on the West Coast and throughout the country, more young people were being diagnosed with cancer—or at least there were more stories about them in the news. Most of the time, I'd hear about kids under 18 stricken with the big C. But I'd begun seeing more ads on TV and newspapers about organizations like Stand Up to Cancer, the organization celebrities were embracing to support young adults with cancer, and Stupid Cancer. Both organizations have remained committed to advancing cures.

Rachel, it occurred to me, could have been their poster child. She was out to prove that cancer needn't be a death sentence. "Life is what you make it" became her mantra. And, though it was one of the toughest things ever for us to let our girl with stage 4 cancer and an impaired immune system gallivant around LA, we felt compelled to oblige. By her third day there, we'd learned that she met up with more friends; got tickets to be in the audience at an Ellen DeGeneres Show taping; and went out with more friends in the evenings.

On one of those nights, Rachel stayed out till 2:30 a.m. When I spoke to her the next day, she sounded exhausted but so happy. She'd just eaten lunch with her mentor at the elementary school where Rachel had done her fellowship teaching. Her mentor, perhaps 10 years older than Rachel, had lost her hair from chemotherapy for breast cancer.

When I heard about this, fear and anger gripped me: *There was simply no escape from this scourge.* It seemed as though God was making all kinds of physiological errors. Or, could the culprit be our lifestyles? Our environment? Both?

Intellectually, I knew that cancer biology was genetic, and that genes can take a wrong turn. But shortening lives, especially in children and young adults? And what did our beautiful girl do to deserve this? Or, I worried in lower moments, was it somehow the result of the sins of her parents?

I tried not to dwell on these negative thoughts, though they resurfaced when I least expected them, like soup that boils over, sizzles and hardens on the stovetop. Knowing Rachel was on the other coast without her caregivers unnerved me even more.

Thankfully, a phone call from her soothed my spirits. She'd spent a lovely Shabbat with Mike and Naomi. They'd walked to shul together and visited another friend after services. Now that Shabbat was over, she was getting ready for a planned reunion with friends at a bar.

But when I spoke to her the next night, she told me that she was bruising a lot and had more petechiae, the little red dots that likely signal low platelets. "She really has to be careful now," I wrote in my journal. I could tell that Judah was scared, too.

We cringed but forced ourselves to let her see this trip through. In case of an emergency, we knew we had our dear cousins Alisa and David in LA to turn to. When Rachel told us about her bruising, she rushed through the conversation, as she was getting ready for the Grammys. At 10:30 p.m. our time, we heard the excitement in her raspy voice. She and Joanna had gotten their hair and makeup done. The photos tell the astonishing tale: There was absolutely zero evidence that Rachel looked any less vibrant and healthy than her beautiful friend.

Finally, Rachel arrived home safely on Feb. 14, 2011. Except for all the bruises and petechiae on her arms, she looked darned good. She was so rejuvenated from the trip that I simply couldn't allow myself to wonder anymore whether or not we were irresponsible for supporting her decision to head to the West Coast.

Rachel admitted, however, that she'd turned heads while coughing on the plane to LA. At one point, she turned to the person who seemed most troubled by it and quipped, "Don't worry; it's just cancer!" How could I not laugh out loud?

Once we arrived home, her cough seemed intermittently manageable. But by 9 p.m. that night, it had morphed into a major coughing fit. Rachel was dreading her scheduled chemo and, no doubt, platelet infusions. I thanked God for having returned her safely from her much-needed respite.

The contrast between the LA experience and the chemo unit the next day was stark. Rachel learned that if the pneumonia didn't go away on Cipro, she might need IV antibiotics at home. I was glad I wasn't with her then: Her friend Ally had taken Rachel to chemo and back. They ate lunch together. I wondered what Rachel would do without these devoted friends. I was feeling the same way about ours, who continually found myriad ways to help or show their moral support.

As the chemo coursed through her veins, Rachel was in her usual position on the vinyl chair/bed—knees bent, laptop on her belly. She spent a lot of time choosing and posting photos from her trip to share with her friends. I hoped those moments would sustain her through this difficult week.

Two days later, Dr. Ambinder called to say that he wanted Rachel to meet with an infectious disease specialist. He was becoming more concerned about her lingering pneumonia. Indeed, Dr. A. told her she needed the IV antibiotic (AmbiSome). She'd had one treatment at Hopkins. Dr. A. gave her and me a pep talk—reassuring us that this time, it's an infection causing the cough, *not* the Hodgkin's. Otherwise, he explained, she would not have felt well enough to go to LA.

He was heartened to learn that Rachel and another patient on the experimental cancer treatment (rapamycin and bendamustine) appeared to be doing well.

Still, Rachel would need three weeks of the IV antibiotic three doses every eight hours. But she had a violent allergic reaction to it. She started itching everywhere and called Dr. A. So he put her on another drug.

As the days wore on, Rachel seemed weaker. She had trouble walking without stopping to catch her breath. We worried that things were going downhill fast. But then she'd rally her spirits and go about her life, convincing herself and us (to a lesser extent), that she wasn't giving up.

Her social calendar was filling up again, too. On Feb. 20, we went to see *Jersey Boys* in Baltimore. We took Rachel's friend Julie as our guest. Rachel coughed a little bit and was tired during the first half of the play (probably due to the oxycodone she'd taken). But she perked up and was definitely walking better as we left the theater.

Several days later, Rachel's camp friend Devo and her husband, Mike, arrived from New York for the day and took her out to lunch. Snow and sleet followed and lasted through the night. Rachel felt increasingly worse. Her pallor frightened me. I couldn't help but think of Devo's mother, Lori, and how the leukemia treatments and bone marrow transplant in Baltimore couldn't save her life. But I refused to let myself to slip down into that well of gloom.

Still, there was reason for concern: Rachel's hematocrit had dropped, as had her platelets. I called Dr. Ambinder's nurse, Jane, to let her know how worried I was. The next time Rachel arrived at the outpatient chemo unit for bloodwork and regular chemo treatment,

Dr. A. stopped by a couple of times while Rachel received her meds. The new drug required treatments round the clock: at 6 a.m., noon, 6 p.m. and midnight, then flushed with saline and heparin. My heart ached: *Here we go again.*

The noon dose would be the most difficult because we would not be home. So we arranged some help until Rachel felt confident enough to administer it herself. Once again, our friends, neighbors and Jewish Caring Network stepped up to see us through these infusions.

Rachel continued tutoring and completed her application to social work school, having been inspired all over again by Lacy. Then she drove to Hopkins for a unit of red blood cells (her crit had dropped to 25.5).

A couple days later, Judah's sister, Dena, and her husband, Walter, arrived from Israel—a boon for all of us. Rachel adored Dena ("Deens!" she exclaimed upon seeing her) and was delighted to have her around.

Feeling celebratory, we decided to host mutual friends for Shabbat lunch that weekend. Later, Rachel and Dena visited our dear friend Barbie, who had been diagnosed with a lung ailment and was also being treated at Hopkins. Rachel and Barbie shared a special bond, laughing together whenever they saw outrageous outfits or behavior.

And then, something momentous happened: As our feisty girl continued to fill her social calendar, she learned the exciting news that she'd been accepted to social work school. Rachel was beyond ecstatic, and, of course, we were mighty proud. She wasted no time reviewing the required reading list and writing papers. She also continued nurturing her friendships and even hosted a book club meeting.

Rachel also began spending more time with Barbie. They'd go out for coffee and hot chocolate, comparing notes about managing their coughing and the frustrations of being treated at a behemoth hospital center. The 25-year age difference didn't seem to matter. They discussed pop culture (both followed the latest music trends and The *Bachelor* escapades), chocolate indulgences and fashion.

It occurred to me that all three of my children were blessed with the ability to forge friendships with people of all ages. Their friendship was layered with mutual affection: Growing up, Dena and Barbie were besties. Dena was a bridesmaid at Barbie's wedding. And Barbie was our friend, too, though Judah continues to tease her, as he did when his sister and Barbie were growing up.

By this time, I realized, more than three decades of loving friendships in Baltimore had more than made up for the dearth of friends I had growing up. As for our Rachel, she seemed to have become *everyone's* beloved friend.

On March 1, 2011, Rachel drove herself to Hopkins for bloodwork and learned she had to go right back again because she needed platelets and potassium. Afterwards, she headed to our friend Diane's house, where they cooked up a storm of Italian dairy dishes— Rachel's favorite—which we enjoyed immensely later that evening.

In spite of her having spent much of the day at Hopkins, Rachel looked beautiful and radiant. I marveled at her resilience. Over the ensuing days, she tutored, went for short walks with friends and out to lunch. She even substitute-taught at Beth Tfiloh.

Jon came home for a visit that weekend, nursing a cold and heartache, following a recent breakup. I had plenty of comfort food at the ready, and was glad to see him open up to Rachel.

I'd finally learned how to administer Rachel's antibiotic, but was not disappointed when on March 5, she was informed that after 10 days, she could be taken off of it. Dr. A also told her that he wanted her to get a scan to "see where we are." It was creepy to realize that it had been a year—almost to the day—since Rachel was diagnosed with cancer in her lungs. But that night, she woke up coughing a few times, and the antibiotic had caused more itching. (*Or,* Judah and I wondered, *was it more Hodgkin's?*)

On Shabbat, we went for a walk down Benhurst to visit Barbie and our friends the Leves. En route home, Rachel became short of breath, gasping for air. Then her itching became unbearable, so she took more Benadryl, which made her sleepy.

That's when it hit me that something had changed emotionally for Rachel: She seemed almost defeated. For the first time, I admitted to myself that her spirits were in worse shape than her body was. Perhaps that was because she'd run into a 25-year-old patient who also had Hodgkin's and was dealing with liver problems. "I hope to get compassionate use of SGN-35 [the first immunotherapy for refractory Hodgkin's]," she told Rachel.

The following week, a PET scan revealed that Rachel's tumors were shrinking. But the lung infection was still there. Dr. A was eager to resolve it but needed her to schedule a bronchoscopy to reveal the source of the problem. *Would we ever hear news about her health that wasn't mixed?* I wondered aloud to Judah. And still, Rachel continued to tutor. In between, her blood counts had dropped. She needed a blood transfusion and potassium.

On one particularly bad week, she felt utterly spent. The bronchoscopy and blood work revealed that she had the flu. Her spirits plummeted. She posed an unanswerable question: *"I'm so sick of this! When am I going to feel better??!"*

But we were pleasantly surprised to learn that the lung biopsy samples tested negative for cancer and fungus. I knew we weren't out of the woods until the PET scan told us more, but it was a nice reprieve. And, the fever had vanished. Even the itching seemed to have taken leave.

Nevertheless, Rachel's body and soul were tenuous from all the ups and downs. One night, we watched *Conviction,* a movie about a man wrongfully convicted of murder, whose sister goes to law school to help get him freed. It moved us both. The unspoken parallels to Rachel's life felt palpable to me: Sam's bone marrow donation and Jon's willingness to donate his, if necessary—and anything else—if it could save their sister's life.

As the credits lined our TV screen, Rachel melted down. Her voice breaking, the words tumbled out: *"I'm never going to be able to breathe normally again!"*

My heart was racing. What could I possibly say to comfort our girl? *Absolutely nothing,* I realized. So, choking back tears, I just listened. I wrapped my arms around her shrinking frame, no longer hiding my angst. We shared a good, long cry together.

Rachel admitted that she didn't think she was well enough to go to New York for a trip she'd planned. But, I assured her, we were going to have a better day tomorrow. "Dear God," I wrote in my journal, "please don't make me a liar."

Rachel did, in fact, fare better day the next day, though she threw up several times. The antibiotics had likely ripped her intestines up. Yet she felt well enough that evening to go out for ice cream with Judah. I took that as a good sign, as well as the slight boost in her energy level.

The following day, March 18, 2011, would bring unexpected news.

Rachel had driven herself to the hospital for blood work, then called me to let me know she was there. I had a meeting on campus anyway, so I met her in the chemo area. She said she had some good news to share. Dr. A. told her that he thought she could be going into remission and that the next chemo could be her last. He wanted to give her body a break. For one thing, he didn't like her counts dropping so much, And her lungs seemed to be clear, though she would need a PET scan soon to confirm that. I cried when I heard this update and wished I could stay with her, but I had to get back to work and catch the shuttle.

Later, Rachel told me that Judah had cried, too. But he didn't want to believe it just yet.

As thrilling as this development was—and we were initially elated—I knew better than to believe remission was imminent. Indeed, over the next several weeks, Rachel rallied, until one symptom or another would knock her down. For me, the hardest part was leaving for work every morning, not knowing how her day would play out. Her friends would often call her, making plans to get together. And, as daunting as I'd thought social work school would be for her, it turned out to be a great distraction.

Still, my work was suffering, along with my spirits. It was becoming increasingly difficult to focus on my assignments. The few times I managed to churn out a decent story, I felt buoyed (and relieved). But I couldn't sustain it. My head and heart were consumed with how to keep Rachel strong—physically and mentally—as her health plummeted. It felt like I was mired in quicksand.

Days turned into weeks. Winter was melting into spring, though cold blasts reminded us not to become too used to going coatless. And suddenly it was Purim again. We heard the traditional *megillah* (*Book of Esther*) reading at Beth Tfiloh Congregation/School, where our kids went to school. The tumult of groggers, laughter and gasps at creative costumes distracted us momentarily from our concern about Rachel's health.

The next morning, we went to Suburban Orthodox Congregation to hear the *megillah* once again before heading to New Rochelle, NY, for Judah's brother, Josh's 60th birthday party.

It was wonderful to see so many relatives, and Josh's son Shami and his wife, Elana, and children were extremely gracious hosts. Our other delightful nephew Shachar and his wife, Stephanie, and family were also overjoyed to see us—especially Rachel, of course. I was relieved that her cough had subsided. And, though she looked pale, that high-wattage smile and twinkling eyes assured us that she was enjoying herself.

My father-in-law, still in declining health, seemed pleased. Rachel's trademark "Hi, Saba!" elicited a big smile from him. It was turning out to be a much better Purim than the previous year. We also got to spend time with Jon, Sam and Nikki, as well as extended family. Niti—effusive as ever—recited one of her signature poems to mark the occasion, a sweet, well-deserved tribute to her husband. The living room had been set up with tables; the food was delicious and plentiful.

We slept over and awoke to big snowflakes falling and quickly carpeting the lawn. We sat and watched the peaceful scene, knowing that we'd soon need to make the trip home. The snow was short-lived but left a sparkly coating. It reminded me of a peaceful winter scene in a snowglobe.

I stored that scene from Elana and Shami's kitchen in my mind as a touchstone, something I could summon during a challenging time. Spirits lifted, we left New Rochelle at around 2:30 and made it home at around 6.

Most of all, I mused, despite our fears that some crisis with Rachel might have erupted hundreds of miles from home, the escape from our routine was refreshing. It did us good, even as the reality of returning to the drumbeat of cancer treatment and follow-up loomed large.

Rachel's days at Hopkins seemed endless, and, though I tried to be hopeful, my morale often dipped. The frustration of being part of a complex medical system in an academic hospital fueled an angst that put me on edge. I was grateful when frontline employees would actually smile and greet us. But things rarely moved quickly.

On one particularly long day, Rachel waited hours for platelets—hers had dropped to 6,000. Then, she developed a severe allergic reaction to them. When it was finally time to leave, at around 5:30, Rachel realized that she was out of parking stickers. We walked over to a machine to purchase more, but it wouldn't accept Rachel's credit card. And we were out of cash. By then, we were so frazzled and exhausted that we almost collapsed on the spot. My eyes quickly welled up.

Then—out of nowhere, it seemed—a man who'd witnessed the scene came up to Rachel and pulled out a $10 bill to give the parking attendant. It was the second random act of kindness that day. A few hours earlier, my editor and dear friend Marjorie had presented me with a daffodil plant. The following week, Judah's colleagues chipped in to buy a Target gift certificate for Rachel. Talk about *chesed*!

Moral support from my other colleagues was equally touching, especially Mary Ann, a gifted editor who is deeply spiritual yet quick with a snarky observation. I knew that she, like Marjorie, was praying for Rachel daily. The human capacity for kindness seemed boundless. But these gestures went beyond kindness: They were acts of love that boosted our spirits. Still, there were times when I felt embarrassed to accept all this unbridled generosity. I just hoped I'd have the opportunity to do the same for someone else struggling with a family crisis.

Despite all the recent positive family news, Rachel's ups and downs continued to rattle our nerves. There was a new kind of urgency bubbling up inside of our feisty girl. She started talking nonstop about her dream of becoming a social worker. Meeting with Lacy regularly through good and horrific times no doubt had a profound impact on Rachel's decision. But Rachel had a specific mission: to devote her career to helping the underserved population of young adults with cancer.

I was so proud of her, even though a part of me felt like Rachel was setting herself up for disappointment. We knew that any time, her condition—already weakened by setbacks—could take a turn.

For his part, Dr. Ambinder continued combing the literature on refractory Hodgkin's and weighing the value of treatments to cure her. It pained me sometimes to imagine how he would deliver the next round of bad news. But I knew that if Rachel wasn't giving up, neither would I, so I'd quash the negative thoughts and tried to smile when people told me they were praying for her.

Meanwhile, Rachel's excitement about her mission to become an oncology social worker was intensifying. I'll never forget the soggy day Judah drove Rachel to see the University of Maryland's School of Social Work, located directly across the street from the hospital where her father trained and completed his internal medicine residency, and where Sam and Nikki would end up training together.

It was *pouring*—the torrential kind of rain that blurred vision. I worried that Rachel would be upset that she couldn't walk around the campus much. But when she and Judah returned, Rachel was jubilant. She couldn't wait to start her studies. It was as though she'd found a cure for her recalcitrant disease.

By the end of March 2011, Rachel's platelets had increased to 40K, which was significant. And her crit was 33, higher than usual. So she didn't need to go back to Hopkins after subbing at Beth Tfiloh. On that last weekend in March, we enjoyed a "pajama-Shabbat"—just us three—so nice and quiet. Rachel was tired but looked much better than she had the previous week.

On March 31, Dr. A. called to tell Rachel she needed to come off of the bendamustine drug she'd been taking. It was time to reassess. He wanted her to have a PET scan within the next two weeks. Meanwhile, the stress of preparing for Passover was building again. As if reading my mind, the Jewish Caring Network delivered beautiful paper goods to adorn our table (and reduce the need for washing dishes).

Hope resurfaced when the results of Rachel's PET scan turned out better than we expected. "It was good," Jane reported. "No new tumors." In fact, it looked like there was only one, in her chest, and it had shrunk. A few weeks later, Rachel sent out an update. Its candor and continuing hope for brighter days evoked renewed awe.

From: Rachel Minkove
Friday, April 15, 2011 1:47 PM
Subject: Pre-Pesach update

Dear Friends and Family,
I usually receive bad news before Jewish holidays, so

I'm happy to report that I am going into Pesach in a more positive tone than usual.

I'm not saying things are perfect, but this is a much better way to usher in a holiday. I recently had a PET scan (my favorite test.....) The results were a mixed bag. As always, I am told that I'm complicated. However, the overall impression was encouraging.

Most of the tumors have either resolved or shrunk, which means that my chemo was effective. However, there is still a lot of junk in my lungs which is recurrent pneumonia. Recently, it has been an obstacle for me to breathe and walk, often preventing me from accomplishing small tasks. So that's what has to be dealt with next: how to make my lungs function properly so I can resume daily tasks. I am starting on antibiotics and meeting with some doctors, who will hopefully create a plan to accomplish this.

Additionally, the chemo has caused me to become reliant on platelets, so I am currently going to the hospital at least once a week to receive platelet infusions. This is not a simple process either, because I have developed an allergy to platelets, so they need to concentrate them for me. Overall, my chemo was effective, but it is starting to take a toll on my bone marrow. Therefore, I am now on a break from chemo infusions, but continue to take nightly chemo pills to keep up my progress.

Overall, this is encouraging news, but I remain cautiously optimistic. However, this is a much better way of going into the chag, as opposed to finding out about a relapse on erev [the eve of] Pesach. Also, I have just enrolled in the University of Maryland School of Social Work for the fall to eventually assist patients and families going through illness.

*As always, thanks for your continued concern and
prayers, and have a chag sameach!*

Rachel

In the end, on erev Pesach, the eve of the first Passover seder, we were assaulted with sobering news: Dr. A. had called to say he was very concerned and that Rachel would need to be on antibiotics for a month with two-hour doses. He told her that she might have BOOP or graft v. host—or possibly a tumor, or a serious fungal infection called *Aspergillus*. The infection is 90% fatal. So Rachel would need to have another bronchoscopy ASAP.

Meanwhile, Rachel had developed a fever of 101.3 and was coughing almost incessantly. She'd been up half the night. And her itching became unbearable. I'd prepared an oatmeal bath for her, knowing full well it would likely provide only momentary relief. Once again, Rachel's "antisemitic body" had upended our holiday.

We'd hoped to head over to the Wolfs for the first seder. But we never made it. Throughout that day, Rachel had trouble catching her breath. So we cancelled our plans. But, for the second night, we upheld our tradition of hosting our dear friends Mitch and Janice to join us. We got through the seder fairly quickly. Rachel struggled to breathe and made her way to the couch intermittently throughout the meal.

By the end of the evening, Rachel was exhausted and irritable. But Jon and Sam did their part to entertain her. Once again, they challenged each other to a *maror* competition, ingesting the bitter horseradish root until their faces turned a splotchy red. We couldn't help but laugh, which, I gathered was the goal. Oh, how I loved those guys. And there was no mistaking the love shining through Rachel's tired eyes.

CHAPTER 10

'Man Plans, God Laughs'

W aiting for test results must be akin to awaiting a verdict and sentencing. But in this case, there was no crime. Actually, there was: A young, vibrant woman in the prime of her life is stricken with cancer. The perpetrator was fate, or God, and my patience was wearing thin. *Why, why must our beautiful girl suffer so much? What did she, or we, do to deserve this? And how much more could she take?*

At last, the results were in. Dr. Ambinder called Rachel to inform her that she'd tested positive for *Aspergillus*. We were devastated but not entirely surprised. Her itching had returned with a vengeance. The new drug was likely causing it (and perhaps the emergence of new cancer cells). It was hard to stay positive, knowing that the survival rate for this infection was so slim. But we assured Rachel that we were going to support her every step of the way.

Later that night, when I looked in on her, our little angel was fast asleep. As I gently adjusted her blanket, my heart skipped a beat when I discovered the toilet paper woven between her toes. I prayed that it offered some measure of relief. But it was jarring to recall her initial resourceful approach to quell her toe-itching—now, almost three years since leaving LA. Judah was shattered by this latest news. His face lost all color. How could it not? When he was in med school, *Aspergillus* infection was 100% fatal. Thirty years later, that number has been reduced, but only by 10 percent.

The most dreadful part was that Rachel would need three-hour infusions of antibiotics, twice a day. "She has the worst case of *Aspergillus* this hospital has ever seen," Dr. Ambinder told us. I saw a new and fearful intensity on his face. He went on to explain that Rachel would need those three-hour infusions of the treatment for three months. Then he said three words that pierced my heart: "I am concerned."

For most people, this diagnosis requires hospitalization, but thanks to Judah's training and the wonderful Johns Hopkins Home Care team, we convinced Dr. A. that we could manage this major setback at home. Though Dr. A. seemed a bit skeptical, I knew his respect for Judah's judgment and competence would ultimately win him over.

Still, we were shaken, especially Judah, who knew how serious things had just turned. By this time, Rachel's weight had plummeted to 99.2. She did enjoy Barbie's homemade matzo lasagna and matzo pizza. I hoped it was plenty caloric.

Of all the treatments Rachel had to endure, this one was—hands down—the most grueling. And, almost immediately after the drug coursed her veins, it generated itching and nausea.

After a couple of weeks, the intensity of this treatment began to wear our girl down. She did her best to keep pace with her work, school and social life, but her energy level plummeted. One day, in exasperation, she railed at the unfairness of this latest diagnosis: "I don't want to be sick anymore! When am I going to feel better and go on with my life?" I wished I had an answer, but all I could muster was something like, "We are going to fight this together, Rachie."

Despite receiving the I.V. treatments at home, Rachel still needed to go to Hopkins regularly for bloodwork and other tests. I could feel the dread rising up in us both as we got into our minivan. We knew that even "short" visits would take hours. Afterwards, we'd drag ourselves back to our car and head home. One day, as we were pulling out of the main drop-off and pickup area, a sweet middle-aged woman—herself a cancer patient—tapped on our passenger-side window, I pressed the electric button to open the window. Then, breaking into a big smile, she told Rachel: "I saw you today and how young and beautiful you are. I'm sorry you're going through this. But God will bless you, and you're young and strong and will get better."

I was touched by her kindness and so wanted to believe her. But we were still reeling from the pulmonologist's grim news, following Rachel's bronchoscopy. The infection in Rachel's lungs, he told us, was pervasive. And, though he found no apparent Hodgkin's disease, he encountered something very surprising—and serious, he said: invasive *Aspergillus* in her vocal chords. That explained why she couldn't catch her breath. Rachel would need to be admitted to Hopkins.

"It's airway-centric," he said. "So it's good that she's been treated with amphotericin, but now she'll need it for months—maybe even forever. And she'll need additional antibiotics." Judah wondered aloud: *Is her native immunity so altered that she can't fight infection?* I don't recall hearing an answer. But his eyes said, "It's possible."

By the time we returned to Rachel's outpatient chemo area, we felt utterly defeated. So we were surprised when Dr. A. showed up looking happy. In fact, he was almost ecstatic, saying that this was the best possible news. Yes, *Aspergillus* is a serious infection, but at least it's treatable, and it's probably *not* more Hodgkin's.

Alas, on April 24, just as I was about to light candles to usher in the last holy days of Passover, Dr. Ambinder called to tell Rachel that she needed to think about what would happen if she stopped being able to breathe on her own. "Things might be irreversible at this point," he told her, noting that he did think there was more Hodgkin's, and that she needed to be admitted ASAP. We bought a little time— enough for us to get through the end of Passover and put away the Passover dishes.

Once again, I was struck by how nature sent us signs: On Rachel's admission date—April 27, 2011—there was a tornado watch. It turned out to be a false alarm. How I wished for similar news about Rachel's health!

A few days later, when I arrived at Hopkins, Rachel had just eaten four pieces of French toast. She looked darned good for someone as sick as she was. I was about to speak to her when I noticed that she was *davening* (praying), using an online *siddur* (prayer book). When she was done, she told me how much she disliked Princess Kate's royal wedding dress. The sacred and the mundane. I almost laughed out loud. *That's our Rachie!*

Morning rounds were fairly quick. Dr. A. still sounded upbeat, but he mentioned that they were going to ramp up the amphotericin and add another drug, plus increase her potassium. Rachel's liver values were off, so they'd keep an eye on them, too.

After the care team left the room, Rachel looked up her infec- tion on the Internet and became agitated when she read about the 90 percent mortality rate. Judah told her to stop reading. A little while later, Shmuel Shoham, the infectious disease specialist, stopped by. We immediately bonded with this affable man, also a traditional

Jew. Despite acknowledging the gravity of her condition, he told us he'd seen people recover from this infection, which gave us a much-needed lift.

The next day, Rachel was released from Hopkins, and we began the arduous administration of the two four-hour infusions at home for three straight months. Our lives were suddenly dictated by the treatments, but we were grateful for the opportunity for Rachel to be treated at home, which is almost unheard of because of how serious the condition is. As ever, I was grateful we were blessed with a seasoned M.D. in our household who ensured that his daughter wouldn't miss a single infusion.

The den had again morphed into a sick room; the sterile wipes' scent filled the air, as the TV blared. We sat together as a family and bided our time. What choice did we have?

Miraculously, after three months of treatments and awful side effects, especially vomiting, Rachel overcame the deadly infection. The hospital staff was incredulous; some involved in her care called Jane to verify the news. One nurse told Rachel, "We didn't think you were going to make it."

Yet we knew things had taken a dangerous turn. Although Rachel managed to overcome one of the deadliest infections, her immune system was essentially kaput. And that made her vulnerable to more infections and complications than ever before. The possibility of Rachel's being on AmBisome for the rest of her life made me shudder.

With heavy hearts, we met with her pulmonologist and Dr. Ambinder to discuss the next steps. We knew things didn't bode well. But we were grateful that a few experimental treatments held some promise. We held out hope that the SGN-35 immunotherapy drug Rachel so desperately sought in New York would soon become available at Hopkins.

As for Judah and me, we avoided discussing the impact of Rachel's health woes. It was too fraught.

But one morning, en route to Hopkins, Judah's fears seemed palpable. We left the house early and sat in anguished silence, as he drove through beautiful Mt. Washington. Suddenly, the light at Greenspring and Northern Parkway turned yellow. For once, Judah decided not to rush into the intersection. Facing us was Sinai Hospital, where all three of our children were born.

Judah ran his hands through his hair; I thought he might tear it all out. "*We just keep accepting another level of deterioration,*" he said. My eyes welled up just hearing his tone. I don't recall what I said back, but I was unnerved by his hopelessness. I sat silently, trying to process his comment. Then he added, "I just can't fix this! I can't *fix* this!"

In that moment, I totally understood his helplessness. I'd felt it myself. My heart ached for him—and our family. I wanted to rely on his astute medical opinion, but at this point it seemed the cancer train was veering off the tracks. Even Dr. Ambinder's face, I noticed, had begun to betray his stated expectation that Rachel would recover. The setbacks were wearing me down, too.

At last, on April 30, Rachel was released from the hospital. But several weeks later, while recovering at home, she started feeling especially awful: exhausted and unable to stop coughing, A test Dr. Ambinder ordered revealed that she'd once again developed *Pseudomonas*, pneumonia. Rachel decided it was too nice a word for her latest complication. "From now on," she declared, "I'm no longer calling it *Pseudomonas*. Its new name is '*Doody-coccis*'!"

We laughed out loud, even as I choked back tears, knowing that this new development would mean yet another hospital admission.

Soon we were cracking up together as we, in unison, shouted, "*Ugh!
Doody-coccis! Doody-coccis!*" Resorting to bathroom humor, I
realized, is a tendency that can persist into adulthood. An immature
response to a serious new development? Yes, but in this case, name-
calling the disease seemed to empower Rachel to fight it all the more.

A few other strategies existed for our daughter's "refractory" Hodgkin's
disease, but they, too, proved ineffective. By the time a cancer has
lasted this long, it isn't the same disease that originally strikes. Against
the pressure of the chemo drugs, of cancer genes' natural instabil-
ity and even, likely, of a rampant infection's effects on the immune
system, a cruel sort of evolution takes place that selects for the most
elusive cancer's survival. And so it seemed with the now-distinctive,
singular Rachel's Lymphoma.

We—and anyone who heard about what Rachel was going
through, were in awe of Rachel's resilience. But as time went on, she
cringed when people told her how inspired they were by her. "I'm
tired of being amazing," she said for the hundredth time. "I just want
to be a healthy 27-year-old!"

Around this time, I realized that my difficulties writing for
Hopkins might improve if I could feature exceptional people at the
institution. I'd already written about the bell-ringing ceremony in
radiation oncology after Rachel thought she was in remission. The
story was well received. So, in anticipation of the need for inspiring
Nurses Week stories, I received permission to write a profile on Jane,
Rachel's outpatient chemo nurse.

Jane, who by then had worked alongside Rich Ambinder for
more than a decade, was gracious about the idea. She sent me an

email about her own cancer ordeal as her husband, Pat, was being treated for acute leukemia in 1980. He'd been diagnosed with a brain tumor in the winter of 2000 and died in August of 2001, leaving Jane a single mother with two teenage daughters.

To make things easier for me, Jane chronicled her experience in an email to me. The email also revealed the effect Rachel's illness was having on Jane. I appreciated her candor and concern, even though the email was hard for me to read. I was also touched by the love I felt between the lines.

4/27/2011 email from Jane Diaz

> I would get up every day at 4:30, get Pat settled and then go to work all day (paid for his private duty and medical expenses). My girls were in and out, working and taking him places. He was disabled as soon as the diagnosis came in. Rich [Ambinder] was with us when the doctor told us he was sick and "there was no cure." We endured 8 more long months of strife. He struggled and always wanted to go back to work. I am thankful I don't do brain tumors. They change the personality so much. He actually slapped my youngest daughter and made her cry. He never raised a hand to them, ever! What a sad disease to see. I can look at a patient and pick out someone who has a brain tumor. Thankful I was never assigned to them. Dr. Grossman/ Kleinberg were his docs, but Rich was very helpful as well. One of the hard parts was seeing my girls lose their dad so young. No weddings, no births, etc.
>
> Now, I think of how Rachel struggles. She actually worries me and makes me a little nervous when I see her so labored. I know Rich had a pretty sobering chat with Rachel and Judah on Sunday. I think part of that was from me. I wanted to know what to do "just in case" and sorry this upset you all. It is the part of the job that destroys me. I have had talks about "what

do you do if…" and they are not easy. But with Rachel, I will do whatever it takes to work with her to make her better. As you know, I am here for whatever you need. Ask me more, if I have left other things unsaid.

 Jane

The story on Jane and her family's cancer experience ran in the employee newsletter and was well received. It pained me to learn how much suffering Jane's family had endured, but my fondness for this extraordinary nurse had grown exponentially.

Jane's story was a painful reminder of the universal nature of cancer and the scores of people it continues to affect. At this writing (2022), according to the National Cancer Institute, more than 1.8 million Americans will be diagnosed with some form of cancer, and this year, more than 600,000 will die from complications relating to it. The numbers tell the tale, but I have no doubt that each one of those families affected by cancer has a unique story to share about their loved ones' experience.

CHAPTER 11

Glimmers and Downers

As spring morphed into the summer of 2011, we were treated to some beautiful days, interspersed with our city's trademark oppressive heat and humidity. I encouraged Rachel not to run around too much so she wouldn't become overheated, but she ventured out more than I would have liked. Yet, at this point I was feeling nearly as concerned for Rachel's emotional health as I was for her physical health. So I tried not to worry that she'd overdo it.

One day in late June, she went out for lunch with Barbie, followed by pedicures and then to Field's in Pikesville for snowballs. Rachel managed to keep everything down (lately, her nausea was erupting more often). When I returned home, she looked radiant and scarfed down a turkey avocado wrap. Later, while relaxing on the hammock on the deck, she had a craving for canned corn. About an hour later, she barfed it all up. But her spirits were good, and she told me she was doing well in her course.

Her pallor had worsened in a way that concerned Judah and me. But her numbers and the labs showed improvement. For once, she didn't need platelets or red blood cells, and her kidney and liver functions had improved, albeit slightly. The best news was that both her sinus and chest scans showed improvement.

Yet the vomiting continued. Though Rachel suddenly seemed to relish eating again, she couldn't keep food down. We learned that nausea was a common, lingering side effect from prolonged use of that antifungal drug AmBisome (amphotericin B) she'd been taking. Initially, she'd been taken off of the drug after 10 days. But in light of her recent lung infection, she'd resumed taking it. Finally, Dr. A. informed her that the culprit was likely the megadoses of potassium she was taking, *combined* with the AmBisome.

The ups and downs continued, unabated. Rachel's battered lungs had been through so much. Thankfully, spring weather made it easier for her to breathe outside. Still, we worried that she was venturing out too much on her own. We'd argued about it one night, reminding her that in her fragile state, she needed to be more careful. Her pale face turned red, and I watched her eyes well up.

The next morning, I came downstairs to find a note on the kitchen counter:

> Hi Guys,
>   I know you care about me, but sometimes it's just frustrating when I want to do normal things.
>   I'm not upset. I just wanna be better already.
>   Sorry if I take it out on you.
>   ,
> Rach

Her cough had worsened, and at that point, she needed to have oxygen available, in case she had trouble breathing.

Seeing Rachel tethered to an oxygen tank at home—something I once thought was the exclusive domain of old people—hit me hard. But I knew she needed that security. Just getting up and down the stairs had become difficult. Breathing is something I'd always taken for granted. Swimming laps for decades raised my awareness about breathing properly, but, thankfully, my lungs have always been healthy.

It shocked me to realize that my daughter, who was 29 years younger than her mother, would have lungs so compromised they would likely remain that way indefinitely. But cancer has its own set of rules. The unfairness of it all incensed me, though I tried hard to stay positive for Rachel. But why, *why* did our daughter have to suffer so much? And, still, I prayed every day to a God who seemed oblivious to our agony.

Rachel's fatigue had begun to dog her. She spent more time on the couch, where *Glee* always perked her up. I continued to look for ways to lift Rachel's spirits. One day during my lunch break, I ventured into a toy store and found a Very Hungry Caterpillar musical butterfly and sun mobile that lit up. Rachel was delighted and kept calling it a *be-yooo-tiful* butterfly. Her smile gave me hope, mirroring that Eric Carle story that continued to resonate with Rachel.

The next day was especially trying. Rachel's friend Talia hung out with her at our house. They watched a movie, Rachel strung up to her portable oxygen. Later, Barbie picked her up and took her out for ice cream. She brought along her oxygen, but it had mostly been used up from the earlier part of the day, and she became short of breath at Maggie Moo's, feeling so weak that she had to go outside to throw up.

Tears filled her eyes as she recounted the experience to me. "I vomited on a plant, and a high school girl Barbie knew 'told on me.'"

The teenager—in front of Rachel—said to Barbie, "Can I speak to you outside?"

Rachel knew that conversation would be about her. Afterwards, she kept getting looks. In retelling the exchange, Rachel was so upset that she could barely get the words out to finish the story.

But the fact that she wanted to get out of the house and found the energy to do so was somewhat encouraging. And yet ... it pained me that Rachel had felt so much shame in that moment. Barbie later told me that she informed the girl that Rachel had advanced cancer and that she couldn't control her bout with nausea in that moment. I just hoped that young lady learned a lesson about reserving judgment.

I'm reasonably sure that had the roles were reversed, Rachel would have run over to the sickly girl and asked if she was OK. It reminded me of how Rachel, at a tender age, used to check on me many years before, most memorably, on the day a cicada smacked into my eye.

Every 17 years, during late spring/early summer, a plague of cicadas emerge from the ground and swarm into the mid-Atlantic region to mate—and then they die. Their beady red eyes and deafening call unnerve anyone in their path. Their carcasses overwhelm windshields, lawns, sidewalks and every other outdoor walkway or surface. When Judah and I were dating, he described this surreal proliferation of these insects that resemble grasshoppers, but I simply couldn't fathom such a Biblical scene actually unfolding. It seemed utterly fantastical ... that is, until I experienced it personally.

On a sweltering June day in 1987, I dashed toward our station wagon, clinging to one-year-old Sam. Then I buckled him into his car seat in record time. The cacophony of the screeching creatures was utterly unnerving. Four-year-old Rachel followed me out, brushing away the flying debris. As the cicadas swarmed us, she yelled, "*Eew—gross!*" over and over again. I was grunting right along with her. It was an exciting day for my middle child—her "graduation" from preschool at the Jewish Community Center on Park Heights Avenue. Jon, three and a half years her senior, was already a third-grader at Beth Tfiloh Community School, so he didn't accompany us that day.

As I drove down Park Heights Ave., the windshield swarmed with those feisty insects and their carcasses. I may as well have been driving through a snow squall. The five-minute ride seemed to last a half-hour. But we finally made it.

My relief was palpable. I parked the car and braced myself to push through the bug avalanche. As swiftly as I could, I opened the umbrella stroller, belted Sam, and grabbed Rachel's hand. Then we did our best to dash into the building's side entrance.

Suddenly, a cicada smacked directly into my eye. It so unnerved me that I fell backward ... and lost control of the stroller. Then I heard Rachel scream, "Mommy! Mommy! Are you *OK*?" In that moment, I felt terror—realizing that Sam and possibly Rachel could be run over by a car. Then I started screaming.

It had all happened so fast and resolved itself in a matter of seconds. I managed to get a grip on the stroller and myself. We finally made it up the steps, shaken but relieved that no one was hurt.

Rachel's sweet voice and concern that day became permanently etched into my psyche. The experience has served as a constant reminder of our capacity for empathy and selfless love, even at a tender age.

I recall nothing else about the preschool graduation, except having been shaken to the core. *Not true:* I can still conjure Rachel's sweet smile and translucent eyes popping out later that day as she shared the story of our frightening experience with her friends, commiserating about how gross the insects were. I was still shaking, but she'd taken it all in stride. Thankfully, Sam, who was facing the greatest peril that day, has no recollection of this episode.

Rachel also told her friends that, much to her chagrin, her older brother thought the cicadas were cool. Indeed, Jon would put one in each hand, put them up to his ears, and say, "Look, Mom, I have a Walkman!" I felt such a profound love for these children.

That cicada flashback would revisit me many times as Rachel fought for restored health. It sustained me. But it simply wasn't enough to stem my angst. And still, I smiled as much as I could to provide some measure of hope for my ailing daughter.

The days took on a new rhythm. Mornings were horrid. Rachel couldn't seem to get started. She was sapped of energy; so little air went to her lungs. I was in and out one Sunday, but when I returned home, Rachel was parked on the couch in the den looking washed out. She'd become obsessed with a show called *Prison Break*. I tuned in and was immediately repulsed by the violence and gore. But I couldn't help thinking how apt it was that Rachel identified with the prisoners, who felt trapped and schemed ways to escape.

Rachel's new favorite food was Mexican soy beef with cheese and marinara. I prayed she'd keep it down. Most of the time, she did. Friends would stop by; some took her out for Slurpees.

At this point, people close to us wanted so badly to find a way to lift Rachel's—and our—spirits. The Backstreet Boys were coming to Baltimore in a couple of weeks, and the Jewish Caring Network folks knew Rachel would love to go with a friend. Sheera, who also loved the band, made a special trip in to accompany Rachel. Leading up to the concert, I saw our girl's grit reemerge. I came home from work one day to an unusual sight: Tethered to her oxygen tank, Rachel was doing leg lifts while holding on to a dining room chair.

The home care physical therapist told her that she had to walk a flight of stairs, get up from her bed and toilet for a PT assessment. Not much older than Rachel, the blondish Ed was muscular, with a kind demeanor. He thought Rachel could benefit from PT three times a week. After he left, Rachel told me how weak she felt and how poor her balance was. She suddenly became hyper-focused on doing those exercises on her own, three times a week, and once again, when the physical therapist returned.

A week later, her vigor resurfaced, but her cough seemed to worsen. And so did Judah's mood. He was furious that Rachel was so determined to attend the concert, especially because she wasn't even the biggest fan of the Backstreet Boys. I told him that wasn't the point. It was the idea of going to any concert at this juncture that excited her.

"If you can't catch your breath," he scolded, "someone will call 911! Even the nurses are scared when they see you short of breath!" The prediction and his giving voice to his own deepest fears in such a harsh tone crushed Rachel. It frightened me, too. She and I simultaneously burst into tears.

Sheera, who'd witnessed the exchange, came up with a compromise: they'd go to the concert late, after the crowds dissipated. That way, they could pull right up. I felt a burst of affection for Rachel's dearest friend.

In the end, though, Rachel decided not to go. Instead, she headed to the movies with Sheera and her boyfriend Mike and a few other friends. When she came home, she was indignant. "I did *fine* at the theater … *and I could have gone to the concert!*" Judah and I felt some regret, but knowing how weak she'd been feeling, we weren't convinced Rachel would have fared well.

Rachel was holding out hope that a June 16 concert in New Jersey to see the cast of *Glee* would work out. But first, we needed to gear up for the next Jewish holiday, Shavuot, which commemorates the giving of the Torah at Mt. Sinai.

The dread on Judah's face sometimes scared me. His medical experience fueled his concerns, and so far, his doubts had proved warranted. And it seemed like bad news often emerged during Jewish holidays. But we were granted another reprieve.

Over the Shavuot holiday, Rachel had a bunch of friends over, and later, we walked with her to our neighbors, the Scharfs, despite the oppressive heat, which nearly hit 100 degrees. She'd made it there and back without much difficulty.

The best news emerged the next day, when Rachel went to Hopkins and learned that she was making platelets. Her numbers had gone up to 59K, from 36K, so she was able to just get her blood drawn at Hopkins. But, of course, even that consumed hours. Still, we considered that to be progress. It meant her lymphocytes were multiplying.

That said, she'd been vomiting a lot. We thought Avelox, the medication she was on was likely the culprit. But even when she stopped taking it, the vomiting continued.

And yet ... despite her frustration, Rachel walked up and down the block. She seemed more animated than we'd seen her in many months.

She'd begun her online psych development course, a requirement for social work school, in earnest and told me about her "virtual child"—a hypothetical daughter she named "Olivia." Rachel poured over her textbook and took two quizzes.

From the moment she started her summer prerequisite course, she embraced the challenge of balancing school work and treatment. There was an intensity on Rachel's face I hadn't seen for a long while, and she didn't seem as pale as usual. I kept pinching myself. *Could she finally be close to remission again?*

I marveled at her focus. She'd lie on the couch at home or in a chair-bed while getting an infusion at Hopkins. Computer on her stomach, Rachel typed paper after paper. By then, the clicking had become my favorite kind of music.

It occurred to me that prednisone could have been fueling this burst of productivity. But I saw something else: urgency, determination, passion. And, of course, there was hope, which had once again sprouted, despite the eff-ing cancer cells' resurgence.

Good news—well, maybe just glimmers—continued to build our hopes that maybe, just maybe, our resilient girl would beat the odds. In the days that followed, Rachel's pulmonologist scheduled a bronchoscopy. After the procedure, he was pleased to report "much improvement" in her lungs. He removed a lingering *Aspergillus* bump near her vocal cord but wrote in his report that she still has bronchiolitis—inflammation in the small airways, and he may need to do a repeat scan in four to six weeks.

He was typically negative, so we were pleased to hear this news. Rachel *was* able to walk longer distances and looked better all around. She did need platelets, however. Still, we found ourselves cautiously hopeful. I suppose we'd reached the point of savoring even slight improvements to her health.

Five days later, as promised, Judah and Rachel took off for New York. It was the second anniversary of her bone marrow transplant, and she celebrated by going to the *Glee* concert she'd been looking forward to with her friend Leora. I was amazed that Rachel felt well enough to make the trip.

Judah reported that she'd eaten well (had a calzone and kept it down). Actually, she ate three solid meals that day. While the girls attended the concert, Judah met up with Sam, Nikki and Nikki's family at Noi Due in Manhattan. I was grateful that Judah enjoyed a night out. Meantime, I headed to DC with a couple of friends to see my niece, Leah, who was leading a kosher cooking demo, using recipes from her new cookbook. It was wonderful catching up with my brother Harold and his wife, Rena, there, too.

By Shabbat, however, Rachel was utterly exhausted. And so was her father. She spent a couple of hours on the hammock outside, delighted about an email she'd received from her psych professor telling Rachel how well she was doing. The next day—Father's Day—she fussed over her dad, who took it easy most of the day. Rachel also managed to write a nine-page paper in less than three hours.

Not wanting the beautiful weather to pass us by, we loaded up the car and drove to the Inner Harbor. Judah pushed Rachel in the wheelchair, but she insisted on walking sometimes. All told, we probably covered about three miles. For once, we felt like a normal family. Back at home, we enjoyed a festive steak dinner, and Rachel actually ate well.

That idyllic day remains a cherished memory. But, like so many others, it was followed by sobering developments. Rachel had begun to cough more and suffered more shortness of breath. Dr. A. told her that he was concerned about her vomiting and that if it continued, she'd need parenteral (intravenous) feeding—a last resort. Her weight was holding steady at 95.5 lbs. He also told her that he wasn't pleased about her kidney function. So he scheduled a CT of her sinuses and a chest CT. Sam and Nikki came in, which gave Rachel a huge lift. And, she continued to plug away at her coursework.

The weather seemed to mimic our ups and downs. Some days were oppressively hot; others delightful. By now, flowers were in full bloom. Gentle breezes eased the sweat on our brows as we pushed Rachel in a wheelchair on our brief walks. It was the kind of weather that rekindles hopes. Often, Rachel insisted on walking; that is, until she acknowledged that she could no longer catch her breath. I hated seeing her look so defeated.

On the last weekend in June, Jon came home to spend time with us. He kept making us laugh and was evasive as ever about his social life. But he seemed happier than he'd been in a long time.

His visit did wonders for all of us, especially because Rachel had thrown up six times over the previous two days. She'd also tested positive for *cornyeabactrum*, a bacterial infection that's the basis for diphtheria. So she had to be put on yet another antibiotic, which could have contributed to her extreme nausea.

Dr. A. also told her that the radiation oncologist wanted to talk to her about a suspicious area on her spine. After expressing concern about Rachel's complaints of back pain, Dr. A. had ordered an MRI. We couldn't imagine Rachel getting radiation at this point, on top of everything else.

If all that weren't enough, Rachel received a major blow—virtually—from an instructor. The online course Rachel was taking required a term paper that followed APA style for references (author, date). But, thanks to a computer glitch, she didn't see those instructions initially. When Rachel informed the instructor about this snag, she wasn't buying it. Rachel also mentioned that she was getting chemo, but, apparently, that didn't arouse any sympathy. The professor gave Rachel a zero. Indignant, our girl looked up the professor's rating and found that it was 2.3 out of 10. It was turning into a dreadful weekend.

We also needed to pay a shiva call to Judah's longtime work

partner, also a dear friend, whose son had died in a car accident as a result of an overdose. We were heartbroken by the news. It was a shocking reminder of how fragile our children's lives are.

Nevertheless, Rachel somehow managed to function better, though her coughing and low energy became constant companions. One night in late June, however, the focus turned to me. I had a severe case of urinary retention. The pressure was unbearable. I was so bloated and distended that I needed to be seen immediately. Sam drove me to Patient First. My weight revealed a 12-lb. weight gain since the week before. I needed to be catheterized.

A few days later, I saw a urologist. Rachel had a good laugh when she told me to take an oxycodone for the pain and saw how much it had helped me. That little wonder drug worked immediately. I was floating and suddenly understood how easily and unexpectedly one could become addicted. I prayed that Rachel wouldn't succumb to its power, though I would hardly be able to blame her.

By this time, we were in something of a holding pattern. Rachel continued to work on her social work assignments. There were days when she had me convinced that her determination to overcome her advanced disease, aided by targeted treatments, would succeed. If she didn't give up hope, how could we? It was clear to me, though, that Judah never believed it. So often, he looked defeated, or would express his concern privately to me about how tenuous Rachel's health was. And that sometimes shook me to the core. I just prayed that Rachel didn't pick up on our fears as often as I did.

To escape our reality, we watched TV together more than ever. Rachel was ecstatic when Javier Colon won *The Voice*. Besides being blessed with an operatic voice, he was utterly charming. I would often need to cook or do housework in the evenings, but sometimes I'd make my way to the den and watch TV with Judah and Rachel.

We'd all become enthralled with a new show called *Smash*, about rising Broadway stars, particularly a blonde bombshell with a big voice, played by Megan Hilty. She'd been cast as Marilyn Monroe in a musical but was suddenly replaced by a movie star. I knew Rachel could relate to the crushing disappointment.

In one episode, when the pressure of performing and feeling rejected hit this lead character hard, she and her boyfriend sing a duo called "Mr. and Mrs. Smith." The song captures the joy of normalcy—just being ordinary Americans with none of the pressures behind seeking and sustaining fame. I recall exchanging a look with Rachel. In that moment, it hit me how much that idea of normalcy resonated with her. And it pained me to the core. I was reminded of her profound disappointment when she learned she'd landed a lead role in a musical with a theatre group in LA but had to turn it down because of her diagnosis and move back to Baltimore.

That said, as sick as she was, there *were* moments of normalcy still (such as sitting on the Estersons' porch and catching up with our wonderful neighbors). And, I continued to marvel at the way Rachel would do whatever possible to lead a normal life herself: making plans with friends, driving to Staples for school supplies, and staying on top of assignments. Striving for predictability became more important than ever as her health teetered.

> *From: Rachel Minkove <rminkove@gmail.com>*
> *Date: Mon, Jul 18, 2011 at 1:33 PM*
> *Subject: the last few months*
>
> *Dear Friends and Family,*
> *I've had a pretty debilitating few months since Pesach. Since my immune system is so weak, I am more susceptible to infection. As a result, I got a severe fungal infection in my lungs. For the past three months, I have*

been fighting it, at home, with IV antibiotics. I was taking the antibiotics every night for 3 hours, but I am now down to 3 nights a week, as the infection is improving. Additionally, it really impaired my breathing, and I was relying on oxygen for a while to get around. I am now off of oxygen, but still have trouble walking far and climbing stairs, and still use a wheel chair when I need to go far distances.

My doctors are encouraged that the infection is healing, and I am getting better. I have been working with a physical therapist to improve my strength. But, a lot of the antibiotics cause additional side effects, such as lowering my potassium. I was then put on high levels of oral potassium, but they hurt my stomach, causing me to be severely nauseous. To combat the nausea, I am now taking 8 hours of IV potassium while I sleep, but now it's been a little difficult to get a good night's rest. I have another bronchoscopy in a month to check the status of the infection. If it is cleared, then I can get off of the antibiotics and the potassium. So that is what I am hoping for.

In the meantime, since I get the IV potassium at home, I am spending less time at the hospital, and able to get out and about more. I am finally starting to feel better, and am hoping this trend continues.

Hope you all are having a great summer!

Rachel

CHAPTER 12

Renewed Purpose

Tisha B'Av, the 9th day of Av, the saddest day on the Jewish calendar, commemorates the destruction of the two Jewish Temples in Jerusalem. Long ago, the rabbis declared it a time for national fasting and the recitation of the Book of Jeremiah. The somber day on the Jewish lunar calendar happens in late July or early August, making it a longer fast day than Yom Kippur. In 2011, it fell on August 9.

I knew Rachel would insist on fasting—at least for part of the day. She didn't eat until 1 p.m. that day, and when she broke the fast, she ate and drank very little. Finally, at around 6 p.m., she asked me to warm the baked ziti I'd made to break the fast. She'd thrown up earlier in the day and looked devoid of color.

There was another reason for her pallor: She'd just finished reading *Leap Into Darkness*, by Leo Bretholtz, a Holocaust survivor and member of our synagogue. The book recounts his extraordinary escape from a train bound for Auschwitz. I'd recently finished reading it myself and had interviewed Leo for an article I was writing about hope for the *Baltimore Jewish Times*. Judah and I, both busy at work, endured the fast fairly well, and I continued to chip away at the article later in the day. I would never forget something Leo said to me about hope: "I have hope, but my hope is wounded."

The next day, Rachel seemed transformed. She looked rested and perky. That afternoon, she'd taken Sam's car to get her hair highlighted and then treated herself to soft frozen yogurt. And that evening, she and Sam went to an Orioles game. They left the game early because it was going into extra innings, but ultimately the final batter for the O's hit a homerun to win the game, breaking their losing streak. We all watched the winning play on TV together. I wrote in my journal that night: "Go Rach, and break your slump!"

My father-in-law turned 89 the following day. Unsolicited, Rachel picked up the phone and called him. Raising her voice so he could hear her, she exclaimed, "Hi, Saba! This is Rachel!" We could hear his response through the receiver: "I know!" And, though we couldn't see his face, we knew he was delighted to hear that sweet voice.

Afterwards, Rachel straightened the den, where she was spending most of her time. The clutter—from her work, magazines and medical supplies—was getting to her. Then she headed to our friend Pam's house. A school psychologist, Pam had a preternatural gift for relating to younger people. Rachel had once called her "one of the coolest moms ever." Later that evening, Rachel went to the movies with her friend Mira.

But I felt the angst rising again, as the MRI and potential bone biopsy in her spine loomed. Incredibly, when she had the MRI, it showed no change. Dr. A. had a long talk with Rachel and Judah and said, much to their relief, that she probably wouldn't need the bone biopsy after all and that he was "very happy about how good Rachel looked." Dr. A. added that we should continue to make our plans. Those, Rachel insisted, would involve a beach.

As I'd expounded in the *Jewish Times* article I'd just submitted, hope is a funny thing. Even during our most skeptical moments, we cling to imaginary lifeboats. Rabbi Maurice Lamm said it best in his memoir, *The Power of Hope*: "We know in our hearts that hope is everything. In the back of our minds, we suspect it's nothing at all." Ironically, he, too, had a daughter who was diagnosed with Hodgkin's. She survived, married and gave birth to seven children. I was moved to learn her story, and a bit envious.

Rachel, too, was the kind of girl who could convince you that she'd be OK, no matter how many challenges came her way. She was also clearly frustrated about living with her parents all this time and lacking autonomy, which is one reason she'd insisted that Judah and I attend our dear friends' son Yonah's wedding in New York on August 14. It seemed like a viable option. After all, there was a chartered bus going back and forth on the same day, and Rachel had friends around (as did we) who could come to her aid, if necessary.

So we went. That late August day began with a drenching rain and persisted, worsening. We crawled for much of the trip and barely made it for the last 15 minutes of the smorgasbord. "Could have been worse," I wrote in my journal.

Well, not much, as it turned out. Yes, we'd had a wonderful time celebrating with friends, and our bus ride back to Baltimore left promptly at 5:15 p.m. But the rain never let up, and we soon encountered heavy traffic. About an hour and a half later, the driver pulled over because of "engine trouble." Long story short, we had to wait for another bus.

Judah was utterly panic-stricken. "It's way past time for Rachel's intravenous AmBisome treatment! We should have been home hours ago!" Fortunately, we learned that our friends Larry and Laura were driving back to Baltimore, so we called Larry, asking him to meet us at the rest stop where we were waiting for a second bus to take us home. We were so thankful but arrived home at 1:20 a.m. Judah decided to forego the one treatment and just let Rachel sleep.

Meanwhile, I fantasized that Rachel had enjoyed a wonderful day at home. She, too, had attended a wedding—of her friends, Shaanan and Rachel.

Our Rachel, it turns out, had what might have been called a normal day. Mira took her to get her makeup done for the wedding, and Shoshi gave her a ride. Shortly before the wedding, a group of friends, including Rachel, went to the couple's wedding suite to scatter rose petals. Rachel insisted on wearing her new heels and schlepped a luggage bag of theirs up three flights of stairs. Exhausted from all this activity, she'd gone to bed long before we got home.

Reality smacked us hard again the next day. Judah needed to take Rachel to Hopkins for several tests, beginning with a CT. The machine was broken in the Weinberg building, so they went to another building, causing the first delay of the day. We learned that Rachel's CT was "OK," meaning it wasn't showing any worsening features.

And then she had a bronchoscopy. The results of a pulmonary function test she needed to take first did not bode well. She'd failed it again, though there was a slight improvement from the last time. It turned out that the bronchoscopy would have been considered good, had the pulmonologist not given her a pneumothorax—a collapsed lung. It's a common complication during this procedure and ultimately reverses itself. But it's quite painful.

Upon awakening, Rachel felt miserable. Judah suspected that Dr. Y. might have been too aggressive trying to get biopsies. Dr. Y. immediately apologized. Rachel had to be admitted to Weinberg 5 again. It ended up being a "20 percent" pneumothorax. So, it could have been worse. But Rachel needed to wear oxygen and was clearly uncomfortable.

Judah looked crestfallen, as if *his* lung had collapsed. Later that evening, as Rachel slept, I noticed new worry lines on his face. Head in his hands, he suddenly looked up at me. Then he whispered, "I don't know how much more of this I can take. And when I say 'I,' I'm including you."

I was both shaken and touched by his admission. But what choice did we have? We couldn't abandon our daughter. He knew that, too, of course. But physically and emotionally, he was struggling more than ever, it seemed to me. I told him we both needed to get some sleep—and, hopefully, hear some better news.

That night, Rachel was more lethargic than we'd seen her in a long time. Her sugar went up, causing the team to think she might need insulin, but Dr. A. wasn't concerned. Judah fretted that it would cause a sudden sugar drop, possibly causing a fall en route to the bathroom. For a 250-pound person, he said, that might be OK, but not for a 96-pound girl.

The next day, Rachel's friend Jessica—a lovely fellow elementary teacher from L.A.—arrived for a visit. Rachel was thrilled to see her, and so were we; our girl didn't need us hovering over her 24/7. Rachel was clearly still in a lot of pain, and the nurse taking care of her that night was brusque, so, Jessica's big smile and warm embrace proved especially uplifting. I was so grateful she'd made the trip. It was incredibly noble of her, considering the trying circumstances we suddenly found ourselves in.

After Rachel was released from the hospital the next day, she mapped out a plan for her and Jess. Despite the wincing on her face, no doubt caused by pain from her collapsed lung, Rachel insisted they go to Hunt Valley Mall. We all piled into the car, but when we arrived, Judah and I let them go their own way.

It was clear that Jessica's visit rejuvenated Rachel's spirits. The next day, the three of us headed downtown to the social work school to pick up her parking permit. Rachel walked more than she should have and was exhausted, but still insisted on accompanying us to take Jess to the airport.

With each passing day, Rachel's health seemed to improve, but the itching resurfaced, probably from the new antifungal drug, Judah told her. A steady stream of Rachel's girlfriends paraded through the house. It gave me such pleasure. Rachel's spirits appeared to be lifting. She walked around the track at Pikesville High School twice with Judah. And the following day, Judah took off from work to take Rachel to Silver Spring to a new kosher dairy restaurant. They found a theater nearby and went to see *Sarah's Key*. The movie, a Holocaust story based on the book by Tatiana de Rosnay, was depressing, no doubt, but Rachel seemed uplifted by it. After dinner, father and daughter went to the track again. I clung to hope, or at least tried.

Our days continued to be defined by how Rachel looked or felt. Regardless, she pushed for independence as much as she could between treatments. Social work school was demanding. Her typing seemed speedier, her laser-focus unshakeable. I was in awe.

After completing a big assignment, Rachel would reward herself by going out with friends and accepting invitations to gatherings. Of course, we worried about the cesspool of germs that could threaten her already fragile existence. But what choice did we have? Rachel was an adult and deserved some normalcy.

The morning Hurricane Irene was in the forecast, the sun was beaming and the weather was unseasonably mild for August. It was also a beautiful day in other respects: Rachel received news from Dr. A that her health was improving. I would have heard it myself, but my car battery had died, and I'd been waiting for AAA to come to my aid. No matter: I was grateful that she and Judah had heard the words directly from Dr. A's mouth. He'd even announced that he thought Rachel was in remission but wouldn't put it on paper. Her numbers were good. Rachel felt well enough to do five loads of laundry.

But the next day, Hurricane Irene struck, and we lost power, which seemed ominous. Indeed, Rachel threw up more than a few times. Right before the power went out, we watched three episodes of *The Big C*. I was incredulous we'd have the emotional wherewithal to watch the series about a young woman who learns she has stage 4 colon cancer and becomes reckless in her marriage. But the acting was superb—I've always been a Laura Linney fan.

During the last episode we watched, her character finally told her family that she had cancer. It suddenly felt weird to be watching this with Rachel, *but maybe it's a good thing*, I wrote in my journal.

After a summer of ups and downs and oppressive heat, I prayed that fall would bring burst of color and crisp air. But first, our country marked a tragic milestone: The 10th anniversary of 9/11 arrived. It reminded me that time marches on, even in the face of unspeakable tragedy. In a way, it seemed like yesterday. And yet it also felt like an eternity since things had been normal for us and for the world. *Nothing like a national tragedy*, I wrote in my journal, *to make you reflect on your blessings, even when trauma strikes your own household.*

I knew we had so much to be thankful for. That day, Rachel received a flu shot, just as we and much of the nation had.

With Rachel's prerequisites for social work school behind her, she was finally heading to in-person classes. Seeing Rachel get ready for school fueled renewed hopes for some normalcy. She looked downright perky in her plaid shirt and black jeans and a little makeup. When she came home after the first day, she said she'd barely slept the night before but so enjoyed being at school. Her courses included social theory and human development. She'd discovered that a single mother in our community, Miriam, was also starting social work school. I was thrilled to learn that Miriam was happy to give Rachel rides to and from school whenever possible.

On one of those days, I picked up a prescription for Rachel at Hopkins and ran into Dr. Ambinder. He was so pleased with Rachel's progress and reiterated that he didn't think a bone biopsy of her back was necessary, at least not at this point, because, he explained, "We don't want to go too deep … it's pretty painful, and you might not get enough of a sample anyway."

He could not have missed the relief on my face. Then he told me that he thought Rachel was incredibly inspiring. He paid me and Judah a compliment, too, for being such supportive parents. I assured him that Rachel set the tone, and that it was almost always positive. This "chance" meeting did wonders for my soul, and I thanked God profusely for it on my way home.

Rachel's life had filled up outside of school, too. She began tutoring Miriam's son and another friend's sister, and even taking Rabbi Silber's young adult class. The next day, Rachel drove herself to Beth Tfiloh for these commitments, but I'd almost refused to let her go because she'd thrown up her dinner immediately before. Judah hoped it wasn't because of the new antifungal drug she was on. She'd started itching terribly, and he knew the drug wasn't agreeing with her, even though she was eating better.

Privately, though, I worried that Rachel's itching meant more Hodgkin's. Dr. A. emailed Rachel to discontinue the drug, and thankfully, the itching vanished. Judah and Rachel began taking walks on the crisp, colorful fall days that followed.

As we went about our work, it pleased us to no end to learn that Rachel was enjoying social work school. She told us she was already making friends. Several were sorority sisters. When they complained about how far from campus their cars were parked from school and asked Rachel where she'd parked, she told them she had "a slight disability," so had gotten authorization to park across the street.

I was in awe of our girl all over again. One morning she came downstairs wearing jeans and a favorite oversized shirt. Her half-ponytail and fresh, freckled face made her look like she was 18. She kept up with her assignments but allowed herself to watch the new seasons of her favorite TV shows.

Fatigue plagued her, though, and I worried that she was expending too much energy on too many pursuits. She continued to tutor and walked with us for more than a mile after dinner a couple of times a week. But she was crushed when Dr. A. called to tell her that, as a precaution, she had to resume the antifungal drug that had been making her throw up. Her itching came right back.

Incredibly, she managed to laugh a lot the night she got that news, especially when I plopped down on the balance ball the physical therapist had left her. I must have been quite a sight, and we laughed about it, and then turned on the season premiere of *Modern Family*, which made us cackle in unison. I loved the way Rachel's laugh caught in her throat and made her eyes sparkle, like marbles rolling down a sunlit sidewalk.

Two nights later, she packed for yet another trip to New York. Privately, I worried that we were reckless parents for letting her go. But wasn't she entitled to have some control over her life? As was our custom, we snuggled up to read *The Very Hungry Caterpillar* together. But before we got started, she had me feel something that felt like a pebble on her right breast and asked me if I thought it felt normal. We exchanged a look of concern, and I made her promise that she'd show it to Dr. Ambinder. She'd just seen a gynecologist, who hadn't felt anything problematic. I hoped and prayed it was just a cyst.

While Rachel was in New York for Shabbat, Judah and I caught up. We tried to relax and spent time with friends. On Saturday night we watched *The Help*, which we enjoyed. I couldn't wait to tell Rachel how much she would like it, too. We'd all read the book.

When we spoke to Rachel after Shabbat, she sounded very tired but happy, and Jon told us she looked good to him. The next morning we drove to New York so we could all attend the wedding of our dear friends' son Ari. Jon, Rachel and Sam were already in New York, and the plan was for us to drive Rachel home with us afterwards.

Rachel was exhausted but looked stunning in her sleek black

dress. A friend had helped her with her makeup. Whenever I spotted her that evening, she radiated love and gratitude. Both of our sons looked dapper, too. Jon walked down the aisle, smiling big.

For the next several hours, we felt normalcy and unbridled joy for our dear friends.

We returned home safely, tired but grateful for that magical time together. Yet I knew we were all feeling unsettled. The newest elephant in the room lived inside Rachel's right breast. It was becoming harder to quell my fears. In the end, Dr. A. examined her and told her that he was "unimpressed." We breathed a huge sigh of relief.

But Rosh Hashanah was the following weekend, and the holidays always brought a sense of foreboding. Still, we enjoyed the reflective but festive few days—bearable, thanks to Rachel's dear friend Sheera's visit.

The cover story I wrote about hope came out that weekend in the *Baltimore Jewish Times* (Sept. 30, 2011). It generated great interest, especially the sidebar Rachel wrote about what hope meant to her:

> Hope means having the foresight to overcome adversity. This entails making plans for the future—looking forward to vacations and life events. Hope means placing a blind eye to negative outcomes and statistics. It is not about focusing on what could happen; rather, it's believing that there is light at the end of the tunnel. I did not envision running a marathon in a few months, but taking baby steps (walks around the hospital unit or block) and setting attainable goals that make me appreciate life. These include weekend getaways with friends, attending weddings, parties and other social events, in addition to teaching, reading and learning.
>
> When I have something on my calendar, I'm motivated to build my stamina physically and mentally. Sure, there have been times when it's been hard to harness hope, like

when scans are not ideal. But for me the key is to always look to the next possible step, and ask, "Where am I going from here?" The most important thing is to not always listen to prognoses and statistics. It is holding onto the belief that you—or your situation—will get better.

Rachel had always loved celebrating birthdays, but as her own neared, I worried about her precarious health. On Oct. 2, 2011, the night before Rachel's actual birthday, she stayed up late to watch the Ravens game. She was feeling optimistic and continued to receive positive feedback about her *Jewish Times* sidebar on hope. On top of that, The Ravens came through to win the game at 11:40 p.m.

I awakened the next morning feeling hopeful and determined to make our daughter feel loved and deserving of some nonmedical fuss on her birthday. It turned out to be a memorably upbeat day. At 28, our daughter was beautiful, smart, strong, life-affirming and inspirational. She'd called me from school, noting that she wasn't feeling great. I told her I'd pick her up, but she managed to get a second wind.

We went out for a festive birthday dinner, where Rachel scarfed down most of an order of penne pasta with vodka, her favorite dish. Her Facebook page was stacked with good wishes, and her phone rang incessantly. A package of red velvet mini-cupcakes with metallic stars from Faith greeted Rachel when we got home, with a card attached that read *Rach for the stars.*

Alas, the celebratory spirit was quashed a few days later, when Rachel had to endure four rounds of mammograms, followed by a sonogram and a needle biopsy, because of several suspicious areas. It was painful for her, physically and emotionally. The radiologist wasn't forthcoming about his feelings, but the expression on his face screamed concern. It didn't help that he kept asking me if I was OK. *Please God*, I begged, *let this lump be benign.*

The next day, Judah called me to report that the lump was, in fact, benign. So we went into Yom Kippur with much better news than we expected. Reprieves were always welcome, even in a time of such intense and constant uncertainty.

There's something so pure and genuine about Yom Kippur. The holiest day on the Jewish calendar, it's a time that we as Jews collectively pray to God that we be granted another year of life. Having just prayed for a healthy and meaningful new year on Rosh Hashanah, we beseech God to forgive our sins over the past year and seal us into the Book of Life. We afflict our souls by fasting for the entire day. Rachel insisted on fasting until 3 p.m., which she did, without a single complaint.

I could only imagine how she was feeling about the likelihood that God would extend her life; at her core, our daughter was an optimist. It seemed to me that her concentration grew more intense with every word. I wrestled with my feelings toward God but prayed with more *kavana* (intention) than ever.

One prayer in particular, however, troubled me: the ancient poem known as *Unesaneh Tokef*: "Let Us Cede Power." Written about a thousand years ago, as antisemitism swept through Europe, the somber narrative of the prayer is central to the High Holiday services. I instantly conjured my father's clear, melodious voice singing those words with conviction:

On Rosh Hashanah it is written, and on Yom Kippur it is
  sealed.
How many will pass and how many will be created?
Who will live and who will die?
Who in their time, and who not their time?
Who by fire and who by water?
Who by sword and who by beast?
Who by hunger and who by thirst?
Who by earthquake and who by drowning?
Who by strangling and who by stoning?
Who will rest and who will wander?
Who will be safe and who will be torn?
Who will be calm and who will be tormented?
Who will become poor and who will get rich?
Who will be made humble and who will be raised up?

The congregation sings the final words—a repeated refrain after each stanza—in unison:

But teshuvah *and* tefillah *and* tzedakah (*return and*
  prayer and righteous acts)
deflect the evil of the decree.

The singing intensified. Everyone seemed to be shuckling back and forth, eyes closed. But all I could feel in that moment was angst. As my tears dripped down into my *siddur*, I stood there feeling the weight of those age-old words. The question of our mortality and the innumerable ways we may or may not survive another year had consumed me from the outset of Rachel's diagnosis.

Could I really believe that repentance and doing good deeds would reverse our bad fortune?

Desperately, I tried to hide my wet face from Rachel. I'm certain she saw it, though, and that she felt plenty troubled herself. How could she not have been? Yet she'd dutifully uttered those Hebrew words. I reached into my tote bag for tissues, and then headed out of the sanctuary—I needed some air. Rachel followed me out.

The weather was gorgeous that day, the sun electrifying the autumn splendor. We walked along the perimeter of the synagogue and caught up with friends. Between those chats, neither of us spoke, but there was a silent acknowledgment of mutual pain. Then, I embraced my beautiful girl with a fierceness that very well might have alarmed her.

Moments later, Rachel told me she was getting anxious about her upcoming midterm exams. I thought to myself, *Please let that be the worst of her concerns.* But in that brief exchange outside the shul, I realized we'd made the right decision in letting Rachel attend social work school. The intellectual stimulation alone was uplifting enough to strengthen her resolve to excel and, ultimately, to help other young adults with cancer.

On that holiest of holy days, I beseeched God to grant Rachel the future she deserved and was working so hard to attain. I almost screamed out loud the words I'd been carrying around for three years: *She could do so much more good in this world, dear God, if you would just heal her!*

The magnificent weather extended into the weekend. We went to Annapolis and took a tour of the Naval Academy. Rachel joked about finding a husband there. As we walked toward the building, we spotted a young man putting up a sukkah with camouflage walls. On our tour, we visited the updated chapel, the site of a Yom Kippur service that attracted 500 people, we'd learned.

Our sukkah at home, made of green canvas, looked more like an outdoor shower stall than a temporary dwelling. But we decorated it with posters and Jewish New Year cards and tried to heed the Biblical directive, *Vsamachta b-chagecha*, "And you should rejoice in the holiday."

If only we could have.

On the eve of the holiday, I returned home from work to find Rachel furiously typing a paper. She had tutored that day and was sniffling and coughing intermittently. And she mentioned that her back was hurting a lot. On top of that, we learned that Margaret, one of the lovely outpatient oncology nurses, had died in her sleep. She was 51. Everyone on the unit, Jane informed us, was in shock. Once again, my questions for God were multiplying.

I was about to light candles to usher in Sukkot—running late, as usual. But first, I decided to run upstairs to check on Rachel. I hadn't heard from her for a while.

My instincts proved prescient. She was lying in bed, wrapped in a towel, her hair soaking-wet. Then I saw tears streaming down her thinning, wan face. Dr. A. had just called to tell her that the spot on her spine was significantly larger. He wanted her to schedule a PET CT to see if the Hodgkin's had spread elsewhere. If it's localized to the spine, he explained, she can get radiation. Then they'll try SGN-35, the new drug she'd fought so desperately to take back in New York.

Our beautiful girl was shaking. Her lips couldn't stop quivering. Nor could mine. We held each other tight. Somehow, we managed to pull ourselves together. We were invited to several holiday meals and almost opted out but realized that some semblance of normalcy tended to distract us from the increasingly troubling scenarios we were about to encounter.

We also bonded in our own sukkah—the temporary dwelling that's meant to remind us that we ultimately depend on God for shelter. Why, though, was God punishing our beautiful girl, who was doing so much good in this world? Her smile alone instantly put people at ease.

During the intermediate days of the eight-day festival of Sukkot, I went to work, carrying with me an overwhelming sense of dread. Rachel looked especially pale when I came home that first day back at work. She coughed more, and her eyes were teary. Rachel told me she went to a spa for a manicure and then headed to Hopkins for blood work. One of the first people she ran into was Dr. A., who told her he wanted her to schedule a biopsy of her spine.

Rachel was not very happy to learn this. But Judah explained that he wanted to be sure they were targeting cancer cells, not infection. Rachel went about her life and made a point of going out as much as possible. She and Judah attended an event at Beth Tfiloh to hear Supreme Court Justice Elena Kagan speak.

The ups and downs of our life revolved around cancer's erratic behavior. But how Rachel endured it all and how we found the strength to give her some leeway continued to surprise me. Our house became a revolving door, even more than before. The constant stream of visitors provided a good distraction, and we ate meals with friends. Rachel worked hard to look her best, taking time to apply makeup. But a phone call from Dr. Ambinder just a couple of hours before Shabbat dashed our spirits.

Rachel learned that the chest x-ray Dr. A. had ordered revealed that her right lung didn't look good. "It could be more *Aspergillus* or Hodgkin's," he told her. She'd need a bronchoscopy ASAP to confirm. But she was still scheduled for the bone biopsy on Wednesday. She couldn't receive radiation to her back, however, until they figured out what's up with her lungs.

When Rachel asked Dr. A. which of the two things would be better to have, he responded, "Neither."

Anxiety was running high, but I kept telling myself that we had to hang tough. There was hope for the SGN treatment, God-willing, but only if she needed it. Something wasn't right, of course. But denial is a comfort sometimes. My self-talk was full of contradictions.

Incredibly, during the bone biopsy, Rachel barely complained. The following week, she experienced newfound independence, thanks to our beloved cousin Gene, who helped her shop for a good used car from a friend. Rachel named the royal blue 2005 Honda Scion "Hope."

Gene's friend, David W., who owned a car dealership in Rockville, Maryland, delivered the car to Rachel with no down payment or obligation and said he'd take it back if she didn't want it. Once again, we were touched by the human capacity for generosity.

Rachel stood looking outside as Gene and David pulled up. It was love at first sight. Her face lit up, and she thanked both them and us profusely. Though we'd never purchased a used car, worried about potential problems, this decision made sense to us. I'd been ambivalent—how could I *not* worry about her being alone in the car, feeling too sick to drive?—but, we just knew our gift to Rachel would become a valuable one: Finally, she could feel empowered. And, incredibly, Rachel succeeded in getting to and from her destinations regularly without incident.

On top of that, Rachel was finally able to celebrate her birthday with friends, at a belated celebration in downtown Baltimore. Our girl looked radiant. She dressed up, determined to have a wonderful time, even though she wasn't feeling great. Unfortunately, the weather had turned bitter cold; it snowed and rained intermittently all day long, and the friend who'd picked her up parked three blocks away from the bar. Rachel struggled to catch her breath.

The next day, Judah went to a Ravens game with Jack, one of his closest friends. I caught up on housework, as the drone of the sportscaster reported the game on TV. Rachel had settled into her spot on the couch. She was becoming frustrated with the way the Ravens were screwing up. And then, when it seemed they had no chance, they came back to a dramatic win. I told Rachel it was a metaphor for her illness. "You're also coming in from behind, but you *will* conquer this." I knew I said those words to shore myself up, too.

An hour later, Dr. A. called with sobering news. The PET scan showed Hodgkin's under her right arm, in her neck and back, "So, she may not need the biopsy or bronchoscopy just yet," he said. He planned to move forward and had already ordered the SGN-35—our last hope. Encouraging results from studies showed that 84% of patients on the immunotherapy had a response rate, and 34% went into complete remission. We had no choice but to hope that Rachel would be one of the lucky ones. The demons persisted, however, though we used every ounce of restraint to hide our deepest fears from her. The agony of her now-prolonged illness consumed us. But, if she could stay strong, how could we not?

Our new rhythm featured the ups and downs we'd come to expect with every treatment. But this time we hoped against hope that remission would follow.

Finally—*finally!*—on Nov. 3, 2011, after a yearlong wait, Dr. A received the first batch of brentuximab, aka SGN-35. It was now available at Hopkins: the first-ever immunotherapy for refractory Hodgkin's lymphoma—an approach just out of the experimental gate, for which Rachel hadn't been eligible until now. A swirl of emotions consumed me, as we marked a milestone for Sam as well: celebrating his white coat ceremony, a rite of passage for first-year medical students. I'd taken off work to attend, and even though Rachel couldn't go, we enjoyed it immensely and felt mighty proud. Nikki even made a surprise appearance in pink scrubs (from her Shock Trauma rotation).

Back at home, Rachel was sore from her bone biopsy, but Erica came over to help her out. A little later, we went out for Slurpees, but Rachel was in a lot of pain and was coughing up a lot of green stuff. We remained hopeful, though, as the SGN treatment would begin the next day. Serendipitously, at the ceremony earlier, we'd run into one of Judah's former med school classmates who worked in oncology at the National Cancer Institute and told us about "this new wonder drug called SGN," noting how effective it was. All we could do was hope he was right and that this drug would *finally* provide the cure for our girl.

The very next day Rachel's friends Ally and Amy picked her up for her first SGN treatment. I recall having prayed fervently that morning, beseeching God to make this new treatment work.

The highlight of Rachel's day came a few hours later, when Shmuel Shoham, the infectious disease specialist stopped by, greeting Rachel with a big smile and pulling out his iPad to play her "Don't Stop Believing," by Journey. He also told her he was putting her on an antibiotic. Too bad Rachel couldn't seem to cough up enough sputum for a sample, so she'd have to try again in a couple of days.

When Rachel returned home, she looked spent. She recapped her day: First, she needed bloodwork and had had to wait more than an hour and a half for results. Then she learned that the doctors needed a mucous sample. Rach told us that the tech "violently" stuck the swab up Rachel's nose without even warning her that it would be uncomfortable. She hadn't even bothered to greet her patient.

We wanted so badly to believe the treatment would work. Rachel's resolve intensified. Her parents—especially her father—were hopeful but somewhat skeptical. Cure or no cure, I dreaded the probable side effects. They included the usual nausea and fatigue, mouth sores and neuropathy, or nerve damage.

Meanwhile, we tried our best to live our lives. A few days after that first SGN treatment, Rachel wrote a paper for school. She was chained to her computer for hours. She and Judah watched a Ravens game that Sunday. Afterwards, we had a "tailgate" barbeque to celebrate the Ravens' 16 to 6 victory over the Steelers, which we took as a good sign. Everything those days was taking on new meaning.

Still, I was wrestling with my fears, and I knew Judah was, too, even though neither of us acknowledged it much. Writing daily in my journals not only helped clarify Rachel's complicated trajectory; it also provided an opportunity to capture how we were dealing with our troubling reality as caregivers.

One night, after a horrific day at Hopkins (Rachel had to wait about four hours for her drug), the stress caught up with me. I grabbed the notebook and spilled out my anger in ink.

> No words most times—
> Just anxious glances
> For fear that one of us
> Might utter a painful truth.
> Yet it's a relief when those words burst forth.
> "No matter what, it's not good."
> "Mmm-hmm," I respond.
> Whither hope?
> Whither mercy?
> Whither God?
> Please come to our aid.
> Save our beautiful daughter.
> What has she/we done to deserve this?

That first SGN infusion was short—it took less than an hour to administer. But Rachel was upset to see Dean, one of the other two patients on SGN. She'd learned that he had to shave his head because he was losing his hair again. Hair loss was apparently an uncommon

SGN side effect; diarrhea was far more common. By the time Rachel came home late that afternoon, she was terribly itchy and coughed a lot. But mostly, she was exhausted and likely shaken up. She confessed that she'd barely slept the night before.

I was beyond proud of Rachel and wanted some quality time with her outside of the hospital, so I scheduled a girls' day out. We went to a spa for massages, manis and pedis. I packed lunches, which we enjoyed inside the mall. But then we needed to head over to Hopkins for Rachel's radiation treatment. Afterwards, we went to a café for hot chocolates. It was a raw fall day, but we'd made the most of it, I assured myself.

Rachel awoke early the next day to register online for her next semester at social work school. She was exuberant when she learned that she'd found a spot in a class with a beloved professor. But the following day, a meeting with Dr. A. turned worrisome. The results of her scan showed that the Hodgkin's was back and in her bones, mostly in her spine. She would need radiation ASAP so her back wouldn't collapse. On the upside, her lungs looked better. Rachel was frustrated. A lunch date with her friend Adena provided a welcome diversion. And, in spite of Rachel's overwhelming fatigue, she managed to write a six-page paper.

That night, I heard Rachel cough more than usual. She admitted that for the past three days her cough had gotten progressively worse. We wondered if it was a new infection or a side effect of SGN. Rachel was loving her "adorable" Toyota, but we worried about her driving herself to the hospital alone. In the end, we let her but insisted that she wear her medical bracelet.

Our days proceeded with uncertainty. Fearing the worst was something I often saw on Judah's face. New worry lines were continually emerging, and his eyes were ever redder. I hoped the anxiety wasn't quite as obvious on mine. To combat it, I'd continued to employ my strategy of smiling as much as possible when I was with Rachel or even with friends. I'm sure it didn't always seem sincere. Hope had begun to elude me. It felt like a wet bar of soap. No matter how hard I tried, it seemed impossible to maintain for days on end, and staying positive was becoming exhausting. But how could I not, when our daughter, who'd endured one setback after another, continued to greet people with that magnetic smile?

Rachel's email update that week captured the troubling new reality we were now facing. Seeing it all from her point of view made it all the more difficult to accept.

> --------- Forwarded message ---------
> From: Rachel Minkove <rminkove@gmail.com>
> Date: Sun, Nov 13, 2011 at 7:56 PM
> Subject: I had hoped this was the end of my nightmare
>
> Dear Friends and Family,
> I was planning on sending out an email that there was finally no evidence of cancer in my body. This has been what the doctors have been telling me for months. As a result, I started school and finally felt like I started to get my life back. That all changed on erev Succot. I got an MRI and biopsy, again showing recurrence of Hodgkin's. To say I'm distraught by the news would be an understatement. I now have to start a new type of chemo and radiation to my back. I have not needed any chemo since March, so this came a little as a shock.
> I also had another pre-Yom Kippur scare. I don't know what it's like anymore not to have an erev yom tov crisis. I discovered a lump, which ended up looking suspicious, and I needed a biopsy. Thankfully, my biopsy was benign, which was such a meaningful way to go into

Yom Kippur. I had so much to be thankful for. But it was incredibly scary and bought back painful memories from my original diagnosis three years ago. I experienced some post-traumatic stress, and it shook me up. But that wasn't as bad as receiving a positive result the following week.

My new chemo drug, SGN-35, looks promising, at least. It's the first drug specific for relapsed Hodgkin's patients that has come out since 1977. It targets the cancer cells, with minimal side effects. And it's targeted to attack my exact cell type. So, for the first time in a while, I am very optimistic about a chemo drug and hope it will finally do the trick. In addition, I need several weeks of radiation to my spine, which will hopefully alleviate some of my back pain.

So here we go again. I was ready to be finished, but that wasn't the plan for me right now. Yet, as I continue social work school and recently purchased a car, I am working toward getting completely healthy again and regaining my life. With this recent turn of events, however, I am feeling more limited physically. Still, I remain hopeful that this treatment will finally be successful in curing this awful disease.

Meanwhile, though I'm busy with school, I have plenty of free time during the day. So let me know if any of you are ever around Baltimore.

Thanks so much for your continued support.

Rachel

A couple days later, Rachel drove herself to Hopkins for treatment, and, after parking, texted me four words that made my day: "I LOVE MY CAR." I suspected she loved the independence the vehicle brought, more than the car itself. And I loved that she'd named her new car "Hope." I continued to worry that her fatigue might impair her ability to drive and—Heaven forbid—cause an accident. But it pleased me to know she finally could feel some empowerment from behind the wheel. She'd need all the inner strength she could get as she braced herself for 12 sessions of radiation to target new cancer cells and relieve her back pain.

There were times I'd insist on driving her or making sure she got rides to radiation oncology. Sitting in the waiting area, she got to know Barbara, whose husband, Nick was being treated for brain cancer. They had many overlapping appointments, and Barbara, a charming French and Spanish teacher, instantly bonded with Rachel. I, too, had the pleasure of getting to know Barbara, as we awaited our loved ones' return to the waiting room after treatments.

Rachel and I had a new rhythm. Once we arrived home, after getting Rachel settled in the den to work on assignments, I dashed to the kitchen to prepare some of Rachel's favorite foods—the more fattening, the better: pasta salad, minestrone, rich chocolate desserts. The aromas permeating the kitchen soothed our senses, and I was thrilled to see Rachel finding her appetite. But her itching became a constant companion, and her extended coughing fits alarmed us. She became more short of breath and needed an inhaler and double doses of Benadryl to stem the itching.

And still, Rachel continued to go out with friends and worked on a presentation for social work school. She and her two team members worked together virtually and on the phone, and, though she was exhausted the day of the presentation—Nov. 14—she'd put together a crisp blue and white striped shirt, long sweater and a new pair of jeans I bought to fit her thinning legs. It went well, Rachel reported, and they'd earned a 98% on their presentation.

Time marched on; yet another "new normal" rhythm emerged. Rachel continued to fill her calendar with social events. It seemed that everyone reveled in her presence. It pleased us that she wasn't excluded from her social network, but as her friends continued to marry and have baby-naming ceremonies, I worried that she would feel increasingly bereft.

By the week of Thanksgiving 2011, I began to notice that Rachel seemed more short of breath and was coughing more. When she was out one night, I shared my concern with Judah, whose silences and somber demeanor were beginning to worry me as much as Rachel's condition was. But I needed to hear what he was thinking. So I asked him. "It's one of two things," he said, "neither of which can be good. One is pneumonia. The other is the elephant in the living room." I knew he meant that her life was in great peril.

I choked back tears, until I couldn't. There was no adequate response for what sounded like the truth, but I clung to hope none-theless. And—so, it seemed—did Rachel.

A couple of days after Judah's dark predictions, Rachel came home after tutoring in the afternoon and having dinner with her friend Gabrielle. The first thing she showed me when she returned home was a picture of Uggs sparkly black boots she told me she'd just ordered. "I'll pay you back," she said. "I deserve them for what I'm going to have to go through." Her words pierced my heart. She was going out with our dear cousins, Tammy and Gene, the next day and would pick up the boots at Nordstrom. Against her protests, they'd insisted on paying for them.

From that day on, Rachel became something of a celebrity in the outpatient center. Those sparkly boots and her signature jeans and T-shirt drew notice. But that smile she wore sparkled as much her boots did. And it pleased me to see the magnetic effect she had on other patients and staff, though the long waits and rudeness among the frontline staff persisted.

On Dec. 2, just as I was about to light Shabbat candles, I heard Rachel talking on the phone. After she hung up, I went to check on her. She looked crestfallen. Her voice breaking, she reported that Dr. A. spoke to a radiologist, who told him that Rachel's right lung didn't look good. It could be more *Aspergillus* or Hodgkin's. Either way, Rachel would need another bronchoscopy. She was still scheduled for a bone biopsy the following Wednesday. But she couldn't get radiation to her back until they figured out what was up with her lungs.

And so, our lives proceeded with angst-ridden uncertainty. It's like driving a beloved, reliable car you've had for years that suddenly stalls, then lurches forward. The mechanic tells you it might be time for a new one, but you decide to sink money into a new transmission, and it feels brand new … until the alternator starts acting up.

But cars don't have feelings, memories and hope. By now, we felt as if we were hanging from a cliff, consumed with worry for our beautiful girl.

Actor Ethan Zohn, of *Survivor* fame, we'd just learned, had also experienced a relapse of his Hodgkin's lymphoma in his lungs and would be receiving SGN-35 as well. "Weird coincidence," I wrote in my journal. I made a mental note to follow how he was doing.

I also decided we all needed some social time. So I invited our dear friends the Neumans over for Shabbat dinner. Rachel was especially pleased because their sweet daughter-in-law Zipporah was in social work school with Rachel. Moments before they arrived, Rachel had a major "barf-owitz," as she'd begun to refer to her sudden bouts with nausea. Thank Heavens for Zofran, the miracle anti-nausea drug, which worked its magic within minutes. We never mentioned it to our guests, though; normalcy was what Rachel craved most, after all.

Rachel enjoyed the evening immensely. Good friends, as we well knew, could provide the best kind of medicine, we continued to discover. The Neumans' two-year-old granddaughter Nava charmed us all. Later, Judah and I agreed that we'd instantly fallen in love with that child because she reminded us so much of Rachel at that age: so vibrant and naturally outgoing—her eyes twinkling as she spoke.

The Ravens and Netflix continued to provide welcome escapes for Rachel, as well, even as she managed to complete all her assignments. I was in awe of our girl's resilience and determination to lead as normal a life as she could.

Judah and I wondered how long Rachel could continue attending social work school, but didn't dare bring it up. How could we, when she'd finally found a purpose so fulfilling and personal? Besides, it served as the perfect distraction from her disease; the disease that had inspired her to pursue this field in the first place.

One day, a new social work school friend confided in Rachel that she was newly pregnant. The pregnancy was unplanned, and the girl hadn't told her parents yet, and Rachel was amazed that this girl trusted her with this news first. Could it have been because Rachel had cancer? Maybe Rachel's openness and vulnerability resonated with this classmate. But I like to think that was simply because Rachel comes across as so empathetic and kind—*and* someone you could always trust.

That night, Rachel cleaned her dinner plate. She was always ravenous on Mondays—her most hectic school day. Earlier that day, she'd walked blocks to the registrar's office and admitted to becoming short of breath afterwards. I couldn't help but wonder, *Were we being responsible parents by exposing her to so many people and trusting that she had the strength to endure all the walking and hours-long classes??* Rachel was an adult, though, and had the right to advocate for herself and take on a certain amount of risk.

Later, as she watched TV with Judah while doing *People* crossword puzzles, I kept sneaking looks at her. Wearing that new long striped sweater and jeans, she looked about 15. Her eyes glistened with intensity and *purpose.*

The next day was miserably rainy. Rachel drove herself to Hopkins, then to Beth Tfiloh to tutor, then to radiation. She needed to get a tattoo with dots for radiation to pinpoint where to be zapped every day. She texted me that her weight had hit 100 lbs. *Finally,* I mused. *Her appetite is better; she seems perkier... Could the SGN be working?*

After a long, enjoyable Thanksgiving weekend with our family and friends, a troubling "patient experience," as we at Johns Hopkins referred to interactions with caregivers, hit hard. Rachel had a horrible afternoon waiting for the radiation oncologist to show up for her appointment, scheduled for 2:30. He didn't arrive until 4:45. Rachel texted me that she'd been sitting on an uncomfortable metal folding chair in his office all that time. The *nerve,* I thought! I dashed over there from my office and told him how frustrated I was about how much time waiting Rachel has to endure, on top of her symptoms.

He was apologetic, but I was seething. I simply couldn't believe he'd had the nerve to tell Rachel that he "got called into a conference and forgot about her appointment." The only silver lining during that long wait was that Rachel managed to study for her test the next day without interruption. Small consolation.

Rituals grounded me somehow, as our lives as caregivers began to unravel. I got up early every day to pray, beseeching God to restore our girl to good health. After work, and on weekends, I continued to cook Rachel's favorite foods.

Rachel also prayed, using the siddur we'd bought her for her bat mitzvah—and then doubled down into her social work studies. Her brow, furrowed with determination, had a direct line to her fingers which typed in their familiar, hurried two-fingered fashion.

When she wasn't doing schoolwork, Rachel emailed or texted with friends. Thankfully, they hadn't abandoned her, though she worried they'd tire of keeping up a friendship that was becoming difficult to nurture in person. Rachel's calendar also filled with Hopkins appointments and social work school commitments.

Sports, I had to acknowledge once again, continued to be a wonderful outlet for Rachel. On Sunday afternoons, she followed the Ravens religiously. Before the games started, she'd don her oversized purple Ravens jersey and claim her spot on the couch. She yelled at the players when they blew their lead; cheered when they rallied.

I was often in the kitchen most of that time, but hearing Rachel clap and scream, "*Go, go, go!*" delighted me to no end. And, though Judah never mentioned it, I knew he treasured that sports bonding time with his middle child. During commercials, phones started ringing: Jon and Sam would call with their take on the game. Together, they'd commiserate about missed opportunities and debate about which play may or may not have saved the game.

I wouldn't have admitted to it aloud, but all I kept thinking was, *How can we save Rachel's life?*

CHAPTER 13

Getting Back on Track

The handwriting in my journal was beginning to look like ocean waves as dark clouds begin to gather. I knew I needed to continue to document Rachel's cancer journey, if for no other reason than to note her symptoms. But when I'd periodically look back, my heart ached to see all the ups and downs. I continued to pray every day for a miracle.

On Dec. 2, 2011, Rachel awoke at noon and went to Hopkins with Judah. Dr. A. told her she had new bacteria in her lungs, so he put her on a new antibiotic. But he also told her that her lungs looked great and that, overall, had improved. He added that she'd need at least 16 more treatments, unless she went into remission.

Rachel came home very tired, and when I helped comb her hair, it began coming out in clumps. She was very upset. Dr. A. mentioned that he wanted to hear more about any hair loss. But he gave Rachel his blessing on her trip to LA. I was incredulous.

A few days later, my birthday brought lovely surprises. After presenting me with roses and a beautiful card, Rachel posted a sweet Facebook post about my being "the best mom ever." I had a simple response to that one: She was the best *daughter* ever. Indeed, what would I do if Rachel were half as positive about her situation and continually gave me grief?

That evening, she and Judah presented me with two beautiful cashmere sweaters from Macy's. Their gift did my heart good. I wore the red one to work the next day. The sweaters' coziness made me feel enveloped in their love and kept me warm through the rest of that winter.

As Rachel's trip to LA neared, however, Judah and I were becoming more concerned. He'd also become much more short-tempered, which was making Rachel say more often that she *needed* to get away.

Of course, as I noted in my journal, Rachel mainly needed to escape "these damn treatments and the drudgery of her medical routine at home and at Hopkins." I was so proud of her strength and fighting spirit—and her passion for living. But, all things equal, there was no denying that I, too, was scared for her to be that far away.

Once again, the Jewish Caring Network celebrated Rachel, this time with a basket of travel goodies and treats for her upcoming trip. But the night before her trip, she coughed a lot. All day, she'd struggled with nausea, fatigue, some shortness of breath and coughing. And still, we let her go. *Had we lost control of our senses?*

On Dec. 14, 2011, our friend and neighbor Hersch took Rachel to the airport. After landing in LA, she called to report that she didn't cough once on the flight. A few hours later, we spoke as she was eating dinner with friends at the Israeli laffa place she liked so much. She struggled with the time change but managed to get some sleep and to attend a screening of Wheel of Fortune. She even met Pat Sajack, who seemed like a nice guy, but when she mentioned that she'd love to be on the show and had been fighting cancer for three years, he responded, "You'll have to go to the website, like everybody else."

While Rachel was away, Judah and I decided to spend the weekend in New York to visit Jon, Judah's father and the extended family. Elana and the New Rochelle Minkove family made a festive brunch. My father-in-law looked good, but he was nodding off a lot. I suppose at age 89, he was entitled. Jon's visit perked him up a little. They had a special relationship.

We'd had a relaxing Shabbos but, of course, worried about Rach.

When we finally spoke to her again, she was starting her day watching a Ravens game with the guys in LA. She was having such a good time that she threatened to delay chemo and stay in LA for another week. I told her I wished she could, and meant it. It was clear we'd made the right decision letting her make the trip. She came home tired but rejuvenated.

Reality hit hard the next day, Dec. 21. I'd scheduled the day off to take Rachel to chemo. Still on LA time, she had a lot of trouble getting up. We finally arrived at around 10:30 but had to wait more than an hour for Rachel to be taken back for blood work. From the parking lot to the registration area, we encountered countless technical difficulties and frustrations.

On top of that, it took hours for Rachel's blood results to come back and there were delays delivering her drug. Finally—*finally!*—someone came over to us to let us know that the drug wouldn't be available until after Rachel's 2:45 p.m. appointment. I was so incensed that I marched over to the director of nursing for the cancer center to complain. It turned out I wasn't the only one. How cruel, I raged, to keep people—cancer patients, for God's sake—waiting this long! Even as we finally left at 4:15, the valet guy took a long time to retrieve our car. The lot was full.

Yet, through it all, Rachel held up well. Barbara and Nick, the lovely couple we'd met in radiation oncology, greeted us once again with warm smiles. Barbara, whose demeanor and voice exuded calm, made a point of telling me that she thought Rachel looked much better. That pleased me greatly.

Nevertheless, I was frazzled from the hospital and technology hurdles. Exasperating days like this were not uncommon, but our moods soured as day turned into evening.

Rachel had decided to repeat the Chanukah party she'd thrown for friends the prior year. Judah and I would be going out for the night, so that she could entertain on her own. I was determined to find time to bake cookies for the party And so I did. The cookies burned. Then I dropped them. I felt sucker-punched and couldn't stop crying.

Two nights later, I dreamt that I'd dashed over to the infusion center and the nurses, including Jane, Rachel's chemo nurse, were abuzz with how important it was to be with your child every step of the way to observe things that may not be quite right. In the dream, I told them I worked full time, and that would be impossible. The next thing I knew, I was transported to my office, where a beloved male colleague who had been treated for breast cancer charmed me with his stories. He assured me that I was doing remarkably well, under the circumstances.

But was I? Navigating cancer treatment with our determined girl had become increasingly fraught. My work was suffering, and my boss seemed only perfunctorily sympathetic, which pained me and shattered whatever confidence I had left. He and my immediate supervisor told me I should no longer try to work on projects from home. Of course, I understood their concerns. But I couldn't help but worry that on top of everything else, I might lose my job.

It didn't help that the Chanukah party Rachel hosted turned out to be a major disappointment. Afterward, she just kept saying *I need to move back to LA*. To make matters worse, she'd needed platelets the day before and had received a new radiation approach, all of which exhausted her. Her cough and pallor seemed more pronounced, but what was most evident was how defeated she'd felt.

Thank Heavens for music. I'd just bought Rachel the newest *Glee* DVD from the concert she'd attended last June. A few nights after the Chanukah debacle, we sat and watched the DVD. It was hard not to dance, so I gave in and pranced around the living room as Rachel belted out the lyrics. For someone with bad lungs, she sure could have fooled me.

The next day—December 26—was our 35th wedding anniversary. Our kids bought us a digital picture frame and a gift certificate to an elegant kosher French restaurant in New York. It was generous of them, even though we had no idea when a trip to New York would be possible, given Rachel's uncertain health. No matter. We were determined to make the most of our time off locally, driving to see the elaborate Christmas lights on *the other* 34th Street, in Hampden, about a 20-minute drive from our house.

Earlier in the day, Rachel had met with her social worker, Lacy, for coffee, and had asked her if any internships were available. Lacy told her that none would be available for a couple of years, but it was good for Rachel to get a foot in the door, and even more importantly, to see her hold on to hope and make plans for the future.

Yet the fragile state of our nerves resurfaced, sometimes before Rachel's eyes. Judah, an avid reader, had become accustomed to carrying around his Kindle to read novels during the long waits at

Hopkins. One day, it suddenly stopped working. He had a major fit. He slammed it down and yelled, "Damn it, *damn* it! Why won't this work anymore?" Instinctively, I knew it was misplaced anger. Cancer brings out all kinds of emotions, I was learning.

I wasn't immune to this angst. Immunity: *lack of susceptibility; resistant*, says the online dictionary. I thought a lot about emotional immunity, and it struck me that I'd used the word almost exclusively in a medical sense.

Sometimes during Rachel's coughing fits, I'd have a flashback to the horrific day we learned of her recurrence. After that fateful meeting, after Judah drove Rachel home, I dashed to the parking garage, only to realize I'd misplaced my ticket. I'd burst into a sobbing fit and unleashed my frustration onto the parking attendant. The cost of a lost ticket was something like $15. I was angry with myself for misplacing it but way more outraged that my daughter's condition was worsening. I informed the attendant about the horrible news we'd just received. He kindly waived the fee and gave me a pass to use instead.

Small consolation, I thought. Still, acts of compassion like these truly make a difference. Mulling over this later, I realized how often such a scenario probably occurs, given how many patients are seen at the hospital every day. And, of course, when I cleaned out my purse the next day, I found the ticket buried behind some papers. My frazzled state in the parking lot had rendered me blind.

After Rachel's final radiation treatment, she once again rang the radiation oncology bell, but this time we didn't make a fuss. The clapping in the waiting area was heartwarming but muted. To call the experience anticlimactic would be an understatement. Still, it was a milestone.

So we celebrated by taking Rachel to Philly. An American history buff (it was her college major), she wanted to revisit the museums and see the Liberty Bell. Seeing her posing beside the cracked bell instantly moved me. I was reminded of the deepening fissure in her cancer trajectory. The City of Freedom uplifted us nonetheless, and we enjoyed the sites—and each other's company.

Two nights earlier, surreptitiously, from the upstairs hallway, I'd watched Rachel prepare for a video chat. While in LA, she'd met a guy—a friend of a friend—who knew nothing of her illness. They'd been in touch intermittently ever since. Because of his work schedule and the time difference, however, he asked that they video-chat at around 10 p.m.

He couldn't know it was a struggle for Rachel to stay up that late, but she was highly motivated. After all, it had been a long time since she'd had a real social life, even from afar. I saw her put on makeup and adjust her fall, topping it off with her Ravens hat to match her Ravens sweatshirt. She closed her door, but I could hear her giggling all the way down the hall. It did my heart good.

Yet I worried about the fate of this relationship. When the blow would come—as it most surely would—once this guy learned he was pursuing a girl with stage 4 refractory cancer, he would skedaddle. I dreaded that day.

Rachel's CT scan a few days later showed slight improvement in her lungs, but there were areas of "serious disease," Dr. A. noted. Still, he was encouraged and told Rachel she'd need more treatment, followed by a PET scan. After that appointment, Rachel went with Judah to see *The Girl with the Dragon Tattoo*, which they reported was very good. I couldn't fathom watching such a violent movie in my precarious emotional state, especially one about a young girl who was being abused.

Meanwhile, the video chats with the guy from LA continued. Incredibly, he didn't seem to have a clue about his lovely new friend's declining health. *Good for her*, I thought. The low-grade fevers persisted, and a cough that produced greenish-yellow sputum that Rachel nicknamed *shuchas*. It sounded like a pejorative, ugly, guttural Yiddish word—exactly what she'd intended by the nickname.

Because schools weren't in session during that week between Christmas and New Year's, this window of time felt like a reprieve. Sam and Nikki came in from New Jersey and watched the Ravens best the Bengals, 24-16. And, in the evenings, Rachel pulled herself together for video chats with her new friend. She'd begun talking more about how much she liked this guy. They chatted all day long, and Rachel told us he was planning to visit her in a few weeks. I didn't dare believe it, nor did I tell her that it was highly unlikely. My heart ached in anticipation of the letdown this breakup could bring.

The new calendar year arrived without fanfare, but, as usual, it took me a while to adjust to the correct year in my journal. I realize that's a universal problem, but by this time, we seemed to be in a perpetual time warp. I willed myself all over again to cling to hope.

On the evening of Jan. 3, 2012, I headed downstairs to watch *Srugim*, an Israeli show about Orthodox singles and relationships, with Rachel. She'd had a tough day running errands. I thought she might, considering the frigid temperatures this morning and 30 mph wind gusts. I'd suggested she take her inhaler with her. She did go out to the Post Office (no handicap parking spots) and to the bank (also no parking spots). She was so short of breath from walking that she called me.

It didn't help that she didn't eat much that day, beyond cereal at noon and water. "She eats like a prisoner . . . well, she kind of is one," I wrote in my journal.

The next day was even worse for Rachel—and for Judah. The plan was for her to go with him to work and then to an eye appointment with Dr. H. But Rachel wasn't feeling well at all and could not catch her breath. Plus, Dr. H. cancelled on Rach (for the second time). Uncle Ronnie ended up taking Rachel home and stayed with her. She was really bad off and needed oxygen.

Ronnie was wonderful: He made her toast after she threw up and then brought down the oxygen tank and hooked her up.

By the time I got home, she was better but looked flushed, and by 8 p.m., her low-grade fever had climbed to 100.2.

Later that night, I helped her get settled after her shower. She couldn't stop coughing—to the point where it made her throw up. She took another oxycodone, and then managed to put on her wig and makeup for an hourlong chat with her new friend in LA.

In the days that followed, Rachel remained lethargic and weak. I stayed home for half-days and made sure she took it easy. She mostly stayed in her PJs and wrote some thank you notes. On one of those days, as I was leaving for work, she found out she'd received an A+ in her social behavior class and an A in social policy. I wasn't the least bit surprised, but was mighty proud.

She'd finally convinced us that she needed to go to Miami for a few days to visit her former roommate and dear friend Sheera. The plan was that she would meet up with two other girlfriends there, and they would make sure to look out for her. But as the date neared, Rachel had trouble catching her breath, even walking short distances. Judah told her that if she went to Florida in this condition, she'd end up in an ER. I had to agree.

Of course, she was crushed to hear this. And Judah once again bemoaned the fact that he always had to be the bad guy. My heart ached for them both.

But I knew we'd made the right decision. The coughing fits intensified, and more *shuchas* poured out of her mouth. She would likely need another bronchoscopy. Of course, she was terrified about the possibility of getting another collapsed lung. But more than anything else, she was so tired of this wretched illness calling the shots. Could we blame her?

That night we laughed together over *The Bachelor*, which Rachel normally watched with her friend Julie. It was a good distraction from the reality that the next day Rachel was scheduled for chemo. She mentioned that she wanted to talk to a doctor who could fix her lungs, "because I can't go on like this."

Just as I'd come to expect, Rachel and Judah spent the entire day at Hopkins. There were no seats available while Rachel awaited her bloodwork results and for the chemo to be ordered. By 11:30 a.m., she was coughing so much and was so uncomfortable that she and Judah moved to the first floor. Rachel decided to call Dr. A., but just as she was about to dial his number, she saw him walk through the door. Her pulmonologist also happened to come by. Dr. A. told Rach that she shouldn't go to Miami and that she needed a chest X-ray.

Later that night Rachel learned that her chest X-ray was normal—improved, in fact, but that there was still fibrosis, whatever that meant. (When I got home, I looked it up; it meant thickening and scarring of the connective tissue.) Dr. A. prescribed another antibiotic. We were relieved when we realized how close we had come to another hospitalization. But how many more breaks could we get?

The weekend brought frigid weather, souring our moods even more. Rachel struggled to breathe. But Sam and Nikki had invited us for Shabbat dinner at their apartment, just a few blocks behind our house. Sam came to our house first to help Judah push Rachel in the wheelchair. She was swaddled in wool, but the cold ripped the color from her face.

Their apartment was on the third floor. Miraculously, Rachel climbed the steps and collapsed on the couch, gasping for air. She ate little but managed to relax and nearly fell asleep. Nikki's parents were in town, so we enjoyed catching up with them. We kvelled together about Sam and Nikki's commitment and dedication to their medical training, and I was in awe of their understated taste and tidiness. They were in this for the long haul. Resilience, I mused, was in full view that night.

Shabbat lunch the next day at the Lefkowitzes was lovely, though Rachel insisted on wearing black. "I'm in mourning for not going to Florida," she said. During lunch, she barely cracked a smile. She'd expressed worry about her upcoming courses but fretted even more about when she would be done with her cough and shortness of breath. She was also excited but anxious about her new LA friend's upcoming visit.

Nikki's parents told us they were planning another trip to Baltimore soon to visit Nikki and Sam and to watch the second half of the Giants game together.

Ah, sports—always the great equalizer. Rachel's illness and our rooting for her had come to seem like its own team sport. As always, seeing our growing family mesmerized by plays on the screen and debating players' talent was a refreshing change from sitting in waiting areas at Hopkins. It gave me tremendous pleasure to see Rachel escape and bond with the Minkove menfolk and friends as she cheered and clapped for her beloved Ravens and Orioles.

Earlier that day, the Ravens beat the Giants 20 to 13. After all the sports watching, we all went out to David Chu's, the kosher Chinese restaurant. Rachel coughed quite a bit during the meal, but she managed to ingest some soup and lo mein.

It pleased me to see that her fortune cookie read: "Don't give up. Everyone is cheering for you." That was a welcome sign, as her breathing problems seemed to be worsening.

Two days later, despite the biting winds that greeted her when she opened the front door, Rachel dragged herself to Beth Tfiloh to tutor. Then she headed to Hopkins for blood work and chemo. I met her at around 12:30. By the time I arrived, Rachel was upset because Dr. A. wasn't coming, and she'd had an encounter with a mean nurse. And, of course, the waiting seemed endless. Finally, another, much kinder nurse came back to Rachel's pod with the results from her sputum sample.

Rachel had tested positive for *Corneyabactrum* and miscellaneous flora, as well as "rare epithelial cells." So Dr. A. put her on another antibiotic. Though Rachel was short of breath and coughed intermittently, she seemed slightly better.

She didn't leave the house the next day, but something exciting flashed across her computer screen. It was an email from the dean of the social work school. It seemed that the executive director of the National Association for Social Workers in Washington, D.C., who subscribed to the *Baltimore Jewish Times*, had seen the sidebar Rachel wrote about hope and was blown away by it. He wanted Rachel to have lunch with him the following week in D.C.

The news couldn't have arrived at a better time. She was so excited. The prospect of sharing her experience and advocacy for young adults with cancer intrigued and excited Rachel. She wrote back that she couldn't make it for the lunch because of some health issues, but that she would be delighted to speak by phone.

Sports, meanwhile, continued to play a vital role in Rachel's and my guys' lives. But on Sunday, Jan. 22, 2012, my family and the entire city of Baltimore, it seemed, would descend into a major funk. The Ravens lost to the Patriots in the playoff game 23-20 because of a bad kicker. I wasn't home at that time; I was shopping for purple things, assuming—or at least hoping—that the Ravens would win. They *were* winning when I left the house.

My family was crushed, and it struck me how charged sports metaphors had become for us—ominous, at times. I kept thinking back to Rachel's spectacular pitch at Camden Yards, and how much we rooted for the O's to win. But they'd lost that game, by a lot. Now cancer was overwhelming Rachel. This was no game, but we clung to those metaphors. After all this time, I still hadn't embraced sports. But I'd come to recognize their power.

About a year after Rachel was diagnosed, I was asked to write a story for a newsletter from the Johns Hopkins Packard Center for ALS Research about O.J. Brigance, director of player development for the Baltimore Ravens. He was diagnosed with ALS—amyotrophic lateral sclerosis—aka Lou Gehrig's disease, in May 2007 and was being treated at Hopkins. Among the most dreaded ailments, the progressive, fatal disorder destroys the nerve cells that control movement. O.J. had made a substantial donation to the center in gratitude for his care and to help advance research.

At the time of my interview with him—just months after Rachel was diagnosed—I headed to Ravens headquarters in Owings Mills. My family was incredulous that I, of all people, would be writing a profile about a football player. And so was I. I just hoped my ignorance about football wouldn't hamper our meeting.

I needn't have worried. O.J., then 38 years old, couldn't have been more charming. The former Ravens linebacker, credited for the first tackle at the 2001 Super Bowl, now had to tackle everyday tasks, like holding a cup or dialing a phone number.

From the outset, O.J.'s optimism was palpable. He most certainly knew the statistics—that most patients with ALS die within five years of diagnosis. But O.J. told me he was optimistic that he would be cured. "The only one who determines the length of life is God," he said. "You've got to believe in the possibility of everything." O.J. also told me that he didn't want to be treated differently. "I have no time for a pity party," he said. "This diagnosis doesn't have to be the end of life. It's an opportunity for us all to fight, to come together to try to find a cure."

O.J. went on to tell me he was used to disproving naysayers. His coach at the University of Houston told him he'd never play football professionally because he was too small [he's 6 feet tall]. Yet he played for the CFL and NFL for 12 years. O.J. also had a back injury and was told he'd never play again. He recovered and was recruited by the Ravens.

Then he looked at me intently and shared his philosophy of life: "When people tell me I can't do things, I say, *Watch me do it.* You can call it stubborn or hard-headed, but I believe that once you have faith, everything falls into place." Then he showed me his Super Bowl rings.

It was hard not to lose my composure. Actually, it was impossible. The floodgates had opened. I quickly reached into my purse for a tissue. After O.J. gave me a tour of Ravens headquarters via electric wheelchair, I told him about Rachel and how much she, too, was doing her best to stay positive. He offered consoling words and reassured me that he would keep Rachel in his prayers.

Not long after that, I had the pleasure of seeing O.J. again and meeting his lovely, supportive wife, Chanda, at an event. It struck me how powerful love, faith and, yes, even sports, can be in the face of a dreadful diagnosis.

Some days it seemed like sports was the *only* outlet Rachel had left. True, she had many wonderful, loyal friends. But they were getting on with their own lives—marriage, children, careers. I begged God to give our girl a home team victory, at the very least.

We went about our lives almost robotically, it seemed—every day defined by how Rachel was feeling. By this time, she looked waiflike, as if a slight breeze could knock out all the breath she had left.

Rachel mentioned that she had to leave class three times that day because of coughing fits, but she refused to call me to pick her up because, she pleaded, "I didn't want to miss school." But she was exhausted and had to do it again the next day.

A couple of days later, I dashed home from work early. Rachel had called me, saying, "I can't do nothing." She loved using the double negative because she knew how much it upset her grammar-snob mom. As soon as I saw her, my heart sank. Her pallor frightened me, and she'd developed a fever of 101 and couldn't stop coughing. So she called Dr. A. as I headed into the kitchen to fix her a grilled cheese sandwich.

Dr. A. told her that he thought her condition was viral because she was also chilled. He wanted to see her, but he was heading to Singapore for a conference. He called her back at 8 and told her that he wanted her to get a complete workup.

Judah had missed all this back and forth—he was at a Terps game with our dear friend Jack, who had an extra ticket. Judah hadn't been sure he should go, but I was so glad he could escape the stress for a few hours. Meanwhile, Rachel and I watched the final episodes of *Srugim*. Then we watched a Gabby Giffords special (inspiring) and *Glee*.

Judah returned home close to midnight. I hated to break the news about Rachel's latest symptoms to him, but I couldn't hide my concern. He looked crestfallen. Rachel spent a long night grappling with chills, headache and exhaustion. *Please God, I wrote in my journal. Please let it be a better day tomorrow.*

Miraculously, my prayers were answered. Though Rachel's blood counts were low, her chest X-ray was unchanged from two weeks before. So she wasn't admitted. Dr. A. told her to stop taking Zyvox, the $1400/week pill she'd been on (thankfully, mostly covered by insurance). He suspected it was bringing her counts down.

On Friday, Jan. 27, 2012, we were awakened at 5:45 a.m. by a call from the person on call, who found out that Rachel's blood cultures came back positive. That meant that she probably had a staph infection. Judah thought she'd need to be admitted.

But things got better as the day wore on. I stayed home from work to take Rachel to the hospital at 10:30. Her counts were still low, but her white count went up 200 points, and she looked better. Her pulse was 148, but that was because she insisted on walking up herself.

Later that day, she went to get her nails done with Erica. And Rachel told me she wrote a paper while she was at Hopkins. She seemed determined; unstoppable.

But when I woke her up to give her that bad news that she might have to be admitted, she was angry—and adamant that she was absolutely not going to stay at the hospital. Of course, we'd have to wait and see what the cultures revealed the next morning.

We were awakened that Shabbat morning by the dreaded call that Rachel's cultures were positive again. Judah was truly scared, though he later told me he hadn't slept because he suspected that call would come.

It was so hard convincing Rachel to get up and go to the hospital. She was very upset. I told her that none of this was fair, but that we had no choice but to get those antibiotics into her.

The admission to Weinberg 5B went very smoothly. The first person we saw was the director of the bone marrow transplant unit. He suspected that her port was infected. Fortunately, the cultures came back positive for *Staph. Coag. Neg* (epidermis), instead of *Staph. Aureus*, which could have been devastating.

But Rachel developed a fever of 101.6 and was shaking with chills when they touched her port. By 12:30, the vancomycin started to course through her veins. She was totally exhausted and irritable.

Her hematocrit was 26, which certainly didn't help. We learned that her sputum that day contained another bacteria. We were told that we might be able to take her home, and arrange for Johns Hopkins Home Care to take charge of sending over drugs and a nurse. But we'd have to see how Rachel would feel overnight.

She emailed the guy she met in LA not to come—that *something had come up* and that he should plan to come the following weekend.

Later, Sam and Nikki came by with pizza for Rach, which she ate.

We had a wonderful intern—Tom, and we were lucky to have Carla at Rachel's side again, and Karen, the night nurse. At least we knew Rachel was in good hands.

During rounds the next morning, we learned that Rachel's port was infected, and they would need to take it out. Our girl was not happy, yet we were all relieved that nothing else had deteriorated, at least physically.

But there was no denying this: Being in the hospital all day is utterly mind-numbing. Yet, I acknowledged to myself, within 24 hours, Rachel had come a long way. It didn't hurt that she had lots of visitors—relatives, her friends and ours. Malka and Sammy brought dinner one night. That home-cooked meal, made and delivered with love, reminded me all over again how blessed we were to have such extraordinary people in our lives. Too bad those feelings were often overshadowed by my dread about another potential crisis.

As I was pulling out of the hospital parking lot that night, I saw a Virginia license plate that read, "Ki Tov." That's Hebrew for "that it was good." It's a reference to the Book of Genesis: After each of God's daily creations—the Heavens and the Earth, the Light, etc., the text reads "*Vayomer Hashem ki tov;*" translated, "And God saw *that it was good.*" I had to take that as a positive sign, knowing full well I was clinging to any shred of hope left after yet another setback.

The surgery the following day to remove Rachel's port went well. Her pain was manageable, and her doctors were pleased. Dr. Matsui, an intense but kind, articulate man, talked to us for a while. He spoke directly to Rachel as we listened, turning toward us at times, explaining how the antibody SGN she was taking binds to cancer cells. But, he warned, particles of the immunotherapy can "break off" and cause side effects, like hair loss.

After 13 hours at the hospital, I felt utterly spent. I couldn't believe it was only Monday. My thoughts were interrupted as a woman with a kind face followed me inside. We exchanged tired smiles and got to talking. She told me her husband was being treated for a brain tumor. She still had a long drive home, alone—to Gettysburg, Pennsylvania. I wished her well and safe travels. Our brief conversation made me appreciate my 20-minute drive home. *Cancer so sucks*, I muttered to myself—no matter how it manifests itself.

Winter churned on. Incredibly, despite the ups and downs since Rachel was released from the hospital on Jan. 31, 2012, she had begun to recoup much of her strength. The surgical site was healing. We'd become used to seeing our pale, waiflike daughter camped out on the couch. Like rosebuds poking through icicles, glimmers reemerged. Rachel mustered the energy to chip away at her social work school assignments, usually while reclined, with the laptop perched on her flat belly. These days, she had little time or energy to be a *silly goose,* as I loved to call her.

But at night, we'd relax together in front of the TV. A new series, called *Touch,* starring Kiefer Sutherland, captivated us. It was about a former newspaper reporter whose wife died in the 9/11 attacks on the World Trade Center, and who is trying to raise his 11-year-old autistic son, Jake, alone. Rachel told us that the talented young actor playing the son had been a student of one of Rachel's friends, Jessica, at the LA Jewish day school where both girls taught. Knowing that made the show all the more riveting.

Though Jake struggles, he is also gifted with clairvoyance through numbers and patterns related to numbers. He writes them down in notebooks, his touch-screen tablet or sometimes using objects (e.g., popcorn kernels). Because of this gift, he can predict events before they happened. But his severe autism has rendered him speechless, so his father has to try to figure out how to intervene when the events might have dire consequences.

We all looked forward to that hour together, predicting aloud at times how the drama might play out. Sutherland manages to resolve these potential crises/mysteries in the nick of time. The show reminded me of a modern-day *Mission Impossible*. But by the end of the hour, when those nail-bitingly close calls were resolved, I found my hopes for Rachel rekindled—at least for a little while.

Our girl was finally getting back into the swing of things. One night she dashed into the kitchen looking for a scissors, her face a study in determination. Waving a pair of slipper socks, she flashed a big, conspiratorial smile. Then she proceeded to cut off the tops and bottoms. And, voila! She'd created "sleeves" to cover her PIC chemo port that had recently been surgically implanted under the skin, in the right side of her chest. With its thin, silicone tube, the small device attaches to a vein, in the underside of the upper arm, making it possible for nurses to draw blood and administer fluids and treatments directly into her system—without the need for needle sticks. But she hated that the port was so conspicuous.

Our resourceful girl— our silly Goose—was at it again. Indeed, she'd found her groove again, and a creative way to hide her port, but I knew better than to expect much more.

Yet, over the ensuing 10 days, as the antibiotics kicked in, Rachel looked really good to me. One evening, I heard her talking to her friend Talia animatedly, and the entire conversation went by without a single cough. By the following Shabbat, when Sam and Nikki came over for dinner, she insisted that we walk them home—it was about five blocks from our house. Rachel made it up the hill and to Fallstaff, the first street behind our house. Judah thought we should head back because she was getting short of breath. Thankfully, she didn't protest.

The next day we hosted 10 people—mostly Rachel's friends—for Shabbat lunch. Rachel ate fairly well and sat for hours, coughing little. After Shabbat, we watched a movie called *50/50*, which turned out to be disappointing. Every woman in the movie was weak and shallow.

There was some humor about a character's cancer experience, but it hit too close to home. As the credits appeared, Judah had but one pithy comment: *"No more cancer movies."*

Super Bowl Sunday 2012 brought long faces: the Ravens had blown their chance. I ran out to get a pizza, and Rachel's friend Stacy came over to watch the game. All agreed that the Ravens could have beaten either team (the Giants or the Patriots). Rachel was rooting for the Patriots. All I could think about was rooting for our sick girl. *Could she ever get a break?*

The Sunday night dread in anticipating another challenging work/treatment week visited me later that night. Our growing frustrations about Rachel's health plagued us. Social work school did prove a good distraction for her, but I was concerned that it would sap every ounce of energy she had left. And yet ... just when I thought things couldn't get worse, glimmers would emerge.

On Feb. 6, when I called Rachel from work, she sounded tired, even defeated. She had every reason to feel that way, of course, having just been released from the hospital and at school for six hours.

We picked her up from school, and she coughed the entire way home. She mentioned that her classroom had been super-hot and she looked exhausted, but she was ravenous and ate every last bite of her turkey sandwich, after which she asked for warmed-up chocolate chip cookies. I took that as a good sign.

I was also pleased that, despite her having had chemo the next day, she looked much better than she had in weeks. Her bloodwork validated my impression. Her hematocrit was 36.5, though I wasn't happy to learn that her weight was down to 96.5 lbs.

Rachel waited an hour to be taken back for bloodwork and then another hour and a half for results and mixing the SGN (brentuximab). But the actual drug delivery into her port took only 35-40 minutes.

Afterward, we headed to Hunt Valley Mall. Rachel redeemed a gift certificate from Mira, and we both bought shoes, and then went to Greetings & Readings for hot cocoa. A wet snow was falling, and we were so happy to be out together. Rachel displayed a vitality I hadn't seen for a long time. I learned that she liked a couple of Vera Bradley patterns, and G&R had a huge line of her accessories. We bought a tote for Sheera's birthday.

Incredibly, during that time we shopped together, Rachel didn't cough once, nor did she feel nauseated. But fatigue continued to dog her.

The ups and downs continued, and so did reminders of human mortality. We spent a Sunday morning at a tribute lunch for our friend Sheldon, who was being treated for a glioblastoma brain tumor. It was a beautiful event—funny, poignant and uplifting. But Rachel couldn't attend. She hadn't slept well, and her back was hurting. She pulled herself together to meet with our friend Aaron, an insurance agent, who helped her review her changeover to Maryland health insurance.

Rachel's friends, meanwhile, continued to pick her up and take her out. And suddenly it was time for the Grammys again. Whitney Houston had recently died from an overdose, and the videotaped tribute moved us all, as her exquisite voice reverberated through our den. Of course, we reminisced about Rachel's phenomenal experience at the Grammys the previous year. She told us again how spectacular it was to see so many of those stars in person.

I couldn't help but think that our girl had taken on a starring role herself—as the "amazing" cancer patient. By now, I'd lost track of how many people used that word to describe their awe for our daughter. But I knew for certain that Rachel was sick and tired of hearing it. And, if I'm honest, by then, so was I, even though I agreed with that assessment.

Fatigue and setbacks notwithstanding, Rachel continued to attend classes, treatment at Hopkins and social events. On Feb. 16, I took Rachel to her appointment with Dr. A. When he learned that her weight had dropped to 93.5, he decided to increase her thyroid medication. He was also concerned about a new pain in Rachel's back. It had been bothering her intermittently. Rachel, of course, was upset at the prospect of more radiation, but Dr. A. wanted an MRI as soon as possible.

I began to see the effect of these new developments chip away at her confidence. One night, after she showered, it seemed as though a nest had formed on her head. The hair bundle appeared to be loosening away from her scalp. She wouldn't let me comb it for fear that it would all come out. I let her be, my poor baby. Choking back tears, I thought to myself how utterly unfair this new development was. It had taken an entire year for her to grow that hair back. *Dear God*, I later railed, *what did she do to deserve this?*

If that weren't enough, Rachel told me about something she'd read online about a woman on SGN whose muscles in her legs were so weak, she could barely walk. Neuropathy, as we knew, was a common side effect, and Rachel had recently been complaining about pain in her feet and legs.

The very next day, Friday, Feb. 17, a new crisis erupted. While out at Starbucks with her friend Erica, Rachel noticed blood spurting from her PICC line (port). Judah took her to Hopkins to stop the bleeding. Her caregiver thought Rachel would need platelets, but they came in at 26,000—low, but not at critical level. That said, Rachel was a mess. She threw up and then told me that Dr. A. was very concerned that this could well be Hodgkin's again. If so, they would need to talk about radiation. He'd also said something about how if the SGN wasn't working, there really weren't any other options. He'd also gingerly broached the subject of ventilator assistance. In other words, there might come a time when Rachel's lungs would shut down, and she wouldn't be able to breathe on her own. She told him she would want ventilator assitance and wasn't going to give up hope.

What a lovely way to usher in Shabbat, I thought to myself. Judah and I were shaken by these developments, but Sam and Nikki were coming for dinner, along with Nikki's parents, and we felt compelled to stay positive. We actually enjoyed ourselves, though it was obvious Rachel felt crappy and defeated.

By Monday, she felt better. Dr. A. had put her back on antibiotics. Choosing meds for Rachel was always tricky. Her shrinking body often rejected them or reacted violently to their effects. This time, however, they seemed to help, even as her back started hurting more. Nevertheless, Rachel continued to eat more and go out with friends. I was cautiously optimistic when I realized she'd barely coughed. But we knew a big test lay ahead. She told us she needed to be at social work school for nine straight hours of classes.

In the days that followed, we watched our girl go on with her life like nothing was wrong. She got up early for her classes and kept tutoring at Beth Tfiloh. Rachel seemed much perkier: Her back pain wasn't as intense, nor was her cough, and she'd also started paying more attention to her appearance.

One morning she came downstairs wearing a Kelly-green smock shirt, skinny black jeans and long black suede boots. She wore a cream-colored knit hat over her fall. And her darker eyebrows, touched up by a beautician the day before, made her eyes pop more than usual. She gobbled down some cereal and made her way to social work school. I thought my heart would burst.

After classes, Rachel drove herself to Hopkins, and on the way back had a craving for a Coke Slurpee, so she stopped at a 7/11. Maybe it was the caffeine in that drink, but the energy boost lifted her—and our—spirits.

February was in its last week by then. On the last Shabbat of the month, we commemorated Judah's mother's yahrzeit, the anniversary of her premature death after failed cancer treatments, 28 years before. As I lit the yahrtzeit candle in her memory, the unspoken significance of her loss rankled.

We missed my mother-in-law, and, as Rachel geared up for her upcoming MRI and PET scan, I had to hope Bootsie was rooting for us from above. There was also the fact that Jon had arrived late that Friday afternoon from New York, and would surely provide comic relief with his cynical sense of humor and sports banter.

Rachel awoke at noon that Shabbat morning, and got dressed at my prodding. I was pleased to see her eat the solid lunch I'd prepared: soup, pasta and chicken, rice, chocolate cupcake. Not long after, several of Jon's and Rachel's friends dropped by.

That Saturday night, Judah accompanied Jon back to New York to see my father-in-law. Ever since he entered his 80s, he'd begun a steady decline. I just hoped the visit would go well, though my heart broke for Judah, knowing that he was consumed with caring for ailing loved ones.

Left alone with Rachel, I looked forward to the girl talk we could enjoy together. But it was not to be. At 12:15 a.m. that Sunday, after she showered, I helped her comb what was left of her hair. She was trying to convince me, jokingly, that she'd already had her MRI and that Dr. A. called to tell her everything was OK. I told her I wished that were true, and I hoped and prayed that would be the case the next day. It was becoming more and more difficult to choke back my tears.

We read *The Very Hungry Caterpillar* for the umpteenth time. Afterwards, as part of our new routine, I pulled the caterpillar/butterfly mobile to activate the lullaby music in hopes that it would soothe both of our spirits. I gave Rachel a big smile, followed by a hug, hoping the quiver in my lip didn't betray my fears about the MRI. She returned a hopeful smile. *Oh, how I loved that girl.*

While Judah was still in New York that Sunday, Rachel and I were preparing for her friend Natan's wedding. Rachel looked stunning in a Marc Jacobs dress from Loehmann's with an asymmetrical neckline. She'd had to buy new shoes so that she could walk more easily in lower heels than usual, and donned her old wig, the one she'd just gotten updated. It pained me to realize Rachel was 10 lbs. thinner than she was the last time she'd worn that same dress to another friend's wedding.

How *normal* this all seemed—finally an escape from our *not-so-normal* routine! But then my thoughts took me back to our tough start that morning. I'd had to wake Rachel up at 7 a.m. for her 7:40 a.m. MRI. She got through it OK, but her back had been hurting her a lot. The fact that the MRI had been scheduled for a Sunday made me worry that Dr. A. was more concerned. Thankfully, the technicians couldn't have been nicer. And Rachel got her wish: to listen to *Glee* during the MRI. How she recouped enough energy to attend the wedding remains a mystery.

I pushed those thoughts aside. Somehow, Rachel pulled herself together for the wedding and managed to look radiant. She even got up to dance a little and caught up with Michael, a friend from college, at dinner, where he told her about his journey to Columbia's social work school.

Later, we changed out of our clothes and watched the Oscars. Coughs erupted from Rachel as she claimed her spot on the couch. She asked me for her puffer. I dashed upstairs to grab it. Incredibly, her spirits seemed to be OK. Then, during a commercial, she mentioned that she'd joined a Facebook group for people on SGN-35. She went on to report that three of the people on the drug had died, and one girl was writing that it didn't work for her but that she was having some success with another drug. My heart skipped a beat; I was at a total loss as to how to respond.

Jon had advised Rachel not to read these updates. I had to agree and told her so. In the midst of this discussion, Rachel received an email from Dr. A with the results of her MRI: "No stress fracture, and nothing new that looks like cancer."

That news, of course, buoyed us, but Rachel's fatigue had become unshakeable. The following day, she had a tour of Healthcare for the Homeless in downtown Baltimore, not far from the School of Social Work. Everyone walked there together. She admitted to me that she'd almost collapsed in the process, in large part, because the building was so hot. But for someone as sick, thin and exhausted as she was, she sure looked beautiful that day.

Reading novels and nonfiction remains a sacred part of my life. For decades, I've been involved in two book clubs, one of which I lead.

This started when Jon was five and Rachel was two, and I was feeling overwhelmed by motherhood, working part time and frustrated by Judah's demanding schedule. Then, one Saturday night we were invited to a party. We found a babysitter and went, and I struck up a conversation with a lovely woman named Mary Lou. She mentioned that she was in a women's book club, and I was immediately intrigued. The idea of a group of women choosing a book and meeting to discuss it every month or two delighted me.

Almost three decades later, that book group feels like a second family. We discuss recurring themes, often touching on parts of our lives we may not have thought about for years. For a time I'd also joined a Jewish women's book group—HBI (Hadassah Brandeis Institute) Conversations—in which members paid to bring authors to Baltimore speak about their work. Reading these books also provided a welcome escape as Rachel's health struggles continued. Each memoir or novel was completely different, and meeting these writers and hearing them describe how they went about writing their novel or memoir inspired me, both professionally and personally.

From an early age, Rachel also loved reading and had recently joined a less formal book group, led by her friend Julie. These discussions, mostly about novels, provided a welcome diversion for her, too. More importantly, it seemed like such a normal thing for a young adult to do, as opposed to having weekly blood draws and a chemotherapy regimen that may or may not be effective.

But the person who devours books the most ravenously in our family is Judah. In his quiet, cerebral way, he's never without one. After Rachel was diagnosed, he began choosing longer books—in anticipation of hours-long hospital appointments and admissions. Thank Heavens for the distraction books bring to us all.

As the last day of February neared, Rachel geared up for yet another PET scan and chemotherapy treatment. Thankfully, her appetite had improved. She couldn't stop raving about a salad she purchased in the Hopkins cafeteria: a prepackaged kosher one. Then, for dinner, she scarfed down an entire turkey avocado wrap, followed by a cupcake.

March arrived in the form of a glorious day: 65 degrees and no wind. Rachel was going to meet her friend Erica at Starbucks in Quarry Lake, and it was a perfect day for it. Her spirits were up; "Good vibes," she posted as a Facebook status. Sure enough, Dr. Ambinder called her that night to report that her PET scan looked "marvelous." Everything was smaller—the cancer in her back and lungs. So he planned to keep her on SGN. We felt cautiously optimistic.

Rachel decided to send out another update, as her friends had continued to inquire about how she was doing. Given how many friends she had, it was always easier for her to send out a single message. As ever, I was struck by her openness. I also always appreciated having a glimpse into her psyche through all the ups and downs.

From: Rachel Minkove <rminkove@gmail.com>
Date: Fri, Mar 2, 2012 at 11:55 AM
Subject: long overdue update

Dear Friends and Family,
I apologize for my lack of correspondence for a while. Things have been pretty stable for the most part. As always, there have been many hurdles to overcome. Around a month ago, I was hospitalized for a few days with sepsis in my bloodstream, which was rooted in my port. They surgically removed the port, and I have a temporary PICC line in my arm, but I'm hoping to soon have no medical implantation, so long as my veins hold up. For now, I have stylish arm bands.
I've been extremely busy in social work school, taking

three classes this semester. And, as a result of my sidebar in my mother's article about hope this past summer, I was invited to speak at the National Association of Social Workers' conference in Washington, DC. I will be speaking in front of 1,000 people in July, regarding how my personal experiences have led me to social work and what hope I can impart to others.

I completed my radiation treatment, and have been continuing with my chemo every three weeks. Fortunately, the side effects are pretty minimal, allowing me to have more energy to hang out with friends and be more physically active. Additionally, I still have been tutoring part-time at Beth Tfiloh. Walking continues to remain a struggle, but I'm making slow progress.

I just received a PET scan and MRI this past week showing improvement. The treatment seems to be slowly working, so let's hope this is the magic bullet that cures me. I still have a long road ahead, having completed 6 of my intended 16 treatments. But, after a few setbacks I am finally back on the right track.

We, too, did our best to convey a sense of measured optimism for our girl—and for our friends, whose concern sometimes seemed unbearably intense. I was grateful to those people kind enough not to ask a million questions.

Meanwhile, Rachel convinced us to let her go to Washington, D.C., for Shabbos with friends. When I caught up with her that Saturday night, she told me she'd thrown up three times after going to bed Friday night, partly from coughing, but also from nausea. Still, she'd had a good time. But by the time we saw her on Sunday afternoon, she looked utterly exhausted.

Somehow, the next day, Rachel looked refreshed. She barely coughed, though she was wiped out after having attended two classes at social work school. As I baked hamentaschen for Purim, I tiptoed near the den to make sure I wasn't missing any coughs. *Not a peep.* I almost had to pinch myself as hard as I did the dough after filling it with fruit jam.

Was I just imagining it, or was our pale, thin girl fighting cancer rebounding? Could the SGN-35 be kicking in? Rachel had an intensity about her that had only recently surfaced when she was furiously typing papers, but that I hadn't seen otherwise. She told us it was Erica's birthday, and that she wanted to make a fuss. So she went out to buy her a scarf and took Erica out for lunch. There was no stopping our girl, I kept thinking … or, if I'm honest, *hoping so*, with all my heart.

In the midst of all these ups and downs, Zippy Schorr, the director of education for Beth Tfiloh, emailed me to ask if Rachel would be willing to speak at Beth Tfiloh's graduation. She noted that she'd been blown away by Rachel's latest update and thought Rach would be "incredibly inspiring."

I was touched by the suggestion/invitation. But Rachel squawked at the idea. She thought Mrs. Schorr could surely find someone better to speak. Besides, it had occurred to our girl, the idea was too similar to having Steve Jobs—who died in Oct. 2011 of a rare form of pancreatic cancer—speak at graduation. Rachel had a point. It did seem a bit morbid. And, of course, it was her decision. She turned down the offer. No doubt Mrs. Schorr was disappointed.

Going into Purim, Rachel's fatigue dogged her, but she did get out on yet another beautiful day. She and Erica studied together at an outdoor table at the Quarry Lake Starbucks. Erica snapped a photo of Rachel that day which I love—her knees bent, laughing before her open computer. Except for intermittent "*shucha*s," Rachel had enjoyed that morning with her friend immensely.

That night, as we headed to Beth Tfiloh for Purim, she came downstairs dressed as a Baltimore Raven. She looked no different from how she dressed up to watch Ravens games, but she owned it and looked perky as she assembled a few *shalach manot* (food gifts) with hamentaschen. We heard the *megillah* reading at Beth Tfiloh, where Rachel caught up with friends and enjoyed everyone's creative costumes.

Purim day was chaotic, as usual, with the constant stream of food basket deliveries. We were inundated. It all felt rather normal, except for the fact that our daughter was being ravaged by stage 4 cancer.

At the Purim *seudah* (feast) later, hosted by our friends Shosh and Brian at their home, Rachel was the star attraction. Her back was hurting a bit, but her appetite was hearty, which pleased me to see. She was downright chatty, regaling everyone with humorous stories about her teaching experiences in LA. All eyes were on our sparkling daughter. The joy on everyone's faces as they caught up with her was uplifting.

The next day Rachel had an interview for a case work position at Roland Park Place retirement home. The woman who interviewed her liked Rachel so much that she was hired on the spot.

Sheera arrived to stay with us the following Shabbat. Her visit did wonders for us all, especially Rachel. I marveled that the two girls who were so different shared such a special bond. Sheera was far more introverted and cautious. But over the years, Rachel had brought out a gregarious side in her friend that Sheera hadn't realized she had. Now, they were close, and shared many common friends.

On the afternoon Sheera arrived, Rachel learned she had cataracts. The optometrist at Johns Hopkins told her that it had likely been caused by prolonged use of prednisone. But it was just in its early stages, so all Rachel would need for now was a new glasses prescription. Still, she was distressed by this new development. When I returned home from work that day, she greeted me with: "Can you believe that on top of everything else, I have cataracts? That's what *old* people get!"

Her platelets that day had soared to 92,000, and she'd walked all the way to her optical appointment from the parking lot. Hopkins is such a big place, and without a wheelchair escort, it's easy to rack up miles of walking without realizing it. She'd also driven herself to Roland Park Place, as part of her social work requirement. Rachel seemed to enjoy working with the elderly population, and I have no doubt that just seeing her smile gave them and their families a lift. I was in awe but more than a little anxious about the cumulative effect of all this exertion.

Having Sheera around made Rachel more animated than usual, though that night Rachel's cough resurfaced, and she told us she needed to take an oxycodone pill and Nyquil.

By Sunday, Rachel and Sheera were inseparable. Sheera insisted on making her delicious chocolate chip pancakes. I was thrilled to see how Rachel devoured them, given that my daughter's weight had plummeted to 93.9 lbs. Afterwards, Judah drove Sheera to the train station, Rachel sitting in the front seat. It had all turned out well, and Rachel was so energized that she studied most of the day, took a Coke Slurpee break, and walked twice around the track with Judah.

The weather had turned mild—nearly perfect, at 75 degrees and sunny. We were heartened, and I realized that Rachel was in a better place than she'd been a month ago. Spring break had begun for her. She was perkier than usual and continued to insist on pushing herself to walk in the neighborhood. But she had trouble catching her breath when she returned. My worry intensified. How much longer could she keep up this pace?

In the middle of that night, March 28, 2012, my fears proved warranted. At around 4:15 a.m., Rach came to our room holding her side and crying in excruciating pain. She had a low-grade fever, but the biggest complaint was about a spot under her left rib. We almost took her to the ED, but Judah thought it best to let her be (after giving her oxycodone and oxygen). She was also nauseated, so he gave her a Zofran.

I took off from work and brought her in to see Dr. A. Judah had no idea what was going on.

Neither did Dr. A. or Jane. It could have been one of 10 things, including a clot in her lung, pericarditis, or more Hodgkin's.

We arrived at Hopkins at around 1, after Rach slept fitfully. But she was in excruciating pain. Her PICC line wasn't working, so they had to poke a vein. Actually, Michelle got one pretty fast, as Rachel spoke to the insurance person about authorization for her CT.

Rachel had to wait a good long while for the scan—abdominal and chest—and had to first consume an awful drink for the contrast.

Afterward, Rachel ate the salad she likes me to get for her. We waited for hours in pod C, but when—at around 4:15—Dr. A came by, he looked *happy*.

"So … so, you have this way of scaring us, but then things turn out pretty OK," he said. Not that a broken rib and pneumonia are good, but there was no evidence of Hodgkin's. In fact, the scan was better than the last one: There was no evidence of tumors. Still, pneumonia is serious stuff, so she needed to take Avelox again. She'd also been taking oxycodone more often, so she was feeling miserable, thanks to the cycle of pain, drug-induced exhaustion and loopiness.

My heart was breaking for Rachel. Yet I was relieved that the news was so much better than it could have been. Her labs were decent, too. Her hematocrit had climbed to 38! Nevertheless, it was a harrowing 12- hour ordeal.

That night, our girl scarfed down steak, rice and popsicles. I was thrilled to see her eat so well. But we were all so tired and drained.

It turned out that the broken rib was likely the result of all the daily coughing over the past few months. The X-ray from the previous day revealed that her sixth rib on her left side showed a "subacute fracture" and continued to give her grief. I bought a Velcro abdominal wrap to help stabilize her rib cage. But the cycle of pain meds and constipation made her loopy.

The very next morning, March 29, at 1 a.m., our phone rang. Rachel had had some blood drawn the previous day, and the oncology fellow told Judah that Rachel had bacteria in her blood again. This time, the culture was gram-negative, meaning that the bacteria could cause pneumonia and infection; gram-negative bacteria are resistant to most drugs. Still, Rachel was prescribed antibiotics in hopes that the medication would kill—or at least hamper—the growth of bacteria.

Nevertheless, it was a scare. Judah took Rachel in. They waited a solid hour before being taken back. Then they removed her PICC line. She screamed in pain, though it only took a minute to yank it out.

In spite of this setback, Rachel attacked her social work assignments with a vengeance, though I noticed that at times her eyes rolled with fatigue, and she had to stop to rest. But her usual rhythm, albeit slower, seemed restored. Rabbi Silber came over later that day to study that week's Torah portion with her. And Judah took her to the optician to pick up her new glasses, which perked up her face and made her look both brainy and stylish.

By Shabbat, however, Rachel looked utterly spent. In the morning, I came downstairs to fix myself a cup of coffee. After two sips, the phone rang. The moment I saw Rachel's name pop up, I sprinted up the stairs. I knew she wouldn't use her phone on Shabbat unless she absolutely had to.

Rachel was in excruciating pain again, stemming from her rib. I grabbed some tissues to wipe her tears. We spent the entire day trying to help her feel comfortable. She barely ate and never got dressed. Eventually, she made her way downstairs and vegged out on the couch.

It was becoming more difficult than ever to watch our girl suffer. Thankfully, Sam and Nikki came over, and then later, our friends Faith and Ed and Malka. Sometimes, we shunned visitors, especially after exhausting days, but we knew how much Rachel thrived on socializing. Besides, by this point, our friends had become extended family. We badly needed the boost they provided.

Once again, our girl rallied. The following day, she spent four hours on schoolwork. She looked perkier, more engaged. At one point her phone rang. It was Zippy Schorr calling again to ask Rachel to speak at graduation, and saying she wouldn't take no for an answer. Rachel agreed to do it. I knew she was nervous about what she would say to the graduating seniors and their proud family members, but I could also tell she was flattered to have been asked.

One evening a few days later, Rachel and I sat in the den working on our computers. She took a break to look at Facebook, and suddenly, she gasped, looking outraged. I asked her what was wrong. Then she went on a diatribe about a posting she'd just read:

You might want a new car and a vacation, etc., but a cancer patient wants only one thing: good health.

Rachel's eyes blazed as she explained why she was so infuriated. "I want all those things, too. But just because I have cancer doesn't mean my life is over, and all I can do is sit and wish I were better. I go after the things I want!"

Motherly pride swelling, I informed Rachel that she'd just found the perfect way to open her upcoming talk at the NASW conference. She agreed, rewarding me with a smile and said she couldn't wait to get started on it.

By this time, the routine of going to Hopkins for bloodwork was getting old. And yet, its relative normalcy provided relief. It sure was better than the thought of Rachel's being an inpatient who developed more complications. Still, it pained me to see how some people involved in Rachel's care would make thoughtless, cruel remarks.

One Friday, for example, we'd been waiting a ridiculously long time for bloodwork, and a new phlebotomy nurse complained aloud about the need to change Rachel's bandage. She wanted to go to lunch and said so. "We *never* go to lunch," responded the other nurse.

It was difficult to decide which of those two women troubled me the most. Regardless, the experience made me realize that low morale among staff can trickle down to patients—especially when it's shared out loud. Rachel said nothing, of course, but we exchanged a mutual look of exasperation.

Thankfully, Rachel's numbers were improving. Her platelets had reached 12,000. But she'd developed sinus trouble and let Sam know how upset she was about having inherited (from his DNA, no doubt) his allergies.

That said, I was touched to see how much closer the two siblings had become. Sam was on spring break, so he took Rachel to chemo treatments that week. He and I both expressed concern that Rachel appeared to be developing neuropathy in her feet. I found a stress ball for her to squeeze, which seemed to help a little.

The upcoming NASW presentation became a focal point for Rachel. She continued to mull over her presentation and fretted about what she should wear. One day in late March, our dear cousin Linda came to Baltimore from Rockville and offered to take Rachel to Loehmann's. When I returned home from work, Rachel was pleased to show me a lovely black and white dress she'd picked out. It featured a white blousy empire top and a straight black bottom. She slipped it on. Instantly, our girl exuded class and confidence. No matter what she wore, I had no doubt she'd rock that presentation.

Glimmers of renewal continued to surface. By early April, spring seemed to emerge stronger: Birds chirped louder, and bright green leaves seemed to burst from trees defiantly, even on cold days—as did Rachel's will. On two consecutive days, she walked around the track three times. Her legs were sore, but she was so proud of herself. Even Judah was impressed. He reminded Rachel that in January, she'd needed oxygen just to go to the bathroom.

Our girl tried to reclaim her life. She went out to lunch with friends and entertained family and friends at home. I was more than happy to take on the additional cooking. Yet Rachel expressed frustration about her social life here. She wanted so badly to return to New York, where most of her friends now lived. But I knew it was more than that. She simply wanted the independence young adulthood brings. *If only I had the power to make that happen*, I thought.

CHAPTER 14

Grappling with Loss and Travel Plans

Passover, the festival of redemption, freedom and harbinger of spring, has always brought our family together, making up for the stress that turning over the kitchen brings: putting away leavened foods, covering countertops and reviewing Passover recipes. Things were different now, however. Rachel's illness had progressively worsened. We all knew it but couldn't dwell on it. For one thing, Rachel would resent that. For another, it was profoundly depressing.

Exhausted from the preparations and feeling the dread that came with Rachel's notorious crises on Jewish holidays, I tried to focus on the laborious tasks ahead.

Fortunately, Jon had arrived, and we were eager to spend the first seder night at the Wolfs. The day before, Rachel had rallied. Other than fatigue and a "barfowitz" in the yellow plastic hospital bin next to the couch, she seemed perkier. The weather cooperated, too. For once, we didn't need raincoats. We were heartened to see green lawns, tulips and the blossoms of forsythias and dogwood trees emerge. Those bursts of color reminded me of the joy in a new box of crayons.

Yet we knew better than to count on an uneventful holiday. As Rachel often reminded us, she had an "antisemitic body." And, of course, Jewish holidays crop up fairly regularly. Indeed, if you count the Sabbath, that's one every week.

Much to our surprise, the eve of Passover 2012 brought zero drama. I willed myself to stay positive, despite my angst about a potential crisis. Rachel had her usual coughing fits and green sputum, but she didn't seem quite as weary. She dove into her social work assignments and, when she felt she'd accomplished enough work, went out to get her nails done. Normalcy became her *raison d'etre*.

Jon's presence gave us all a boost. Much like Judah and my father, he always manages to find the humor in everyday life, as does Sam. That night, our entire family headed to the Wolfs for the first seder. The weather was glorious, my hopes buoyed. I wanted so much to believe that this spring would be the harbinger of good health.

God answered our prayers. For once, we had a reprieve. Both seder nights were beautiful. Not that Rachel was feeling terrific. She coughed plenty, especially during the second seder.

The first seder at the Wolfs was a delight. Matzo—traditionally an ingredient in many Passover dishes—is not a favorite in our household, but thanks to Faith's culinary gifts, in most of the food she made, you'd never notice the difference. And the presentation! The table looked elegant, yet whimsical. Plastic frogs, representing the second of the ten plagues God foisted on the Egyptians, graced the table. We left after 11 p.m. with extended bellies, uplifted by the profound love a decades-long friendship across generations brings—and grateful that Rachel had made it through the evening without a crisis.

The next day, another dear friend, Sandy, hosted her annual kiddush in memory of her beloved father, a Hungarian Holocaust survivor, who'd passed away a decade earlier. Sandy's mother, a charming matriarch and phenomenal baker, always greeted everyone with a warm smile and a twinkle in her eye. Her sweet disposition belied the unspeakable horrors she'd endured at Auschwitz.

We worried about Rachel's ability to attend the kiddush, but she insisted. Sandy's house was a fairly short distance from our house, so we gave in. On most recent outings, we'd insisted on using the wheelchair to save Rachel's energy. This time, as we approached the house, Rachel asked to walk the rest of the way. I totally understood why and found myself in awe all over again of our plucky girl. Judah went ahead with Rachel on his arm, as I pushed the empty wheelchair and parked it out of conspicuous sight.

When Sandy and her mother spotted Rachel, they glowed with delight, as did others who hadn't seen Rachel for a while. And, I could tell Rachie was enjoying the quasi-normalcy this experience offered.

But on the way home from the kiddush, a wind gust blew her wig off as Jon pushed the wheelchair. I quickly snatched it off the ground, and we all had a good laugh. At the same time, it broke my heart to realize how vulnerable Rachel was—not only because of her persistent illness, but also because of the increased potential of unexpected embarrassing moments like this one.

I couldn't deny that she was beginning to look like a stick figure. But at least we'd managed to celebrate two seders together with dear friends, and for once, had entered Passover without more devastating news. Rachel's fragile state frightened me, but when she smiled, her eyes offered as much possibility as a cloudless sky. As we basked in that early spring sunshine, Rachie's face radiated hope. After the holiday ended, I'd captured my relief at this sight in my journal: *Our girl is mighty sick, but at least we got through the sedarim [Seders]. There were no test results that brought devastating news; and Rach was no longer suffering with Aspergillus. But she is so fragile … yet always so beautiful. And when she smiles, her eyes dance and send sparks of hope.*

Those first two days of Passover also brought a steady stream of visitors into our den. I found myself sneaking looks at Rachel for signs of fatigue. We kept lots of antibacterial gel nearby and asked people to use it. But what I remember most was the unbridled joy on her pale face and the musical cadences and laughter emanating from the very same spot where Rachel spent most of her time alone or with her parents.

By the evening, Rachel was wiped out, but clearly uplifted. I was moved by how much she nurtured her friendships. As her friend Sarah aptly observed, Rachel was blessed with the *opposite* of social anxiety.

We'd even had a reprieve on the last days of Passover. Rachel gave a presentation at social work school, which she told us had gone well. She looked forward to catching up with Sheera, who was en route to Baltimore by train for the last days of Passover. The two girls' bond had continued to deepen, and with each visit, Sheera seemed more like extended family.

When the holiday began, of course, Rachel also had to put up with a revolving door of visitors. Magnificent weather enticed every-one to get out and visit. Every time we wanted to venture out, another friend would knock on our door. The visits, constant as they were, as always, boosted our spirits.

Once again, we'd been spared a Passover crisis. There had been plenty of coughing, but Rachel had socialized her heart out and even felt well enough for me to take her to shul via wheelchair. She received a warm public welcome from Rabbi Silber. By the time the holiday ended, I was utterly spent but greatly relieved and happier than I'd expected. Would we finally get a reprieve? *Could our girl continue to live this way, even with no apparent response to treatment?*

As always, the ups and downs continued. Rachel's prolonged coughing fits led to shortness of breath, robbing her face of color. At times she looked so defeated that I felt sure we'd need to rush to the hospital again. And the look on her face appeared so forlorn that I felt a profound sadness for her—and for us all.

But then, come morning, Rachel would rally. We clung to our routines. She'd work all day on an assignment, taking a couple of breaks in between. At night, I continued to read *The Very Hungry Caterpillar* to her. And, during the day, seeing the intensity on her face while tackling her assignments made me think of another book whose persona she'd unwittingly embodied: *The Little Engine That Could.*

Judah, meanwhile, reworked his schedule, so he could take her to chemo, which would sap much of what was left of her strength and turn her into a rag doll.

Television and games continued to be helpful distractions. One night during this turbulent time, we played an online game called "Re-Mission," where you get to shoot cancer cells. Of course, Rachel loved this.

She'd also treated herself to another wig—more blonde and lighter in weight. Jumping at the chance to boost her spirits even more, that evening, I dashed over to Old Navy to buy Rachel a few things for the warmer weather. I found a cute, green maxi dress with a ruffled top and flowers—a throwback to the fashions I'd loved as a teenager. While I was out, I ran a few more errands I'd been putting off.

Getting out of the house to tackle mundane errands seemed like a reprieve. But the restlessness in my heart would surface regularly; the panic that something worse was about to happen to Rachel.

And for good reason: Dr. A. seemed more concerned about Rachel's coughing. He asked Rachel to collect some sputum in a sterile plastic container for the lab. It took only moments for Rachel to produce enough *shuchas* for me to bring to Hopkins the next morning for analysis.

After Rachel went up to bed, Judah lingered with me in the kitchen. We locked eyes. I could feel mine starting to moisten. His pale blue eyes, the ones our daughter had inherited, blazed. Then he uttered five words I will never forget: *"Something's going on with her."*

And still, Rachel refused to surrender hope. She kept rereading the letter from the director of the National Association of Social Workers inviting her to speak at the 2012 conference on hope from a young adult's perspective. She was so excited and wasted no time preparing her remarks:

> *Although mortality rates for pediatric and older adult cancer patients have steadily decreased in the last few years, young adults with cancer have seen no improvement. This is often due to lack of insurance, late diagnoses and a feeling of being invincible that keeps them from going to a doctor. I hope, one day, to make people more aware of this often-underserved population.*
>
> *I would love to say that my cancer nightmare has concluded, but after several relapses, I am still fighting. But I now have a new life goal. Having just completed my*

second semester at the University Maryland School of
Social Work, I am determined to complete my degree and
assist other young adults facing cancer.

There was no denying that Rachel's fatigue was getting worse. That week, despite her exhaustion, we had to keep a follow-up appointment for a mammogram with Peggy, a friend of mine from book club, who also happened to be the chief radiologist at Green Spring Station, where Johns Hopkins doctors have offices.

It turned out that the suspicious lump hadn't changed in size, but the calcifications were worrisome. There was a two percent chance they could be cancerous, Peggy informed us. We could either do nothing and schedule follow-up mammograms every six months, or do a mammo-guided needle biopsy.

Peggy told Rachel that with everything she'd been through, she didn't have to do anything at that point. The relief on Rachel's face was visible. I suspected that's how we would proceed, and, in six months, if the mammogram was worrisome again, we would schedule a biopsy. Judah was inclined to agree with that approach.

Time and time again, we—and anyone who heard about what Rachel was going through—were in awe of Rachel's resilience. But hearing people tell her how inspired they were by Rachel became increasingly hard for her to accept. In public, she'd smile and thank people for their kind words. But in private, she unleashed what had by now become a Pavlovian response: "I don't want to be amazing anymore! I just want to be a normal, healthy 27-year-old."

Who could argue with that? Yet I couldn't help but acknowledge, at least to myself, that she *was* incredibly, *amazing*ly resilient.

In the days that followed, Rachel's coughing fits and fatigue intensified. She produced more of those horrible green *shuchas,* enough sputum for me to capture in a plastic container and bring in for lab analysis at Hopkins. If all that weren't enough, her itching returned.

I was feeling scared all over again. Judah's angst was also intensifying. Before hitting my pillow for the night, I grabbed a pen, my head swirling with conflicting emotions.

4/22/12

I know what he's thinking,
But I don't dare ask.
No need anyway.
I'm well aware of how sick she is.
But optimism is her strongest medicine.
Its elixir benefits us all,
I like to think.
Besides, what's the point of living
Without hope?
Yes, I mourn for the vibrancy that never flagged.
For the career derailed by sudden illness.
For the relationships that couldn't morph into
A lifetime commitment.
For the friends she lost to coupling.
For the grandchildren we can't have right now.
And yet I rejoice
For her resilience
For her joie de vivre
For her existence.

Two days after I wrote those words, Judah's father died at an assisted living facility in Riverdale, New York. He was 89. We were deeply saddened by the news but forced to turn our focus to Rachel, who had coughed for more than two straight hours, delivering dreaded green *shuchas* into tissues. The wastebasket we'd placed next to the couch in the den filled quickly, and I braced myself for a challenging, emotionally charged week.

Soon, loved ones with long faces paraded into the house. Josh and Niti arrived at around 5; I didn't return home from work until 6. I would have left immediately upon hearing the news, but I'd already taken off so much time because of Rachel's health and my own health problems. I rationalized that the loss of Judah's father was truly sad but not unexpected, given his age and medical conditions.

Shortly after I came home, Rabbi Silber arrived to express his condolences, talk about the funeral and review the laws of *shiva*. Sam and Nikki came over, and we ate dinner on the deck, commiserating about our loss. I was surprised and relieved to see that Rachel consumed one-and-a-half mushroom calzones and then returned to her computer, pecking out a paper for one of her classes. But I also heard intermittent coughing.

The funeral for my father-in-law proved uplifting. Rabbi Silber spoke, capturing Dad's persona: understated—a man of few words, but with a steady reliability. He'd been a devoted husband to Bootsie and, much later, for a decade, to Ida. Mickey Minkove had been deeply supportive of the synagogue, serving as president at one point, and always made sure anything in the shul that needed fixing got taken care of, even when it was inconvenient. And he was blessed to have lived long enough to welcome 10 grandchildren and seven great-grandchildren to the family.

Yet he'd remained worldly, too. He'd served overseas during

World War II, and always started his day by reading the newspaper cover to cover, before donning tefillin for morning prayers. Born into a poor family in a row house in East Baltimore, the youngest of 10, he'd been an electrician with little secondary education. But he devoted his life to family—oh, how he'd adored Bootsie, who'd died so young! I was struck early on by how much he'd also loved her family. Of course, I'd felt the same way upon meeting them.

Jon spoke at the funeral, and his words echoed the rabbi's, his voice cracking as he described his Saba (or "Sabs," as Jon had lovingly nicknamed him). "He was a man of few words but a constant kind of force," he said. I was touched and proud of Jon for sharing those poignant remembrances. I kept thinking about how frightened I was by my father-in-law the first time I'd met him because he was so quiet. It wouldn't take me long to realize that he was just naturally reserved and preferred to let his loquacious wife and her family to do most of the talking.

Rachel had trouble suppressing her cough during the funeral, especially outside at the cemetery. Someone had kindly set up a chair for her near the grave. It frightened me to see her taking in this sad moment in such a fragile state. But overall, she fared remarkably well. Rachel, too, had adored her Saba. And, though he hadn't verbalized it, I knew he loved her, too.

I'd forgotten how difficult sitting shiva can be: being confined to the living room and kitchen, receiving guests, repeating stories over and over again. Yet it was incredibly comforting to hear people recount their own experiences with my father-in-law. Throughout that week, Rachel was either asleep, doing homework or in class—intermittently joining us as people came by. Her cough punctuated every conversation. After taking a couple of days off from work, I returned to my office, helping out with meals and receiving visitors when I got home every day.

As we counted down to Shavuot, the holiday that commemorates the giving of the Torah at Mt. Sinai, Rachel became obsessed with her latest mission. She was determined to convince us that we desperately needed to get away to Florida for the holiday. Sheera's parents had a condo in Miami where we could stay and walk on the beach, and had kindly invited us to stay there. The idea had merit: We all desperately needed a break from our grueling routine. And, she reminded us, we wouldn't have to miss much work: In 2012, Shavuot coincided with Memorial Day Weekend.

Touched by Rachel's thoughtfulness and Sheera's family's generosity, I wanted to make it happen. But Judah thought it was a bad idea, being that far away from the hospital where Rachel was receiving care. *Hadn't we learned how vulnerable Rachel was?* He voiced his concerns to her more than a few times, but Rachel was determined to change his mind, remaining adamant. My eyes welled up, and so did Rachel's. Judah pushed back, but she was having none of it.

One night, after I helped Rachel edit a social work paper she'd written, she confessed that she was looking into flights to Miami, no matter how much Judah objected. I remember thinking that this was a good sign. She was always making plans and living every day to the fullest. Yet I wondered, *Did she have any idea just how fragile she was?* The arguments between Rachel and Judah continued. His face became a study in angst. He wasn't sleeping well either. And so, I began to worry as much about his health as our daughter's. How much more could his heart take?

And yet ... here we were, in the middle of May 2012, wondering how Rachel managed to have driven herself to her CT appointment, gotten her eyebrows dyed and then headed to Staples for padded envelopes to mail her schoolbooks she hoped to sell on Amazon. On a whim, she'd called her friend Mira about meeting for lunch. Rachel scarfed down an entire veggie cheese wrap. She'd also received CT scan results forwarded from Dr. A. with the subject line: "Looks pretty good." There was a new "infiltrate" in her lung, and she still had a fractured rib, but nothing too worrisome showed up.

The trip to Florida for Shavuot became Rachel's Holy Grail. We watched her redouble her efforts to stay healthy and active. She started walking with Judah around the track, and, when she felt up to it, she accompanied him to shul to say *kaddish* and studied hard for her courses. On Mother's Day an e-card popped up in my box:

> *Dear Mommy,*
> *Happy Mother's Day to the best mommy in the world.*
> *I am so lucky to have you as my mom. I apologize for*
> *not getting a tangible card, but I ran out of energy the*
> *other day. I just wanted to tell you I love you, and I can't*
> *imagine having a better mom!*
> *You're the best Mom ever!*
> *Love,*
> *Scootchy [one of several silly nicknames I'd given her:*
> *She used to say "Scootch over" whenever she wanted*
> *someone to make room for her on the couch.]*

Those sentiments blew me away. Our girl's love was boundless, and she wanted so much for us to get a break.

In the end, we caved. We let Rachel book a flight to Miami for all three of us. I beseeched God to let us go in good health. *Please let us go, and give this girl some joy and an escape from her grueling routine! It would do us all good*, I convinced myself. Judah was seething, but outnumbered.

By then, spring was in full bloom. Sunday, May 20, 2012, was a glorious day—perfect weather for the Jewish Caring Network (JCN) fundraising 5K/run/walk, to be held in Druid Hill Park. It was also Judah's birthday. My dear friends/college roommates Cheryl and Leah had come in for the weekend to contribute to the cause and to accompany me for the walk. Many other friends joined us, as well. Rachel, of course, couldn't muster the walk. But our friend Barb kindly offered to bring her to the zoo to celebrate at the end. Clusters of flowers and trees brightened our view, fueling hope.

As people finished walking or running, Rachel slowly made her way to the megaphone. Suddenly, our girl flashed her megawatt smile and thanked JCN for all the moral support and kindnesses the organization had bestowed on our family. The race raised $80,000 for the Tikva House, a rowhouse JCN had purchased near Johns Hopkins Hospital for families in need of housing over Shabbat or holidays, as loved ones received treatment at the hospital.

Feeling celebratory, we headed to Goldberg's Bagels for lunch. Rachel devoured a Mexican veggie cheese wrap. But she experienced a painful episode of neuropathy in her feet. Between bites, she could no longer hide her discomfort. "Ow, ow, *ow!*" she said, stretching her legs to the side.

Judah's face turned crimson. I knew he was stewing about our plans to go to Florida. And still, at least on that beautiful day, I willed myself to stay positive. I took it as a good sign to have learned that same day that Ethan Zohn, from *Survivor*, was now getting better after taking SGN-35 and receiving a bone marrow transplant from his brother.

A few days before we left for Miami, I received a text from Rachel:

I got 100 on my midterm.

Of course, I wasn't surprised, but she so needed that. The research course she was taking was making her nuts. The teacher was tough on everyone, and Rachel hadn't expected anything higher than a B. If a B were the worst thing that happened to her, I could live with that, and I was sure Rachel felt the same way. *If only grades were the biggest stressor facing her,* I thought.

But I also wanted so badly for her to get a break, and was thrilled to see that perfect score validating her hard work.

Anxiety about the planned trip to Miami had begun to consume me, though I didn't verbalize it to Rachel. In private, Judah kept telling me it was a terrible idea. My journal captures our angst.

> 5/24/12
>
> Rach has a terrible stomachache. She's very constipated, but, of course, on the day before our trip, we're worried that it could be something worse. Not that this is so great. She can barely walk, and she's wiped out from this intense week of classes.
>
> Yet she seems to really like the teacher and is getting to know the 11 classmates—they're becoming friends.
>
> Sure hope we can make the trip to Miami tomorrow.
>
> 5/25/12
>
> We're in Judah's car en route to the airport. WBAL is blaring. Dave Lefkowitz is driving—he'll hold onto our car for the long weekend. Rach is sitting next to me in the back seat, looking green. She's still constipated and can't pee. Judah shot her an exasperated look this morning, as if to repeat what he said yesterday: "This is why I can't make plans."
>
> Rach ate some Honey Nut Cheerios and took a "fizzly bubbly" laxative last night. Hope she can go to the bathroom at the airport. It's drizzling, and traffic is stacked up on I-695.
>
> Memorial Day weekend is off to a bumpy start for lots of other

people, too. Just hope God will give us a break and let us all enjoy
this long-awaited, much-deserved vacation. Please, God?

From the moment we arrived in Miami and headed to Boca, some 45 minutes away, Rachel was clutching her belly. She couldn't go to the bathroom. Laxatives couldn't penetrate whatever blockage she was experiencing.

We tried our best to enjoy celebrating Shavuot with Sheera and her parents, but Rachel's discomfort had become unbearable. Clutching her distended belly, Rachel made her way to the couch. Even during the best of times with Rachel, I worried about her health, but now I was really getting scared. At this point, we were beyond feeling any embarrassment about Rachel's need to keep running to the bathroom. In between those mad dashes, she laid on the couch, too exhausted to participate in conversation. There was no question that Rachel's worsening state soured the long-awaited holiday visit, even though Sheera and her parents could not have been more supportive.

Dread engulfed us, but we knew we needed to act quickly. We called Dr. A., who told us to take the next available flight home and head straight to Hopkins. We had no choice but to travel on Shavuot. Because it was Memorial Day weekend, there were only a few seats left on the flight—two together in first class and one in coach. Judah decided that Rachel and I should take the first-class seats.

Stooped over in a wheelchair as we rushed to the gate, our girl was clearly in agony, devoid of color, shivering and utterly exhausted. As we got settled, Rachel couldn't get warm. I shed my denim jacket and draped it over her thin shoulders By then, all the color had drained from our shrinking girl's face.

When I asked the stewardess for a blanket, she responded that they didn't have any. Incredulous, I responded something like, "You're kidding me, right? My daughter is not well, and she can't get warm!"

She offered a perfunctory apology, then headed down the aisle. My pleas to another flight attendant also proved worthless, so I cuddled with Rachel to keep her warm, with hours until landing.

Finally, we arrived—via taxi—at Hopkins at around 5 p.m. A room on Weinberg 4B was ready for Rachel. By 8:30 p.m., she'd had a line and feeding tube placed. Though these were painful procedures, Rachel clearly felt relieved that she was finally getting treated. So were we, of course, but it was becoming increasingly more difficult to hide our fears.

Dr. Braunstein, who was filling in for Dr. Ambinder, pointed out that while, as we knew, SGN-35 could cause neuropathy, it could also spread to the GI tract and cause paralysis/intestinal blockage in the gut. (Later, Judah told me he'd suspected this all along.) Rachel would need nutrition and fluid via an IV and possibly a nasogastric tube, from the nose and into the stomach, to remove what was in her belly and to prevent more pain.

Meanwhile, her emotional state was plummeting. She begged us to take her home. But they wouldn't let her, so I decided to sleep over for a couple of nights. At one point, I saw Rachel's eyes rolling, and her pallor turned scarier than ever. She was in agony. I actually thought at that moment that she was slipping away from this world. Panicked, I yelled for help and buzzed for a nurse, who gave Rachel a sedative. By the second night in that unit, Rachel looked utterly defeated. I grabbed my journal and wrote furiously, desperate to document her experience.

> 5/31/12
> Hopes were dashed after Judah left at around 10:30. Rachel
> started throwing up, and her platelets dropped to 12,000. She has

bruises all over her arms. And she still has a lot of belly pain. Her liver enzymes are elevated. The doctors ordered an ultrasound.

It took an agonizing two weeks for Rachel's caregivers to determine that disseminated herpes zoster virus had invaded Rachel's organs. Evidence finally emerged in the form of small pustules on her forehead, which soon spread to her arms. During rounds one morning, I said aloud to Dr. Shoham, "This kind of looks like chickenpox, doesn't it?" Instantly, his typically low-key demeanor darkened, as he nodded in agreement. I would soon learn that "herpes zoster" is the medical term for chickenpox. Shingles—the acutely painful inflammation of nerve ganglia that causes a skin eruption—is caused by the same virus as chickenpox.

The too-familiar severe itching resurfaced with a vengeance. Wincing, I recalled that anytime I heard about a person suffering with "shingles," the words "incredibly painful" would follow. Rachel had had chickenpox as a child, but, as I would learn, even if you've had that affliction, the virus lies inactive in nerve tissue near your spinal cord and brain. Years later, the virus may reactivate as shingles.

At this juncture, Rachel's poor body appeared to be incapable of fighting the infection. We felt defeated and helpless: Our girl was in agony, unable to find relief.

And suddenly, there was a flurry of activity. The infection that likely began in Rachel's pancreas, we learned, was rapidly heading for her lungs.

CHAPTER 15

Final Gifts

O n June 5, 2012—Sam's 26th birthday—it became obvious that Rachel could no longer breathe on her own. Watching Rachel gasp for air made me think of watching someone drown from a distance. Judah and I felt utterly helpless in what had become our ocean of grief. Rachel's translucent eyes beseeched us to stay close. She needn't have worried. We were glued to her at this point.

Seconds before being sedated and intubated, between staccato breaths, she mustered the strength to yell, "I'm coming back! I know you're sick of me, but I'm coming back." As we sat there, terrified that her condition would soon overwhelm her and end her life, she added, as though reading our minds, "You've been such great parents. I love you."

Those would be the last words we'd hear her utter. As they wheeled Rachel into the unit's ICU room, Sam let out a primal cry. It reminded me of a shofar—a wake-up call that we needed to savor these likely final moments with our precious daughter. We told Rachel how amazing she was and how much we love her. I told her to hang tough and dream about the beach.

By 11 p.m., Rachel was barely recognizable. Now connected to the ventilator in the ICU-equipped room on Weinberg 5, she was all puffed up, covered with chickenpox on her face, arms and scalp. We knew our time together was running out, but it wasn't clear just how much longer she could survive.

During the two-month-long hospitalization that followed, the reality of Rachel's decline felt like a sucker-punch. We knew she was withering away, but we could only connect with our eyes. Our poor girl was unable to speak. Rachel's dear friends Sheera and Jessica had come in from LA to visit her, lift her spirits and to let Rachel know how much she meant to them.

It was becoming increasingly difficult to watch our girl deteriorate with each passing day. She was exhausted. But she perked up a little when I read her *The Very Hungry Caterpillar* and turned on the musical mobile with the Eric Carle-inspired butterfly and flowers. The ritual did us both good.

In the beginning, Rachel could communicate only by pointing to magnetic letters. One day, Rachel seemed desperate to ask me a question that took me a long while to decipher as she tried to mouth the words. Finally, I thought I'd figured it out. I repeated the words that I believed she was asking: "Am I making sense?" She nodded as vigorously as she could: a minor victory. I assured Rachel that she was making sense, but suddenly felt an overwhelming ache. I could tell she was afraid she was losing her grip—her sanity—and descending into another sphere. It was hard to choke back my tears. I began to play CDs with her favorite music. And there were moments when she did rally, especially when she heard Sheera, Talia or Erica on her phone and when they visited. Rabbi Silber also visited often.

To our surprise, during the first few weeks of Rachel's crisis, Dr. Ambinder remained upbeat. "I'm one of the few who's optimistic," he'd say, his words paining me. But efforts to get Rachel off the ventilator ultimately failed. She actually breathed on her own for 25 minutes one day, during one of her spontaneous breathing trials—the first stage of weaning her off life support, wherein her caregivers unhook the respirator to see how long she could go without gasping and safely breathe on her own. Ultimately, though, she simply didn't have the strength to get through any more than one of these.

Our friends and family, meanwhile, came for brief visits, often bringing home-cooked meals. And our phones, which we rarely answered, were filling up with loving messages.

On June 29, 2012, Mother Nature struck Baltimore and the mid-Atlantic region with a derecho, a large, fast-moving series of thunderstorms with powerful, destructive winds. It's often preceded and accompanied by extreme heat. For five consecutive days that week, the temperature outside climbed as high as 100 degrees.

By the time the devastating storms ended, some 26 hours later, the derecho had killed at least 29 people and caused $19 million in damage. Although it did not affect the hospital's power, our power at home was out for more than a week. In a way, the disaster seemed Biblical, as if God was trying to send us a message.

Rachel's friend Jessica had come in from LA to visit Rachel, and stayed at Liz and David's house.

Without air conditioning, the temperature upstairs in our house became so unbearably hot that we had to relocate to the basement to sleep. We actually found ourselves looking forward to heading to the hospital, so we could experience the relief air conditioning brought.

But that was hardly enough to soothe our spirits, as Rachel's health continued to plummet. The pustules on her body were multiplying, and she was itching like crazy, twitching her head and wanting to scratch but unable to, having been rendered immobile. Medically, as Judah explained, the intubation had caused her muscles to atrophy—typical in an ICU scenario. The weakness and neuropathy were so profound that she simply didn't have the strength to move very much. The worst part of it all was not being able to hear her sweet voice.

One day, as the shingles overtook her liver, enlarging and distorting our beautiful girl, Rich Ambinder ushered us into a conference room. Running his hands through his hair, he looked utterly defeated. "I'm afraid there's nothing more we can do for Rachel," he said, "and there's not a single person involved in her care who isn't heartbroken." We were deeply touched—albeit pained—by his words.

All that preparation Rachel had done for her talk at the NASW conference was for naught. She was inconsolable and mouthed the words, "I want to go!" It was then that I noticed yet another cruelty: Rachel looked as though she was crying, but no tears emerged. I realized that shingles had likely caused paralysis of her tear ducts.

The next day, July 26, Rachel was barely responsive. Lacy recalls going into Rachel's room, "and I just sort of acknowledged that things weren't working out the way she wanted—that this was the way her life was going to end," she told me. "It was a Friday, and I remember asking her if she wanted to go home. She said *yes* with her eyes. I just knew she wanted to be home for the Sabbath." Lacy set the wheels in motion, bringing in staff from Hopkins' fledgling palliative care unit.

Rachel was open, honest and "real," recalls Lacy. "Her authenticity fostered connections in return—connections of caring, respect and love. It was wordless; it 'leaked out' with a glance and a smile on

Rachel's face. And I hope she saw it in mine." Lacy also told us how grateful she was to feel this bond with Rachel and our family.

Though unable to speak, Rachel beseeched us with her eyes to take her home, confirming what Lacy told us. I prayed that Rachel would survive until the arrangements could be made and that we could settle her there safely.

Again, following her lead, we *adjusted* our hopes.

The palliative care team isn't in the habit of sending home people on ventilators. It takes many hours to orchestrate; things can easily go terribly wrong. In fact, neither Lacy nor Dr. Ambinder had ever seen it done. But once the team learned Rachel wanted to go home, they mobilized to fulfill her wish, lining up a portable respirator. Swiftly, and with extraordinary compassion, Gilchrist Hospice, our house-keeper and our dear friends rushed to set up our den.

We met with Lacy, the palliative care team and local hospice people to go over what to expect. A numbness had swept over me. Lynn, a nurse and palliative care pain specialist, reassured us that the team was committed to getting Rachel home and managing her pain.

During that surreal two-month hospitalization—I later came to realize—we were connected to a staff that cocooned us in kindness. I recall how freely tears flowed among them and that kindnesses abounded. Rachel's caregivers were open with their compassion, but not so emotional as to cross a line that would leave us raw.

There was Meghan, the clinical technician, who kept Rachel company in the middle of the night and polished Rachel's nails when she couldn't sleep. Tracy, the unit's director, who knew to arrange a massage for her, one with the gentlest, gradual, compression over her body. Dalal, then the senior vice president of Johns Hopkins Medicine Marketing and Communications, who not only supported me emotionally, but had "adopted" the entire oncology unit; visiting often, arranging massages, and asking colleagues on our marketing team to keep Rachel in their prayers. Most every day, Dalal showed up long enough to wish us courage, with both words and hugs.

And there was Karen, the night nurse supervisor and member of our synagogue, who asked me if I wanted her to explain to Rachel what happens physically as you die. I couldn't muster enough emotional strength to admit how close the end was; I still prayed for a miracle. But I told Karen, *yes, please do.*

The next morning, I saw a calmness on Rachel's face I hadn't seen before. I even perceived a smile. At the foot of her bed lay a colorful, oversized scarf Karen left for her. And then we found a handwritten note from Terry Langbaum, then administrator of the Johns Hopkins Kimmel Cancer Center, and a Hodgkin's lymphoma survivor.

> Dear Rachel,
>
> I understand that you will be going home, and I didn't want you to leave without sharing a few thoughts.
>
> First, I consider you to be one of my heroes. You are brave, strong and full of spirit. You face adversity with grace and you put others first. Rachel, you have the life skills of someone who has lived a long and wonderful life.
>
> You are loved, unconditionally, by your family and by your friends and those that care for you and know you in Hopkins' family. We have all learned from you and your parents—about love, compassion, and about living well for the days we are given.
>
> We meet many people on our journey through life. Only a few teach us to be better people, and Rachel, you are one of those.
>
> With great admiration,
>
> Terry

And so, despite myriad challenges, a miraculous feat had occurred: Rachel spent the final two days of her life—including Shabbat, the day of rest—at home among her loved ones. She died on Sunday morning, July 29, 2012, which happened to fall on Tisha B'Av—the saddest day on the Jewish calendar. She was 28.

At around 9 a.m. that morning, Rachel's breathing had become labored. We were with her in the den but had stepped out of the room momentarily. I don't recall why. But when we returned, she was gone. It was almost as if she'd waited for us to leave. And yet, even though we knew her death was imminent, we were overcome with grief. To this day, it is still so overwhelming that I'm unable to express what that moment felt like for me and Judah. Of course, Jon and Sam were also devastated.

Rachel was buried at 4 p.m. that same day. Rabbi Silber arrived at our house shortly after she'd passed away. He was visibly shaken and expressed his deepest condolences. Then, patiently, he went over the mourning rites. He wanted to make sure we understood how things would proceed. The morticians from Sol Levinson Funeral Home had arrived less than a half-hour after Rachel died. It was surreal to see a hearse parked in front of our house. The men were kind and efficient, yet extraordinarily gentle and attentive to our grief.

We sobbed as we said our final goodbyes to Rachel before they covered the casket with a velvet cloth, emblazoned with a gold Jewish star. I thought I would pass out watching the hearse leave our block. Our neighbors respected our privacy, but I knew some of our dear friends were shaken as they watched the spectacle. We later learned that one of them had fainted.

That old adage is true: There's really nothing worse than burying a child. And yet … there was some modicum of peace in knowing that finally, our beautiful girl was no longer suffering.

Looking back, I can still conjure the audible sobbing as people filed into Sol Levinson's Funeral Home for Rachel's late-afternoon, Tisha B'Av funeral. Row after row filled quickly. Soon there were no seats left in the oversized chapel. The back door had to be held open to accommodate latecomers.

More than 900 people attended Rachel's funeral, among them Jane Diaz, Rich Ambinder, Lacy Fetting, Terry Langbaum and oncology chaplain Rhonda Cooper. Rabbi Silber spoke eloquently for 40 minutes. He was shuckling throughout, overcome with emotion, as he recalled how sick Rachel was but how she insisted on learning Torah with him and smiling through that time together. Then, each member of our immediate family spoke. I was so moved by each perspective and the love that fueled those heartfelt reflections on Rachel's extraordinary life.

The hour-and-a-half service unfolded with moving tributes from each of us. We knew the hardest part was about to come. We had no choice but to steel ourselves so that people could hear our words and learn as much as possible about our wondrous girl, whose life was cut short.

What came through in every remembrance on that unforgettable Tisha B'Av was this: Our beautiful daughter lived only 28 years, but she managed to teach us and everyone she touched about the power of resilience and hope. Judah said it best at the end of his eulogy, "In other words, she taught us how to live." She also taught us how to die—yes, fighting with every fiber left of her being to survive, but accepting her fate and allowing us to envelop her in a final collective embrace.

After the service, we entered the hearse with Rachel's body. We felt a wave of comfort accompanying us from the scores of people

Rachel touched. We scooted into (*scootched*, Rachel would have said, in her strong Baltimore accent) the plush leather seats, absorbing our strange new reality, numbed by grief.

Seconds later, something caught our eyes simultaneously: A goose had sauntered directly in front of the vehicle. We let out a collective gasp, then a laugh. I've always had ambivalent feelings about reincarnation, but it struck all of us in that moment, that one of Rachel's pet nicknames had been "Silly Goose," which later simply became "The Goose." She'd always been always so playful.

My eyes welled up when I saw the incredulous look on my bereft guys' faces. Then my voice cracked as I uttered something I knew we were all thinking simultaneously: "It's Rachie!"

That moment is seared into our hearts. We've recalled it many times since then to remind ourselves that it actually happened. Nevertheless, the grim reality of the imminent burial made me shudder. We looked out the coated windows, amazed and touched once more by the hordes of people walking somberly, wiping tears. Many of them followed us to the cemetery. So much love our girl generated.

Rabbi Silber gently guided us through the rituals before the undertakers lowered the coffin into the ground. The scene was surreal, forever etched into our collective memories. My boys took turns shoveling the dirt over the casket. The sound reverberated in my ears, its finality utterly shocking. I knew it was a mitzvah to blanket her casket with dirt, the ultimate gift to a loved one. But I couldn't bring myself to participate. It felt all wrong—*horribly* wrong. I simply watched, in awe of my guys' strength, hoping God would forgive me for opting out of this sacred rite.

When the coffin was finally covered, the rabbi led us in the *Kaddish* prayer. A numbness swept over me. Shock, grief, anger, love, gratitude for family and friends: I felt all these things simultaneously.

But what choice did we have? Our girl got the regal funeral she so deserved. Small comfort, yes, but it's something.

Shiva—the Hebrew word for seven, signifying a week of mourning—is truly an out-of-body experience. It's a warm blanket of love emerging from kind, loving visitors from near and far paying their respects. Many shared uplifting stories about Rachel. Others who came simply felt obligated to pay their respects.

The *Kaddish* prayer we said in unison acknowledged our gratitude to God for Rachel's existence. After each morning, afternoon and evening prayer gatherings, in one unified pained voice, we uttered the devotional mourner's *Kaddish*, "*Yisgadal v'yiskadash shemay rabbah* …" "Glorified and hallowed is God's great name …"

Certain moments stand out from that sacred time. On the day after the funeral, a young woman we'd never met before walked in. She stepped confidently into our living room waving a condolence card.

"Hi," she said. "My name is Miesha. You don't know me, but I was in Rachel's class in social work school. My mom died of cancer, and I'm fighting it now myself. There were Sunday nights when I thought I didn't have the strength to make to school the next day. But then, all I had to do was picture Rachel—weak as she was and coughing a lot—sitting in class with a big smile on her face and participating in discussions. I thought to myself, *If she can do it, so can I.*"

We were speechless, awestruck. But we found our tongues and thanked her profusely. I was delighted to realize that it was around dinner time, and we invited her to join us. Incredibly, through a mutual friend discovered through working on this book, I was able to track Miesha down recently. We had a delightful lunch at Goldberg's.

I learned that Miesha at that point worked for the State's Attorney's Office as a social worker and still thinks of Rachel often. Miesha has informed me that she's going to be part of a documentary, titled *Hush*, which focuses on mental health in the Black community.

There would be many more standout moments from that intense week of shiva: people who traveled great distances to comfort us; daily deliveries of condolence letters and donation acknowledgments in Rachel's memory.

Rachel, our beautiful butterfly, died on the saddest day on the Jewish calendar. Yet *Tisha B'Av* is the very same date that the rabbis predict the arrival of *Moshiach* (the Messiah) to deliver us all from our earthly chains—the grueling hardships, illness and dashed hopes that occur daily in this world. I do believe that God and Rachel were trying to send us a message of hope.

There's no denying that we miss our beautiful daughter/sister/sister-in-law terribly. Yet Rachel remains present in so many peoples' lives and in myriad ways. With this memoir, I aimed to honor the way-too-short life of an extraordinary girl, whose ripples will no doubt inspire people for generations to come. Our beloved Rachel, of blessed memory, deserves nothing less.

Epilogue/Ripples

It's been 11 years since Rachel died; 15 years since she was diagnosed. So much has changed in the world, in our world, too. Yet I feel her presence daily—in every blue sky, which reminds me of her crystalline eyes, and the accompanying sunshine, conjuring her electric smile. We all carry her spirit with us in our own, often unspoken, ways.

About 10 days after Rachel died, as the temperature topped 95 degrees, Sam and I drove to Rita's for flavored ices—one of our first outings since Rachel died. We found a bench outside and sat down, the scorching sun nearly blinding us.

As we reminisced about Rachel, a beautiful Monarch butterfly suddenly darted between us and then flitted around nearby for a few seconds. Sam and I instantly exchanged a smile, wiping tears as we made the connection. Since then, other signs of her presence or unexpected human connections have offered hope that her spirit thrives.

Thankfully, Rachel continues to send us messages. I still grapple with faith and probably will until my final days. I've come to realize that sooner or later all humans will struggle with their faith—through all kinds of challenges. But some traumas are impossible to reconcile. All I can say is that opening myself up to hope has provided tremendous comfort.

In July 2019, on the 25th anniversary of Tour De Court, another butterfly flitted around us. This one was black with two patches of blue at the bottom of its wings. Ultimately, it settled on a spot on the black pavement, moving its wings slowly. I felt its eyes locking onto mine. The light blue patches on its wings captivated me. I had no doubt that our girl had made a cameo appearance again. Rachel must be so proud of her brothers, I thought, for their having raised more than $250,000 for blood cancer research.

Unexpected acts of loving kindness from the hospital staff and others Rachel had touched continued well after her death. Terry Langbaum sent us another letter on behalf of the cancer center, acknowledging the purchase of a block of Orioles tickets—one renewed every year in perpetuity—so that families staying near the main campus as loved ones underwent treatment could enjoy a ballgame in Rachel's memory. When I had lunch with Terry in 2019, a few months before Terry died from a recurrence of her cancer, she assured me those Orioles tickets have continued to provide a lift for families.

Rachel would be immortalized in a new social work textbook, titled *Hope Matters* (published in 2014), in a chapter on preserving hope for young adult oncology patients. Lacy Fetting and Corey Shdaimah, one of Rachel's social work professors, were co-authors. They attested to Rachel's resilience and determination to make things better for young adults with cancer. The book has become a source text for social work students.

In her introduction, Lacy compared Rachel's fortitude to that of Holocaust survivor's Viktor Frankl's. In his book *Man's Search for Meaning*, he wrote, "Everything can be taken from a man, but one thing." He went on to define that one thing as, "The last of the human freedoms—to choose one's attitude in any given set of circumstances" (p. 75).

Corey recalls an intensive summer course she taught that required students to spend four eight-hour days together, during which time they were asked to reveal personal information and motivations for their work. "Rachel made a deep impression on me," she says. "I am glad, together with Lacy, to have the opportunity to highlight Rachel's spirit and her contributions. Rachel wrote parts of an assignment from my course from the hospital and was determined to eventually use her research to make things better for others."

As for Rich Ambinder, he says it pains him that Rachel didn't live long enough to benefit from the advances in treatment for refractory Hodgkin's disease. "There's so much excitement about the new approaches," he says, and he's seen several patients go into remission. He envisions a day when chemo infusions won't be necessary as the first line of treatment—just a few pills to swallow. But, he adds, "It tears me up to lose patients; I have cried with many families."

He said he considered Rachel a model patient: always smiling, fully engaged but also instructive whenever she complained about what might have been handled better. In retrospect, I asked if he thought it was crazy to send Rachel home on a ventilator. He closed his eyes, then said, after some 30 seconds, "I didn't think it was crazy. I think part of our job is to help patients do what's in the realm of the possible. I just wasn't sure we were in that realm."

The ripples continue. Closest to home, there are now 11 little girls named after Rachel—including our two granddaughters. After a time, I rejoined Johns Hopkins Hospital's Patient and Family Advisory Council in hopes of applying some of what I learned from Rachel's long hospital stays. I also found myself overseeing the creation of a new patient and family handbook.

My sons have found their own ways to honor their sister's memory. Jon continues to ensure that Tour De Court stays relevant. Now an incorporated nonprofit, TDC continues to thrive. The annual event has raised enough money to set up a continuing portfolio to support Hodgkin's lymphoma research, as well as other supportive projects for young adults with debilitating illness in her honor. Jon and his wife, Elizabeth, also a lawyer, named their beautiful first child—our first grandchild—Sadie Rae (in Hebrew, Sivan Rachayl), now five; and they have a darling two-year-old son, named Jacob Mickey (Yochanan Mordechai).

When Jon and Elizabeth first started dating seriously, we learned about an incredible coincidence—or something I prefer to think of as the hand of God. One summer weekend in 2011, during the time of Rachel's treatment, Elizabeth had taken a train from New York to Baltimore to spend the Shabbat with her former Barnard roommate and Rachel's friend—Adena. It just so happened to be the same humid Shabbat that Adena had invited Rachel over to join them for Shabbat lunch. Judah and I recall having walked Rachel to Adena's apartment that day.

I asked Elizabeth if she remembered Rachel. "Of course!" she responded, unequivocally. "You don't forget someone like Rachel." I suddenly got choked up, feeling Rachel's spirit upon us. Yet it pained me that Rachel was robbed of the opportunity to participate in Jon and Elizabeth's wedding and to bond with their beautiful children.

For Sam, Rachel's illness inspired a direct commitment to patients and their families. He'd been a medical student, not yet graduated and unsure of a specialty area. We now realize that, beyond the intense concern for his sister, he was also taking in the medical lessons swirling around him throughout her illness and treatment.

In his application essay for his internal medicine residency, Sam wrote of the time his sister's shingles had eluded everyone:

> I had just completed my first year of medical school and had learned the basics of anatomy and physiology, as well the intricate pathways of biochemistry and neuroscience. But I felt utterly helpless. I had some knowledge but lacked clinical experience. I marveled at Rachel's team of primary doctors who would come up with a plan each morning to elucidate her condition, always keeping a broad differential. Nothing showed up on scans to explain the source of my sister's pain.
>
> I listened intently as the senior resident would explain the care team's collective thought process. "We have consulted with the gastroenterologists, and today we'll be performing a procedure called an ERCP." Or, "The infectious disease doctors and the oncologists are coming by today." "We ordered some tests that will tell us how her liver is functioning." Sadly, days passed, and we were left without a diagnosis. Rachel got sicker.
>
> Each day, my family, including my internist father, would rush to the hospital to be on time for morning rounds. What would be the plan today? What was the thought process? Ten long days later, Rachel broke out in a rash on her forehead. Finally, we learned that the lesions tested positive for herpes zoster, suggesting that the infection had begun internally and was disseminating—not following a textbook presentation. She fought for her life for ten weeks as shingles invaded her organs, ultimately causing liver failure. . . .
>
> I always knew I wanted to be a doctor. But Rachel's illness and death at 28 helped crystallize the kind of doctor I hope to become. As I watched clinicians care for her. . . they became role models— her true champions. Their approach left an indelible impression; they helped me realize how much I wanted to pursue a career in internal medicine.
>
> . . . The team carried our trust, guiding us through what to

expect to the very end. Even slight changes in her plan, like getting physical therapy involved or consulting with palliative care, instilled confidence.

Now, as a fourth-year medical student, when I see patients on the wards, I recall how much faith my family had in Rachel's primary care team, and I treat every patient as if they were my family. In each case, compassion and hard work guide me.

Today, Sam, who completed an internal medicine residency at the University of Maryland Medical Center, recently completed a fellowship in pulmonary medicine and critical care at The National Institutes of Health/Johns Hopkins Hospital. His fellowship included rotations on the Weinberg bone marrow transplant unit, where Rachel was and where he donated bone marrow to his sister. Several of her former nurses reconnected with him, remembering Rachel fondly. Sam also served on the COVID-19 unit during the height of the pandemic and was called back to assist at an affiliate hospital. He then returned to the NIH, studying the effect of COVID-19 on rats and mice and seeing patients in a pulmonary clinic. He is currently practicing pulmonary and critical care medicine at St. Joseph's Hospital in Baltimore.

Sam's wife, Nikki, also profoundly affected by Rachel's experience, completed her internal medicine residency at Johns Hopkins and went on to complete a fellowship in cardiology at the University of Maryland. She currently works in Judah's multi-specialty group as a cardiologist. In October of 2017, Sam and Nikki became parents of beautiful twins, Matthew Isaac and Rae Isabelle. (Rae's Hebrew name is "Rachayl Chaya," which means "Rachel lives"). Their youngest son, Simon Or, arrived in September of 2021.

As for me, enough time has passed to bring a rough sense of perspective, on occasion, on my daughter's life. The enormity of what she suffered hasn't yet dulled, but I'm comforted by realizing what must be eternal truths about her: Though Rachel's life ended tragically, she taught us and everyone around her how to live and how to love. And she was rewarded by being enveloped in love to the very end of her life.

I often find myself reliving the Shabbat after Thanksgiving 2019. Everyone is home. We've just finished lunch and, after cleaning up, have congregated to the den—all eight of us: Judah and I; Jon and Elizabeth and their precious children, two-year-old Sadie Rae, and Jacob Mickey (two months); Sam and Nikki and their two-year-old twins, Matthew Isaac and Rae Isabelle.

Seconds later, the floor morphs into an obstacle course: colorful blocks, books, stuffed animals and pull-toys. I let myself relax about the mess. It's happy clutter, created by squealing toddlers, except for newborn Jacob ("Jakey"). But soon enough, he will also become part of it.

I'm stretched out on the couch, resting my right leg as I recover from a knee replacement, which had taken place a week earlier. The pain remains intense: it awakens me several times every night. I wonder how much more discomfort I can take. But as I look around the room, joyful distractions abound. I'm reveling in the cuteness surrounding me—or, as the Yiddish term captures so beautifully— I'm *kvelling*. It is unbridled love.

Suddenly, a framed photo on an end table captures Rae's eye. She breaks into a smile, looks at me, then back to the picture and points to the thin, smiley girl standing between Judah and me. Then she exclaims, "That's Aunt Rachie!"

In that moment, I know our daughter's spirit has permeated the room. Then, Rae's slightly older cousin Sadie runs over to the table and repeats those three magical words.

And then, Rae points to Judah. "That's Saba!" she says. Her smile still strong, she points to the third person in the photo, meets my eyes and announces, "That's Savta!" Though she can't quite verbalize it, Rae seems to laugh at the realization that her Savta is both smiling in the photo and, in this moment, smiling back at her in real life.

I study the photo again, and I'm transported to that gorgeous fall day in 2010. Judah and Rachel and I were sitting on a bench just outside the Cancer Research Building at Hopkins, where the kosher food kiosk is located, eating lunch just after Rachel's treatment. Moments later, I spotted Keith, the kind, talented photographer I'd worked with for years on newsletter assignments. Schlepping his equipment, he walked toward us. "Hi, Judy!" he exclaimed. "Say, let me take a picture of the three of you!"

At first, Judah scoffed. "Nah, that's OK," he said. Instantly, I overruled him: "Sure—let's do it!" Rachel's hair had finally started growing back after the bone marrow transplant. Her dirty-blonde spiked pixie framed her face. The coral jacket draped around her shoulders provided a splash of color, brightening her pallor.

The sun made us squint, but all three of us fair-skinned adults—even Judah—flashed jubilant smiles. It's one of the happiest photos I'd ever seen of us, and the only one taken on the hospital campus.

A week later, Keith sent me several copies of the photos. Now, each of our sons has the identical photo framed in their living rooms. It was yet another example of a random act of kindness. What we didn't realize then was just how much joy—albeit tinged with pain—that photo would bring. It moves me to think about how many times my boys quiz their children: "Who are these people"?

So much has happened since that day at Hopkins. Despite their tender age, those babies epitomize resilience and vivaciousness. The twins were tiny miracles at birth: Rae weighed less than two pounds;

her brother, less than four pounds. They were in the neonatal intensive care unit for two months. But you'd never know it now. Rae has become obsessed with books and egging her brother on in playful ways. They are besties, and now proud older siblings to Simon.

Sadie, the oldest of the grandchildren, seems to have perfect pitch: After hearing a song just once, she belts it out on key, reminding me of her Aunt Rachie's gift for music. Sadie is also articulate and has a delightful imagination. Her younger brother, Jakey, has similar coloring and a sweet disposition and hangs on to Sadie's every word.

I've no doubt that these precocious children will keep their beautiful aunt's spirit, her *neshama*, alive. Their parents will make sure of that. Besides, it's already in their DNA: I see sparks of Rachel's persona in them whenever they get silly; when Sadie bursts into song; and, of course, whenever we read *The Very Hungry Caterpillar* together.

Afterword

BY DOUG ULMAN

I n the Jewish faith, hope isn't just a wishful longing. Hope, or *tikvah*, is about very real progress toward better days. We cling to hope as a sign of our belief that a brighter, better world is within reach.

Rachel Minkove never stopped hoping for better outcomes for adolescents and young adults (AYA) facing cancer. Nearly 15 years after her diagnosis, there have been dramatic improvements for the AYA population that would make Rachel proud: increased education, more access to fertility preservation and more widespread psychosocial support. Yet, there is still so much work to be done, as we improve the odds for young adults with cancer.

At the time of this publishing, 89,000 young adults continue to be diagnosed with cancer every year, representing just five percent of all cancer diagnoses. Despite advances in early detection, treatment and prevention, there has been no substantial improvement in survival rates since Rachel's diagnosis. In the wake of the COVID-19 pandemic, AYA patients are also reporting higher instances of significant barriers, including increased social isolation; a need for mental health support; challenges navigating the health care system; and the need for more help understanding a diagnosis. Rachel personally experienced many of these barriers—which fueled her desire to make people aware of the resources and support that the AYA population deserves.

As a young adult survivor, I can relate firsthand to Rachel's experience. I was just 19 years old and a rising sophomore at Brown University when I was first diagnosed with chondrosarcoma, a type of bone cancer that develops in cartilage cells. Almost overnight, I became someone else entirely. I was someone with cancer, facing a surgery that might lead to a future I would not recognize. After being diagnosed with cancer twice more that same year, I wondered if I could count on any future at all. Like Rachel, I was inspired to do more—and together with my parents, I founded a nonprofit to support other young survivors.

More than 25 years later, the Ulman Foundation still exists and is changing lives by creating a community of support for young adults and their loved ones impacted by cancer. The Foundation envisions a world where no young adult faces cancer alone and offers a myriad of programs—from dedicated AYA navigators to a new, 12,000 square foot "home away from home" for patients and their families receiving treatment in Baltimore. I am so proud of the Foundation's work, and my professional career has also taken me to organizations including the LIVESTRONG Foundation and Pelotonia, which are leading the charge in advocacy, survivorship and cancer research.

Today, Rachel's legacy continues to bring me hope. Sharing her powerful story and determined spirit through this book will inspire countless others, and I am so grateful to Judith and the entire Minkove family for including others in this very special project. Those of us touched by AYA cancer live with an urgency to ensure a brighter future for others—a future defined by hope, made possible through advocacy, and strengthened by a common goal. It is an honor to further this work that meant so much to Rachel.

Acknowledgments

Writing a memoir, I've discovered, can be agonizingly difficult—especially one centered on the loss of a loved one. When the words flowed, the experience was magical, like watching daybreak emerge on an overnight road trip. As a professional writer, I know this instinctively. But grief has its own rhythm. Reliving so many difficult moments from a time when our daughter's health was declining took a toll. There were days when I simply had to put the manuscript aside. Yet, somehow, I found the strength to persevere—just as my daughter had done.

My gratitude begins with God for bringing me to this juncture: to finally tell Rachel's story, even as I railed against Him for all the suffering she endured. That said, this memoir would never have come to fruition without the encouragement, input and moral support from dear friends, family, caregivers and colleagues. Over the course of Rachel's way-too-short life, our beautiful girl touched scores of people, many of whom remain in close touch with our family—truly a blessing.

Special thanks to the Johns Hopkins Sidney Kimmel Comprehensive Cancer Center staff, particularly: Rich Ambinder, Jane Diaz, Lacy Fetting, Carla Taylor, Amy DeZern, Shmuel Shoham, Karen Katz and Terry Langbaum (of blessed memory), for their extraordinary care and moral support, as well as Amy Mone, director of the center's public affairs; and Vanessa Wasta, Johns Hopkins science and medical writer.

I am also profoundly grateful to Stacey Goldenberg and the extraordinary volunteers at Jewish Caring Network, as well as Rabbi Shmuel Silber, for his moral and spiritual support, and his wife, Aviva, for her delicious cakes (true comfort food). Special thanks to Dr. Zipora Schorr, whose love for Rachel continues to touch us beyond words; as well as Rabbi Mitchell Wohlberg and Rachel's inspiring teachers at Beth Tfiloh. I also want to recognize the wonderful Gilchrist Hospice staff, for making Rachel as comfortable as possible during the last few days of her way-too-short life. We are also grateful for the Chevra Ahavas Chesed burial society and Sol Levinson Bros. for their holy work in preparing our beloved daughter for burial.

Our family, friends and neighbors who supported us throughout Rachel's illness remain treasures: Faith and Ed Wolf; Sandy and Aryeh Guttenberg; Mark and Diane Krasna; Janice and Mitch Posner; Liz and David Lefkowitz; Malka and Sammy Esterson; Rachel and Alan Rosenblatt; Barbara and Steve Scharf; Mindy and Chaim Landau; Patty and Chuck Leve; Yossi and Jackie Greenfield; Sandy and Ronnie Rosenbluth; Shaindy and Alan Kelman; Ester and Roni Matyas; Barbie and Glenn Porcelain; Ruth Klein and Todd Heller; Bette and Jack Gladstein; Pam and Neil Weissman; Barbara and Henry Rosenbaum; Sonia and Bernie Kozlovsky; Barbara and Larry Marder; Israela and Mike Meyerstein; Helen and Jesse Mashbaum; Susan and Jeff Posner; Cheryl and Norman Gras; Leah and Richie Zelkowitz; Barbara and Craig Neuman; Diane and Dan Berkowitz; Sharon and

David Zuckerbrod; Cris and Gary Manko; Elyse Michaelson and Rick Schraeder; Mini and Jacob Panikar; Sherri and Gary Bauman; Debbie and Aaron Rapoport; Michelle and Eddie Schwartz; Laura and Larry Cohen; Barbara Mangraviti; Toby Devens, Vicky Sery—among others. I apologize profusely for any unintended omissions.

Incredibly, many of Rachel's adoring friends continue to stay in touch, buoying my spirits. These include Sheera Hopkins; Naomi and Mike Burgher; Talia Lefkowitz Ackerman; Talia Landau Shorr; Atara Kelman; Sarah Feldman Horowitz; Gabrielle Mashbaum Heilman; Jessica Walch; Joanna Friner Millman; Jamie Chubak; Rachel Travis; Erica Sirkis Zimmerman; Shoshi Wolf Ponczak; Hudi Schorr; Julie Lowe Blumenfeld; Amy Hershkovitz; Adena Jurkowitz; Andrea Brem Wolf; Miesha Rice; and Leora Allen Hyatt (again, apologies for any omissions).

I'm also deeply grateful to my writing gurus, wonderful colleagues, gifted editors and cheerleaders: Tracy Gold; Daphne Gray-Grant; Linell Smith; Michael Keating; Justin Kovalsky; Mary Ann Ayd; Marjorie Centofanti; Alan Feiler; Neil Grauer, Mary Ellen Miller; Karen Nitkin; Lisa Rademakers Eddy; Tori Banks; Ron Hube; Patrick Smith; Marc Shapiro; Maureen Martin; Elizabeth Tracey; Sue DePasquale; Amy Goodwin; and Karen Diesenberg, our office manager, who was wonderful and supportive throughout Rachel's illness and beyond.

My incredibly talented niece, writer/wordsmith Temim Fruchter, deserves effusive praise for polishing the narrative and seeing it through to its end. And thank you, graphic designer extraordinaire Lisa Carta, for shepherding me through publishing the manuscript via Amazon, with patience and reassurance.

A special shout-out to Dalal Haldeman, former vice president for marketing and communications at Johns Hopkins Medicine, who encouraged me to tell Rachel's story, as part of a book project, which, alas, never came to fruition. I will never forget Dalal's constant love and support throughout Rachel's illness—and beyond. Heartfelt thanks, Dalal. I must also recognize the vital work of the Ulman Foundation, founded by Doug Ulman and his mother, Diana, to provide resources for young adults with cancer. Special thanks to you, Doug, for your poignant, inspiring reflections in this memoir's Afterword.

Finally, I am *beyond* grateful to my husband, Judah, for his loving support and medical expertise, as well as to our awesome children and their spouses: Jon and Elizabeth; Sam and Nikki. I also want to recognize my siblings and their spouses: Debbie Robinson; David Fruchter and Amy Supraner; Harold and Rena Fruchter; Hannah Heller; as well as cousins Charlotte, Jodi and Steven Reches, and extended family on Judah's side—Josh and Niti Minkove; Dena and Walter Zalcman and their families; and cousins Linda and Arturo Garzon; Tammy and Gene Berman; Alisa Shudofsky and David Cohen; as well as Aunt Ruthie and Uncle Ronnie Friedman; and Uncle Simmy and Aunt Dorothy Friedman and their families.

Although the sharpest moments of grief for our extraordinary daughter have diminished over time, difficult memories resurface, sometimes unexpectedly. The late Elizabeth Kubler-Ross, who pioneered "the five stages of grief," said it best:

> The reality is that you will grieve forever. You will not 'get over' the loss of a loved one; you will learn to live with it. You will heal and you will rebuild yourself around the loss you have suffered. You will be whole again, but you will never be the same. Nor should be the same, nor would you want to.

Our beautiful Rachel, of blessed memory, deserves nothing less.

POSTSCRIPT

Below are links to two extraordinary videos my colleague Maureen Martin produced about Rachel. The first showcases Rachel ringing the radiation oncology bell and celebration, when we thought she was done with treatment; and the second, an intimate "reflections" video Maureen crafted for us that contained footage that didn't make it into the original video. Both videos are priceless, albeit bittersweet to watch.

https://studio.youtube.com/video/tZz3kI-KyJo/edit

https://studio.youtube.com/video/Ss_tZAyusJQ/edit

Judy Minkove

Judy Fruchter Minkove served as a senior writer at Johns Hopkins Medicine (JHM), where she worked since 2002. In this role, she wrote for and managed two of the health system's newsletters: *Hopkins Brain Wise* (Dept. of Psychiatry) and *Aequanimitas* (for Osler Medical Residency alumni). She also wrote regularly for *Dome*, JHM's flagship employee newsletter. In addition, her work has appeared in *Hopkins Medicine Magazine* (the medical school's alumni publication). Minkove has won several national writing awards, including the Association of American Medical College (AAMC) Group on Institutional Advancement (GIA) Awards for Excellence and the Robert G. Fenley Writing Award of Distinction, in 2005.

A self-described grammar nerd, she also enjoyed her role as a Johns Hopkins copy editor for assorted publications, press releases and Web content. Prior to joining Editorial Services in 2003, Minkove managed publications, events and transplant patient volunteers at the Johns Hopkins Comprehensive Transplant Center.

All told, Minkove has more than 35 years of editorial experience, including four years as manager of public relations at Levindale Hebrew Geriatric Center and Hospital and 13 years as a medical textbook copy editor for Williams & Wilkins/Waverly Press. She has also published essays in *The Baltimore Jewish Times, The Baltimore Sun, The Forward* and *The New York Jewish Week.*

A rabbi's daughter—raised in a modern Orthodox home in communities across the country—Minkove is probably best known for her family's close ties to young Elvis Presley, whose family shared a duplex with the Fruchters in Memphis.

Outside of work, Minkove relishes reading, swimming, cooking and spending time with family—especially her five grandchildren, two of whom are named after her daughter, Rachel, who died in 2012 from complications of Hodgkin's lymphoma. At this juncture, Minkove, who retired in April of 2023, continues to chronicle Rachel's impactful, albeit way-too-short, life.

judyminkove.com

www.ingramcontent.com/pod-product-compliance
Lightning Source LLC
Chambersburg PA
CBHW030242030726
47493CB00023B/518